Susan Sallis is one of the most popular writers of women's fiction today. Her *Rising* family sequence of novels has now become an established classic saga, and *Summer Visitors, By Sun and Candlelight, An Ordinary Woman, Daughters of the Moon, Sweeter Than Wine, Water Under the Bridge, Touched by Angels, Choices, Come Rain or Shine, The Keys to the Garden, The Apple Barrel* and *Sea of Dreams* are well-known bestsellers.

D0885256

www.**booksattransworld**.co.uk

CHOICES

Susan Sallis

CORGI BOOKS

CHOICES
A CORGI BOOK : 0 552 14549 1

Originally published in Great Britain by Bantam Press,
a division of Transworld Publishers

PRINTING HISTORY
Bantam Press edition published 1997
Corgi edition published 1997

7 9 10 8 6

Set in New Baskerville by
Phoenix Typesetting, Ilkley, West Yorkshire.

Corgi Books are published by Transworld Publishers,
61–63 Uxbridge Road, London W5 5SA,
a division of The Random House Group Ltd,
in Australia by Random House Australia (Pty) Ltd,
20 Alfred Street, Milsons Point, Sydney, NSW 2061, Australia,
and in New Zealand by Random House New Zealand Ltd,
18 Poland Road, Glenfield, Auckland 10, New Zealand
and in South Africa by Random House (Pty) Ltd,
Endulini, 5a Jubilee Road, Parktown 2193, South Africa.

Printed and bound in Great Britain by
Cox & Wyman Ltd, Reading, Berkshire.

To Jane and Mike

One

The man looked through the interior window of the single-bedded ward and drew in a sharp breath. The girl lying on the high bed was unnaturally still and waxen; her blond hair, permanently damp with sweat, was scraped back from her face and curled into her neck to lie lankly over her thin shoulders. But her face was still a perfect oval and though the eyes were closed they were set wide apart and he could see that they were long-lashed and large. She looked raw and scrubbed, yet beautiful in her plainness. The man's hands clenched at his sides.

The sister said, 'Are you a relative?'

He said in an almost awestruck tone, 'No. I never saw her before.'

Sister's surprise was evident in the sudden turn of her head. 'Then why are you visiting?'

'I know of her. We are . . . connected.' He gave a quick sideways glance and added quickly. 'It's complicated.'

She smiled reassuringly; he was conventional enough. 'I know how it is with big families.' She continued to look at him although he turned back to the window. She said, 'Do go in. You can wake her.'

'Oh no.' Suddenly he was decisive. 'Oh no, she

doesn't know me. I simply wanted to see her.'

Sister frowned. 'She had visitors at first, but now . . . please go on in. It will do her good. She needs . . .'

He smiled without amusement. 'She doesn't need me. I know that.' He gave the still figure a last farewell glance and turned. 'I am the very last person she would want to see.'

He began to walk along the wide corridor past all the other single rooms. He moved aside for a wheel-chair and looked back once more. 'Thank you so much for showing me where she is.'

And he was gone.

Three months before, on Wednesday 12 May 1993, on a showery, Hardyesque day of mild breezes and blown chestnut spikes, Helen Wilson, aged twenty-six and a bit, was involved in a car crash on the M5 and was subsequently paralysed from the waist down. She was a passenger in her father's car, sitting behind him and next to her husband-to-be, Miles Gorman. Her mother was sitting in the front passenger seat. They were driving to Taunton where they intended to turn off to one of the villages on the Somerset Levels and visit a very special boutique owned by a friend of the Wilsons. Helen hoped to buy her wedding dress, and Miles was going because he couldn't bear to be parted from Helen for a whole day. There was not much traffic on the road; it was mid-week and halfway between the May Day and the Spring Bank Holidays. Helen, who was a teacher, had an in-service training day and felt mildly guilty about using it for shopping, even though it was with the permission of her headmistress. Jock Wilson pulled into the outside lane to overtake an enormous delivery lorry and coming straight for him was an open-topped sports car decked with balloons. It was a driver's nightmare: a vehicle on the wrong carriageway. There was nothing anyone could do. The central reservation was narrow at that point and Jock was hemmed in on his left by the high-sided lorry. The sports car turned onto the rough grass, bounced off the crash barrier and hit the Wilsons' Rover head on. Miles, Barbara and Jock Wilson probably died instantly, certainly they would have done in the subsequent fire. Helen, who had not fastened her seat-belt, threw up her arms instinctively, was pitched forward onto her father's back and slid upwards and through the sun-roof as if shot from a cannon. Afterwards she remembered it was a Safeway lorry . . . the flames were flame-orange but also black. The sports car seemed to burst like a balloon and spewed people everywhere. Afterwards, she did not care.

At first there was some hope for her. The spinal cord was not so much severed as misplaced; there was a kink in it where two vertebrae had been smashed against the roof of the car. She endured two long operations, then was put in plaster for the rest of the summer. Everyone else thought it was a poor summer; Helen found it stiflingly hot even when they wheeled her bed onto a covered verandah and she could look across Frenchay Common. She wanted very much to die and tried to starve herself, but the heat made her so thirsty and her treacherous body demanded more and more liquid. She asked angrily for plain water, but she was given fruit juices and milk shakes. When the nurses washed her flaccid legs, she saw with revulsion that the calves were still rounded and firm. Hockey-player's legs, her mother had called them. 'Don't wish for the long thin kind, Helen,' she had adjured when Helen bemoaned her appearance. 'Your legs are good and strong. They'll carry you till the end of your days and not protest.' Helen recalled that in the middle of one of her sleepless nights and moaned aloud involuntarily. The nurse was with her instantly.

'You in pain, dear?' she whispered.

Helen said wearily, 'How can I be in pain? I can't feel anything!'

'You will,' the nurse said in the tone of voice Helen already recognized. Encouraging. There were two grades of encouraging tones. The treacly kind and the bracing kind. It was 2 a.m. so this was the treacly one.

'Oh goody,' Helen said. 'Then I'll be able to writhe in pain.'

The nurse actually started to laugh and then stopped herself. There was an embarrassed pause before she said, 'Would you like a cup of tea?'

Helen managed to control the violence in her refusal. After all, how could this twenty-year-old be expected to understand? How could anybody be expected to understand?

The case was heard in August. The other car, an open-topped sports model, had contained three men returning from a stag party. Because it had hit the Rover sideways on, two of the men had survived,

10

one of whom was the bridegroom-to-be. Helen, reading the newspaper reports, murmured, 'Two bridegrooms . . . car crash . . . now there is one.' It had the resonance of a playground rhyme. When she read later in a gossip column that the surviving groom had never, after all, married, she said slowly, 'Two weddings . . . car crash . . . and now there are none.'

The insurance company made an interim payment immediately and there would be subsequent payments until the case was finally decided. The total sum promised to be a substantial amount; as far as Helen could tell from the solemn reports made by her social worker, it really depended on whether she made a recovery or died. Her consultant was called as a witness and he agreed, with 'reservations' that there was a hope Helen's nervous system might one day 'reconnect'.

Helen had a flurry of visitors. An aunt by marriage, a distant cousin. Her best friend and fellow-teacher who was to have been bridesmaid . . . other friends.

'You'll have to be very careful,' her Aunt Mildred cautioned, after she had said that really now Helen was sitting up there seemed to be nothing wrong with her. 'Money attracts the wrong kind, you know. When your uncle died it wasn't long before my insurance agent tried to get his legs under the table. He knew what policies I'd got, of course. And the house was worth over three thousand, and in those days three thousand pounds was worth three thousand pounds.' She spoke with enormous significance, tapping Helen's knee with the handle of her umbrella. Helen felt nothing.

'In your case . . .' She raised her shoulders and brows simultaneously. 'Well. It's in all the papers. They'll come from far and wide.'

Helen almost laughed. She and her mother had always laughed at Aunt Mildred. Her mother had bemoaned the fact that she would have to be invited to the wedding. 'Uncle Ernie was such a lovely man. We must have her for his sake.' And . . . here she was. Helen tried to take it all seriously. 'I hardly think . . .' She thought suddenly of Miles. Miles quibbling about wearing a topper. Miles laughing and then suddenly intently serious and unable to look away from her. 'Auntie . . , I was engaged to be married. To Miles. You had an invitation. Surely you remember?'

'Oh I know, my dear. And your heart is still with him. Of course. That is natural and right and how it should be. But in a year's time . . .' Aunt Mildred leaned forward. 'You'll be fed up with this place, Helen dear. If someone – someone very nice I daresay – someone good-looking too – offers to make a home for you and look after you . . . for a price . . .'

Helen said nothing.

Mildred went on, 'I'm going to leave you my number, dear. When this money comes through, just give me a ring and we'll arrange for you to share my house. And I will look after you. Myself.' She wrote carefully, precisely, then tucked the piece of pasteboard – obviously brought for this reason – into Helen's bag.

'I won't let you feel beholden, Helen. You can buy half the house and there will be plenty of money to employ nurses and things.'

Helen said, 'So you would not, in fact, look after me yourself?'

Mildred smiled understandingly. 'Of course I would! But all the . . . you know . . . washing and things. You wouldn't want me doing that. I think the impersonal touch is so much better, don't you?'

'Oh yes,' Helen said. She bore Mildred's continuing smile for as long as she could, then said, 'When can I expect the men?'

'Men?'

'The insurance men. Who might want to get their legs under my table . . . or wheelchair.'

Mildred flushed slightly. 'Helen . . . are you teasing your old auntie?'

'Absolutely not. It sounded rather fun. I wondered when I could expect it to happen.'

Mildred's lips disappeared around her dentures. 'I simply wanted to put you on your guard, child. It's a great deal of money and men are unscrupulous as we well know . . .'

Helen had thought she was enjoying the exchange. Suddenly the little spark of anger disappeared and she was infinitely tired again.

'Just go, Aunt Mildred. And please don't come back.'

'If that's how you feel . . . only trying to fill the shoes of your dear . . .'

'Don't say it!' Helen's voice sharpened uncontrollably. 'Just leave!'

Visibly bristling, Mildred did so.

Sister said, 'You look better tonight, Helen. That

little spat with your aunt did you good. Put colour in your cheeks.'

Helen remembered that she too had almost relished it for a while.

Sister said thoughtfully, 'Anger need not be a negative emotion, of course.'

Just for a moment Helen's eyes met the other woman's. All she said was, 'Oh.' But Sister pursued her theory no further.

That night Helen allowed herself to remember. The night sounds of the hospital were all around her. Further down the long ward, male voices chaffed the nurses. One voice sounded like her father's. She had a sudden vivid mind-picture of him, glancing sideways as he drove that day; smiling conspiratorially at Barbara because they both knew what the silence from the back seat meant. Somehow she had felt embarrassed by that look and had pushed Miles away and looked out of the side window at the flat fields of the Levels. Miles had reached for her hand and squeezed it gently to let her know he understood. He had always understood. They had known each other for one short year but he had known her, understood her, better than her parents even. Miles . . . with his round English face, slate-grey eyes and snub nose, brown hair which flopped across his eyes and made him look like a schoolboy . . . how he had endeared himself to her. He had insisted that their eyes had met across a crowded room and he had known instantly that they were meant for each other. Had it really been like that?

She closed her eyes. She had allowed herself the

agony of remembering, only to find she could no longer remember.

The door opened and Sister said, 'I'm going to give you something, my dear. You need a night's sleep after all the excitement.'

As if it had been a party seeing Aunt Mildred . . . what had Jock always called her? . . . Aunt Putrid.

Christmas Day came and went. There was no physio; but there were balloons and carols around a tree and the Queen on the television. The old rituals trundled on as if nothing had happened. Halfway through the afternoon Helen wondered what would happen if she started to scream and did not stop. Could not stop. Instead she closed her eyes and pretended to be asleep.

The new year of 1994 brought another social worker. This one was called Dorry Latimer. She was short with mousy hair, small, humorous brown eyes and a rosebud mouth. She had been sent to plan Helen's future because the National Health could not afford to keep her in the hospital for much longer and of course she would want to be as independent as possible.

'There are various sheltered housing schemes,' Dorry said. 'But you may well prefer to look through some brochures and find something for yourself.'

'After all, I can afford it,' Helen said.

Dorry smiled without embarrassment. 'Quite,' she agreed.

She produced brochures, all brightly coloured and very shiny. Helen rolled a corner of the cover between thumb and finger; the paper had a pliancy all of its own. The sort of paper ideal for sculpture. She had enjoyed paper sculpting with Year Five at school. Art and craft had been her speciality. It was how she had met Miles.

'What you must decide,' Dorry exchanged the brochures and smoothed down the rolled corner carefully, 'is whether you want to be somewhere with a mix of abilities. Or whether you would prefer to be with other disabled people who would understand your problems.' She turned a page to show a purpose-built block of flats, single-storeyed, notched with an abundance of concrete ramps. 'The everyday world is still pretty difficult for wheelchairs. A new functional development like this one has its advantages whatever one might think of segregation.'

A whole hideous new world seemed to yawn at the step of Helen's wheelchair. Segregation. A word connected in her mind with South Africa. And now . . . was she to be segregated?

She said abruptly, 'I don't want to think about it. Make decisions.'

Dorry just saved the pile of brochures from falling to the ground. She sat back with them on her lap. 'Yes. It's a bit much, isn't it? We'll take it slowly.'

Helen actually managed to laugh though it sounded more like a snort. 'I haven't been rushing about these past eight months,' she said.

'Not even inside your head?' Dorry asked.

'Especially not inside my head. I'm in no man's land.' It was the furthest Helen had ever come to revealing her feelings. And to this dumpling of a woman with button eyes.

16

'You mean you never think of Jock and Barbara? Miles Gorman? Your wedding day?'

Helen was staggered at the woman's complete lack of tact. She stammered, 'How do you know the names of my parents? And Miles?'

Dorry said prosaically, 'I've read your file. Obviously. And I've talked to the Gormans. And your fellow-teachers at Barton Primary.'

'You've what?'

Dorry began to repeat her list. Helen said fiercely, 'How dare you? How *dare* you?'

'Because it's my job. How can I help you if I don't know anything about you? And my predecessor's notes are scant to say the least. You haven't been very forthcoming!'

Helen hissed, 'Does that not tell you anything? Does it not indicate – just slightly – that I want to be left alone? That I don't want – need – any help from anyone?'

Dorry shrugged. 'Sorry. Whether you want it or not doesn't really matter. It's my job and I'm going to do the best I can. So I've called on your friends and asked them to tell me about you.'

'Go away!' Helen heard her voice escalating and was surprised at its force. It was so long since she had raised it past a monotone. 'I don't want to see you again! Do you understand?'

Dorry picked up a briefcase and began packing away the brochures. 'OK. But they'll only send someone else. I am, after all, the devil you know!' She smiled and her rosebud mouth flowered, showing good square teeth.

Helen rested her elbows on the arms of the

17

wheelchair and put her head in her hands and fought not to cry. She hadn't cried. At all.

Dorry said gently, 'I will go. But I want you to try something. Keep a diary. Put anything into it. The weather, whether Sister is smiling or miserable. The day you see the first snowdrop. Visitors. Anything.'

She stood up and gathered her umbrella, case, gloves and scarf.

Helen said, 'I don't get visitors. Not any more.'

Dorry pulled on her knitted hat. 'So I gather.'

'The Gormans . . . Miles' parents . . . they've never been.'

'No.' The scarf went round once, twice.

'D'you know why?'

'Not really. They were very . . . discreet.'

'Discreet?' Helen looked up. 'There's nothing to be discreet about! Anyone would think . . .'

Dorry pulled on woollen gloves and went to the door. 'Would you like to see them?' she asked.

Helen wondered whether she would like to see anyone, do anything, think anything . . . ever again.

She said, 'Yes.'

'OK,' said Dorry and left.

A week passed. It rained every day. The railway line from Exeter to Newton Abbot was closed because of flooding. The hospital chaplain asked if she would like Eucharist and she said no. A sore appeared on her heel and wept plasma copiously. She could not feel it but it gave the nurses something else to do.

She wrote these things on pieces of notepaper, dated them and pushed them to the back of her writing case. All they did was to reinforce her

18

realization of the pointlessness of her existence. She was strangely disappointed. She had wanted Dorry Latimer to be right. But, just like everyone else in the world, she simply did not understand. And her powers of persuasion could not be that good either, because the Gormans did not appear. Helen had not wondered about this before; now she did. Grief and horror must surely have eased enough for them to visit their dead son's fiancée.

On 10 January when the flooding was at its height, Dorry Latimer appeared again. The rain had got through her anorak and her hair was plastered to her small round head. Her eyes looked more like buttons than ever and her small mouth was screwed into a tight bud of discomfort.

She took off sodden gloves and placed them over the radiator, then draped her anorak over the back of her chair where it dripped miserably.

'Sorry about all this. Messing up your room.'

Helen was surprised to hear herself say, 'I like it. The rain.'

'Do you?' Dorry sat on the edge of the chair, well away from the anorak. 'Funny. I had you down as a summer girl. That blond hair under a straw hat . . . flowery cotton dresses, all Laura Ashley.'

Helen made a face. 'Yes. That was me. Now, I like this weather. The summer . . . the sunshine . . . it seems cruel.'

'It is. Uncaring. The rain is easier for you to bear.'

'Yes.' Helen said, still surprised.

Dorry said, 'Would you like to go out in it? I could wheel you down to the verandah and there's a ramp there—'

'No!' Helen interrupted violently. 'Never! I don't want to go out. Ever!'

Dorry said comfortably, 'That's because you're at last beginning to feel some sense of place in here. That's excellent. Soon it will be a stepping-off place for somewhere else.'

'I told you – I don't want to think about that. Don't produce those brochures again, for God's sake. And where are the Gormans? You said you'd ask them to come and see me. They haven't been.'

'No.' Dorry frowned and sleeked back her wet hair. 'It's odd that. They sort of buttoned up when I suggested it. Had there been a row? Anything?'

'Of course not.' Helen frowned too, forcing herself to remember. 'I didn't have much to do with them really. I mean, they were all right. Miles said they were shy but they liked me. That's all that seemed to . . . matter.'

Dorry nodded. 'You were an only child. You had always had what you wanted. It never occurred to you that the Gormans might not approve?'

Helen said, 'How can you be so – so callous? Do you dislike me so much? Why can't someone else do your job – I don't want to speak to you again!'

Dorry was surprised. 'Helen . . . I didn't mean to be callous. Forgive me . . . I was trying to work it out. The Gormans seemed a nice decent couple, they are slightly bitter perhaps . . . I'm not sure. I was simply trying to work out why they seem unwilling to visit you. That's all.' She leaned forward. 'I'm very sorry. I simply talk to you as if you were a friend. Directly. Honestly. I mean it as a compliment.'

Helen did not reply. Her colour was better than it had been since the accident.

Dorry said, 'Look. We should talk about a great many things. Practical things. Like, where you go from here. I know the brochures were unappealing. So think about your own home. The kind of help you would need. What you can do for yourself. Whether you want to live locally or move right away . . .'

Helen felt terror surge inside her like nausea.

'I couldn't look after myself! What are you talking about? A nurse or companion or something? I should absolutely hate it!'

'Haven't you a friend? A cousin or maybe an older relative?'

'My aunt.' Helen laughed briefly. 'Lord preserve me from my aunt!'

Dorry grinned. 'I've got one like that too. My father calls her old Horseface.'

'Mine was known as Aunt Putrid – for Aunt Mildred,' Helen said, her hard laughter softening slightly.

Dorry said quickly, 'Was that your father's name for her?'

'Yes,' said Helen. Her laughter died and she looked at Dorry and said, 'And I am not going to reminisce about my parents. Is that part of the treatment?'

'No. I was curious.' Dorry stared back. 'Funny. Your eyes have gone dead again. Sorry.'

This time Helen did not take umbrage. She leaned back in her chair wearily.

'I should have died too. Back there in the car. I feel . . . my presence here . . . like an insult.'

Dorry made a sound of protest, quickly cut off. After a moment she said very flatly, 'I think there's self-pity there somewhere. But it won't last, Helen. Please believe me. You're going to be busy again. Not thinking about how you feel – accepting what has happened.' She suddenly put out a hand and covered Helen's thin knuckles. Her voice lifted. 'Do you know something? You're going to be happy again!'

Helen said nothing, did nothing. After a while Dorry withdrew her hand and reached inside her bag.

'I brought you a diary.' Suddenly she sounded tired. 'Try to record something each day.'

She placed a large desk diary for 1994 on Helen's lap where it immediately began to slide to the floor. Helen roused herself and grabbed it. She looked at Dorry standing there, wet and dishevelled.

She said, 'I did write things down. On notepaper.'

Dorry's face was transformed. She dug her arms into the wet anorak and reached for her steaming gloves.

'Good! Copy it all into the diary. And then go to it.' She was still grinning as she zipped herself up vigorously. 'And . . . I'll have another go at the Gormans. Perhaps they're feeling guilty. Embarrassed. You might have a job with them. Are you sure you want to see them?'

Helen had not wanted anything since the accident except death.

She said, 'I think so. Yes.'

'Right,' said Dorry. 'See you soon.'

Helen copied her notes into the diary because it kept on raining and gave her something to do which stopped people talking to her. She read her entries. The chaplain had called. She wondered vaguely what his name was. It could be Oswald. He looked like an Oswald. Her foot had been sore. She glanced down at it. They insisted on putting slippers on her feet although there was no sense of heat or cold. She wondered – still vaguely – how the sore was now. She had eaten a poached egg for her supper two days before. And it had rained.

The weekend passed by and on Monday it was suddenly bright and blustery. Helen stared out of the window and shivered because a new spring and a new summer were approaching and there was nothing she could do to stop it. If only Miles' parents would come today . . . perhaps they were ill. Grief made some people ill. She wondered how she had survived. Surely no-one's grief could be worse than hers? The Gormans had each other; she had no brothers, sisters; no parents; no Miles. She shivered again. Why wasn't she ill . . . properly ill . . . dying or dead?

The door opened and Sister said, 'You've got a visitor, Helen. Are you decent?'

A visitor? A single visitor. Perhaps Mrs Gorman had come alone. Unexpectedly, Helen felt her heart race. Miles was so like his mother. Brown hair and grey eyes, round face . . . typically English.

She said, 'Of course. I think so.' She looked down at herself. She was wearing an Aran sweater which sapped what little colour there was in her skin.

Track-suit bottoms covered her useless legs. And the slippers looked enormous. But she was decent enough. She wasn't supposed to look anything but decent.

Sister came in and pulled out the visitor's chair, so rarely used now. Behind her came a woman, certainly not Mrs Gorman. A young woman, younger than Helen probably, with luxuriant red hair and brown eyes that picked up the same colour and glowed in her freckled face.

Helen's heart stopped racing abruptly. This was surely another social worker. Someone with terrific verve who was going to jolt her back to life. Helen closed her eyes momentarily.

'I'm Peggy,' the girl said. Helen heard her settling herself in the chair. The door closed behind Sister. The girl gave a small, unamused laugh. 'I see you've heard of me. Miles doubtless referred to me as Piggy. He could be very . . . unkind.'

Helen's eyes snapped open. The girl had opened her coat and was obviously plump. But she was pretty. More than pretty; striking. Those freckles highlighted a thick creamy skin . . . one of Barbara Wilson's old saws had been 'freckle said as he went in, I'll never enter a tawny skin.' Helen swallowed audibly.

'I'm afraid . . .'

The girl said, 'Please don't be embarrassed. I haven't come to make things worse.' She laughed again. 'They couldn't be much worse, could they?' She opened her bag. 'I'm not going to stop – I can see it's hard for you. But . . . well, May can't bear to see you. And I felt you deserved something. So I've

24

brought some photographs. May said I could have them. Frankly, I don't want them. But you might.' She put an envelope on Helen's locker. 'They're of Miles. Of course. School groups. Things like that.'

She waited for some response and when none came she closed her bag and stood up. 'Sorry. I know it's all impossible. But when that nice Miss Latimer said how much you would like to see May . . . and Alf too . . . well, I knew she wouldn't come. And I thought I would.'

Helen was in a complete fog. She grasped at the one fact that might be clarified by a question.

'Why won't Mrs Gorman come to see me? Is she very . . . you know . . . grief-stricken?' For the life of her Helen could not think of an alternative to that hackneyed phrase.

'She's bitter. That's what it is.'

'Against me.' Helen accepted the blame unprotestingly. After all, if it hadn't been for her wedding dress none of them would have been killed. 'We met twice. I didn't think she liked me. But Miles said she was very reserved.'

'I don't think she likes or dislikes you. She told Miles he was doing the wrong thing. She is bitter about him.'

Unexpectedly Helen flushed. 'Miles was a grown man! If she had no objection to me I really cannot see why she thought he was doing the wrong thing!'

Peggy opened her eyes suddenly and her mouth formed a perfect circle.

'Oh! Oh my God! You don't know about me, do you? I'm Peggy Gorman. Miles' wife! We were divorced of course. But I had nowhere to go and there was Rosetta and so I sort of stayed on in the flat in the Gormans' house. And Mrs Gorman – May – seemed to think that meant we were still married – she is very narrow-minded really.' Peggy put up a hand and covered her mouth. 'Oh, I am so sorry! Miles said he had told you. He really did. We all thought you knew. I . . . I don't know what to say!'

Neither did Helen. She stared at Peggy, her own mouth clamped tight; she felt her eyes were burning back into her head.

At last she whispered, 'Rosetta?'

Peggy visibly swallowed. 'Our daughter. My daughter now, I suppose. She's four. She'll go to school next September and then perhaps I can . . . get myself together.'

'I see.'

Amazingly, Helen did see. Miles was so sweet, so easy-going. As assistant to the Chief Education Officer he had been a governor of the school and had first met Helen when she applied for the reception teacher's post. He had said it was a look across a crowded room. Actually there had been the chairman of the governors, the head teacher, the local rector and another governor besides Miles himself in the room. But those famous looks . . . they had gone in for looks in a big way, deliberately meeting each other's eyes, shutting out whatever was happening.

And he had shut out his wife and daughter.

'It was sexual. Just sexual.' She spoke aloud, remembering the long looks which she had always thought of as a meeting of their souls. When Peggy frowned, she asked quickly, 'When were you divorced?'

Peggy nodded, knowing the importance of the question. 'The final papers came through almost exactly a year ago,' she said. 'It was all legal.'

But only just. They had probably got engaged before the Decree Absolute. So naturally Mrs Gorman thought Helen had deliberately split her son's marriage right down the middle.

Without thinking she said, 'Thank you.'

Peggy fidgeted where she stood. 'No. I should thank you. For being so understanding. I didn't dream you – you . . .'

Helen said steadily, 'I didn't know Miles very well. Not really. It was a sexual attraction. Oh I suppose we talked about the films and plays we saw. But not for long.' She smiled. 'And now Miles is dead and I haven't got any sensation below the waist. So sex seems pretty ironic, doesn't it?'

Peggy drew in her lips and gripped them with her teeth for a long moment, then let them go in a sob. She picked up her bag. 'I really am . . . so sorry,' she gasped, making for the door. 'I hope the snaps . . . I hope they . . .' She was gone.

Two

Coincidentally, the flowers started to arrive the next day. Helen did not think it was a coincidence at all. She thought they came from Peggy Gorman and were sent from a sense of pity. She watched Nurse Gillings arrange them by the wash basin, Nurse Gillings was small and round and very brisk. She split each stem with great care and shook in the powdered preserver from the packet. 'Someone thinks a lot of you,' she said archly. 'These are from Blooms Best just outside the hospital – they're terribly expensive.'

Helen thought of Peggy. Somehow she had exuded hard-upness. Why else would she be living with Miles' parents?

The nurse went on, 'It's exciting not knowing who sent them, isn't it? Like a guessing game.'

Could it be Dorry, in that case? It was the sort of thing she might do to force Helen into thinking of something – anything. Especially if she had known about Peggy and Rosetta all the time. Helen narrowed her eyes. Dorry had visited the Gormans. She must have known about Peggy. Had she engineered the whole thing? Just the suspicion made Helen feel sick. She had lost Miles twice . . . no, not even that – she had never had Miles in the first place. He had been married to Peggy. He had a daughter called Rosetta. Oh God. Somehow she had thought Dorry was on her side.

She said, 'Perhaps the card was in the wrapping. Could you just look in the bin – to check?'

Nurse Gillings checked. There was no card.

'They're probably from Dorry. My social worker.' She tried to smile at Gillings who had turned her mouth down in disappointment. 'She's giving me something to put in my diary. That was another of her ideas.' She laughed lightly. 'She's full of ideas.'

She was surprised at how hurt and angry she felt, as if Dorry had betrayed her. The next time she came Helen intended to ignore her completely. She intended to retreat into her shell again and not come out for anyone. But it was difficult to resurrect the shell now that Dorry had breached it and Peggy had smashed it completely. Even when she managed to get it halfway up, she found herself having furious conversations inside it. Sometimes with Miles. More often with Dorry. And during one of her confrontations with Miles she discovered that she could not afford to re-erect the shell. Not yet. She must still communicate with the outside world because there was something to be done.

Dorry arrived two days later. The rain had stayed away and it was still blustery, but colder and sunny. Dorry wore felted knitted gloves and a matching hat. She pulled them off, turning her short brown hair inside out and revealing chapped fingers.

'Chilblains,' she said briefly. She went to the radiator. 'Shouldn't warm them really. They'll start to itch.' She grinned at Helen. 'Any luck with the Gormans?'

Helen took a deep breath. She had rehearsed the invective with which she intended to annihilate Dorry. She hadn't allowed for the chilblains. The trouble with Dorry was that she *was* so ordinary. She let the breath go quite slowly and said, 'Oh God. Did you know – please tell me the truth – did you know that Miles was married? Did you ask his wife to visit me and let the cat out of the bag?' She watched Dorry's eyes widening and repeated flatly, 'I just want to know. That's all.'

Dorry too took a breath and said explosively, 'What sort of person d'you think I am? Christ – he was *married*? What the hell was he doing with you? I don't get it!'

Helen felt her heart lift, just a little.

'He *was* married. He got a divorce when he met me. So I suppose the Gormans thought I'd broken up his marriage. They disapproved of what he'd done. They must have hated me. Though Peggy said they didn't.'

'Peggy?' Dorry continued to stare incredulously. 'Peggy! I've met her. She was there when I called once. Red hair. Freckles.' Helen nodded. 'Why didn't they tell me? Why didn't someone tell me?' She spread her red hands, her face seemed to fall apart. 'And she came to see you? Oh God, Helen, I'm so sorry. What kind of support have I turned out to be!' She waved her hands helplessly. 'I've met her! Nobody said a word! Nobody even introduced her! Nothing in your file! I should have found out about her . . . Helen, I am deeply sorry.'

Helen smiled properly for the first time since the accident. 'I'm not. I thought you were up to something. Shock therapy . . . you know. I'm glad you're—' She searched for suitable words and spoke her previous thought. 'I'm glad you're on my side.'

Dorry stared for a long moment, then pulled a chair towards the wheelchair and sat down. She did not take her eyes off Helen. 'How do you feel about Miles now?' she asked directly.

Helen shrugged and her smile disappeared. 'I don't know. I wanted to shut myself away again. I mean, I've been living in a fool's paradise, haven't I? Looking back now, all that wedding business. It was so ridiculous. I just wanted to hide.'

'From who?'

'Miles? Myself? You? The Gormans? Peggy and Rosetta?'

Dorry frowned. 'Rosetta?'

'Their daughter.' Helen smiled again, this time at Dorry's expression. 'She's four and starts school soon.' She dropped her head. 'Miles was a bit of an amateur Egyptologist, you know. He must have named her after the Rosetta Stone.'

Dorry groaned aloud then burst out, 'He must have been an absolute . . . prig!'

Helen sighed. 'Probably. He said he chose me because my CV mentioned I had specialized in classics at college.'

'Chose you?' Dorry's voice escalated still more.

'He was a governor of the school, remember. He was on the interview panel.' Helen shook her head. 'He wasn't as bad as you think. He also said he thought I looked like a fairytale princess and the little ones would all love me.'

'Condescending,' Dorry condemned.

Helen thought of Miles; he had not been condescending. He had been besotted with her. And he had been weak too; that was why he could not tell her about Peggy and Rosetta.

She said, 'I thought he was perfect husband material. That was the trouble. He thought if he told me he was so recently divorced, I would be totally disillusioned.'

'Would you have been?'

'I don't know. I might have been.'

'I think you would.' Dorry sat back suddenly. 'My God, Helen. You couldn't talk like this if you loved him. You'd be cut to ribbons over this whole business. Oh I know it's pretty bad – one more thing on top of all the other things. But surely it's your pride that is hurt? Be honest with me now.'

Helen shrugged helplessly. 'It could be. I simply don't know.' She looked at Dorry ruefully. 'I haven't talked to anyone like this – at all in fact – since the accident. I feel strange. As if I'm . . . sort of . . . free.'

Dorry spoke carefully. 'Is that good?'

'It's not bad.'

Dorry relaxed further against the hard back of her chair. With her hair standing on end and her small eyes gleaming, she looked an odd creature. Helen thought she was beautiful.

She said, 'Can you do something for me?' Dorry nodded automatically and Helen rushed on, 'All that money. I don't need it. And I think Peggy is hard up – I got the impression she has to stay with the

Gormans and she isn't that keen. Can I give her some money? After all, she has lost Miles too.'

'The award was to provide you with a home and help,' Dorry reminded gently.

'Yes. But there's more than enough. Will you see her for me, Dorry? Sound her out?'

'All right. But your solicitor will have to be brought in. I can't do more than make the suggestion.'

'I know. Of course.' Helen too seemed to relax. There was a curious ache running from her abdomen to her chest. She said nothing; the thought occurred to her that sensation was returning.

Dorry said, 'You look tired. Such a lot has happened. Shall I go?'

Helen hesitated, then said, 'All right. Will you come again soon?'

'Of course. I'll call on Peggy today.'

Helen nodded, well satisfied. 'And thank you for the flowers,' she said.

'Flowers?' Dorry glanced at them appreciatively. 'They're lovely, aren't they? Hothouse of course. But I didn't send them. Gifts, one way or another, are frowned on!'

She left. And Helen let her head fall back and closed her eyes, forcing herself not to think of Miles or Rosetta, or anything about the accident. Instead, she wondered who had sent her the hothouse carnations.

The next day the ache was in her shoulder and unconnected with her legs. She felt a strange lassitude and it was mid-afternoon before she could bring herself to write in her diary. The events of yesterday and the previous weekend now seemed less incredible and she wondered dully about the sense of freedom they had given her. The bright cold weather continued. The staff seemed ridiculously cheerful. Helen huddled into her wheelchair and asked for another blanket around her shoulders.

The next day she thought was going to be exactly the same, but mid-morning brought some more flowers. This time freesias, a small sheaf of them encased in a cellophane sheath, oozing fragrance. Nurse Gillings could hardly contain herself.

'A secret admirer! Isn't it exciting?'

Helen explained with chilly brevity that she had no secret admirers and that her old friends had other things to do with their lives now. She thought, momentarily regretful, of Jan who had been so excited at the prospect of 'bridesmaiding' . . . of Meg who had been at college with her, of the many people invited to the wedding. Family friends, schoolfriends. She had seen their helplessness and told them not to visit her any more. Jan had insisted on coming in spite of Helen's coldness, but then she had got a job in Brussels . . . Meg was engaged herself . . . Helen cleared her throat and said, 'There's only one person who could have sent them. And she can't afford it. But . . .' she recalled the fiercely red hair and freckles. 'It's a nice thought.' She stared at the flowers ranged either side of the door. It was as if Peggy was a reminder of Miles' fallibility. They had that in common.

On Thursday Dorry arrived after lunch. She went through the usual business of taking off hat, gloves and scarf. She had had a haircut and looked more like a boy than ever.

'Did you see Peggy?' Helen asked immediately. It was the one thing left from all the revelations of last week: her gift to Peggy.

'Yes. I rang for an appointment. I didn't want May or Alf around when I passed on your suggestion.' She turned her mouth down. 'It's no good, I'm afraid, Helen. She turned it down flat.'

That had not occurred to Helen. Her eyes opened with astonishment. Before she could begin to protest, Dorry went on. 'The court awarded her maintenance for the child, Helen. And I believe there is more than just maintenance. Money in trust . . . Anyway, my dear, even if there hadn't been, what did you expect? Really? Put yourself in her position.'

'But she must need the money? Why is she still living with the Gormans? Dependent on them?'

'They're the closest she has to a family. And in a way, she does them a favour . . . it's their grandchild.'

'Rosetta. The little girl is called Rosetta.'

'I know.' Dorry shook her head. 'Peggy is quite like you. She's got a lot of pride—'

'And where does that get you?' Helen was unaccountably disappointed. She had wanted to do this . . . the first thing she had positively wanted since the accident. Except death.

'All right, not pride. Self-respect. I think . . . talking to her . . . Peggy lost most of her self-respect between Miles and the Gormans.' Dorry sat down; Helen registered that she looked tired. 'She wants to

35

get a job and a flat as soon as Rosetta goes to school. Be independent for the first time since she met Miles.'

Helen flinched. Dorry went on quickly, 'Let it go, Helen. The whole thing. You can't help Peggy. And you're so dissimilar. There's nothing you can do for her and nothing she can do for you.'

Helen shrugged and the ache in her shoulder was a sudden pain. She said, 'She is doing something for me. The flowers.'

'Are you all right?' Dorry was sharply anxious. 'Pain?'

'I've pulled my shoulder in some way.' Helen looked into Dorry's brown eyes. 'It might be . . . mightn't it? Sensation. Returning.'

'Is it anywhere else?'

'No,' Helen admitted reluctantly.

'Take it day by day.'

Helen closed her eyes. 'I know what you're saying. I'm not going to get better, am I? These kinks don't put themselves right. I'm going to stay like this all my life.'

Dorry leaned forward. 'Listen to me, Helen. There are many ways of getting better. You are completely different from the person I met at the beginning of the month. You are already getting better. We couldn't have talked like this at the beginning of the month. Could we?'

'No,' Helen said again. 'But you know what I mean. I'm going to be in this bloody chair for ever.'

'You don't know that. There are people who have to accept their disablement however bad it is. For you, there is hope.' Dorry sat back with an air of finality.

'Meanwhile I think you should have some physio for that shoulder. I'll mention it on my way out.'

'Are you going?'

'Not yet.' Dorry reached for her bag. 'We've talked enough about the Gormans. Let's leave it until we've both had time to think again.' She brought out more papers. 'What is concerning me is where you go from here.' She darted a humorous look upwards at Helen's low groan and went on briskly, 'Listen. One day you're going to wake up and not want to stay here a minute longer. So at least know what your options are.' She held up a folder. 'Stuff from house agents. You're not keen on hotels, residential homes, et cetera et cetera. So how about setting up your own place?'

Helen felt the old weariness coming upon her. 'Who sees to my catheter? Who lifts me into bed? Puts me on a commode? Changes all the padding?' She drew a breath. 'For God's sake, Dorry! What choices do I have? Really?'

'Well, of course you can't live alone—'

'A trained nurse? I think I might kill her in the first week.'

'Someone congenial. Someone you could even like!' Dorry rolled her bright eyes incredulously.

Helen felt a tiny surge of interest. 'You? Would you come and live with me?' she said and then could have bitten her tongue at Dorry's expression.

'My dear . . . I couldn't. Oh, I'm sorry – did you think I was leading up to that?' She was genuinely distressed. 'Helen, I'm married and my husband works from the house. He's an osteopath. I'm so sorry.'

'Please – it's me again. I think the world should stop for me.' Helen was horrified to discover tears of disappointment in her throat. It could have worked. She was certain it could have worked.

'Don't be silly. You're entitled to make enquiries – in fact you must if you are to find someone who would help. And I'll be around.' Dorry bit her lip. 'Listen – we seem to be capable of honesty, the two of us. Tell me, if I had been free and able to come and help you, would you have been interested in setting up your own home?'

Helen swallowed. She was going to say no. For her stubborn pride's sake, she was going to say no. But instead she said, 'I might have been. I'm not sure.'

'Come on. Think about it. You and me in a flat. Or a country cottage even. People going by. The seasons changing right outside the window. Sunsets, daily walks, Christmas trees.'

'Stop it.' The tears were there again, making her voice hoarse. 'What do you think?'

'In that case . . .' Dorry sat up straight. 'We're halfway there. You've thought of something you would like. We now take each problem as it happens. And we deal with it.'

'You're supposed to be practical.'

'Well, if you can't see that I am being practical—'

'The problems are insurmountable. Surely that is being practical?'

'They would be more problematical, if you did not have funds. As it is, a house can be adapted so that you are no longer disabled. Someone congenial can be found to help you.' She smiled almost smugly. 'It will happen, Helen. Next Christmas I'll come with

38

you when you do your shopping. How's that?'

Helen said, 'Time you went. Supper will be here at any moment and presumably you have to cook yours.'

'Yes.' Dorry put the folder on Helen's locker and stood up. 'I've got a slow cooker and it's been cooking away all day.' She drew on her gloves. 'I can recommend them. And of course microwaves are useful too.' She wound her scarf diligently. 'Don't discard the houses because of the stairs either. Those stair lifts are marvellous—'

'Dorry. Stop,' Helen said, and there was no mistaking the weariness in her voice. 'It's just too much.'

'Sorry.' Dorry rammed on her hat. 'I can't help getting carried away. Tom says it's because I prefer to live vicariously than face up to my own life.'

Tom must be the husband. Helen hoped he realized how lucky he was. She said, suddenly curious, 'How many people do you have . . . on your books? Besides me.'

Dorry was sniffing the freesias. 'Hard to say. People come and go.'

'Except me,' Helen pointed out.

Dorry grinned. 'Except you.' She opened the door. 'You know, those flowers are jolly expensive. Peggy must have liked you. A lot.'

Dorry almost ran down the corridor; she had two more clients to visit before she could get home to her slow cooker and Tom. A man was coming towards her carrying – self-consciously – a nosegay of snowdrops. Dorry slowed and then stopped in front of him. She knew she was a fool; wasn't Tom always telling her about rushing in? Nevertheless she said, 'Forgive me. Are those for Helen Wilson?'

He was wearing a woollen cap rather like her own; he was dark-complexioned, his eyes almost black. She was used to seeing this kind of face; it was an unhappy face. Even so, it smiled gratefully.

'Oh yes. Would you take them?' He glanced over his shoulder almost convincingly. 'I'm just visiting. Someone handed them to me.'

Dorry smiled. 'How mysterious. Man or woman?'

'Woman. Thank you so much. I'm in rather a hurry—'

Dorry's smile widened. 'Same here! She's number fourteen. On the right.'

She sped on; the swing door whipped behind her and she dashed to one side, breathed carefully, then risked a look through the porthole window. He was standing where she had left him, obviously waiting for staff to appear. Everyone was busy with the supper. Dorry hugged herself. He'd have to go and deliver the snowdrops himself. Who was he? Had he sent the other flowers? Peggy Gorman wasn't the sort to send flowers regularly. Then the trolley arrived at the top of the corridor and he moved purposefully towards it. Dorry muttered her disappointment. She could ask Sister of course, but this man was not going to give anything away. She rushed through the foyer praying that her car would start. It really was cold.

Helen did her best. The days began to lengthen imperceptibly. She watched the television when Torvill and Dean won the gold and she duly entered

40

it into her diary. She began to read again: Dorry brought her old favourites from her schooldays and then tried to interest her in contemporary fiction. A spell of dry frosty weather seemed to clear up the ache in her shoulder and in a strange way she was disappointed because she had wondered whether pain – any kind of pain – could be the beginning of sensation returning. Dorry suggested viewing some of the houses in the lists she kept bringing. They were all disappointingly inaccessible. 'You could have a ramp put at the front door—' Dorry began. Helen cut her short. 'I simply don't like it. I can't see myself there.'

The flowers kept coming and at last when British Summer Time began on 27 March, Helen wrote a letter to Peggy Gorman. It was difficult and she made several attempts. She intended to thank her for the flowers but ask that they should now stop. She wanted to wish her well so that any peculiar guilt between them could finish. She wanted to send good wishes to Rosetta and hope that she would enjoy school next year. Finally she said none of those things. Instead she wrote, 'Dear Peggy, I hope you are well and have found yourself a job. I would so much like to see you again if you have time. Thank you for the flowers. Yours sincerely, Helen Wilson.' It looked a strange note, written in thick black biro in the large writing she had developed for the blackboard. She gave it to Sister before she could change her mind. She knew that she had written the truth: she did want to see Miles' wife again.

Peggy Gorman arrived on Tuesday afternoon, the

same day she must have received the letter. Helen watched her, her head framed in the window of the door as she exchanged a few words with Sister. She was attractive in a vibrant, vivid way. It was very easy to understand her attraction for Miles.

She opened the door diffidently. Seen full-length she looked distinctly shabby. Her cotton skirt and double-knit cardigan were obviously home-made and were too thin for March. As if pre-empting any such thoughts, she said immediately, 'My goodness, it's hot in here. Hospitals are always much too warm, aren't they? So unnatural.'

'Yes.' Helen forced a smile. 'I'm sorry. I shouldn't have asked you to come.'

'Oh, I didn't mean . . . I wanted to come. I just felt rather awkward about the money. It was nice to get your note because I wondered if you were annoyed. I had to say no about the money. I'm twenty-three! I must begin to look after myself! But it was ever so kind of you. Honestly.'

Helen was thrown by the girl's frankness. And she was only twenty-three.

'Well . . . I just wanted to help. After all, your loss was the same as mine.'

Peggy looked shocked. 'Oh no! How can you say that? You're stuck there and I'm here.'

No-one had been so direct before. Helen pressed her lips together for a moment in case they trembled, then nodded.

'I meant Miles. We both lost Miles.'

Peggy sat in the visitor's chair and drew her full skirt well over her knees as if ashamed of her legs.

'Well . . . yes. But of course, I had lost him before. Really.'

Helen listened for resentment but could hear none. She said tentatively, 'Perhaps. But I feel now as if I never really knew him. So in a way, that was a loss.'

There was a pause. Peggy bit at her lip. Lipstick came off on her top tooth. 'I never thought of it like that. He should have told you about me.'

'His parents should have told me.' As Helen spoke she realized the full truth of this. 'Someone should have told me,' she said emphatically. 'Miles, of course. But if he didn't, then—'

'I didn't know he hadn't told you!' Peggy said defensively. 'Anyway, it wasn't up to me to say anything, was it? If he was that ashamed of Rosie and me, who was I to—'

Helen was horrified. 'Peggy! I didn't mean that you should have said anything!' In her anxiety she leaned forward and put a hand on the girl's knee. She thought with another part of her mind that this was the first time she had touched someone of her own accord since . . . since it happened. The knee was plump beneath the thin cotton covering.

She said, 'It just seemed so incredible that I didn't know. Somehow.'

There was a little silence and she sat back in her wheelchair. An audible crack came from the area of her hip bone and she was aghast. But it must have been inside her own head because Peggy made no comment. Instead her creamy, freckled face coloured.

'Sorry. Didn't mean to let fly. Miles always said I was a typical redhead. Mouth before brain, he said.'

'Did he?' It sounded a horrible thing to say to this young, strangely innocent girl. But then, she had known such a small part of Miles Gorman.

It seemed Peggy was intent on frankness; she rushed on, 'He had to marry me, you see. I was only nineteen when Rosetta . . . started. He had a good job in the Municipal and he used to come over the road for his lunch.' She gnawed her lipstick again and added, 'I was a waitress. I couldn't go on when I started to show. And anyway, he loved me then.'

Helen could no longer stop the tears; they flooded her eyes. Peggy said, 'I'm sorry, Miss Wilson. I didn't mean to say that. But . . . well, it wasn't just because of Rosie that he married me. I want you to know that. Even if it does hurt you.'

'It doesn't hurt. Not in the way you mean. It's just that . . . you were so young. And probably if I hadn't arrived on the scene two years later, you and Miles and Rosetta would still be together.'

Peggy tightened her full mouth and frowned, thinking about it. 'I don't think so,' she said at last, almost judiciously. 'He was a good father up to a point. I mean, he put her name down for St Margaret's and used to do all kinds of work. Voluntary.'

Her eyes were earnest with sincerity and Helen nodded and murmured agreement. A sudden traitorous thought occurred: Miles had been a good father outside his home, away from his daughter.

Peggy's voice dropped. 'But we didn't talk much. When he wanted to name the baby after some stone,

I said that was awful. But then Rosetta grew on me. And I wasn't all that keen on Tracy anyway.'

Helen started to laugh and wipe her eyes. Peggy might be naïve but her directness was a kind of relief. As Dorry's was in a different way. Peggy smiled too, a little reluctantly, and pulled her skirt down again. 'You sound much better,' she observed.

Helen sobered and thought about it. 'I am,' she discovered. 'Dorry was right. I am better.'

'Dorry? Is that Mrs Latimer? She seems nice. May doesn't like her. She says social workers always interfere.'

'Dorry doesn't interfere,' Helen said definitely. She hesitated then asked bluntly, 'Aren't you fed up living with your in-laws? When Rosetta goes to school and you get a job, will you be able to afford a flat on your own?'

'I hope so.' Peggy made a face. 'I hope I can get a job full-stop. I don't want to leave Rosie with a child-minder or anything. She's all I've got. I could stay at Farnsworth Avenue – they want me to because of Rosie. But May will spoil her when I'm not there.' She sighed. 'It's going to be difficult.'

Helen nodded slowly. 'Yes. Why don't you go and see the head at St Margaret's? Mrs Whitaker. She's so easy to talk to. If you could get a job as an assistant – something with school hours—'

Peggy's fox-brown eyes shone. 'D'you think they'd consider me? That would be wonderful. Besides, we'd be sharing something. Rosie and me.'

Helen made up her mind quickly. 'Listen. I'll write a reference for you. And a note to Mrs Whitaker.' She rubbed at the blanket covering her knees. 'They all came to see me at first. When it happened. I wasn't nice. I told them I didn't want to see anyone.' She sighed. 'But they must have understood. I'm sure if Mrs Whitaker can help, she will.'

Peggy seemed to sparkle with excitement. 'It would be great – absolutely great! I can't thank you enough—'

'Hang on,' Helen warned. 'If there's no job available, that will be that.'

'Yes, but you're trying to help! I can't get over it! Why on earth should you want to help me?'

Helen almost admitted the real reason. Guilt. Then she said, 'Well, look how you've helped me.' She smiled as she indicated the banked flowers. 'My goodness, once a week, twice a week sometimes. You shouldn't do it, Peggy. Please don't any more.'

'The flowers? I wondered what you meant in your note.' Peggy gazed, surprised. 'I haven't sent you any flowers, Miss Wilson. I never thought of it. I'm sorry . . . I wish I had.'

Helen too was surprised. 'Oh! But then, who . . .?' She shook her head. 'Don't be silly. I'm glad they're not from you. I worried that you were spending too much anyway and with Rosetta to look after . . . Listen. Please don't call me Miss Wilson. If you come again, call me Helen.'

'I will come again. If you don't mind.'

'No, of course not. I'd like to see you.'

'All right then. Helen.' Peggy smiled self-consciously, then brightened as she stood up. 'And I always call Rosetta, Rosie. Unless you'd rather . . . probably you would. Miles always called her Rosetta.'

'Rosie is much prettier.'

They smiled at each other and then actually shook hands. Peggy waved through the window and was gone. And Helen reached for her diary and frowned at the flowers in complete puzzlement. The fact that Peggy had not sent them did not alleviate the sense of guilt. She just hoped Mrs Whitaker could find Peggy a job; that might help. She began to write and then stopped and stared at the flowers again. If Peggy hadn't sent them and Dorry hadn't sent them, who had?

Three

Tom Latimer knew he was by no means the ideal husband. But then, Dorry was certainly not the ideal wife. And if they were scoring points – which, he hastily told himself while he checked the traction machine, they were not and never would – Dorry would certainly be in the minus column.

'Is that comfortable, Mrs Thorne? Yes? Good. And you can feel a pull from the hips?'

He went to his desk and added some details to Mrs Thorne's file, then went into the second cubicle to put an ice-bag on John Jennings' knee. They made desultory conversation about the football results and how soon it would be before John Jennings could get between the goalposts again. Tom glanced at the clock on the wall. He had told Dorry he would put the potatoes on at six. No hope of that. A great many clients were at work during the day and there was always a full house between five and seven-thirty. He was suddenly furious with her and her wretched time-and-emotion-consuming job. She should be here like any normal wife, cooking their evening meal, enquiring about Eileen Thorne. After all, his clients needed support as much – more so – than hers. Anyone could go and sit by someone and listen to their grumbles. He had to iron out their muscles and bones . . .

Mrs Thorne called from behind her curtain. Her timing bell had rung, yet the machine had not released its grip. He switched it off, apologizing profusely. He must get that cut-out looked at. She smiled up at him forgivingly. 'I wish you would call me Eileen. And you know I don't mind an extra few minutes on traction. It is such a relief not to have that constant pain.'

It should also have released her trapped nerve by now. Tom advised her to relax for five minutes before getting dressed and wondered whether Eileen Thorne was simply bored. Dorry would know.

He eventually went through into the kitchen at six-thirty and when Dorry tore in ten minutes later the potatoes were still hard and he had not salted them.

It made it worse that she was instantly forgiving.

'Darling, don't worry,' she said, aiming a kiss at his nose as she dashed past him to the stairs. 'I can eat later. You have yours.'

'You're not going out *again?*' He forced incredulity into his voice. She often had to go out in the evenings. Like his clients, hers were sometimes occupied elsewhere during the day. But he always knew his timetable. Hers changed 'on the hoof' as she so ludicrously put it.

'I've got an appointment to see a house,' she said, already half inside the bathroom. 'No time tomorrow.'

He followed her up the stairs. 'Not Helen Wilson again? I don't think I can bear it.'

'Don't be dramatic, darling.' She splashed water

onto her face and looked up, eyes closed. He passed her a towel and she snuffled her thanks.

'I'm not being dramatic.' He tried not to sound petulant. 'But she's more than the call of duty and you know it.'

Dorry paused, then hung the towel on its rail. 'Yes. You're right. We're friends. We're completely different. But we're friends.' She did not wait for more analysis but plunged past him down the stairs. 'Can you look at my wipers before work tomorrow, darling?' she called back. 'They're sort of making a chuttering noise.'

'What on earth is a chuttering noise?' he asked. But she had gone and the potatoes were boiling over on the stove. He ran down the stairs, turned down the heat and looked at their bland bulbousness in the saucepan as they fidgeted and knocked against each other. 'OK. That's chuttering,' he said gloomily, and began to lay the table.

Dorry wanted to see the house in the daylight and it would be dark in an hour. She had picked up the keys earlier that day and she drove quickly out of town and on to the motorway. The house was on the spit of land called Stormy Point just outside Weston-super-Mare. It seemed a ridiculous site for a disabled girl, yet Dorry had a feeling about it. However unsuitable, Helen's house had to capture her imagination. And this one might. It just might.

It was almost seven-thirty as she nosed the car along the private road which overlooked the sea on both sides. Years ago a few fishermen had run their strange sledge-like crafts over the mud here and caught eels. The boats had been called flatners and the cottage for sale was called Flatners Cottage. It was one in a group of three dwellings built in a semi-circle of land which protected them from the prevailing south-westerlies and led naturally down to a stony cove, covered at high tide. Opposite them a similar line of typical coastguard cottages looked out to sea. She parked the car, got out and surveyed the view. It was stupendous. The watery spring sun was halfway into the sea and a pinkish-orange path of light glittered almost up to the base of the cove. To the left the lights of Weston were beginning to appear. Even as she stood there, a lamp was lit in one of the cottages and behind her a hideous sodium street light illuminated the road back to civilization. She drew in her breath: that was it . . . this place was outside civilization yet within easy reach. She had checked things like main drainage and electricity. The small group of cottages was far from being uncivilized. The other two were let as holiday cottages and had to meet the high standards of the local tourist board. But perhaps that was a snag. It meant that through the winter, Helen would have no neighbours to call on. Dorry frowned slightly and waited another few seconds for some of the other houses to show signs of life. None of them did.

She left the car and walked down the track to Flatners. Small stones rolled under her shoes and she slowed her pace, not wanting to fall in this deserted place. Of course, Helen would need a hand-controlled car, then she would be able to drive almost up to her front door; nevertheless if there were an accident of any kind, it was rather isolated.

Dorry had had such high hopes of this place; the girl at Vallender's Properties had taken one look at her long cardigan and woolly hat and had enthused about Stormy Point unreservedly. Dorry fitted the key in the front door and smiled rather grimly. If she had confessed that far from being a potter or an artist she was a social worker looking at properties on behalf of a paraplegic girl, it might have been very different. The staff at Vallender's would have thought she was mad probably. Tom would definitely think she was mad.

The front door led straight into the living room; in fact the living space. It was a small cottage and had been converted back in the sixties when open-plan was all the rage. Weight-bearing joists criss-crossed the ceiling and were still hung with paper decorations from last Christmas, ragged and dusty. The stairs were steep and without banisters; well, a lift would solve that one. And once inside there were no more doors for a wheelchair to negotiate. A counter separated a small kitchen from the rest of the room; that would have to be lowered, as would the sink and worktop. But what dominated the room was the window. When it was put in, it was doubtless called a picture window, and did in fact frame the picture that Dorry had admired five minutes before. Now the lights of Weston were a symmetrical half moon strung across the bay, and very faintly against the darkening sky, the outline of the Mendips was an indigo backdrop. Dorry stood for some time admiring it, not seeing the rotten floorboards and general neglect. What she could see was Helen inhabiting this space, filling it with books and

52

pictures. Helen, gradually coming back to life, gradually healing. She sighed sharply and reached for the light switch. Nothing happened. She took to the stairs quickly before the dusk slipped into total darkness. Not that the bedrooms mattered. Helen would doubtless use the ground floor as a studio apartment. Dorry poked her head into the three square boxes and then into an antiquated bathroom and descended immediately. There would have to be a new bathroom built beyond the kitchen. She locked up carefully and trudged back to the car. Maybe the picture window could be replaced by patio doors with a ramp leading to the garden . . . She grinned and shook her head. Probably Helen would hate it anyway.

Mr Edwards was bald and blue-eyed with small hands which Helen could not imagine probing vertebrae and nerve ends. She had decided a long time ago that she hated him because he was utterly useless, but she knew that the only person she should hate was the driver of the balloon-bedecked car that had driven at them that May morning almost a year ago. Mr Edwards was kind and courteous even when she was rude. He had a way of lowering his bald and clever head as if to take the blows and accusations she hurled at him, accept them, maybe earth them like lightning bolts.

He stood up and came to her as she wheeled into his office. He held out his hand although she had ignored it before, and when she put her own into it, he held it, shaking it gently as if in congratulation. But his blue eyes were still wary.

She said, 'It's all right. I've made progress in some ways. Perhaps I'm beginning to accept my fate.'

He was non-committal, unsmiling, releasing her hand, returning to his desk where her notes and X-rays were aligned methodically. He said, 'I understand from your social worker that you hope to move into your own home some time this summer.'

'It depends.' Helen laced her fingers tightly. She had been so excited when she saw Flatners. Just as Dorry had thought, her imagination had been captured by the view, the big space, the strangely accessible isolation. But doubts were already crowding in. 'There is so much work to be done. And I shall need a companion. That is the real snag. I don't like the idea of sharing.'

He nodded, suddenly empathizing. 'Yes. I would hate that too.'

She looked at him again. If he had some hair he would be good-looking in a plain kind of way. She smiled. 'Well, there is no way around that.'

He looked at her consideringly. He was wearing a pristine suit and there was a carnation in his buttonhole. She thought of her own flowers. Dorry had said ages ago that she had seen a man carrying snowdrops, but he might have just been a messenger. Helen had nodded. It could be Aunt Mildred, but that was unlikely; it could be the children at school. Maybe the new teacher had organized something . . .

Mr Edwards said, 'It might . . . it just might be possible to manage with a daily nurse. I am not sure. I thought, during this interim period, we might experiment.'

She felt sick. What had they in store for her now? 'Experiment?' she croaked.

'I want to remove your catheter and the colostomy,' he said bluntly, placing his fingertips on her notes and leaning forward. 'That would do away with the need for a live-in nurse.'

She tightened her woven fingers. 'But that would mean . . .' She had always forced herself to accept her double incontinence at its basic level.

He smiled slightly, reassuringly. 'I don't think so.' He lifted his fingertips and consulted the notes. 'Interestingly enough, your sweat glands are working all over your body. This means that your temperature remains normal – a great blessing as you can imagine.' He smiled fleetingly upwards, again congratulating her. 'I am certain that if that bodily function continues to operate in the paralysed half of your body, then the other functions would follow.'

Helen bleated a protest. 'But I never know when I want to – to – urinate, or—'

He looked up properly, surprised. 'Are you unwilling to try this, Miss Wilson? It would make you independent of a great deal of help. Also the risk of infection from catheters et cetera is quite high. Hygiene would require a daily saline bath, but apart from that—'

'I think I'm frightened,' Helen confessed suddenly.

His eyes met hers again and their blueness was suddenly warm.

'Don't be. You have nothing to lose and a great deal to gain.'

'I'm frightened of failure.'

He lifted his shoulders. 'Success . . . failure . . . out of your hands. If your body is responding as I think it is – almost on automatic pilot – then success will follow just as automatically. If not, it won't.'

'Automatic pilot . . .' She murmured the words, finding them infinitely comforting. Was it possible that her damaged body was capable of continuing to work without volition? She leaned forward and touched her knees. She hated touching her paralysed limbs; it was as if they no longer belonged to her. Dead meat, attached to her living body. Now she touched them firmly. They were her knees. They continued, unfeelingly, to sweat.

She grinned. 'Do my feet smell?'

He raised his brows. 'I don't think so.'

'How did they know about the sweating?' She shook her head. 'Sorry, silly question. It's rather marvellous though, isn't it? Maybe when I start living again, I shall get hot and my feet *will* smell!'

He too grinned. 'Maybe,' he said.

She suddenly felt very close to him and said without thinking, 'Are you married?'

'Yes. My wife is a theatre Sister.'

Helen made a disappointed moue. 'Pity,' she commented and was glad when he laughed aloud, delightedly.

'I say!' He sounded boyish. 'You really are recovering!'

She was surprised, embarrassed at her own pertness. 'Am I? I think I've changed, too. That is not the kind of thing I would have said before.'

But when she wheeled herself down the corridor

again, she wondered whether that were quite true. Miles had been captivated by what he called her honesty; she tried to recall what he had meant by that. Those looks . . . had she instigated those looks? That first time – across the crowded room at the interview – she could have looked away. And she had not; she had let the fleeting glance lock into something poignant, something significant. When he had seen her in town during her lunch break and had told her he always lunched at the Spinning Wheel – and she realized now that that was the restaurant where he had met Peggy – she had been the one to say, 'May I join you? The school dinners are rather boring.' It had been across the polished oak tables that the famous looks had developed into a unique form of communication. And she had been right: they were entirely sexual.

She had been going to wheel herself to the verandah and watch for Dorry coming up the drive in her awful old car with one windscreen wiper still missing. Now, suddenly, her face hot, she turned sharply into her room, catching her foot on the door jamb and registering a reflected pain leaping above her waist.

She addressed her lower half with some passion. 'I hate you! Getting in the way . . . dead as mutton . . .' And stopped abruptly as she saw she was not alone. A man in a conventional dark suit was standing by her locker, apparently looking at the array of flowers. No white coat so he wasn't a doctor. A thin, dark, brooding sort of face. Intelligent. Another social worker? She put her hands on the arms of her chair very firmly. She would deal with Dorry Latimer and no-one else.

He said nothing, staring at her with a kind of pain. Or pity.

She said, 'Yes?'

'Ah. Excuse me. I think I have the wrong room. I am looking for Mr Welch. Mr William Welch.'

She shrugged. 'I haven't the faintest. I don't socialize.'

'I see. I don't blame you. I wouldn't either.'

She narrowed her eyes. 'Shame? Embarrassment? Or do you prefer your own company?'

He looked confused for an instant, then rallied. 'I think I meant that I would find it necessary to get to know myself – my new self – before I tried to know others.'

She was startled and felt her eyes widen and lose their fury. It was so exactly how she had felt before Dorry. And still felt about a great many people.

The silence lengthened. At last he broke it. 'I'm sorry. That sounds pretentious and presumptuous. I think you are right. I would simply prefer my own company.' He moved around the bed. She would need to wheel to the other side if he were to get out of the door. She stayed where she was.

'Don't apologize. It's just that . . . perhaps you need to know other people before you can know yourself.' She shook her head, confused and frustrated. 'I don't know. I'm not sure about things . . . some things. Not any more. I was certain of everything before this happened.' She nodded at her legs. The left foot had been knocked from the step of the chair. She tugged at the knee but he was there before her, crouching in front of the chair, gently lifting her slippered foot back into place.

She said, 'Thanks.' It sounded ungracious and she repeated the single word with more emphasis.

He glanced up. His saturnine face was unnaturally thin; she wondered whether he had been ill. He said awkwardly, 'I can't say it's a pleasure, can I? Let me use an Americanism. You're welcome.'

She said 'Thanks' again. He stood up straight; not easily. She moved the chair into the bed. He nodded and went to the door. She said, 'The men's rooms are right at the end of the ward. The other end.'

'The men?' He stared at her uncomprehendingly for an instant and then recovered himself. 'Of course.' He smiled and his face was transformed. 'I'd forgotten.'

'Mr Welch,' she reminded him gently.

He nodded. 'Bill Welch.'

She could so easily have suggested going with him to the far end of the ward where the male patients had their rooms. But she did not. She was convinced already that there was no such person as William Welch, but she was curious about this thin-faced man who had been examining her flowers so carefully. If he was playing charades, she needed a few more clues. She was so certain that she would see him again she did not even bother to enquire his name.

'Goodbye,' she said.

'I suppose so. Yes.' He held the handle of the door. 'Goodbye then.' And he closed the door after him with great care.

She went over to the set of bookshelves which now contained her flowers; there were eight vases displayed there, two of them beginning to fade in the heat of the room. She fingered them, frowning slightly. And then, unbidden, came a surge of feeling. Rather like excitement. And she smiled.

Harry Vallender walked slowly to the hospital car park and unlocked his Rover. He had thought Helen Wilson was beautiful when he had first seen her last August. Angelically beautiful; waxwork beautiful. Now he knew she was more than that. She was fiery; full of passion which could ferment into acidity if something wasn't done. Soon. Quite soon.

He drove to Westbury village slowly and with great care; that was how he drove now and probably always would. The office reception was still open and three or four people milled around its large space, looking at illustrations of various properties for sale. He parked across the road and sat still, staring at the shop front, wondering why he was still running it. Wondering if he was like the hens who would run headless around a farmyard on some kind of automatic pilot. Nothing had much meaning for him any longer. Keeping tabs on Helen Wilson, sending her flowers, had been like a lifeline, the only meaningful things he did now.

He read the words across the shop front. Vallender and Son, Auctioneers, established 1890. The first Vallender had been his grandfather. In those days his father had been the Son. And then when grandfather died, his father had become Vallender and he himself the Son. And now there was no Son. Never would be. Because he was incapable of feeling anything any more, let alone love or passion.

He locked the car and went into the office. Margaret, his assistant, smiled above the heads of a young couple who were going through the details of Flatners Cottage. That had been his father's special place. The little group of cottages, owned by Trinity House, perched on the side of Stormy Point above the Bristol Channel, had been bought by Henry Vallender back in 1950 for his bride. Harry remembered many happy days spent with the flatner fishermen skimming over the shallow tide, literally scooping the eels out of the mud of Bridgwater Bay. Perhaps that was why he kept the office going: in memory of his father and those days by the sea when time had no meaning. And now Flatners was up for sale and as the other cottages emptied their summer visitors, he would sell them too. And that would be the end of yet another chapter.

He went through the outer office and up the stairs to his flat where he worked, ate and slept. The desk was neat, too neat for a busy auctioneer's. He glanced at the pad for any telephone messages. Margaret's neat handwriting informed him that Arnold had rung at midday and would be at the Bristol site until the end of the month. Harry sat down and dialled a number. He had no wish to speak to Arnold, but after all they had shared . . . something. He might have cut himself off from everyone, but he could not ignore a message from Arnold.

A female voice responded to the phone.

'Davison's. Site office.'

'Ah. Yes. Is Arnold Davison around? I have a message to call him. Harry Vallender here.'

'Certainly, Mr Vallender. Would you hold please.'

And then Arnold's voice, hearty as ever. As if nothing had happened. 'Harry! Where were you?'

'Out.' Harry wondered why he had never 'recovered' as Arnold had. They had told him he was traumatized. But Arnold had been there and he did not appear to be traumatized.

Arnold laughed. 'I gathered that. I wanted to give you lunch, old man. Tomorrow?'

'Sorry, I've got an engagement.'

'And another the next day, I expect.' Arnold's voice was suddenly heavy. 'You don't want to see me, do you?'

'There's no point in meeting, Arnold. You know that. We're both trying to forget. You've succeeded. And I will one day, I expect.'

There was a long pause. Harry wondered if Arnold might be going to tell him something important. Tell him that he did not sleep at nights either; tell him that his life had lost its meaning, too.

Arnold began to speak again with sudden resolution. 'OK. We'll take it from there. I wanted to tell you face to face, but if you won't . . . the thing is, Harry, you treated Cheryl very badly. Very badly indeed. The poor girl was distraught.'

Harry felt the task of explaining how he had felt about Cheryl loom like a mountain above his head. He said inadequately, 'She wasn't there so she couldn't possibly understand. She wanted everything to go on as if nothing had happened—'

'Of course she did! Dammit all, Harry, you were going to get married the next bloody day!'

'Well . . .' If Arnold could not see the impossibility of that, it was hopeless to try to explain. Harry said helplessly, 'I couldn't. You see, I couldn't.'

Arnold heaved an audible sigh and reached for his patience. 'Listen. Do you love her? Do you feel anything for her still? Tell me the truth, Harry.'

'That's easy.' Harry almost laughed because at last here was something straightforward. 'The answer is no.'

Arnold said, 'Then I can tell you. No hard feelings. Cheryl and I are going to be spliced. She wanted you to know. Four weeks.'

Harry battled with incredulity. 'You? And Cheryl? You always said she got on your nerves! And she—' He stopped speaking, remembering with dreadful clarity what Cheryl had said about Arnold.

'Well, it's different now. I was sorry for her at first. She turned to me when you let her down. And . . . I suppose I got to know her properly. Her . . . fussing. That's because she cares. It's important to have someone who cares about you, Harry.'

'Yes. Yes, it is.'

'How do you feel about it?'

He could not very well say he felt as if one of the weights around his neck had dropped away. Because even without the dull ache of having let Cheryl down, he still felt nothing. He forced enthusiasm into his voice. 'My God. It's wonderful. Like – like a happy ending.'

'Yes. Yes, that's exactly how I felt. And Cheryl feels the same. And now she knows that you don't mind

. . . You honestly don't mind, Harry old man?'

'Of course not! Am I some dog in the manger?'

'Never were, never will be.' Arnold's relief sang across the wires. 'Any good sending you an invite?'

'I don't think so.'

'I told her that. And so long as we've got your good wishes—'

'You've got those.'

Arnold went on for a little longer and then made his awkward farewells. And Harry replaced the receiver and stared out of the window. Cheryl Mason. He had to concentrate hard to recall her face. She had short, naturally curly hair, brown; blue eyes and a retroussé nose. Mick had called her a nut-brown maid and had told Harry, 'A very suitable mother for your sons, old man! But no more messing about in the mud at Stormy Point. And –' he had grinned wolfishly '– we'll have to meet in secret! Cherry-ripe doesn't approve of me.'

And now Mick was dead and Cheryl was marrying Arnold.

Harry picked up the phone and dialled the hospital and then got through to the orthopaedic ward. He recognized Nurse Gillings' voice; he had spoken to her before. She enjoyed any hint of intrigue.

'I am enquiring for Miss Wilson,' he said.

She said, 'Ah yes. The mysterious admirer!'

He tried to laugh. 'Just a friend of the family who prefers to remain anonymous.' He cleared his throat and said, 'Sister tells me she is doing really well. I wondered how soon before she is discharged?'

'I couldn't say that. She is to have a small op soon.

And then perhaps she will be able to lead a more independent life.'

He replaced the receiver carefully. So, Helen Wilson was going to be independent. She was going to live and things were going to get better. It was what he wanted – the only thing he had wanted. But it meant it was time for him to disappear. Time for the flowers to stop.

There was a tap on the door and Margaret appeared.

'The young couple downstairs. They're quite keen on Flatners Cottage. But that social worker who was looking at it for one of her clients . . . she hasn't come back yet. I doubt very much if she's really interested. It was for a disabled girl and there would have to be a lot of alterations.'

Harry looked out of the window, frowning slightly. He knew that the social worker was Mrs Latimer and she was Helen Wilson's key worker. He had been amazed – almost excited – when Margaret had told him that the two of them were viewing Flatners. It had seemed as if fate intended him to be part of Helen Wilson's life. But, of course, on reflection, he had known better than that. He had already played his ghastly part in Helen Wilson's life and if she knew . . . yes, it was definitely time for the flowers to stop.

He sighed sharply and turned back to Margaret and then – in spite of all his careful logic – found himself saying, 'Look. Hang on to it for a while. See if Mrs Latimer comes back.'

'You know her?' Margaret looked surprised.

'No.' He closed his eyes for a moment. 'I don't know her. Nor her client.'

*   *   *

Mr Edwards gave Helen no time to think up any objections: her reverse operation took place the next day. Dorry was by her bed when she opened her eyes.

'You said you'd come yesterday,' Helen accused, speaking slowly and carefully as if she were drunk.

'Thanks for the greeting,' Dorry grinned as usual, but her small dark eyes seemed lacklustre. 'I take it, from that typically aggressive opener, you are feeling OK.'

Helen licked her lips and enunciated, 'I don't like that word. Feeling.' She allowed herself to be propped and took a sip of water. 'Better.' She closed her eyes then opened them quickly in case she went to sleep. 'Where were you?' she persisted.

'At home. I've got a cold. Thought I'd better not spread it.'

'Phone?' Helen suggested.

'All right. I'm sorry. I should have phoned. There. Is that what you wanted?'

Helen wanted to open her eyes in surprise at Dorry's tone which edged into bitterness. But the lids refused to lift. 'No,' she said very clearly before she slept again.

The next day she remembered very clearly the small exchange between them and knew she hadn't been mistaken. Dorry, who had always squared up to her aggression before, had suddenly and reluctantly caved in. Helen lay in bed, her head turned sideways towards the window, watching the day begin and wondering why she felt no sense of triumph. She and Dorry sparred often and Dorry always won with her sheer practical common sense. Suddenly she had stopped sparring and it was the strangest feeling. As if, in some way, Helen herself had cheated.

She could let her mind range around these days; since January there had been safe things to think about. Sometimes she even reached for her diary to refresh her memory about small hospital events so she could think about them. Now she started with Dorry, got nowhere, then went to Nurse Gillings who was determined to make a romance about the flowers. Then to Mr Edwards for whom Gillings had a definite penchant, and from there to yesterday's operation and the possibility of gaining a little more independence. She did not hang around that thought in case it was hopeless. If she let it lead on to the cottage at Stormy Point it might mean she was piling up disappointment after disappointment. She let her mind turn instead to the dark, thin-faced man who might possibly have sent the flowers – Gillings would lap that up. But it was her secret; not even Dorry knew about him. Not yet anyway. He might turn out to be another kind of social worker. Or a lawyer come to find out whether she was as incapacitated as she had been. Yes. That was really the only explanation for the little mystery. Of course he hadn't sent the flowers; why would he have been examining them so closely if he had actually sent them? That was ridiculous. The trouble was she was starved of male company. That was probably why she had been so – so . . . Aunt Putrid would call it 'forward', and of course that was exactly what it was – she had been 'forward' with Mr Edwards too. She made a face at the long view of the Common where two cyclists were using their mountain bikes like bucking broncos. They were in another world; her world was here in the hospital, peopled by doctors and nurses and social workers. Just that. No mystery men; no men at all who might be interested romantically in a girl who had no feeling from her waist to her toes.

And then, suddenly, almost shockingly, her thoughts turned to Miles.

Before the advent of Peggy Gorman, Miles had had to be excluded from her thoughts in case she began to scream aloud. Since Peggy, she had been unable to imagine him any more. He had somehow transferred himself to another woman. He no longer belonged to her . . . how had she ever had the effrontery to believe anyone could actually belong to anyone else? Yet now, Miles Gorman seemed inevitably to have belonged to Peggy all the time. She'd had no right to remember him; to visualize him. His sudden arrival inside her head was so real – as real as the two cyclists racing on upended bikes over the grass – that she actually gasped. And then relaxed and stared at him. And remembered.

He came closer; his slate-grey eyes fixed on Helen. As she focused him clearly, the quiff of brown hair which he always called his forelock fell over his right brow and he smiled quizzically at her. Like a schoolboy – wanting a favour from his teacher. They were somehow in the Spinning Wheel, coffee cups and soup bowls littering the table between them. He said, 'My God. How can I wait until tomorrow to see you again? What are you doing tonight?'

'Making a farmyard collage.'

'May I come and help?'

'No.'

'Why not?'

'Because you don't help.'

He looked crestfallen. It tugged at her heart. Was that why she said out of the blue, 'Listen, Miles. Will you marry me?'

His widened eyes flattered her. He whispered, 'Nobody asked me that question before.'

'So you don't know what to say? You need time?'

'I know what to say.'

'Go on.'

'The answer is yes.'

'When?'

Why was she so pushy? Was it her fault he didn't tell her that he was married already?

He said, 'Money.'

'I've got enough for both of us.'

That was the trouble. He had called her his silver-spoon girl before then. Her parents were not rich but they were 'comfortable'. They had bought her the house and most of the contents when she left college.

He said, 'No. You have more than enough for you. And that's fine. But I'm not going to be a kept man.'

She lowered her eyes provocatively. 'How else can I keep you?' Then she raised her eyes and deliberately locked their gazes. She felt the surroundings of the little restaurant fade away; it was happening for him too. He breathed, 'Oh God, Helen. I've dreamed of you. I've known you were somewhere. I can't lose you. Not ever.'

'You'll never lose me.'

But, even as she remembered looking into his English face with the snub nose and mobile mouth, she could see Peggy beside him . . . and behind Peggy was Rosetta. His child. He had not lost Helen; but she had lost him. Twice she had lost him, once when he died and again when she discovered that he already had a wife and daughter.

She turned her head from the window as the two cyclists blurred into unexpected tears. God. Was she going to cry for him after all this time? When she knew about Peggy and Rosetta? Or was she crying because she had ruined his life and then lost it?

Dorry said, 'It's just the effect of the anaesthetic. Lift your head slightly, otherwise you'll get all bunged up.'

She blinked hard and looked up.

'Charmingly put.' Nevertheless she helped as best she could with the propping-up and blew her nose hard into the proffered tissue. 'I didn't hear you come in.'

'Not surprised. You were enjoying your wallow.'

'You have a way with words.' Helen blew again and watched Dorry over the top of the tissue. The cold she had mentioned seemed to be dehydrating her. She looked shrivelled. Helen said, 'How are you anyway? You look terrible.'

'I always look terrible. It's the way I am.' But Dorry managed a smile as she folded her cardigan over her chest as if she were indeed cold. 'I'm fine. How about you? Apart from the wallow.'

Helen shrugged. 'The same. I can't see how it will work.'

'Even if it doesn't, it's still a problem we can over-

come. There must be somebody around who is qualified, bearable and needs a job.'

'Well spoken, but without your usual optimism.'
Helen narrowed her eyes. 'Has Flatners been sold to
someone else?'

'No.' Dorry looked surprised. 'Why do you ask
that?'

'Something's up. I can tell. The builders say they
can't do anything with it?'

'Tom's got a patient who is a partner in a building
firm. He says it can be done.'

Helen made her eyes into slits. 'I know what it is.
He *was* some kind of lawyer. And he's going to stop
my money, isn't he? He's going to say I need day and
night care and should go into a state-run home
and—'

'What are you talking about?'

'There was a man here. Yesterday . . . my God, was
it only yesterday? No, the day before. Anyway, he was
an odd fish. Thin and dark and – and – probing. He
looked at the flowers – probably thought I had some
rich relatives who could provide for me – and he
asked questions. Sort of psychological—'

Dorry said, 'Stop squinting in that hideous way,
Helen! And stop talking like a neurotic hen!' She
sighed. 'That's not how the legal profession works.
And they'd hardly employ a private detective on a
case like yours! I told you. Your compensation will
be reviewed at intervals, but you will be notified,
interviewed . . . oh, the usual. It will be sickening, but
it certainly won't be a cloak and dagger affair!' She
leaned back suddenly, smiling, looking better. 'As a
matter of fact, the chap I saw last winter with the

snowdrops . . . remember? He was dark and thin and looked sort of introspective.'

Helen collapsed against the pillows and closed her eyes. 'Those bloody flowers! I've had to hang on to see whether they'd keep coming!'

'Exactly. Perhaps that was the idea.'

Helen opened her eyes again. 'You're sure they're nothing to do with you?'

Dorry made a noise like a squib and Helen said hastily, 'All right. Sorry.' She tried to smile. 'We're not usually so abrasive as this, are we?'

Dorry smiled back. 'We're fairly abrasive. Nothing wrong with that.'

'A bit more so this time. You've got a cold and I'm still full of anaesthetic.' Helen paused then went on, 'I've been thinking . . . remembering. Dorry, I'm not very nice. I'm sorry.'

Dorry said unemotionally, 'I like you. Most people have nasty habits but they're not all likeable.'

Helen said steadily, 'I wanted Miles Gorman. I didn't enquire as to his availability. I just—'

'It takes two to tango, remember.'

Helen persisted. 'I found myself flirting with Mr Edwards. And this man who was here . . . oh God, Dorry. I don't think I can bear myself.'

Dorry took a deep breath and let it go. Her voice was small when she began to speak. 'Tom said I looked like something the cat brought in . . . he said other women looked after themselves and their property and I threw everything away. I couldn't even maintain my car, let alone my hair and my clothes. As for cooking a meal now and then, or cleaning the house . . .' She stopped, swallowed, then went on normally, 'I haven't had a cold. We had an almighty row. I think he's having a bit of a fling with one of his patients. I don't blame him really. I'm hopeless at being a wife.'

Gillings came in, wrinkling her nose.

'Oh dear, oh dear. Bit of an accident? Not to get downhearted. We'll soon clean you up.' She turned and called through the door and the sound of a trolley could be heard coming fast.

Helen began to cry. 'Oh Dorry . . .'

Dorry went to her and held her. 'It can't happen all at once. There's bound to be accidents. It's going to be all right.'

Helen said, 'I'm so sorry. About Tom. So very sorry.'

Dorry said robustly, 'It'll all come out in the wash.' She peered down into Helen's blue eyes and began to laugh. 'Did you hear what I said? It'll all come out in the wash!'

Helen sobbed a laugh and Gillings, entering again towing a trolley, said, 'That's the style! Are we downhearted?'

Dorry said, 'No!' And after a momentary hesitation, Helen echoed her.

Four

By the end of August the house was ready. Dorry brought a glowing report from the builder and reported that the carpet-layer hoped to have all the carpets down by the end of the week.

Helen said, 'I'm so excited.'

'Yes.' Dorry gave a tight upside-down smile. Between them they had interviewed a dozen applicants for the job of live-in carer with nursing experience. None of them had been taken on. Either they baulked at the prospect of lifting Helen on and off commodes and changing her underwear, or Helen herself had declined their help. Her comments were mostly humorous.

'She thinks I'll die early and leave everything to her . . .' 'Did you notice how she sort of hummed tunelessly now and then?' But more often it was simply, 'Sorry . . . I didn't like her.' Usually Dorry agreed sadly, 'Neither did I.'

In spite of four months of disappointment, Helen still asked, 'Why are you looking like that?'

'Like what?' Dorry asked.

'All rueful. It's your job to be optimistic. That smile was not optimistic.'

'Sorry. It's just that . . . well, I can see your point.

You've got to get on really well with someone to live with them all the time.'

'They can have the upstairs. You know I said when I saw it first, the ground floor will be my studio apartment.'

'That means you can't have visitors.'

'I don't want visitors. No-one would want to stay with me anyway. I'm too irritable.'

Dorry laughed. 'You're not irritable. The right person would find you stimulating.'

Helen made a hideous face. 'Not when they've got to change me.'

'You know what Mr Edwards said. Give it time. It might just happen. Perhaps even now your body is working out a pattern to deal with all that.'

Helen said deliberately, 'The crap, d'you mean?'

Dorry looked her in the eye. 'Yes. The crap.'

Helen said, 'Oh . . . shit!'

'OK, if you'd prefer,' Dorry came back.

'I wouldn't. I've got no preferences in that direction. I just want control of some sort.' She leaned back in her chair. 'I was reading a book. Did you know that paraplegics are a high risk for kidney or liver failure?'

'Yes,' Dorry said levelly.

'At least I could have some control.'

'Yes.'

'Did you also know that one week after the reversal op, when it was obvious nothing had worked, the flowers stopped coming?'

'I . . . yes. I didn't work out the precise date, but obviously I've noticed they haven't been arriving.'

'So . . . supposing it *was* the dark man of mystery. Supposing he's something to do with the hospital. Supposing he thought it was all rather romantic. Until he heard that I filled my pants on a regular basis.'

'For God's sake, Helen!'

'It changes things.' Helen spoke lightly. 'For instance, I would have loved to share a house with you. But now . . . I couldn't bear to have you deal with my . . .' she smiled '. . . my waste matter.'

Dorry said, 'Are you testing me? As a matter of fact I trained as a nurse. That's how I met Tom. I could cope with the sort of nursing you need.'

Helen was silent for a while. Then she said, 'Funny how sometimes you make me feel almost cheap.' She held up a hand at Dorry's instant protest. 'It's not you, it's me. Change the subject. Are you and Tom OK now? And I'm not asking that from any ulterior motive! Because even if you could cope with my kind of nursing, I couldn't cope with it from you. You're a friend.'

Dorry said, 'You've got to stop pigeon-holing relationships. I am a friend who could nurse you if I were free. Your nurse will become your friend.' She shook her head at Helen's expression and added, 'Yes. Tom and I are all right now. I was wrong. He wasn't having it off with Elaine . . .'

Helen said, 'Of course he wasn't. He'd be mad.'

Dorry shrugged. She had never mentioned the row with Tom after that first confession, and Helen had not enquired. Dorry said now, 'I've got some more applicants to meet at the office this afternoon. I'll let you know if there's anyone possible.' She stood up, raked her short hair with her fingers and added, 'The furniture you chose goes in tomorrow. Perhaps we could go and look at it next weekend?'

'Next weekend?' Helen repeated. 'It's the bank holiday. What about Tom?'

'He's working too.' Dorry picked up her bag and slung it over her shoulder. She wore a cotton dress that managed to look rumpled. 'I'll see you on Saturday afternoon then.'

Helen wheeled herself to the door and watched Dorry walk down the long ward. There was something consciously gallant about the way she strode to the swing doors and shoved them open. It was Monday. Saturday seemed a long way off. But Helen told herself – as she often did – that Dorry had other clients. And a husband who might still be behaving badly. She went back to her locker and began writing in her diary before the claustrophobia of the ward could enclose her.

That same afternoon Helen had an unexpected visitor. She had wheeled herself onto the verandah and was playing Snakes and Ladders with two twelve-year-olds when she heard Gillings conducting someone down the ward. It was Mrs Whitaker, the headmistress of St Margaret's.

'My dear. Am I interrupting other visitors?'

The older woman had always reminded Helen of the Queen Mother. Her erect bearing drew instant respect from all schoolchildren; she wore a loose chiffon dress and pearls. The boys looked up and stared, fascinated by such elegance.

Helen said, 'Mrs Whitaker! How kind of you to

call.' She introduced the boys. 'Mark and Luke. They were in a canoeing accident, but they're both going home tomorrow.' She smiled at them. 'Mrs Whitaker is headmistress of the school where I taught.'

'You never said you was a teacher, Helen!' Mark sounded reproachful. 'You don't look like a teacher.'

Luke grinned and began to expound on his ideas about teachers.

'Short hair. Glasses. Face like this—' he pulled a long and solemn face and Mrs Whitaker interrupted smoothly.

'Now boys, that's enough. I would like to have a chat with Miss Wilson. You can manage Snakes and Ladders without her for a while, I feel sure.'

She wheeled Helen firmly along the verandah. 'Some boys find it difficult to speak a word. Obviously not those two.'

Helen took control of the chair and manoeuvred it around a table. 'I can manage, really. Do sit down, Mrs Whitaker.' She felt some of her resentment from last winter stir itself again. Had Mrs Whitaker always been so unbearably bossy?

'You look better, Helen.' The small woman settled herself gracefully, facing the wheelchair. 'And you sound better too. I wish I'd kept in touch more, but the spring and summer terms were difficult. Your successor left to have a baby and really some of the supply teachers were . . . anyway, my dear, you don't want to hear about my problems. I've just had a very pleasant rest with my sister and thought it was about time I came to see you.'

Helen had to make a conscious effort to remember St Margaret's and to imagine the 'problems'. Even now, Mrs Whitaker was able to make her feel guilty for having caused them.

She said, 'I've often wondered . . . did you find a place for Peggy Gorman? D'you remember I wrote to you about her?'

'I remember.' Mrs Whitaker turned her mouth down. 'I understood your motives of course, Helen. You were always very kind. Very thoughtful. But I imagine even you realized it just would not do.'

Helen was surprised. 'But it seemed ideal to me. Peggy's daughter will be starting at school and she needs a job to fit in with school hours.'

'Of course. That's why we get so many applications. However, I didn't think Mrs Gorman was suitable. I realize you felt bound to make the gesture, but of course after everything that has happened . . . there has been so much talk about Miles Gorman. When you and he . . . I intended to speak to you then, my dear. It was not a good idea to go out with a married man and a governor of the school to boot. And you were not discreet about it.'

Helen felt her face stretch. She almost bleated, 'But I didn't know he was married, Mrs Whitaker! Nobody told me! Did you know?'

'Well, of course, child. He would hardly have been a governor of St Margaret's if he had not been married with a child who would one day attend—'

'Why didn't you tell me?'

'But it was so obvious! Everyone thought you knew! Are you now saying you did not?'

'I am.' Helen made a sound like a sob. 'I knew

nothing about Peggy Gorman until she visited me here last winter!'

Mrs Whitaker's brows remained lifted in polite disbelief. Then she shrugged.

'It's all in the past now, Helen. Don't distress yourself. But you must understand that if I took Peggy Gorman onto my staff, some parents would see it as condoning what happened. I have also suggested to her that she sends Rosetta to another school.'

Helen was horrified. 'When – when did this happen?'

'When the girl came to see me with your letter. Around the spring half-term I believe it was.'

Helen said angrily, 'So that is why she has not come to see me again!' She flashed a bitter look at the bland woman before her. 'It must be quite a relief to you that I am not going to be able to come back to school! That would really have started the gossip again, wouldn't it?'

Mrs Whitaker lowered her brows but gave no other sign of shock. She said blandly, 'That is one of the reasons I have come today, my dear. I am quite prepared to weather any storm about your return. If you can make arrangements to come into school at any time, we would be delighted to see you. You could listen to the readers, maybe even take an art group – that was your special subject, wasn't it?' She smiled and added quickly, 'On a voluntary basis of course.'

Helen stared at her, trying desperately to find words at once exquisitely polite yet scathing. The woman gave a new dimension to the phrase bare-faced cheek. Helen imagined herself recounting all this to Dorry. Barefaced cheek. She almost smiled.

She said gently, 'I will bear it in mind, Mrs Whitaker. Thank you for coming. It's been so interesting talking to you.' She turned her chair and moved it towards the boys again. 'Will you excuse me now?'

It was the kind of classic dismissal that Mrs Whitaker prided herself on. She stood up, flustered, her chiffon skirt winding itself around her short legs so that for a moment she looked more rumpled than Dorry.

'Well. Yes. It has been interesting.' She paused by the Snakes and Ladders board. 'You are not offended in any way, Helen. Are you?'

'How could I possibly be offended?' Helen smiled brilliantly and picking up the shaker she threw a six. 'That gives me another chance,' she told the boys.

When she looked up Mrs Whitaker was receding fast down the ward. And quite suddenly and unexpectedly Helen felt a ripple in her chest cavity.

'Oh no.' She made a move to follow Mrs Whitaker. 'Boys, I must go. I think that dratted woman has made me feel sick.'

They grinned sympathetically and Helen made for her bathroom. But when she got there she no longer felt sick. Frowning, she called for Gillings and between them they pulled down her trousers and pants and she sat on the commode.

And then she smiled beatifically. 'I think I love you, Gillings,' she said.

'This is so sudden.' But Gillings was as excited as she was. And later Mr Edwards and Sister came to talk to her. Mr Edwards made notes. Sister suggested that she should now learn to move from her chair to the commode without assistance.

'Mrs Latimer tells me you can transfer fairly easily into her car,' she commented. 'So this should not be impossible.'

Helen thought of the gargantuan struggle which had resulted in her and Dorry getting her into the passenger seat of Dorry's old car. It would never be 'fairly easy'. Nevertheless she felt suddenly that nothing was impossible.

She desperately wanted to phone Dorry but she waited two days to make certain that the longed-for control was not a fluke and even then she did not pick up the receiver. It was a delicious treat to be savoured in anticipation. And it was going to make an enormous difference to the situation at Flatners.

On Thursday she did make a phone call, but it was to Peggy Gorman. She had to screw herself up to do it, almost certain that it would be May Gorman who picked up the receiver at the other end. However, it was a male voice. Mr Gorman. Alf, as Peggy had called him.

'Mr Gorman, this is Helen Wilson. How are you?'

There was a startled pause then the reply came pat, 'Just a minute. I'll fetch the wife.'

'No!' Helen almost shouted. 'No, don't do that – I want to speak to Peggy actually.'

'Ah.' She remembered he had a moustache; she could almost imagine him chewing it anxiously. 'She's taken the little 'un to Weston. Bucket and spade. You know.'

'I see. How is she?'

His voice gained some confidence. 'She's all right. We're all right now. You heard there was a partial settlement from the insurance?'

'No.' Dorry had probably mentioned it. 'I tend not to – to hear—'

'Aye. I know.' His voice dropped a tone. Was May Gorman coming within earshot? 'We don't talk about it. But it does mean Peggy and the little 'un will be able to take a flat somewhere. Better for 'em. Really.'

'Yes. Yes, I expect so. I – I'm so sorry, Mr Gorman.'

'It is hard for you. I know that. Try to bear up, my girl. Miles would want you to bear up. It were your strength and independence that he admired most.'

'Did he?' She could have wept then. She forced herself to say coherently, 'I meant I am sorry for what happened. Just to try on a wedding dress.' She swallowed. 'I know Mrs Gorman blames me and I expect you do too. And you're right of course. I—'

'Now listen here, my girl! May can't help herself. She looks round for people to blame. For everything. Peggy and you – you share it more or less equally, 'cept that Peggy has got Rosetta.' His voice softened momentarily then hardened again. 'You know yourself – you're a clever girl so you must know – it weren't your fault.'

Helen could taste her own tears. She thought of her own father, tall and thin – she took after him – always pretending to be henpecked, knowing full well he was cherished. She thought of her mother, short, pretty . . . so pretty. And Miles . . .

She said, 'You don't think I am paying for being

selfish and – and – vain.' It was a thought, a dark and terrible thought, which had visited her often in the night.

Mr Gorman's voice was rough. 'I think no such thing. Is that what May said to you, lass? You mustn't listen! It's a wicked thing to say to anyone—'

'No! No, she didn't say it. I've thought it. Sometimes. When I can't sleep.'

'When you can't sleep, think how happy you made my son. I know that for a fact. He talked to me sometimes. He was sad about Peggy and Rosie. But he said to me that when life offered you something wonderful you would be churlish to turn it down. He said that, my girl. He wouldn't have lied to me. There was no point in lying to me.' There was a pause, then Mr Gorman said, 'You believe me – don't you?'

'Yes. Yes, I do.' Helen dashed her hand across her face. 'Thank you, Mr Gorman . . . for telling me that. Thank you.'

'Someone should have told you before now, lass. I'm ashamed of myself. So busy trying to keep the peace here, I never thought about it.'

'You have now. And I hope you can . . . manage. Somehow. You and Mrs Gorman. And Peggy and Rosetta.'

'I'll tell her you called, shall I?'

They both knew he was not referring to his wife.

Helen said, 'Please. And can you ask her to drop in some time? I would like to see her again.'

He said he would and then rang off so quickly she knew May Gorman had come into the room. She replaced her receiver slowly. Then she picked up a notepad and began to write.

*   *   *

Peggy came the next day. It was five months since her last visit; she was thinner and her fox-brown eyes were puffy.

Helen said directly, 'You know I had a talk with your father-in-law. I gathered that life in that house is taking its toll.'

Peggy smiled fleetingly. 'I'm looking at flats. Did he tell you our first lot of money has come through? I can afford to move out.'

Helen looked at the small square hands emerging from the cuffs of a cardigan not unlike the kind Dorry favoured. But Dorry managed to look shabbily special in her outfits; Peggy simply looked shabby.

'I was sorry Mrs Whitaker turned you down. Especially sorry that Rosetta cannot go to St Margaret's.'

'I don't want her to go there. Not now.'

Helen nodded. 'I agree. Mrs Whitaker came to see me last Monday. I wouldn't want a child of mine to go there either.'

Peggy sighed. 'Miles never said she was such a snob.'

'He didn't know. I didn't know.' Helen shrugged. 'Never mind. Have you got something else lined up?'

'Not until I can find a flat. I'm not sure where I shall be living, you see.'

Helen leaned forward in her chair. 'Does Weston appeal to you? Outside Weston actually. Stormy Point.'

Peggy said unenthusiastically, 'It's all right. But those cottages are just for the summer visitors. And it would be miles to go into school from there.'

'Well actually the village school is about half a mile away. And you could use a car.'

'I can't drive.'

'You could learn.' Helen bit her bottom lip. 'Listen, Peggy. I've got a proposition for you. But it might be embarrassing for you to say no to my face.' She grinned. 'You know, me being pathetic and disabled and all!' Peggy laughed unaffectedly and Helen relaxed. At least there would be no embarrassment in that direction. She picked up her notepad and ripped off the top two sheets. 'I've written it down. My proposition. Take it away with you now. If you don't like it, throw it away and forget it – you need not get in touch with me. If you like it . . . or you're even slightly curious . . . then come back and ask questions.'

Peggy took the folded sheets gingerly. 'You know I can't accept any money – don't need to, honestly.'

'If there was any exchange of money it would be for services rendered.' Helen gestured her away. 'But I rather think you'll turn me down. After all, we don't know each other.'

Peggy stood up slowly, still fingering the sheets of notepaper with some apprehension. 'I'd like to know you. After all, we've got Miles . . . sort of . . . between us.'

Helen laughed. 'There is that. But he is between us. Probably keeping us apart.' She turned the chair towards her locker. 'Whatever you decide, Peggy, I wish you good luck. And of course – Rosetta too.'

'Thank you.' She heard Peggy go to the door. 'Good luck to you, too.' Then came the sound of the door closing. That was something else in her favour.

86

She did not linger helplessly when it came to departing. Miles had never known how to leave a room. Helen dropped her head onto her chest and closed her eyes. She wondered whether she should have waited for Dorry's arrival tomorrow before taking this step. Was it just another example of her impetuosity?

And then the door was flung open again. She turned her chair and confronted Peggy; a very different Peggy.

'I think it's the best idea since sliced bread!' she said without preamble. 'It would make me feel so much better – about Miles and about you and about the Gormans! And I know you'll like Rosetta the moment you set eyes on her! I'm not a nurse of course, but I'm a good worker! A hard worker! I can cook and hang curtains and I dress Rosie, so I'll be able to help you! And all this business about your knickers and everything – that doesn't worry me! I lived with my Gran before I got married and she was incontinent! I always helped her!'

Helen gazed up at her, smiling in spite of her sudden reservations. 'I thought I explained. I am not incontinent any more! Well, sometimes I wet my pants but . . .' She laughed. 'Are you sure, Peggy? I want you to feel this is a proper job, not undertaken because you're sorry for me or feel any sense of responsibility because of Miles . . . I must pay you a proper salary. You do understand that? It's for my sake, not yours.'

'Oh yes! But I'll be working for it, so it will be different. I didn't want any more hand-outs. Any more charity.' Peggy sat down again, her eyes level with Helen's. 'You say here that I need not live in. That I could rent one of the cottages.'

'What about the school? You'd have to walk at first. I could buy a car but you'll have to learn how to drive. It'll all take time.'

'I don't care about walking – Rosie will love it!' Peggy clasped her hands. 'Will you have second thoughts? You won't, will you? You're not just doing this because of Mrs Whitaker or anything?'

'I'm doing it because it seems an ideal arrangement. I've been trying to get someone to help me for ages. I thought you were already fixed up.' Helen smiled and then sobered, 'Listen. If you have second thoughts—'

'Or if you do.'

'OK, or if I do. Then we talk about it. OK?' Helen laughed again at the girl's sheer vitality, she could scarcely sit still. 'Leave it stewing in your mind over the weekend. I'll talk to my social worker—'

'Mrs Latimer?'

'I forgot you knew her. Yes. She'll see if there are any snags. She'll get in touch with you. It puts it . . . sort of . . . on a more official footing. If we do it through her.'

'Yes. I see that.' Peggy clasped her hands again. 'Oh . . . Helen!' She chuckled – it was a good deep chuckle, not one that would get on anyone's nerves. 'It will be so good to have some purpose! I haven't had any purpose since . . . since . . .'

Helen said steadily, 'Since Miles started seeing me.'

Peggy looked down at her hands. 'I suppose it was then. I'm not blaming you. But this is so . . . right!

D'you know what I mean? That we can help each other seems so right.' She swallowed. 'I think . . . don't be offended . . . I think it would please Miles.'

'Yes,' Helen replied. She knew suddenly that she was wet. And it did not worry her too much.

She could not help being pleased that she had actually done something about her own future. She almost gloated at the thought of telling Dorry the next day. She drank her tea, glanced at her watch, wondered whether she should ring Dorry at home. But it was only three-thirty and if Tom answered the phone it could be awkward. The evening stretched ahead interminably. At four o'clock, she rang her solicitor.

'Miss Wilson?' He sounded surprised. 'Is everything all right? I understood you were going out to see the cottage tomorrow?'

'Sorry to bother you.' Roger Whitmore had been anxious about what he saw as an unwise purchase. Even now he was expecting trouble. She injected lightness into her voice. 'I simply wanted the telephone number of the agents who dealt with the sale. Have you got it to hand?'

'I believe I have . . . is something wrong, Miss Wilson?'

'No. Not at all. I am enquiring about renting one of the other cottages. For my helper.'

'You have engaged someone?'

'I think so. I am almost certain.'

'Oh, well done! I am pleased! Mrs Latimer has seemed pessimistic for a few weeks now.' That was true. Dorry's practical common sense had certainly taken a downward trend. 'Yes. Here it is. Double four, double eight, four, eight. And it's Vallender and Son.'

She jotted the number onto her pad, thanked him and replaced the receiver. It was Friday afternoon; past four o'clock. She dialled quickly.

A woman's voice replied. 'Mr Vallender's secretary here. May I help you?'

Helen explained that she was enquiring about the holiday cottages on Stormy Point.

'They are, of course, let at the moment,' the secretary said. 'But it's a short season. I would think by the second week in September most of them will become vacant and I would imagine a long let would be most acceptable to the owners. Let me put you through to Mr Vallender. He is in touch with the owners and will be able to help you.'

'Thank you.' Helen shifted the receiver to her other ear. The sound of the drugs trolley echoed from the end of the ward. Gillings could be heard chaffing one of the men; she gave a small scream and Sister's disapproving voice cut it short. Helen tried to imagine a life where these background noises had no place at all. What sort of sounds would she hear from Flatners Cottage? The shifting of the sea of course . . . that would be lovely. She would measure her life now by the turning of the tides. And there would be gulls shrieking overhead. And the wind constantly pushing at the scrubby trees along the cliffs so that they all leaned inwards. And there would be smells that were quite different from the all-pervading disinfectants of hospital. The salt smell of the sea, the brackish weed at low tide. The wild flowers in the spring . . .

A voice said into her ear, 'Miss Wilson? May I help you?'

Helen felt a shock run from her chest cavity to her waist. She knew it continued down through her legs too, though how she knew this she could not tell. She moved the receiver to her left ear again and cleared her throat.

'I'm sorry . . . is that Mr Vallender?'

'Yes.'

'I – I – am enquiring about leasing one of the cottages at Stormy Point. As close to Flatners Cottage as possible.'

'Certainly. That will be possible. Most of them become vacant next week. If you could send someone for the keys you may inspect them whenever it is convenient.'

She was suddenly afraid her breathing was much too audible. She controlled it with difficulty.

'Thank you. That is most helpful. Thank you.'

'A great pleasure.'

The line went dead. Helen hung on to her receiver and then replaced it as the trolley arrived at her door.

She was certain that Mr Vallender was her dark man of mystery.

Five

Helen dreaded meeting Rosetta so much that on the morning of her visit she was physically sick. The success or failure of her scheme depended entirely on this one small girl. The fact that the girl happened to be Miles' child made the situation so poignant Helen wondered if she could bear it.

Her fears were not shared by Peggy.

'You'll like her,' she said with unexpected confidence. 'She's not like Miles, so there's nothing to . . . well, you know . . . remind you . . .' Helen told herself that she liked small children, she had happy memories of them from school.

She said huskily, 'I shall like *her*. Of course. But if she doesn't like me . . . well, we can't force a new life on her, Peggy. None of this –' She gestured to her legs, to the hospital room – 'has anything to do with Rosetta.'

Peggy said hesitantly, 'You don't understand. She's had to live with everything going *wrong* all the time. Me especially. When I told her I'd got a job, she was so pleased. I can't tell you.' Peggy twisted her hands. 'And anyway, children like beautiful women. Didn't you find that when you were at school?'

Not for the first time, Helen saw the depths of Peggy's terrible lack of self-esteem.

She said, 'You are beautiful, Peggy. Surely you know that?'

Peggy lifted her shoulders and said nothing.

Rosetta was small for her years; Helen watched her come through the doors at the end of the ward, reaching high to hold her mother's hand. But she was sturdy too: she wore a skimpy sun-dress which showed her arms and legs were rounded and somehow capable. She had creamy skin like her mother, liberally dotted with orange freckles; her hair was brown like her father's. But Peggy was right; she was unlike either of her parents; she was completely herself. Her eyes were brown, bright and curious as a bird's, and she seemed to be expecting good things to happen. Somehow, in spite of everything, Rosetta Gorman looked like any other 'rising-five'. Full of anticipation and excitement.

Helen wheeled her chair forward tentatively and held out her hand. Peggy released her hold on her daughter, standing back, letting her choose her own course of action. Helen thought afterwards that most small girls would have instantly looked at their mother for guidance. Rosetta did not. She transferred her hand from Peggy's to Helen's and grinned a huge grin. Helen found herself grinning back.

'Hello.' The grin flowered into a laugh. 'I'm Helen. And you're . . . ?'

Rosetta realized that this was a social routine.

'I'm Rosetta,' she said in a high voice with a trace of lisp. 'But everyone calls me Rosie.'

Helen pumped the small hand slowly. 'May I call you Rosie? It's a pretty name.'

Rosie nodded vigorously. 'Mummy said I should call you Miss Wilson cos you're a teacher. But I can say Helen.' She relinquished Helen's hand in order to place hers at her waist. 'Helen. See? Helen. Helen.'

'Then please call me Helen. I'm not a teacher now.'

Suddenly Rosetta stopped role-playing, took her hand from her waist and began to talk in earnest. Words poured from her in cascades, tumbling from breath to breath, unstoppable. Helen responded with more smiles, a down-turned mouth, astonished round eyes.

'Mummy can do lots of things. She says she can't but she can. She can make beds and do bandages – she bandaged my doll all over when it dropped out of the bedroom window – she can wash hair and clothes and walls and floors and she can grow flowers and . . .' There was a pause for effect '. . . she can scrape new potatoes!'

'She can?' Helen managed to get in incredulously.

'Oh yes. And you know how difficult that is . . . all those little bits and all.' Helen nodded. Rosetta nodded too.

Helen said very slowly, 'I know she will look after me splendidly. But . . . she will need your help some-times. Your – your co-operation. No, that's too difficult a word. I mean—'

'I know cropperation. Daddy used to say cropper-ation.' Rosie put her hand back at waist level and mimicked without mockery, 'Have I got your full cropperation?'

Helen swallowed hard. 'Yes.' From the edge of her vision she could see Peggy, very still, very wide-eyed.

Rosie said, 'Course. Anyway, it will be easy, won't it?' She looked up at her mother, then turned another grin on Helen. 'See . . . we all loved Daddy, didn't we? So cropperation will be easy.'

Helen waited for her own reaction: a rush of emotion that would probably end in a flood of tears, hysterical laughter. Instead she felt, physically, right inside herself, a core of stillness; almost of acceptance. She glanced at Peggy. The liquid reddish-brown eyes were watching her apprehensively.

She said quietly, 'Yes.' And then she opened her arms and Rosie stepped within them without prompting and kissed her smackingly.

The child turned back to her mother and said, 'See? I knew it would be all right.'

Helen and Peggy laughed. And then they began to discuss Rosie's new school, new house, new clothes, new life.

It was another two months before Helen actually lived in Flatners Cottage, but Peggy and Rosetta moved into the house next door immediately. Peggy attended a course in Weston for carers and Rosie went to the small nearby primary school and took to it instantly. It began to look as if Rosie's easy assertion that it would be all right was coming true. When Dorry heard about it she murmured 'Babes and sucklings'. Then she added, 'She must have *some* faults?'

Helen said, 'She hops quite a bit.'

'Hops?' Dorry queried.

Helen explained gravely. 'On one foot. You know.'

Dorry nodded, equally serious. 'Ah well . . .'

Helen realized over that bank holiday weekend that she would need transport if she wanted to visit Flatners regularly. She had plans for making her own curtains and cushion covers and, as Dorry said with a shrug, why shouldn't she, she could sit at the low worktop in the kitchen and plug in a sewing machine. So while the new bathroom was being built she ordered a hand-controlled car and as soon as it had arrived at the nearby garage, she and Dorry went to see it. It was an adapted Ford Escort with an enormous door on the driver's side which enabled Helen to transfer herself into the seat and then deal with her wheelchair.

It was like climbing a mountain. She knew that once she was halfway up she had to go on. It was all right when the mechanic and Dorry were standing there, but when she was alone it would be different.

'I shall develop muscles like Popeye!' she gasped, leaning back in the driver's seat, her legs somehow wedged beneath the wheel while they dealt with the wheelchair. To Dorry as they drove carefully along the old A38 she confessed, 'I'm scared. I don't know whether I'll have the sheer strength for this.'

Dorry said in her most sensible voice – which showed that she too was anxious, 'You'll have to manage if there's no-one there. And of course you will. In some ways it will be easier to do it without an audience.'

'I am tempted to use a word that rhymes with rowlocks,' Helen said.

'But you're too much of a lady.' Dorry did not laugh. She went on seriously, 'You'll have to watch yourself with Rosie. She's put you on a pedestal.'

Helen said, 'Well, I really have got clay feet and she'll have to know that sooner or later.'

Dorry sighed. 'Yes. I was like Rosie. I used to think people in wheelchairs were angels.'

Helen made a grotesque face. 'And I showed you how wrong you were?'

Dorry was forced to laugh at last. 'Oh no. I learned that from Tom's patients. Sometimes when he manipulates them, their language is shocking.'

'I can't imagine you being shocked.' Helen paused at a road junction and went on. 'I'm beginning to enjoy this driving. But it's funny, when I was doing that hill start just now my left foot felt for the clutch.'

Dorry was startled. 'How do you know that? Do you mean you could feel it?'

'No – of course not! In my head. It happened in my head.'

They were both silent for a while. Then Dorry said, 'That's how it all starts. In the head. One day the message will bypass the kinks and get to your foot. I'm sure of it.'

'Well, I'm not. And I'm planning my life without feet and legs. So that's OK.'

'Yes. Sure.' They were in the wooded lane now that split off to lead to Weston or the headland. 'Take it as slowly as you can,' Dorry advised. 'Then I can point out Rosie's school.' There were some villas in the thicketed hill on their left and then Victorian gates and a flight of stone steps leading to a shelf of asphalt that was the playground of the tiny school. Opposite, a lay-by had been carved out of a field and Helen drew into it.

Dorry said, 'I am so thankful she took to you. When I arrived at the hospital that Saturday – two weeks ago now? You were practically incandescent. And you hadn't even seen Rosie.'

'I know. I realize now I was taking a great deal for granted.'

'You certainly were. You can be sure Grandmother Gorman would have painted you as a marriage-wrecker.'

'I suppose so.' Helen tried to see the whole awful business through the eyes of a four-year-old. She shivered. 'You know, Dorry, if I'd realized Miles had a daughter, I would never – ever – have let it get as far as it did. I had tinies in my reception class who were from single-parent families. I know what it does to kids.'

Dorry said sadly, 'I suppose that's why he couldn't tell you about her. Poor Miles.'

Unexpectedly Helen shook her head. 'Cruel Miles. In the end he was completely selfish. He didn't care about Peggy, Rosie . . . or me. Not really. Eventually I would have found out about the other two and I would have been unhappy about it.' She had been leaning on the wheel staring up at the school, now she sat back and looked at Dorry, startled. 'My God, Dorry! It wouldn't have worked! I suddenly realized . . . it wouldn't have worked!'

Dorry said nothing. After a long while Helen

turned back to the wheel and went carefully through the motions of starting the car as the mechanic had shown her. They pulled out into the lane again and almost immediately turned right for the road to the Point. And then they were on the stony track and edging gently down towards the small clutch of cottages that seemed to have been washed in by the sea.

Helen switched off the engine but neither of them moved for a long time. And then Helen said, 'Yes. This is home. This is where I belong now.' She glanced sideways and was shocked to see tears streaming down Dorry's face.

Dorry put up a hand. 'It's all right. It's just . . . I wish we could all reconstruct our lives as you are being forced to do.' She fished for a handkerchief in her sleeve and blew her nose fiercely. 'I think I've got a cold. Try not to breathe.'

Helen, near tears herself, laughed helplessly. 'You really are crazy,' she said.

Dorry sniffed and mopped her face. 'So I'm told,' she said.

Helen wondered who had told her that and said emphatically, 'That's what makes you so good. Don't you see that? You have to be slightly out of sync to deal with the other oddballs like me.'

Dorry opened her door. 'Let's see you get the chair out and yourself in it,' she said drily. 'Perhaps you'll be less complimentary then. You might even be forced to swear at me again.'

Helen opened the big door wide and reached behind her. 'I've never sworn at you, Dorry Latimer!' she said. She watched as Dorry fitted the key in the specially low-sited lock on the front door. 'Have I?' she asked doubtfully.

'Get on with it!' Dorry called back, opened the door and went inside. Peggy's voice greeted her delightedly and she would have come outside to help, but Dorry would have none of it. Ten minutes later Helen wheeled herself indoors, sweating profusely and looking wild-eyed.

'I'm never going to cope!' she announced tragically, ignoring Peggy's anxious face and addressing Dorry's back.

'Well, you'll have to,' Dorry came back. 'This low working surface is ridiculous – I've already got backache trying to make us all a cup of coffee! Come on, you can take over.'

Helen looked at the table by the newly installed patio windows where Peggy had already laid out coffee cups and a big thermos jug. She said, 'You can stop grinning like a Cheshire cat because I'm not going to swear at you!' Dorry turned and revealed that she was indeed smiling now. 'But actually,' Helen wheeled herself to the table and began to pour. 'Actually, you are a rotten little so-and-so.'

Peggy fetched a biscuit tin. She was giggling and looked more like a schoolgirl than ever. 'This is going to be fun,' she said. 'Isn't it?'

Helen looked at her and smiled determinedly. She was going to make it fun. For Peggy and Rosetta.

'It sure is,' she said.

It was decided that Helen would move on 27 October which was a Thursday. By that time she had made curtains and a duvet cover, Peggy had planted a mass of bulbs around the two cottages and Rosetta had painted a picture of what the garden would look like next spring. Helen stuck it on the wall next to the window. 'I'll have golden daffs inside and outside then,' she said to the little girl, smiling at the enormous piece of paper covered liberally in yellow blobs.

Rosie nodded. 'That's how it will look,' she said. 'Course they can't move. They're painted in place. But that's why I've done this . . . see?' She pointed to the dribbles of paint which Helen had thought were simply dribbles of paint. 'That's when the wind comes out of the sea and blows them this way. And that's when the wind comes over the hill and blows them that way.'

'So it is,' Helen marvelled. 'You are a real primitive painter, Rosie. Did you know that?'

'I knows I'm good,' Rosie said with Dorry's matter-of-factness. 'My daddy told me I was good.'

Helen swallowed. 'Well, he was right. You are,' she said.

Rosie sighed with satisfaction. 'It looks nice there, doesn't it? Everything is nice now. Everything.' She looked at Helen. 'And it will go on and on being nice now, won't it Helen?'

Helen smiled. 'Yes. It will go on and on being nice, Rosie.' And she knew it was a promise.

Thursday the 27th turned out to be sunny and dry. The trees were all colours of yellow and red, dying to a crisp ochre underfoot. The sea, peaty brown from the Severn, picked up reflections of the sky and was a pale grey-blue colour, glinting diamond bright here and there. Everything except

Helen's personal possessions had been moved in by this time, but Dorry had found her a small Victorian commode in a second-hand shop and had loaded that into her car. She followed Helen as they bumped along the stony track to the cottages and wondered whether Helen realized that as from today their official connection was broken. Her area did not extend past the Bristol city boundary.

Peggy and Rosie had made a special meal, Dorry had brought candles which they lit as soon as Rosie returned from school. Then the four of them went to the beach, Helen insisting on wheeling herself down the gravel sweep she had had laid. They threw stones into the sea in a kind of ritual, then looked back up at the candles flickering in the big window of Flatners. The sun disappeared quite suddenly into the sea, leaving a smoky orange glow behind it.

'We'll have our bonfire here,' Peggy said, following her own train of thought. 'Rosie can start collecting wood.'

'If you're talking about November the fifth, it will be a Saturday,' Helen said. 'I was thinking about it too. We can all come down in the afternoon and build it. How do you feel about fireworks, Rosie?'

'Don't like them,' Rosie said glumly.

'Just sparklers?'

'Yes. They're all right,' the little girl said, nodding.

'Good. Because I can manage those too.' She looked up. 'Dorry, will you bring Tom? We've never met him.'

Dorry, who had been smiling at such excitement,

sobered slightly. 'I'll have to see. He may have made plans already.'

Rosie ran down the stony beach and came back lugging a piece of driftwood. 'Here's some wood!' she announced proudly.

Peggy said, 'Let's get it above the tide. It can go on drying out then. And some of this seaweed too, Ro. The dry, crisp stuff.' They ran back and forth, laughing and panting, already just dark shapes in the gathering dark while the two older women watched them.

Helen said suddenly, 'Is it going to work, Dorry?'

'It's working. Already.' Dorry leaned over the wheelchair and spoke in a low voice. 'Just because you can't run around with them—'

'Is that why you're staying with me?' Helen looked into the small brown eyes so close to her own. 'Go on. Don't be an idiot.'

'I don't want to rush around in the dark, thank you.' Dorry straightened. 'In fact I want to sit down. I'm tired. I'm going back to the house.'

She disappeared into the dark face of the cliff and Helen listened to the crunching of the gravel and then saw the candles flicker as Dorry opened the window and stepped inside. She knew, even at this distance, that Dorry was crying again.

Peggy called breathlessly, 'That'll do for our first haul!' She materialized by the chair. 'Come on, Rosie. It's going to be too steep for Helen this time. Let's give her a hand.' Helen started to speak and Peggy said firmly, 'That's why we're here, Helen. Remember?'

Helen subsided. She realized suddenly that she too was tired; bone-tired. And there was still the meal

103

and the clearing-up before she could be blessedly alone.

But when they got inside the living-room, a surprise awaited them. Dorry was wide-eyed, her apparent irritability forgotten.

'Look what was on the front doorstep,' she said and lifted an enormous bouquet onto the table. Grasses, reeds and teasels surrounded chrysanthemums and roses. 'The perfect autumn bouquet,' Dorry commented, almost awestruck. 'And not a card in sight.' She smiled at Helen. 'Have you told Rosie and Peggy about your secret admirer?'

Helen said automatically, 'Don't be silly,' but when Rosie clamoured for details she told them about the flowers which had arrived so regularly last winter. She said nothing about her various suspicions, and Dorry, taking her cue, did not mention her meeting with the man with the snowdrops. But when Peggy went to put Rosie to bed later, Helen told Dorry about the telephone call to Vallender's.

'He sounded like the man you thought was from the insurance company? The solicitor man?' Dorry was amazed. 'I dealt with Vallender's of course. But I've only seen the secretary. It's crazy. There's no connection.'

'I'm probably wrong. In any case, it all stopped a long time ago.' Helen grinned at Dorry. 'You and Tom organized this – admit it!' She nodded towards the glorious flower arrangement.

'No. I wish I'd thought of it. But I didn't.'

'And Tom – would he?'

Dorry said with surprising emphasis, 'You must be joking!'

'I wasn't.' Helen wheeled herself to the dishwasher and placed her cup inside it carefully. 'What's wrong, Dorry? And don't say nothing because I know you're under some sort of strain. Talk about it. Let me into your life.'

Dorry was silent, watching the fair head above the counter.

She said, 'You're supposed to talk to me.'

'There's not much you don't know about me. I know nothing about you. Not really. You're married to an osteopath and things aren't good.'

Dorry sighed and then said tersely, 'Tom had a wonderful childhood. He was spoiled, I suppose. I spoiled him at first. And I don't any more.'

Helen came back to the table. She fingered the drooping blond head of one of the grasses. She said quietly, 'You're giving too much time to your clients.'

'He always knew what my work entailed. We agreed I should go on working.'

'But you don't switch off from some of your clients. Particularly one.'

'All right. He's jealous. It's difficult for him to be jealous of my work. But when that work entails someone in a wheelchair it is more difficult still.'

'I understand that.'

'There are one or two of *his* clients who would gladly . . . divert him. I thought Eileen Thorne might be one of them. We had a row about her.'

'I remember.'

'That's all sorted out now. In fact, everything is sorted out.' Dorry stood up. 'I'd better go.'

'You are certain it is sorted out?'

'Absolutely.' Dorry wound her long scarf around her neck. 'Actually . . .' She glanced at Helen then moved to the door. 'He was delighted to hear you were moving to the cottage.' She shrugged. 'Obviously, you'll be with another department now. He thinks that's a good thing. Social workers shouldn't get involved with their clients.' She laughed. 'A bit like nuns really.'

Helen stared and Dorry, glancing at her said, 'Don't look like that. You must have realized . . . I expect you'll be contacted by your new social worker any day now.'

'I won't be seeing you?'

'I shall come and see you – if you would like me to—'

'But not regularly. I won't be on your list. Someone else will fill my place and you won't have time to . . .' Helen's voice rose with every syllable.

Dorry interrupted quickly. 'It's the nature of the job, Helen. But we've become friends. And friends don't lose touch.'

'Did you know – when you found Flatners – did you realize what it would mean?'

'We were looking all over the place – don't you remember? I didn't work the future out like that. It was just to find somewhere that you would like – love – feel at home—'

'But you knew – you knew all the time – it would also mean the end of our relationship.'

'Helen. Stop it.' Dorry came back into the room. 'This is the sort of thing that shouldn't happen. Really. It's the sort of thing that justifies Tom's gut reaction.' She took Helen's hands and shook them.

106

'Listen. You don't want our relationship to continue on a professional basis – there is no need for that. We're friends now. We stay friends. Can't you see that?'

Helen blinked, then dropped her head. After a moment she said, 'Dorry, I apologize. It was just – for a moment – I felt . . . deserted. Like I did at first. When Mother and Dad and Miles were all killed and I was left. Sorry . . . I'm really sorry.' She looked up. Her eyes were intensely blue. 'Yes. Tom is right. Tom has never met me but he knows instinctively when someone is possessive enough to make demands on his wife.' She squeezed Dorry's hands and released them. 'Will you apologize to him too?'

'No. I see nothing to apologize for.'

'I'd like him to know I'm sorry . . . Have I been a pain, Dorry? Oh, I suppose you've got to shake your head – of course you have. But . . . you didn't seem to mind when I was surly and hateful. It was as if you did not see me as different in any way. I happened to operate my life from a wheelchair and that was that.'

'Yes. That was how it was.' Dorry grinned. 'Listen, I do have to go. Peggy will be in to make sure you're settled for the night. Let her do things for you, Helen. She needs this . . . she needs you as much as you need her, if not more.'

'OK.'

'Yes, well. Mind you remember. She's been going to classes. She's got ideas. Don't wet-blanket them.'

'OK!'

Dorry grinned. 'And let me know if your mystery man materializes.' She patted Helen's hand briskly and moved to the door. 'I'll see you on Bonfire Night. With or without Tom.'

'OK,' Helen said yet again and raised a hand. When the door closed she let the hand fall into her lap. Bonfire Night was over a week away. It was the longest time she had been without Dorry since last January.

Peggy proved almost too much of a treasure and Helen, bound by her promise to Dorry, had to bite her tongue several times when Peggy interrupted her blessed solitude to suggest knitting sessions, Christmas-card making, or discussions about the latest news.

'We could have our very own summary of the newspapers,' she said enthusiastically. 'We could call it something . . . headlines. Something like that.' She grinned delightedly. 'I've never really thought about what is happening in the world, Helen! And when they said it was important for you to look outside your environment, my heart sank! I'm so ignorant! When I left school I took the first job that came along – in the Spinning Wheel – and I stayed there until . . .'

'Yes.' Helen tried to smile. 'The thing is, Peggy, I'm not that mad on knitting. I might do a few watercolours for Christmas cards perhaps . . .'

'Oh, that would be nice!' Peggy said. 'I forgot you were an artist.'

'And I'll try to talk about current affairs with you. But what I liked about this place was that it was away from all the awful things of life. I suppose that's a bit ostrich-like.'

'Ostrich-like?'

'You know, I'm burying my head in sand and pretending things like murders and wars and famine and cruelty don't exist.'

Peggy said doubtfully, 'Well, we'd have to find things that were more cheerful. There's often a page about recipes or fashion.'

Helen laughed genuinely. 'Oh Peggy . . . you are such a good person. I think I'm going to call you Saint Peggy.' She shook her head at Peggy's flushed face. 'I'm not being sarcastic, honestly!' She wheeled herself to the stove. 'Let's have a coffee and you tell me what else you've got in store for me!'

Peggy regained her confidence and said, 'The course was called a rehabilitation course . . . the one I went on. And besides all the occupational therapy stuff, they suggested massage. Now, I am good at that. Miles always said . . .' Her voice trailed off then picked up again like an old gramophone record, 'Alf says I do wonders for his fibrositis – he's got it in his shoulder, you know. And it's very important to keep the circulation going in your legs and feet. So I'm going to give them a good rub morning and evening.' She paused momentarily and added uncertainly, 'If you will let me.'

Helen, who had been going to turn down the offer as gently as possible, found herself saying, 'I'd like that, Peggy.' She looked up at the warm chestnut-brown eyes. 'Thank you.'

It wasn't going to be easy having Peggy fussing around her. She sipped her coffee, kept smiling while Peggy fetched her massage oils and thought grimly that she hoped Dorry would be pleased with the way she was co-operating.

*   *   *

On Saturday Helen insisted that Peggy should take Rosie to see the Gormans. They talked about it the day before, while Rosie was at school. Peggy was reluctant to go and Helen had to remind her that May and Alf were Rosie's grandparents.

'Don't let anything spoil all this,' Helen said, sweeping an arm towards the window where storm clouds were piling up over the distant Devon coast. 'My God, I might even invite my Aunt Putrid for Christmas! Perhaps I'm going to turn into a saint too!'

Peggy spluttered a laugh. She held Helen's heel in one hand and swept the other up the calf towards the knee. Helen imagined for a moment how wonderful it would be if she could say, 'Peggy, I can feel that!' Then she shut that thought down quickly.

Peggy said incredulously, 'Aunt *Put*rid?'

'Mildred by name, putrid by nature,' Helen said. 'And I'm only joking! But I am serious about your in-laws. Please, Peggy. It's still just as awful for them – worse because you and Rosie have gone.'

Peggy towelled Helen's leg and her hands and began to wriggle a pair of trousers over the white feet. Helen forced herself to allow this until the waistband was within easy reach, then took over. '*And* I can put on my own socks!' she forestalled the next piece of assistance. 'They should have told you to encourage me to help myself at that blessed course!'

'They did. Sorry.' Peggy stood up and began to put oil and towels away. 'Yes, all right. I will take Rosie into Bristol. Will you be all right?'

'Of course. As a matter of fact, it will be good for me to have a go at being alone.' Helen tried not to look too happy at the thought. 'I'd take you in the car, but I haven't actually driven alone yet. Dorry was either with me or driving right behind. Once you've got your licence we'll be able to go all over the place! And that's another thing, you must start lessons again.'

Peggy grimaced but then nodded. 'It's part of the job,' she agreed.

'So tiz,' Helen teased her. But privately she thought how wonderful it would be when Peggy was able to drive off for the day and leave her with all this land and sea to herself.

Contrarily, she felt unexpectedly bereft as she waved goodbye to them the next day. The rain that had threatened yesterday had arrived with a vengeance and the two figures crouched under one umbrella looked like something from a Hardy landscape as they trudged up to the spine of the headland. And then, almost as if planned, a sleek black Rover car bounced along to meet them. Peggy leaned towards the driver's window, then turned and waved reassuringly at the cottage. Peggy and Rosie clambered into the back of the car which made a careful three-point turn and jogged sedately back towards the village and the Bristol bus-stop.

Helen wondered whether the visitor could possibly be Dorry. Had Dorry persuaded Tom to visit the cottage after all this time? It had been a man's head at the car window, she was sure of that, but it had been impossible to see whether there was someone else with him. She glanced at her watch:

ten minutes to the village, ten minutes back. She wheeled herself across the living room to the low cooker and plugged in the kettle. Were there any decent biscuits? She wanted to make a good impression on Tom.

She was at the window again when the Rover came back and she was not surprised when it parked at the top of the rise. She had somehow gathered that Tom was the kind of man who would not subject his car to the extra hardship of the gravel track to the cottage. She said grimly and aloud, 'I've got to like him – for Dorry's sake, I've just got to like him!' And then he got out on the driver's side and she knew it was not Tom.

She wheeled her chair away from the window as if he could see her through the driving rain, then she peered around the frame like any nosy housewife with a pair of net curtains. Except that she had no net curtains. Even with a black umbrella shielding face and shoulders, she knew it was the man from Vallender's. Vallender himself of course.

'He's come about Peggy's cottage,' she said aloud in the kind of sensible voice Dorry had so often used and which had a calming effect. 'He said a long lease . . . maybe there's a problem with it.'

But he wasn't making for Flatners and its neighbour at all. Halfway along the drive he veered to his left towards the rank of four cottages which had been empty since the season finished. Rosie had named them the Lookout cottages and it was quite possible that they had indeed been built for local fishermen to watch the progress of the fish shoals in the bay.

Helen spun the chair to the patio windows and craned her neck to watch him open the gate which served them all, and unlock the first one.

She felt not only bereft but deflated.

'Serves you right,' she said angrily. 'Cooking up romantic mysteries! Just like Gillings with Mr Edwards! What is the matter with you!' And as if to remind her just what was the matter, she felt the familiar tickle beneath her ribs which meant she needed to trundle to the bathroom and begin the miserable business of getting out of her trousers and pants, dropping the armrest of the chair, locking the chair into position and shifting her heavy body onto the specially curved lavatory seat. It had been a triumph at first; now for some stupid reason she wept at the weight of her dead legs and when she had finished she sat still for a long time, quite unable to find the energy to move to the adjacent bidet.

She said furiously through her tears, 'It's all so damned undignified!' But it was much less undignified than it had been and by the time she was back in the living room she had reminded herself of that and faced the fact that she was missing Peggy and Rosie and deeply disappointed that the Rover car had not contained Dorry and Tom. Or better still, just Dorry.

'You spineless idiot,' she said to herself and managed a smile at the ironic aptness of the insult. Then, like a report from a sniper's gun, the door knocker fell just once and she was frozen in her chair, staring at the inside of the door across the large expanse of her living area.

Because it had to be Vallender. Unless it was the kind of marauder who would be very unwelcome indeed. She moved slightly sideways and narrowed her eyes at the rain-streaming window by the front door. The Rover was still waveringly outlined on the ridge. So, even if it were a marauder, Vallender was probably within earshot of a scream.

She opened the door on the chain and looked up beneath a large golfing umbrella into the face of the man who had been in her room just before her last operation. He looked a little less apprehensive though his dark eyes were still unsmiling.

'I'm Harry Vallender, Miss Wilson. We've spoken on the telephone and we met once at Frenchay when you were there. Do you remember?'

So . . . not much mystery on his side.

'I remember. Do come in Mr Vallender. Is it something about Peggy Gorman's cottage? Next door?'

She backed away from the door and he followed gingerly, shaking his umbrella outside and leaving it in the old-fashioned stand she had brought from her parents' house.

'Sorry . . . I'm dripping everywhere. After that lovely Indian summer the weather has turned on us.'

'Yes. But it's still rather wonderful. Look.' She wheeled herself to the patio windows. The rain swept across the bay and into Weston like the continuous stroke of a paintbrush. 'It's all having a wash,' she said. 'I know that sounds twee, but just look at it for a moment.'

He stepped out of his shoes and followed her curiously.

'I wondered what you'd done to this room. What

114

a view. And I understand you paint?'

'I thought I'd do a water-colour of this. Rather appropriate wouldn't you say? It's all so . . . watery!'

He seemed determined not to smile. 'Lots of grey wash, of course. But there's blue and some ochre there too.'

She remembered from their brief exchange at the hospital that he had treated every one of her remarks with careful seriousness. She remembered especially how he knelt before her and lifted her misplaced foot back onto the footrest. Her face warmed inexplicably.

'I remember you as someone who looked hard at things. My flowers. And the man you were supposed to be visiting . . . Mr Scott was it?'

He wasn't to be caught out. 'Mr Welch. Mr William Welch.' He stood awkwardly by the window. She remembered he had had difficulty in bending and straightening. She had wondered whether he had been ill. He said, 'I do enjoy looking. Even in this weather the bracken and the hawthorn berries . . . as you drive along the Point . . . it's very beautiful.'

She nodded, suddenly relaxing. She did not need to be on her guard with this man. Surely it was possible to be friendly without despising herself for also being provocative?

'Isn't it a sign of a bad winter? My mother used to say that nature was providing a food store for the birds against a hard winter!'

'Well, there are certainly a great many berries. If it snows, we shall know she was right.'

At last he smiled, but she frowned, catching something odd in his words.

She said directly, 'How do you know she is dead?'

His eyes moved fractionally, more with unease than shock or embarrassment.

'I am so sorry. You did use the past tense when you . . . I am so sorry.'

'So you did not know?' she persisted with her old directness.

'I . . . yes, actually, I did know. When Mrs Latimer was talking to my secretary about the sale of Flatners . . . it was mentioned.'

'I see.'

There was a hiatus while they both stared out at the rain. It now looked colourless and simply depressing. She was angry with herself for forcing the admission out of him. He would now go. And he could have been a friend. She felt something for him . . . an affinity or something.

He cleared his throat.

'I came to check on the Coastguard cottages—'

She interrupted delightedly, 'Is that what they are called? Rosie calls them the Lookout cottages. She will be so interested!'

He did not smile. 'Yes. They were in fact owned by Trinity House. My father bought them after we'd moved into Flatners.'

'You lived in Flatners? Here?' She was astonished.

'He bought it for our summer holidays. He loved it – he'd been in submarines in the war – married late – he wanted me to know the sea.'

'How could you bear to sell it?' she asked.

He said with her own directness, 'He died. I tried letting it with the others. But then the last tenants . . .

well, you know it was in a bad state. I didn't think it would sell.'

'And then I came along. How strange.'

'Yes. I was afraid you might not like it.' He spread his hands. He had long fingers, blunt at the tips. 'If you're not happy . . . I will buy it back. I would hate you to feel trapped down here.'

She was amazed; she did not doubt his sincerity for a moment. 'That is most generous of you, Mr Vallender. But . . . I am extremely happy so far!' She laughed. 'I've been here three days but I can say that with confidence.' She let the feeling of warmth for him sweep through her. 'How kind you are! Is that why you knocked? To make me that offer?'

'Well . . . yes. And I wanted to see you.'

She was suddenly breathless. She did not dare to focus into his dark eyes for too long in case the look she had shared with Miles should overwhelm her. That had proved sham. And totally sexual. This was different. This was friendship.

She said, 'I thought you wanted to see me. Before. I thought you would come again. But you did not.'

'I telephoned. That operation – the reversal – was successful. I thought . . . I knew you were going to be all right.' He said painfully, 'I had no place . . .' His voice petered out.

She looked at the flower arrangement on the table. 'So you stopped sending flowers too.'

There was a long pause. She risked looking back at him and said challengingly, 'Well?'

'How did you know?'

She laughed. 'I didn't. I suspected. Now I know.'

She continued to smile at him. 'Thank you. At last I've got the chance to say that. They sort of . . . kept me going.'

He had been holding his breath. Now he let it go in a sigh. 'I'm glad. That is what was intended. I thought you would have to hang on somehow, just to see if there were any more.'

She changed her smile wryly. 'Another psychologist! Dorry with her damned diary! And you with the flowers!' At last he smiled too. His dark eyes were deep and unfathomable. She said quietly, 'You know all about the loneliness of being ill and in hospital, don't you?'

He said, 'I was in hospital. For a time. Not as long as you.' He made a dismissive gesture and went on, 'Dorry with her diary?'

'Mrs Latimer. My social worker.' Helen nodded. 'My friend, actually. She made me do . . . well, what you like doing. Looking. Thinking. Recording things. She made me look outside myself. At the hospital – what was happening. And outside the hospital . . . the weather. Things.'

He nodded too. 'It's important. Looking at everything.'

She had to stop herself smiling again in case she looked idiotic. But she began to turn her wheelchair towards the kitchen. 'Will you have coffee? I've got some biscuits too.'

He started to decline then changed his mind. 'I'd like that. May I help?'

'No. Sorry, but this is my kitchen now.' She allowed herself a fleeting grin over her shoulder as she switched on the kettle and assembled mugs and plates on a tray. 'Do you understand?'

'Of course.'

'Sit down. Look at the view again and then look at the room. It's not cosy like it was before. But do you approve?'

He sat at the table, his gaze going around him all the time. 'I like it very much,' he said. 'After the way it has been treated I feel . . . I feel it's now in good hands.'

She was deeply pleased and felt herself smiling again as she pushed the trolley ahead of her to the table. They sat companionably, drinking coffee and nibbling biscuits, and the only thing that she could have wished for was that he might show the kind of pleasure she was feeling. They discussed how she would tackle her water-colour and she told him about the new board she had which did not need to be wetted or stretched. And then he told her that he still kept one of the original flatners in the shed at the end of the Coastguard terrace.

She was immediately fascinated.

'Was it your father's?'

'He acquired it somehow. The art of flatner fishing was disappearing anyway. There's an example of a flatner in the City Museum and probably just a few here and there in garages. But this one could still be used. I've kept it tarred and in good condition.'

'Have you ever used it?'

'Only as a sport. It's for catching eels in the mud which has never interested me. I use it like a sledge . . . a ski.'

Her eyes shone. 'I'd love to see you . . . I'd love to see it.'

'If it wasn't raining we could go along now. But of course I'll show you. And you could come out in it, actually. Sit in the prow. I need to be in the stern. You'd enjoy it.'

She felt like a child again. 'Oh, I would!'

He drew her sketch block towards him and outlined the shallow flat-bottomed skiff. She gazed at it, entranced. Suddenly life seemed full of possibilities.

She said, 'I'm so glad you called . . . it was such a kind thought but you can see I am completely hooked on life here.' She laughed. 'I'm glad you sent the flowers in the first place and as for William Welch . . .'

He laughed with her this time and somehow she knew for certain there was no William Welch.

She said, 'Why did you send me flowers? Yes – yes, I know, to interest me, make me curious. But how did you know about me? Why me?'

As soon as the words were out, she knew she should not have said them. The way the smile died from his thin face, the way his eyes concentrated on her so seriously, she knew he was about to tell her something awful.

He spoke at last. Slowly and with total honesty he said, 'I was in the other car. The open-topped car with the balloons.' She made a sound of protest and put a hand to her mouth. He paused and then went on deliberately, 'I was the bridegroom. It was the day after our stag night. When I came out of hospital, I heard about you. Your wedding. Your fiancé. Your parents. I came to see you. You had been in hospital for six months and you'd had two serious operations and you were still paralysed. And it was my fault. I watched you for a time. Asleep. I wanted to do something . . . wake you up . . . see you stand and walk . . . and I knew I couldn't. I was the last person on earth you would want to see.'

He finished speaking and stood up. She watched him take the trolley back to the kitchen and put the mugs and plates into the dishwasher. She could think of nothing to say.

He went to the door and put his feet into his shoes, and picked up his umbrella.

With his back to her he said, 'I thought you were the most beautiful thing I had ever seen. I still do. I cannot ask you to forgive me – I cannot forgive myself. But whether we wish it or not, we share something . . . a moment . . . pain . . . terror. Remember that when you are hating me.'

He opened the door and the rain blew into the room so that she shivered. Then he was gone and she watched through the window as he struggled against the wind back to the headland and the Rover car.

Six

Tom Latimer finished stuffing the morning's sheets and pillow cases into the laundry bag, washed his hands and dried them thoughtfully. He glanced around, checking his treatment room was ready for Monday morning's patients. Then he clicked off the lights and went into the waiting-room. Mrs Raines was 'running a duster', as she put it, over the chairs. He looked at her expectantly.

'Just running a duster over the chairs, Mr L,' she said. 'What time you expecting Dorry?'

Inside his head Tom said, 'Keep perfectly calm. She doesn't know a thing.'

Outside his head he said, 'Any minute now. Why?'

She looked smug. 'Thought so. And she told you to light the gas in the oven I'll bet you a thousand pounds. It's all right. I done it.' This to placate the muffled curse that sprang to his lips.

He was about to tell her that he did not know what they would do without her but then she said, 'I don't know what you'd do without me, I'm sure. She still not happy with you?'

He wanted to throttle the woman. He had insisted when she started with them two years ago that she should call him Mr Latimer. She abbreviated that to

Mr L, and called Dorry, Dorry. She was over-familiar. It was terribly unfortunate that she had come into the room when Dorry had accused him of 'going too far' with Eileen Thorne. But she couldn't possibly know about this morning.

He opened the door into the hall and said stiffly, 'I really don't see what business—'

To his amazement Mrs Raines interrupted sharply, 'I don't like to see her unhappy. That's all. And she hasn't been right since that business with Mrs Thorne.'

He felt himself turning red and said furiously, 'My God, you've gone too far this time! How dare you discuss my private affairs like this!'

Mrs Raines was not to be routed. 'I never have done that, Mr L! You know I wouldn't! You and Dorry – you're like my family! Now then! An' if families can't be concerned for each other—' She gave a juicy sniff and he left the door and passed her a box of tissues from the coffee table.

He felt weary. He had discharged Eileen Thorne that awful day when Dorry had witnessed The Kiss ... he put the whole thing into flippant upper case whenever he thought of it, which was often, because it really had been over-the-top and almost funny. Except for Dorry's unhappiness of course. When Eileen Thorne had turned up this morning saying that no-one else could free her back of the terrible pain, he had known he should have sent her packing. And he had not done.

But Mrs Raines could not possibly know that.

'Come on now. I didn't mean to sound so fierce.

But really . . .' She blew into the tissue with a sound like a fog-horn. '. . . The state of my marriage *is* private. I appreciate your concern for Dorry. Of course. But—'

'Not having no mother of her own, see,' mumbled Mrs Raines. She sniffed lusciously and put the soggy tissue up her sleeve. 'Shall I come and do some spudatoes for you, Mr L?'

'No. I can manage that, believe it or not!' Tom smiled. 'But you're right. We couldn't manage without you, so don't let me stop you any longer.' He whipped back to the door, reminding her about the laundry bag and the clean covers for the treatment tables. As he peeled the potatoes fiercely, hacking at the eyes with unnecessary thoroughness, he calmed himself by remembering that after lunch he and Dorry were taking this precious Saturday afternoon off and driving to Bath for a concert in the Pump Rooms. He would make her laugh by 'doing' Mrs Raines' patter. 'Just running the duster over the chairs Mr L, and then can I do your spudatoes? I don't know what you'd do without me . . .' He stopped himself abruptly. On second thoughts he would not lampoon their cleaning lady. Not until he'd got rid of Eileen Thorne once and for all and could look Dorry in the face again.

He added salt to the potatoes and looked at his watch. Dorry should be running the car onto the drive at any moment now. While she superintended the lunch he would fix her wing mirror and check those wipers again. He said aloud, 'You are spineless, Tom Latimer. All you have to do is to phone Eileen

Thorne's flat . . . now. Right now. Tell her you can't see her on Monday however bad her back is. Give her Nick Williams' number. Go on. Do it.'

He hesitated. She had behaved impeccably this morning, apologizing for having embarrassed him before, pleading with him to continue her treatment. 'I knew if I telephoned, you'd put me off. I had to come and see you face to face.' Did she know he was a moral coward who would be unable to say no to that beautiful, pouting, mature little-girl face? He had looked down at his appointment book. 'All right. There is a slot at ten-thirty on Monday. You must excuse me now, I have a patient on traction.'

He put the saucepan of potatoes on the hob and went to look out of the front door. No sign of Dorry's car. He had time to make that phone call and then he'd be able to enjoy this afternoon to the full. He'd be able to make Dorry happy again. That's what he wanted. Like Mrs Raines. He wanted to make her happy. Make her forget her blasted job and all the down-and-outs and sick people. Make her concentrate on him. Just him. Dammit all, he was her husband.

He was actually reaching for the phone and clicking the phone cards for the Thorne number, when it rang at him. He stared at it. Surely Eileen Thorne wouldn't phone him on the house number? He snatched up the receiver, at last ready to tell her to go away.

'Bristol, five double eight, four double zero,' he said in his professional voice.

A female voice replied; in distress. It was not

Eileen and he felt a droop of disappointment. He would have been forced into it. Now he would have to do it under his own steam.

'Tom? Is that you? Is that Tom Latimer?'

'Speaking.' He frowned into the hall mirror. He had never heard the voice before, yet somehow he knew it.

'I hoped Dorry would be there.'

'She's not home yet. Can I give her a message? Who is this?'

'Helen Wilson. I'm Dorry's—'

'I know. How are you? Is everything all right?'

'Yes. It's fine.' There was a pause. He thought her breathing sounded a bit shaky. 'It's more than fine. She couldn't have found anywhere better.'

He frowned. 'What about you? Are you all right?'

She gave a little laugh. 'Yes. I am all right. I'm being totally ridiculous. I am all right.' She spoke the words slowly with emphasis as if convincing herself. 'I wanted a word with Dorry . . . well, I wanted to tell her something. That's all.'

He knew it was more than that. He imagined her sitting in that blasted wheelchair holding the telephone receiver to her ear much too tightly. Dorry had said she was beautiful. Daffodil hair and cornflower eyes. Spoilt all her life. Having to face desolation. Doing it well.

He straightened his back. That was Dorry's car nosing through the gateway now. He could have called and got her to the phone in half a minute.

'Shall I ask her to telephone you when she comes in?' he said.

The voice warmed. 'Would you? Thanks so much.'

He said something reassuring before replacing the receiver. Dorry was just emerging from the kitchen.

'Who was that?' She unwound her scarf and draped it around the newel post then sat her knitted hat above it. She was in a good mood; if he told her about Helen Wilson she would ring back immediately and there would be a problem. She might even decide to forgo this afternoon and drive to Weston to see her.

He said, 'Someone after an appointment.'

'Not this afternoon?' Her voice sharpened with disappointment.

He grinned and pecked her snub nose. She looked like a schoolgirl, like an urchin. 'Not this afternoon. Nothing is going to spoil this afternoon,' he said.

She wound her arms around his neck and kissed him properly. He thought with delight that she had forgiven him at last. He would phone Eileen and make sure she did not keep that Monday morning appointment. He would.

The rain had stopped. Helen sat by the phone for an hour then went to get some lunch. By two-thirty a watery sun was lighting the sea and she was certain Dorry would drive along the headland at any minute. By three-thirty darkness seemed to be coming up from the ground and she knew there would be no Dorry and no phone call. Tom was not going to pass on any messages at all.

In one way she was glad. The first horror of discovering that Harry Vallender had killed her parents and Miles, had seemed vital information. Information that Dorry must have, must analyse, must talk about objectively. As time dripped slowly away, Helen wondered whether the information had much relevance except to herself. Surely the horror lay in the fact that she had liked him? She wheeled herself angrily to the window and looked out; she had more than liked him. She forced herself to be brutally honest: she had been drawn to him. Very much so. Blast it, she had wanted the man. Friendship indeed! She had been just as she had with Miles. She could have looked into those dark eyes and drowned in them.

She leaned forward and banged her fists on the glass of the window. It was stoutly double-glazed and gave slightly to her pounding and that was all. She whirled back to the kitchen, picked up a cup and hurled it against the wall. It broke. It gave her no pleasure. Peggy would have to get the dustpan and clean it up. That certainly did not give her pleasure. She sobbed drily as she leaned over the arm of her chair picking up the pieces she could see. One of the shards caught her finger and she bled profusely.

'Good!' she said, frustrated beyond belief. 'I don't care. I just don't care.'

And then, suddenly, unexpectedly, thankfully before Peggy and Rosetta returned, she began to cry. She was no longer crying for Miles, or her parents. She was crying for herself.

Bonfire Night came at last. It was typically foggy and mysterious and Rosetta, who had two friends to tea, was delirious with excitement. Peggy had a collection of suitable fireworks and packets of sparklers galore and they spent the afternoon on the beach building their bonfire and settling a lopsided guy in its centre. Dorry arrived just before complete darkness; she was alone and in her curious waif-like clothes she had a forlorn look Helen had not noticed before. She pretended to cower before the vociferous welcome from the three small girls, pecked Helen lightly on the cheek and said, 'Hello, friend.'

Helen laughed. She'd battled all week with a mixed bag of feelings that ranged from a kind of despair to a stolid acceptance of her own volatile nature, but in the centre of herself she too felt forlorn.

'Same to you,' she said lightly. 'Can you help Peggy with that piece of trellis? We found it washed up yesterday and it seems the perfect frame for the Catherine wheels.'

'In other words, get on with it,' Dorry came back. She pulled her gloves higher up her wrists and studied Helen's face in the dusk. 'Are you all right?' she asked.

'I would have phoned you if I hadn't been,' Helen replied.

'I hope you would.' Dorry gave her characteristic grin and crunched her way over the pebbles to where Peggy and the girls were cavorting around a rotten piece of fencing. Helen continued to stack dry seaweed around the base of the bonfire, reaching out with the hooked branch Peggy had found and poking it in as best she could; it was as if Tom had slapped her across the face. She shivered, although the mist swirling around the beach was not cold. Tom Latimer could not possibly be a very nice man. And he was married to Dorry who was kind and vulnerable.

Peggy insisted on taking the children into her cottage for an early tea. Helen and Dorry busied themselves wrapping sausages and potatoes in tinfoil for cooking on the embers of the fire later. They talked desultorily about practical matters, as friends do. Dorry spoke of the concert at Bath the previous weekend. Helen, who had assiduously kept her diary since Harry Vallender's visit so that she would have something to tell Dorry, recounted Rosetta's latest sayings.

'Peggy proving hard work?' Dorry said acutely.

Helen grinned. 'At times. She is so *anxious*! But I have to say I very much enjoy the massage.'

Dorry asked curiously, 'How do you know?'

'Know? Know what?'

'Whether it is enjoyable or not. Surely you can't feel it?'

'Yes. Strange, isn't it? She starts on my neck and shoulders – that's wonderful. She says I'm tense.' Helen grinned again. 'She uses all the jargon. Anyway, whether that sensation remains – sort of residual or something – or whether when she gets to my legs and feet there's a kind of reaction in my upper body . . . I don't know.' She shrugged. 'I feel relaxed, soothed . . . it is good.'

Dorry was sitting on a cushion on the floor so that she was lower than Helen. She stirred her tea thoughtfully and Helen waited for her to say that surely this was a good sign.

At last Dorry said hesitantly, 'Helen, how would

you feel ... now ... if you were certain that you would never walk again?'

Helen was aghast at the question and the questioner. Dorry often surprised and shocked her, but never before like this. She shook her head as Dorry quickly apologized for such insensitivity.

'No – no ... I would want to know. I would ... I would. Are you trying to tell me that I'm in this chair until I die?'

'Oh my God! No! What a fool I am! Tom is so right ...' Dorry was almost overcome with remorse. She knelt and put her arms around Helen's shoulders. 'I spoke as a friend, not as your social worker! It occurred to me that you were coming to terms with the whole thing ... Helen, I am so sorry! Please forgive me!'

'No – No, I do understand,' Helen gasped as if emerging from cold water. 'I think ... I was expecting you to soothe me with empty words – you know, perhaps my spinal kinks were unkinking and that was why I am enjoying Peggy's massages. And then you ...' She snuffled a laugh. '... you turned the whole thing upside-down!' She rested her head on Dorry's arm. It was the first time anyone had held her since the accident ... since Miles. She said, suddenly deadly serious, 'The thing is ... I would like someone to love me. And how can – you know – if I am in this chair and can't feel a thing below my waist – how can anyone ...' Her voice trailed away and she leaned back, telling Dorry that she was free to end the embrace.

Dorry sat back on the cushion very slowly. Then, as usual, cut all the conversational corners.

'There are special courses you could attend. Sex for the disabled.' She saw Helen's face and said, 'Don't knock it, Helen. It's important. You already know that.'

'I . . . couldn't . . .' Helen averted her head in distaste. 'It's too . . . calculating.'

Dorry did not pursue the matter. 'All right. But if ever you want to know more, your social worker will—' Helen gave a squeak and she amended, 'Me then. I'll find out about them. And let you know. As a friend.'

Helen said, 'Change the subject, Dorry, please. I've never been embarrassed with you before and I don't like it.'

Dorry laughed. 'Let's have another cup of tea. Then it will be time to take the low road again and succumb to pyromania!' She stayed where she was and let Helen pour the tea. And when they had finished and were dressed and ready to go out she said seriously, 'One day, Helen, you will meet someone. And then you will be willing to go to one of the courses. For his sake.'

Tom felt his stomach churn with suppressed anger and childish pain. It was as if Dorry had left him. He had been so sure she would stay with him tonight and when she had said, 'But darling, I thought you were coming!' he had replied confidently, 'Not likely! Kids and fireworks? You must be crazy – we've got the whole evening to ourselves – everyone else will be cavorting around bonfires – let's make the most of it!'

She had laughed and kissed him. It had been

a good week. Bath had been wonderful and the whole of Sunday they had slopped around the house catching up on domestic jobs, reading, talking . . . it had been like in the beginning. And he had kept his side of the bargain and telephoned Eileen Thorne the moment Dorry left for work on Monday morning. He had not waited for her to argue or cajole, he had said, 'Ah, Mrs Thorne. I apologize. I've overbooked this morning and must cancel your appointment. I can thoroughly recommend Nick Williams however.' And he had replaced the receiver immediately, sweating and uncomfortable, but deeply thankful that it was done. To see Eileen Thorne on Monday morning would have negated the whole of his wonderful weekend with Dorry.

And now Dorry was smiling at him with her wide, urchin mouth and saying, 'But I have to go, darling. I promised Helen. Do come. She is expecting you and she will be so disappointed.'

He had never thought much of Dorry's devotion to Helen Wilson. Now he wanted to blot the thought of the daffodil hair and blue eyes out of his mind; out of their lives. He had not let himself think again of that telephone call.

'Dorry, Dorry, Dorry . . .' He held her shoulders and spoke in between kisses. 'You've always said disabled people loathe specialist treatment. Helen must take disappointment like the rest of us—'

She jerked away at that and stared at him, her button eyes very round. 'This has got nothing to do with Helen's wheelchair for Christ's sake!' Her anger was so unexpected he released her, shocked.

'Tom – she is a person! She has invited us for the evening. I have said yes.'

'Darling . . .' he changed to pleading. 'You don't really want to go. Admit it. We can light a fire in the sitting room and make love on the rug—'

'Stop it, Tom!' Her anger steadied into something else. Was she disappointed in him? 'You're not a child – stop acting like one!'

He hardened his expression. 'You don't love me.'

She turned away. 'I said stop it. I'm going to get my coat and leave. I want you to come. But if you don't I'm going.'

He watched her reverse out of the gate. She was driving badly because she was upset and he had a moment of terror at the thought of her returning home in the dark along that blasted headland. How could he tell her he could not possibly meet Helen Wilson now? He had already worked out that he would say to Dorry, 'Look, I'm sorry. Yes she did ring but she said she was all right and I completely forgot about it.' And perhaps she wouldn't tell Dorry anyway. But he couldn't meet her. He couldn't watch her manoeuvring a blasted wheelchair around, look into her blue eyes, hear the voice that had asked for . . . something.

He felt his stomach begin to churn and went into the kitchen for an Alka-Seltzer. Then, with a kind of schoolboy defiance, he went into the little-used sitting room and started to lay a fire.

At five-thirty when he was wondering whether a cup of tea would settle him, the doorbell rang.

None of their friends used the front door, so he guessed it was someone collecting for charity and was already digging change out of his pocket as he opened the door. Eileen Thorne stood there. Tears ran down her face. Her hair was standing on end. She looked terrible.

'What has happened?' Automatically he stood aside and she came in, sobbing helplessly. 'My God – what is it?'

'I'm so sorry . . .' She could barely speak. She grabbed the newel post and clung to it for support. He closed the door and came behind her. Damn Dorry! If she'd been here it would be all right.

'Look . . . will you come and sit down . . . are you injured?'

'No – no, of course not.' She lifted her head and smiled determinedly. Her face was now streaked with mascara. 'It's just . . . I don't think I can bear you being angry with me. I've been walking up and down all afternoon trying to find the courage to knock on your door—'

'I'll fetch my wife. She's upstairs,' Tom lied wildly.

'I saw her leave.'

'My God. That was over two hours ago!'

'Yes. It seems a long time. I thought she might come back. And when she didn't I guessed she had gone to a bonfire party and I tried to ring your door-bell and I couldn't and then I fell over and got muddy and wet and then I started to cry and I couldn't stop . . .'

Tom was appalled. He shepherded her into the sitting-room and eased her out of her sheepskin coat. Beneath it she wore a cherry-red woollen frock which showed off her long lean lines to perfection. He had told her once she reminded him of a

135

ballerina. What a terrible mistake that had been. He eased her into an armchair on one side of the fire.

She wailed, 'I must look such a mess! Oh my God . . . my tights!' She lifted her legs. The tights were muddy and torn. He was thankful she made no effort to get out of them. He knew he was going to have to be absolutely straight with this woman; it was certainly flattering that she had worked herself up into such a state about him, but for once in his life he had to be strong. He thought of Dorry and yearned for her presence. But then, after all, it had been she who had left him.

Eileen Thorne lay back in the chair, closed her eyes and stretched her legs to the fire. She murmured, 'Give me a moment. I'm so sorry. Have you got a handkerchief?'

He passed her his handkerchief and she mopped her face. He wondered if he should offer the bathroom, then decided against it. He had to get her out of the house as soon as possible.

She said, 'I must look a sight,' and though he knew he should have kept silent, he said automatically, 'Of course not. You look distressed.'

She began to weep again into his handkerchief.

He said, 'Look. Mrs Thorne. This must stop – I am very sorry to have been the unwitting cause of so much unhappiness, but as you well know, I am married – happily married—'

'Oh, so was I! My husband was a wonderful man—'

He hardened his heart. 'He has been dead for ten years if I remember the details from your file, Mrs Thorne.'

'I know . . . do you think I don't know?'

He gave up on that and said, 'I'll make a cup of tea. Then you must leave. I'll call a taxi.'

She removed the handkerchief and said desperately, 'I just want to talk. That is all – just talk.'

He stared down at her, hesitating. She must have been nearly forty and at the moment she looked older; but her bone structure was amazing: strong, perfectly symmetrical. Tom knew all about bone structure.

She filled the short silence quickly. 'Tom. I probably made it awkward for you the other week. I shouldn't have kissed you. Especially when I was only half-dressed.' She managed a tremulous smile. 'Did your wife . . . was she very angry?'

'She was hurt.'

'You told her it was me . . . I don't mind you telling her it was me.'

'We did not . . . discuss . . . it.'

'It would have been ungallant. You would never be ungallant.'

'Mrs Thorne—'

'Please, Tom. Eileen. Please.'

'Eileen. If you don't want tea then I will call a taxi now. Please excuse me.'

She said, 'I would like tea. Yes. Tea would be splendid.'

He had imagined he was handling it so well but he cursed himself as he went into the kitchen. He should not have offered her an alternative. He was still behaving like a weak fool. She was older than he was, basically beautiful, and obviously had some kind of obsession. It was not a mixture to play with. *And* he had called her Eileen.

*　　*　　*

The bonfire party in the little cove at Stormy Point was an unqualified success. The fireworks did not explode loudly, the Catherine wheels all whizzed without restraint and the guy maintained his erect stance until the last minute when he was satisfyingly engulfed in flames. The barbecue which followed provided 'the best feast ever' according to Rosetta. Peggy came into her own, removing the hot tinfoil with gloved fingertips and popping each sausage inside its roll without dropping one.

'It's because of being a waitress,' she deprecated when Dorry praised her loudly. 'I can't cook very well, but I'm good at serving things up.'

'You cook good, Mummy,' Rosetta said stoutly.

'Not like Granny.' Peggy turned her fire-warmed face to Helen. 'She's so efficient. Never let me into the kitchen.'

Helen could imagine that. No wonder Peggy had an inferiority complex. She said, 'I was spoiled like that, too. But when I got my own place, I found I could cook as well as most people.'

'Ah well. You're clever,' Peggy said with finality as if that closed the discussion.

Helen restrained her irritation. 'I couldn't have done those hot dogs without burning my fingers. And I'm no masseuse either.'

'Me neither. Or, possibly, too.' Dorry laughed. 'Let's toast Mummy in pop, shall we, girls?' She filled their beakers and showed them how to lift them high. In the glow of the fire their faces might have belonged to cherubs. Helen thought, 'Six women. Six females. Will it always be like this?'

And, as if in reply, she heard a stone roll behind her. She did not turn. She knew who it was and wondered how long he had been standing there, keeping guard over them. She drank her lemonade and tried to control the sudden tears.

It was ten o'clock when Dorry turned into Falcondale Road. She saw the taxi outside the house and slowed down. Tom emerged from the front door and armed someone down the drive. Dorry pulled into the kerb and switched off her lights. She wondered what on earth she was playing at, acting like some private detective. Whoever was with Tom was ill; that much was evident. The figure – it was a woman – leaned heavily on him, head bowed. Dorry should have leapt out and gone to her aid. But she did not.

Tom released one of his arms and opened the taxi door with difficulty. Carefully he helped the woman inside, then closed the door and spoke to the driver. Money changed hands. So he was paying for this woman to be taken somewhere.

The taxi drove away. Tom hurried indoors. Dorry pretended for another five seconds that she had no idea who the woman could be. Then she started her engine again, switched on the lights and drove up the road with great care, swinging wide so that she could manoeuvre through the gates.

She used the back door and put the kettle on before she went through into the hall. Tom met her. His previous anger had disappeared. He clasped her energetically.

'Sorry I was such a bear. Oh, it's lovely to see you.

How did it go? I'll make some tea – I did light the fire in the sitting-room and it's so cosy.'

She said, 'It's not really cold outside.' She hung her coat on the newel post; the polished wood appeared to be muddy.

'How's it gone with you? You should have come. Six women and no men.'

'Six?'

'Rosetta Gorman had two friends. Both four years old. Both female.' She went into the sitting-room. There was a strange smell . . . not unpleasant. Tom had been using an air freshener.

'I wish I had come with you.' His voice was suddenly deep. 'Sorry, love. Sometimes I'm such an idiot.'

She could have told him he was weak, he was emotionally immature, he was soft. Instead she leaned on the mantelpiece and looked into the fire. There was mud on the tiled hearth. 'I knew that when I married you,' she said, as much to herself as to him. She looked up and smiled. 'Well? What have you been doing?'

She held her breath, begging him silently to tell her the truth.

He said, 'I've been bored. But never mind that. I'll go and make some tea and you can tell me about your evening.'

He was gone. She looked back into the fire. She knew Eileen Thorne was a widow. She understood her. That was the trouble with her job, she understood most people. But some people . . . the unhappier they were, the more dangerous they became.

All Tom had to do was tell her . . . it was difficult for him . . . he could share that difficulty.

She whispered, 'You knew he needed looking after – you knew that. And you have neglected him.'

Seven

Just before Christmas Peggy failed her first driving test. She did not appear terribly disappointed. It was the nearest they had come to having a row.

'Well,' she said to Helen on her return in the small Ford driven by the instructor, 'I would have been surprised if I'd passed. And I wouldn't have dared to drive on my own anyway.'

Helen absolutely refused to answer that last remark. She had told Dorry last week that the more things Peggy accomplished, the faster her confidence ebbed. Now it seemed that the same rule applied to her failures too.

She said tightly, 'Well, I'm not really surprised either. If you intend to fail at something, then – obviously – you will fail.' She watched Peggy's freckles stand out against a suddenly white face. The girl stood before the wheelchair like a child waiting to be reprimanded. Helen could have screamed at her. She drew a deep breath and tightened her hold on the chair. 'You need more practice.' She spoke in a level, reasonable voice. 'I'm not allowed to come out with you and Dorry's too busy . . . is there anyone at school who could take you out now and then?'

'I'll never do it,' Peggy said. 'It's not worth trying again.' Helen opened her eyes very wide and Peggy bit her lip. 'Sorry. But it's true. It's a waste of money. Your money.'

Helen struggled to keep her temper but her voice sharpened unconsciously. 'Look. It was my idea that you should learn to drive. I know I've got a car and I can drive it, but there are times when I would like you to do the shopping.'

Peggy's face drained further. 'Oh my God! Are you telling me that unless I drive I can't keep the job? I wouldn't blame you of course. I know I'm pretty hopeless—'

Helen turned her chair, went to the window, looked at the view and very deliberately screamed. Peggy put her hands to her ears and bowed her head. Helen wondered if she had stood like that in front of Miles when Miles told her he had met someone else. She turned her chair and stared up at the girl, narrowing her eyes analytically.

'Sorry. Sorry, Peggy. It's just that – sometimes you give me a pain. What the Americans call a pain in the ass. Only I wouldn't know about that, would I?' She laughed but there was no response from the cowering girl. She moved the chair back from the window and changed her perspective, as if Peggy were sitting for her portrait. 'My God, there you stand on two beautiful legs – gorgeous red hair, creamy skin . . . completely competent – good mother, wonderful carer for me . . . and all I hear is how hopeless you are!' She whirled the chair again and went for the kettle. 'For God's sake, Peggy! You must know in your heart of hearts that I couldn't manage without you? You must see how happy your Rosie is with you? And then you say something like – like—' She banged mugs onto the counter. 'Yes! I might not be able to feel it, but I'm telling you it gives me a pain in the ass! But I'm sorry I screamed. Forgive me.'

Slowly Peggy took her hands from her ears and opened her eyes. She did not move. 'You don't have to say sorry,' she said in a low voice. 'I'd rather know . . . how you're feeling . . . I want you to be . . . honest.'

Helen tried to smile. 'Well, that's how I'm feeling. I'm fed up with you underrating yourself. I'm fed up with your lack of self-esteem.'

Peggy flapped her hands helplessly. 'But, whatever you say, I *have* just failed my driving test.'

'Everyone fails their test the first time!'

'I bet you didn't.'

Helen lied. 'Well you lose that bet anyway.'

'Really?' Peggy sounded incredulous.

'You've been with me in the car. You know I'm not a natural driver.'

'Yes, but it's an adapted car. Not what you're used to.'

Helen made the coffee and said patiently, 'If it were an ordinary car, then it would disable me. Yes. But because it is adapted it *en*ables me. So we're level pegging on that one.' She passed a mug of coffee and said quietly, 'Listen, Peggy. Is it because of Miles? Or is it because I'm in a wheelchair?'

'What do you mean?' Peggy took her coffee and sat down so that she was on a level with Helen. Her colour was coming back and the freckles were less startling.

'You seem to think I am little Miss Perfect. And

144

you're encouraging Rosetta to think the same. Is it because I am disabled? Or because Miles fell for me?' Her calm enquiring voice made the questions even more brutal.

Peggy looked into her coffee mug. She said in a low voice, 'I don't know what you mean. Of course I think you're . . . special. Not because of Miles. You gave me a job and a home for Rosie. You treat me as if I'm the same as you—'

'Christ Almighty, woman! I treat you as if you were paralysed, do you mean?'

Peggy flushed. 'You know I don't mean that. You treat me as if I'm . . . well, clever. Had an education. Like you.'

Helen groaned long and loud. Peggy added defensively, 'And you say I'm beautiful like you. You said just now . . . and competent and things.'

Helen spoke with her eyes closed. 'And so you are. All those things. Why won't you believe me?'

There was a long pause. Peggy stood up. 'I'd better go for Rosie.'

'You can't answer me? Or you won't?' Helen persisted.

Peggy went to the door. She said in a stifled voice, 'Miles said those kinds of things. He was lying.'

Helen pushed her chair across the room. 'I'll go for Rosie,' she said quietly.

'No – really – it's all right.'

'Please let me, Peggy.' Helen looked up at the girl. 'Please trust me to do that.'

Peggy looked startled for an instant. Then she unhooked Helen's car coat and held the door open.

And as Helen wheeled herself across the room, she said, 'All right. I will try again. But only if you let me pay for my lessons.'

Helen smiled. 'Done!' she said.

The next time Peggy took Rosie to see her grandparents, Helen struggled into the car and drove into the city herself. She had looked up the whereabouts of Vallender's office in the phone directory and she negotiated the roads around Westbury village with some caution. Whatever she had said to Peggy, she was still uncertain about using her car in heavy traffic. She parked in a side street and tried to take the whole business of getting out of the car and into her chair as calmly as possible. It did not seem to get any easier. She sat still, panting and close to exhaustion. Then she locked the car and pushed herself onto the pavement. She did not wish to give herself time to examine motives or emotions. This was almost a business call. Yes, almost.

The girl behind the desk leapt to her feet to help her through the door. Her smile was wide and friendly.

'Is it Miss Wilson?' She stayed on the client side of the desk and sat down by Helen. 'Mrs Latimer used to come in about Flatners Cottage. I feel I know you.'

Helen scraped up memory-scraps from what she now fondly called 'the days of Dorry'.

'Margaret, isn't it? Dorry said how helpful you were.'

'Really?' The girl dimpled delightedly. If only Peggy would take compliments so easily. 'Anyway, how are you managing down there? It's very cut off, isn't it?'

'I've got the car,' Helen explained. 'And it's so beautiful. I rather begrudge time spent away from it.'

'Oh, that's wonderful. Mr Vallender will be so happy when I tell him that.'

Helen bit her lip. Of course, everything she said now would be passed on to Harry. The sooner she saw him herself the better.

'I wanted a word with him, actually. Is he in the office today?'

'He's with a client at the moment. He should be back within the hour. May I make you some coffee?'

'No.' Helen could have cursed. Here was the time she did not want. She forced a smile. 'I'll look around the shops. I need a few things. I'll be back about . . .?'

'Make it midday. He'll come in before lunch to pick up any messages.'

Helen wheeled herself outside to a barrage of pleasantries from Margaret. People were so kind . . . she told herself this firmly as she bowled along the narrow High Street. It was nothing to do with her being in a wheelchair . . . people were simply . . . nice.

She was looking in the window of a fabrics shop and wondering about making Peggy a kind of old-fashioned tea-gown in an apple-green velvet, when she saw his reflection in the plate glass. He had seen her some time before, she was certain of it. He hovered, thinking she could not see him, uncertain whether to approach or not.

She turned the chair and waved at him. He came

towards her, as solemn as ever. She did not smile either. They surveyed each other.

'I wanted to see you about something,' she said. 'Is there somewhere we could go? Not the office. Margaret is too . . . interested. And this is personal.'

He looked around. 'There's a coffee shop somewhere. Would you . . . could you . . . have a coffee with me?' He glanced at his watch. 'A sandwich lunch perhaps?'

She was determined not to see any of the trailing complications hedging them around. She had had an accident and he was an estate agent. But of course she knew very well that if it were just that, she would not be here now. She nodded briefly and turned the chair to fall in beside him as he went down the High Street. She looked at the pavement ahead and could see his shoes from the corner of her eye. Brown shoes. A dark trouser leg. She wondered if he was looking down on her. She had tied her hair back that morning, scraping it over her ears, deliberately minimizing it. For a ridiculous moment she wished she had brushed it over her scarf in a wide swathe. For another ridiculous moment she thought how good it was to see him again. How . . . exciting.

He was veering to his right, opening a door and holding it back so that she could wheel herself into the small café. Thank God it wasn't the Spinning Wheel. There were no steps, no carpet, no tablecloths. It was a bare-bone sort of café without anything to trap her wheels or the arms of the chair. He was moving one of the seats away so that she could manoeuvre close to a table. He said, 'Would you like something to eat? What do you think about a sandwich?'

'No thanks.' Coffee, probably black coffee without sugar, would put the meeting on a proper basis. And then she found herself saying, 'A doughnut would be nice.'

She could not believe herself. He went to the high counter and she had a vivid picture of herself biting into a doughnut and jam squirting everywhere. But she wanted a doughnut. They had always been her weakness; she celebrated occasions with doughnuts. So . . . this must be an occasion.

He returned with two cups of coffee and two doughnuts. She liked him for sharing her occasion.

He said directly, 'Are we going to be friends? Friendly acquaintances?'

She was taken aback. She used the abrupt approach as a weapon; but he was asking – still unsmiling – for information. She tried to be as honest as she could.

'I don't know. I'm sorry. Acquaintances, certainly – there's no controlling acquaintanceship. It has happened. But friendly . . . I don't think so, do you?'

'Because of the circumstances,' he stated.

'Certainly.' She stirred sugar into her coffee. She glanced up. 'It makes anything else quite . . . well, unthinkable. Surely you agree?'

He said heavily, 'No.'

She cut the doughnut in half and began to scoop the jam back inside it. 'Well, I don't propose to discuss that.' She smiled brightly and took a bite. It was delicious. She spoke through it. 'I gather – from the flowers and the co-operation about the house, et cetera, et cetera –' she wiped her mouth '– that you are trying to expiate a certain amount of guilt.'

At last she had got through his grave concern. His dark eyes opened wide and for a moment there was a spark in their depths. He was angry. She smiled again.

'It's all right. You need not answer. As I said . . . no debate.' She took another bite. 'However, assuming that, for whatever motive, you are looking for ways to help me—'

'How dare you talk to me like this, Helen!' He shoved his coffee to one side so that it slopped onto the table top. 'I refuse to be patronized like this! I admit when I came to the hospital first, it was in an – an – agony. Of grief. Guilt. Remorse . . . But then . . . I simply wanted you to live.'

'For your sake,' she said, finishing her doughnut and sitting back, replete. 'It would have been much easier – better – for *me*, if I had died with my parents and my fiancé.' She spoke deliberately. 'But that would have been the last straw for you.' She stared at him. 'Admit it to me, Harry Vallender. You wanted me to live for your sake.'

He stared at her for a long moment. She thought he would protest. But at last he said quietly, 'Yes. I wanted you to live for my sake. Does that satisfy you?'

She did not know whether she was satisfied or not. She had wanted to be in control of whatever was happening between them; and she was. But to feel satisfied was another thing.

She nodded nevertheless and leaned forward. 'Drink your coffee. And listen. You feel guilty about me. I feel guilty about Miles' wife, Peggy Gorman. So we understand one another. Do you know about Peggy Gorman?'

He drew his coffee towards him and stirred it. 'Yes,' he admitted reluctantly. He looked over the rim of the cup. 'I found out all I could about you. Sorry, but that was how it was.'

She assimilated this while he finished his coffee. He knew about her. She knew nothing about him.

She ploughed on. 'Peggy's self-esteem is very low. And she has just failed her driving test.' He raised his brows. She continued. 'I know it sounds petty. It is not petty. It is extremely important.'

He inclined his head. 'Yes. All right. I think I understand.'

Helen had known he would. That morning at Flatners in the rain, they had established certain things.

She said, 'Look. This sounds crazy. But she needs someone to take her out. Driving. She needs someone patient and kind. A good driver.'

'You want me to give Peggy Gorman driving lessons?' He was astonished again.

She said defensively, 'I don't know anyone else. I think she needs a man anyway . . . to help her with the driving, I mean.' But she did not mean just that. Peggy needed a man to cherish her and recognize her talents and her obvious beauty.

He was silent for long enough for her to realize she had manipulated herself into the position of including this man in her life. Even once removed, with Peggy, he would be . . . around. She felt her face growing hot because he too would realize all this.

She said, 'Forget it! Sorry – crazy idea. Peggy would have a fit if you turned up in your big car—'

'No.' He put out a hand and she looked at those

long blunt fingers again and felt their familiarity as a sensation in her own hands. 'No, I think it's a good idea. I can call about the rent or something. Ask her how the driving is going . . . it will happen naturally.' He actually smiled. 'I can do that. Yes . . . that is something I can do.'

She said, 'Honestly – I shouldn't have mentioned it. And I practically blackmailed you into it . . . no, it's not on. Really.'

His smile widened and his saturnine face looked almost youthful. 'Nothing to do with being black-mailed. In fact nothing to do with you now. You've put the facts to me and I am delighted to offer my services.'

She would have to see him . . . she would want to see him . . . and she should not. Was this why she had come in the first place? Was this why she did not dare think it through properly? Was she using Peggy?

He stopped smiling. 'It's all right. I know what you're thinking. I won't take advantage of this situation. You won't know I'm there.'

He ate his doughnut and asked her about her own driving and she told him. Then he asked her about Christmas, and she told him of her plans to invite Dorry and her husband and Aunt Mildred.

She smiled suddenly. 'My father used to call her Aunt Putrid.' She stopped smiling. 'Or do you already know that?'

He raised his heavy brows. 'How could I possibly know that?'

She said, 'I thought . . . you know, all the detective work you did . . .'

'It wasn't quite like that! I know facts. Outlines,

silhouettes.' He put his hand on the table again as if reaching for hers. 'I can imagine your father calling her that . . . I *feel* I know you and your parents. I don't suppose . . . I expect I've got it wrong.'

She said brusquely, 'I expect you have.' And then, curiosity overriding everything, 'Why did you do it? Take that kind of trouble? I should have thought you would want to forget everything about that day.'

He looked at her for a while as if wondering whether to answer that. Then he shrugged with a kind of resignation.

'Yes, I did. When I woke in hospital, I made up my mind I would do that. Forget it. I told myself I was not responsible. I wasn't particularly drunk and I didn't drive the car.' He withdrew his hand and gave a sound that could have been a laugh. 'But I knew that I couldn't avoid it for ever. Arnold came to see me. And Cheryl . . . the girl I was going to marry. They seemed like people from a foreign country. When Arnold told me to forget it . . . that was when I knew I must not. I must remember it. It happened. I did not *want* to forget it. Cheryl . . . all that seemed so trivial suddenly.'

She recalled, in another era, reading that his marriage had been cancelled. She murmured, 'I should have thought you could have helped each other.'

'It wasn't like that. She desperately wanted everything to go on as if nothing had happened. I could understand that. Of course I could. But I . . . was different. Because of what had happened. I wasn't injured like you were. But I was different. Changed.'

For some reason she put her hand on the table,

her middle finger touching the pepper pot in the centre.

He said, 'The only person who had shared the experience, who was most definitely changed, who could not go on as if nothing had happened . . . was you.' He looked at her hand: the crescent moons, the paint stain on the thumb. 'I came to see you. Just look through the door. See you. And then I started to make enquiries. I discovered Peggy, and I knew – somehow I knew – that Miles Gorman had not mentioned Peggy to you.'

She whispered, 'No-one else knew that. Except Dorry. Everyone assumed I knew all about her.'

'You wouldn't have agreed to marry him – I was sure you wouldn't – if you'd realized he was in the middle of a divorce.'

'I wouldn't. Especially if I'd realized that Peggy and Rosetta were still living with him. Because that was what it amounted to.'

Her whisper had become hoarse and he put his hand over hers quite suddenly. She almost withdrew hers. And then did not.

There was a small silence. He said, 'They told me you wanted to die. I couldn't have taken that. You were the only person who had been there. Who knew . . . who understood . . .' He forced a little laugh, patted the back of her hand and picked up his coffee cup. 'So I started sending the flowers.' He drained the coffee, doubtless cold, and shrugged. 'It seems pretty futile now. But I didn't know what else to do. I was the last person you would want to see. The villain. But somehow I had to make contact.'

'You stopped sending them – the flowers.'

'You were getting better. You were going to have that little op. To reverse the catheters. I thought it was time to withdraw.'

'And then?'

'And then Mrs Latimer told Margaret – my assistant – that you were interested in Flatners Cottage.' He sighed. 'I'd met Mrs Latimer once. In the corridor at Frenchay Hospital. I knew she was your social worker. And your friend too. She was as involved with you as I was. She would have understood – but I couldn't tell her. It was too . . . private. Not only my privacy, but yours. I didn't show myself. I let Margaret deal with her.' He shook his head. 'She'd been looking all over the place for somewhere . . . immediately she described your needs people sent her to functional flats. The sort of places where you would have died very comfortably.'

She nodded. That was exactly how she had felt about so many of those places.

He shrugged. 'I knew you could manage at Flatners. It's always been a haven.'

'Oh God . . .' She lowered her head. She was going to cry and he mustn't see that. 'Your father's home. And you let it go. To me. And I've stripped it beyond recognition.'

'My dear girl! It's what Flatners is for. To be useful – to be important again. I have never ceased to be delighted.' His hand was over hers again. 'When I think of those hopeless hippies ruining the place. And you went in and organized builders and plumbers and . . . I would have helped, but I knew you had to do it yourself.'

'It was Dorry. I hardly did a thing.'

'Rubbish. I know Harold Jenkins, the man who did the basic construction work. He told me about you.'

'So you've had me under surveillance all the time?' She tried to sound angry and failed.

'I've tried to make sure—'

She interrupted. 'You were there on Bonfire Night. Weren't you? Making sure we didn't ignite ourselves?'

'I happened to walk by.'

'You've been around at other times too.'

'I'm not a Peeping Tom. But if I have to look at the Coastguard cottages, naturally I glance over—'

'Harry! Tell me the truth!'

It was the first time she had used his first name. He picked up her hand and laced his fingers carefully between hers. She closed her eyes. He said in a low voice, 'I am in love with you. Surely that is obvious? I am the one person you cannot even like. So I am forced to haunt you at a distance.'

She drew in a breath so suddenly it sounded like a gasp.

He said, 'You must have known that whoever was sending you the flowers was in love with you. Wanted you to live and be happy again?'

'Harry . . . please.' She tried to pull her hand from his and could not.

He said levelly, persistently, 'I told you before, you are the most beautiful girl I have seen. You are courageous. You are interesting. You are also cunning and devious. And interesting. I want you. Quite desperately.'

She whispered, 'You know . . . that is not possible.

And you know that when I look at you I must see that car with the balloons and the bodies flying everywhere . . . you must know that.'

He released her fingers and sat back. 'I know that.'

There was a long silence. Helen had to force herself to think of the car with the balloons. Because she dared not think of the other reason for repudiating him. She was paralysed from the waist down.

At last she said, 'I have to go. Peggy and Rosie will be back and they will worry.' She put her gloves on and shook her head as he began to get up. 'Stay here. Please.' She drew a breath. 'Listen. I would like you to help Peggy. If that's still on.'

'Of course.'

'But . . . you realize it will not have anything to do with me.'

He said levelly, 'You don't want to see me.'

'I . . .' She bit her lip. 'I must not see you.'

The dark eyes were expressionless as he inclined his head.

She clutched the driving wheels of the chair desperately. 'All right. Thank you. Thank you for the coffee and doughnut.' She turned her chair. Someone was coming in, they held the door wide and she bowled towards it. She turned and looked at him. He looked back. She said, 'Thank you for . . . saying . . . what you said.'

She went down the High Street and turned into the side road where she had left the car. The struggle to get into the driver's seat, fold her chair and lift it into the back, was totally exhausting but she did not dare hang about in case he came around the corner.

She knew he would. He would check that she was all right.

As she drove through Bristol and along the old Weston Road she told herself she must not weep because it was dangerous. But as the darkening hedges and trees whipped past the car windows, she said aloud, 'It's happened again! It's something to do with pity. Maybe guilt. But he wants me. He loves me and he wants me. Oh God, oh God, oh God!' She slowed behind a lorry; she would probably never overtake another vehicle again. She could hear her own breathing and forced her voice past it. 'And I want him!'

She gasped at the admission and then, quite suddenly was calm. 'I am in love again. I am in love again with the wrong man. Again. But I can't do much about it this time.' She smiled grimly at the tail-light on the lorry. Maybe she had already done something about it by sending him to Peggy. Maybe that would balance the books . . . if it happened. Just supposing he fell for Peggy. Would it make amends for Miles' desertion?

She should have felt total despair; indeed there was a part of her that wept for what could never be. But there was another part. And that part surged and bubbled with illicit excitement. She was nearing thirty, she had lost her parents and her bridegroom; she was disabled. But life still held – against all the odds – wonderful possibilities.

She drove through the overhung darkness of the woods and turned left for Stormy Point. Flatners was a darker silhouette against the inky sea. She was tired and the thought of bouncing down the gravel drive and then getting out of the car and into her chair, unlocking the door, switching on the lights and heating before she could even begin to make some tea, was like the thought of climbing a mountain.

But she did it. And she was still smiling.

Eight

The young man standing under the porch was so obviously a social worker, Helen hardly needed to see his card. It was the week before Christmas and the wind was driving from America and funnelling up the Channel with a roar like an express train. He cowered beneath the hood of his duffle-coat, holding his identification towards her and profuse with apologies for the 'delay'.

'The department is especially busy at this time of year as you will doubtless realize . . .'

Helen took off the chain and opened the door wide. He stood in the open doorway, gazing around with admiration.

'This is wonderful! You've made something really special here, Helen. Congratulations.'

Helen might have warmed to such praise had he not looked as if he were playing the part of a social worker. His jeans were deliberately ancient and when he pushed back his hood all she could see was beard and hair. And she hated him calling her Helen before she had introduced herself.

She turned her chair and went towards the kitchen.

'You'd better close the door before the heat disappears,' she advised him. 'And do you take coffee

160

or tea at this time of day, Mr Harrison?'

It was only just past breakfast time. She wondered whether she dared warm up what was left in the teapot. She wished Peggy were here but it was her first driving lesson with Harry Vallender.

'Coffee,' the young man said gladly. 'And do please call me Josh. Everyone does.'

She was about to tell him that she was not everyone, then she caught a flash of nervousness in his eyes. She put the teapot in the sink and reached down two coffee mugs. He was only doing his job after all. Even so it was a pity he did not stop marvelling at everything.

'How on earth do you manage out here on your own?'

'Very easily. I have a friend who helps – you probably know all about that.' She was giving him the benefit of the doubt. He did not look as if he had read her file.

But he said diffidently, 'It looks different on paper. I couldn't imagine anything so . . . nice.'

In spite of herself she warmed with pleasure. She poured boiling water onto the instant coffee and nodded at him. 'Take the mugs over to the table by the window, will you?' She followed him. 'It can't help but be nice, can it? Look at the view.'

He sighed. 'It certainly is something. After . . . other places.'

She glanced at him as he settled himself in a chair. It was hard to make any assessments because of the beard, but his pleasure in his surroundings told a tale of previously bad experiences.

'I'm very lucky,' she said quietly. 'I have enough

161

money to live here in comfort. I don't think you need worry about making regular visits to me. It's a long way to come.'

'But such a pleasure.' He smiled and his face shone out of the beard and hair and suddenly looked young and enthusiastic. 'I'm supposed to call on you at regular intervals to make sure you are all right.'

She sipped her coffee and said, 'I take it if I had a flat in the city, you might not make such regular visits?'

He flushed. 'I'm sorry. That did sound . . . awful, didn't it? I'm on a six-month contract and nothing is quite as I expected. My university course gave me no real idea at all of what to expect – though we had regular placements.'

She softened again. 'You're disillusioned with your job?'

He lifted his shoulders. 'I thought it would be a piece of cake. No deprived inner city areas or anything. But somehow it's not a piece of cake at all. The people I would like to help don't want me to help them. And the ones that should be trying to stand on their own feet a bit, sort of fall all over me!'

She laughed. 'That's how it is. If you'd come a few weeks ago, I might have told you never to darken my doors again.'

'And now?'

She too lifted her shoulders. 'Now, I think I'll give you an open invitation. There's nothing you can do for me, actually. But my previous social worker taught me a lot. You're welcome to a cup of coffee and half an hour with this view when you need it.'

He smiled again. 'That's very generous of you. Though I'm not certain I should accept on those terms. But . . . this is nice.' He drew a breath and opened up a briefcase. 'May I ask you a few questions, however? Just to make me feel . . . better?'

'Of course. Do drink your coffee first – what about a biscuit?' She felt suddenly maternal, in a position of power again. Though this time in a very different way from her power over Vallender.

He accepted a biscuit and sipped appreciatively.

She smiled. 'Why don't you talk to me? Fill in the forms later, but get your information by chatting informally?' She sat back in her chair. 'Tell me about yourself.'

'Well . . . I . . .' He finished his coffee. 'I shouldn't really talk about me . . . but . . .' He grinned. 'My name is Joshua Harrison – you know that from the ID. And I was born in Swansea. Went to Cardiff University. Studied anthropology. Social sciences. Things like that.'

'Girlfriends?' she prompted.

He flushed and she thought for a wonderful moment he might tell her to mind her own business. Then he remembered her legs and said, 'Yes. One. Louise. Another student. It didn't work out.'

'It often doesn't.'

He sat up straight. 'Yes. When I read your file . . . it was so awful. I'm very sorry.'

She said carefully, 'This file . . . how far does it go?'

'You're entitled to see it if you like. But sometimes it upsets clients to read of their problems objectively.' He glanced at the briefcase held on his lap like a shield. 'It's simply a – a list of events.'

163

'I understand that.' Helen too looked at the polished leather case. Dorry's had been rubbed raw. 'I really wanted to know where the list finished.'

'With your move here.' He looked up, surprised. 'You've had no other visits since then? From the department?'

'No.' She sat back, relieved. Obviously Dorry would not have recorded anything about Vallender.

'Is there anything I should enter? Are you quite happy with your companion?'

'Companion? Oh, you mean Peggy of course. She is really good.' Helen smiled, almost forgetting he was not of Dorry's ilk. 'A bit too good at times.'

His grey eyes sharpened. 'How do you mean? No bullying of any kind?'

Helen laughed. 'Peggy bullying? If you knew her . . . no, she worries that she isn't doing a good job. She finds it very difficult to let me have any independence.'

'She's not here this morning,' he pointed out.

'Driving lesson. Once she can drive she will be able to fetch the groceries . . . things like that.' Helen smiled. 'It's a shame you can't meet her. You would like her.'

He said diplomatically, 'I expect so. It's such an odd . . . situation.'

Helen said bluntly, 'You mean our link through Miles?' She smiled at him. 'Don't you see? Because of that link, we need each other.'

He nodded slightly, obviously unconvinced. 'If there was ever any difficulty . . . you would tele-phone me?' He put a card on the table between them and when she made no move to pick it up, he said briskly, 'There is one thing, Helen. You should be having therapy. On a regular basis. Do you think you could drive yourself to Weston hospital once a week?'

She protested. 'Oh what a business! Peggy massages me every morning. My legs . . . feet . . . to keep the circulation going, you know.'

'Something more professional . . . a private physiotherapist would do if you would be happier with that.'

She said, 'We'll see. I think it might hurt Peggy's feelings if I went elsewhere.'

She could have bitten her tongue. His reaction was immediate.

'I think your full recovery must take priority over anyone's feelings, Helen.' He was like an uncle, chiding her gently but firmly. She was cross with herself too; she had somehow put Peggy in a bad light.

She said curtly, 'And I think my full recovery is unlikely. I am trying to learn to live as I am, Mr Harrison. Not as I might be.'

'You must not give up hope – you must never give up hope—'

'Why not? Hope deferred too long becomes acid.' She gathered the two coffee mugs by their handles and pushed herself into the kitchen. 'My last social worker taught me to look outside my own self. To take an interest in what was happening . . .' She glanced at Josh Harrison's face and felt again a pang of sympathy. 'It works,' she concluded simply. 'Oh, and I think this is a car. So you will meet Peggy. I'm glad. I think you need to know her to see that all is well here. I wish you could meet Rosie as well, but she is at school.'

She whirled to the door with an eagerness not usually evoked by the arrival of Peggy. When she opened it against a gust of wind spinning around the house like a dervish, she was in time to see the Rover driving slowly back along the headland while Peggy waved from her own front door. Helen watched the car as it negotiated the exposed road and tried not to feel disappointed.

Peggy came running.

'Are you all right, Helen?'

'Of course. Why wouldn't I be?' Helen said

Peggy held her hair against the wind. 'You opened the door sort of – urgently,' she explained as she jumped an intervening flower bed and came inside. 'I thought you might want to see Mr Vallender. And he was in such a hurry to get back to work – oh!' She stopped in her tracks as she saw Joshua Harrison standing uncertainly in the middle of the big room.

Helen made introductions and tried to feel amused at Joshua's obvious reconstruction of his mental picture of Peggy. Peggy was indeed looking wonderful with her red hair back-combed by the wind, her freckled skin golden, her fox-brown eyes glowing with health. Helen watched them shaking hands, assessing each other, both much too cautious, much too wary. Or aware. Just as she was aware of Harry Vallender.

She said, 'Will you have another coffee, Josh? Peggy would like one I expect.'

'No. I really have to go now.' He sounded regretful.

'And I had one with Mr Vallender,' Peggy confessed unexpectedly.

'Oh? Where did you go?' Helen forced her voice into a low, casual key with some difficulty.

Peggy looked at her, smiling, diffident as ever. 'Would you believe . . . the Spinning Wheel, where I worked as a waitress.'

Helen went back to the kitchen while Peggy saw the young social worker to his car. She washed the mugs and put them away. She felt drained.

Peggy came back and said instantly, 'He's tired you out, hasn't he? Let me give you a massage . . . your neck and shoulders.'

'No.' Helen heard her own voice, sharp, flinty. She softened it. 'No. Not now, Peggy. I think I'll rest on the bed for a while. Did you get on all right?'

'Marvellously. He's so – so – *nice*, isn't he?'

'Josh Harrison?' asked Helen, purposely obtuse.

Peggy laughed. 'No. He's just a boy. Mr Vallender.'

'Yes. He is . . . nice.' Helen remembered that Josh had used that word. Nice. It was the most inadequate word she'd heard for a long time.

Peggy said, 'I'll bring lunch over in a couple of hours. You rest.'

She was gone. None of her usual fussing. Helen looked at the closed door disbelievingly. Of course. That's how it would turn out. The more confidence Peggy gained, the less she would care.

Helen wondered what she had set in train when she had organized the driving lessons. The excitement she had felt last week . . . the feeling of being involved again, of manipulating events in some way

. . . of sheer intrigue . . . had been on the wane in the last two days. Suddenly it disappeared completely. It was plain to her now that by telling her he loved her, Harry Vallender had also been saying goodbye. That was it. He would fulfil his obligation to Peggy, even to making her face the Spinning Wheel again; but there would be no more coffee and doughnuts for Helen, and certainly no trip in the flatner. She flung back the cover on her bed and eased herself onto its softness. Then she leaned over and lifted first her right leg, then her left. Then she lay down and stared at the ceiling. She needed to talk to Dorry. And Dorry was gradually easing away from her. If she did not come for Christmas, Helen knew that would be . . . it.

Dorry also felt that the Christmas arrangements would settle everything. If Tom would agree to stay at home and visit Helen on Christmas afternoon, she would know that he still cared for her. If he insisted on going to his mother's as usual, she would know he did not. Occasionally she allowed herself to doubt this decision: after all they always went to Mrs Latimer's big old house in Birmingham for Christmas. Dorry had no close family and Mrs Latimer loved to see them, and the house was always full with Tom's brothers and nephews and nieces and a funny old aunt from West Bromwich. But Dorry needed Tom to nail his flag to his own mast this year.

In the event she was at first surprised by his instant acceptance of her proposal, and then, as usual, horribly suspicious.

168

'Of course we'll stay home, sweetie.' Tom was over-affectionate these days and he leaned across the table to cover her hand with his. It was her day off and she had made scrambled eggs for lunch. 'If that's what you want . . .'

She moved her hand to cut her toast into triangles. 'I felt sure you'd insist on going to your mother's.'

'Well as a matter of fact, sweetie, it will suit me very well to stay here this year. There's a rally on the beach at Weston on Boxing Day. You won't mind that too much, will you?'

She and Tom had met at the Isle of Man races; she smiled at him warmly. It meant that he had tacitly accepted Helen's invitation to Christmas Day lunch. And, on Boxing Day, if the noise of the motor cycles was too loud, she would slip away for an hour and visit Helen again. The thought of Flatners Cottage, even with Aunt Putrid, was very inviting. She had not seen Helen for a few weeks now. She had been trying so hard to make things work at home . . .

Tom grinned, well pleased. 'And anyway I've got a treat for you on Christmas Day, sweetie. Lunch at the Unicorn, no less. How about that? No family feuding, no washing-up. Sounds good, eh?'

She felt a flutter of something akin to panic. 'We can't do that, Tom. You know Helen will be expecting us for lunch. It's one of the reasons I didn't want to go to Birmingham this year.'

'Helen? Oh you mean Helen Wilson? Why on earth would we go there, pet?'

She said levelly, 'I think you know that, Tom. She is a close friend of mine now – not a client. A friend.

169

I told you ages ago she had invited us for Christmas. When you agreed to stay at home, naturally I thought it was because—'

'Sorry Dorry.' The stupid rhyme was deliberate; it was a joke he had made when they first met. He laughed loudly, then said, 'Seriously darling. I am sorry. But we're the guests at the Unicorn. A few of the patients – husbands, wives, partners and so forth – they sprang it on me yesterday. Surprise gift. Can't look a gift horse in the mouth, you know.'

The panic flutter accelerated. She had a feeling that the unacknowledged duel which she had been fighting ever since the beginning of November was about to explode into something else. She rinsed her hands beneath the tap, turned it off slowly and reached for a towel.

'I take it this is Mrs Thorne's idea?' she said.

'Mrs Thorne?'

She hated him for not facing up to her implicit accusation. She said loudly, 'Eileen Thorne. The patient who kissed you so gratefully for the very special treatment you had given her. The lady who spent Bonfire Night here . . . in my sitting-room . . . in front of the fire. As we used to do.'

He stared up at her in amazement. 'Dorry! All this time . . . you've thought . . .'

Suddenly, furiously, she flipped the towel at his head. The corner caught his eye and he exclaimed and put a hand to it.

'Don't you dare try to make me the guilty party!' she said, ignoring the exclamation, the lowered head, the protective hand. 'Don't you dare try to gloss the whole thing over yet again! I have the evidence of my eyes, Tom! I saw her kiss you – yes, I accepted that you were as taken aback – shocked – as I was! But you weren't standing where I was! She was almost naked, Tom. Reaching up and pulling your head down – can you imagine what that looked like to me? And then – when you refused to come with me to Helen's – when you knew how much it meant to Helen – and to me – it was because you had an – an assignation with her! Here! In my home!'

'Why didn't you ask me . . . my God, I could have explained the whole thing to you.' His voice was a moan from behind his hand. She knew full well he was milking the situation for all it was worth.

'I expect you could! But if it had been so innocent you would have told me anyway! And I've waited for six weeks—'

'Dorry – for God's sake! She watched you leave that night. She was distraught. When she eventually knocked on the door it was because she'd fallen over. Her clothes were muddy and torn . . . I had to bring her inside, call a taxi.'

'And nothing happened. Of course, nothing happened.'

'If you mean – did she make any more advances – no. Nothing happened.'

'You're lying!' Her voice rose and she flicked the towel at him again. He cowered and shouted at her, 'I'm not!' And then suddenly he stood up, his chair fell backwards and he grabbed her.

'I'm not lying!' He held her in a grip of iron, his arms and shoulders were terribly strong from his work. 'I'm not lying when I say that I love you,

171

either! I love you, Dorry!' He tried to kiss her. She leaned back.

'But there's something else . . .' She stared into his eyes. They were full of tears. 'You might love me, but we are lunching with Eileen Thorne on Christmas Day. Aren't we? Aren't we?'

'She might be there.' He tightened his grip as she jerked away. 'All right. She will be there. But . . . she is a patient – an ex-patient. There are other ex-patients . . . they got together and—'

'Bollocks!' she said loudly, just as Helen said it.

He said pleadingly, 'Dorry. Just come and see.' Tears ran unheedingly down his nose. 'If you still love me, just a little, won't you come and see? I haven't seen her since November the fifth. She is coming with a friend – a man friend. It just so happens—'

She could not bear it any longer. 'All right!' She lowered her head but the tears had reached his chin. 'All right, Tom. I'll come. Stop crying – please. I'll come with you to the Unicorn on Christmas Day. And you must come with me to Helen's on Boxing Day.'

He said, 'But the rally . . . couldn't you drop me at Weston and pick me up on your way back?'

She almost hated him then. He was like a child wanting everything his own way.

She said wearily, 'If that's what you want.'

'Dorry, I'm sorry.' He snuffled a laugh. 'There I go again! But darling, it will be all right, won't it? Promise me it will be all right.'

She put up a hand and levered his fingers from her shoulder, then moved away. 'I don't know, Tom.

172

We'll go on trying. But . . . I have to trust you.'

'Darling – trust me in this. I will never hurt you. I promise.'

She heard him blow his nose. She said quickly, 'You'd better start your afternoon visits. It's almost two.'

She could tell he was glad to escape.

She stood where he had left her, gazing mindlessly through the window, until he emerged from the back door and went into the garage. He was still holding a handkerchief to his eyes. He did not turn to wave; he had not come back to kiss her. She felt terrible. The car emerged slowly and then stopped to allow Mrs Raines to come up the drive. Mrs Raines stuck her head through the driver's window and there was an exchange. Then she edged around the bonnet and into the house and the car reversed cautiously and he was gone.

Mrs Raines was all agog.

'What's he done to his eye? All red and runny it is. Said he had no idea.'

Dorry put the kettle on. She knew suddenly Tom had not been crying at all; she really had hurt his eye and it was weeping. She made tea and listened to Mrs Raines' theories on colds of the eye. She felt as if something were dying; was it her love for Tom?

She changed the topic of conversation with great determination.

'Christmas at home this year, Rainy. What about you?'

'Me daughter's I s'pose.' Mrs Raines was unenthusiastic. 'I don't like Bridgwater. It's a smelly old place. And he –' she meant her son-in-law – 'he do work at the nuclearity place. So we're probably full of radium.'

Dorry laughed. 'You'll enjoy it once you're there. You know you will.'

'You going to see that special of yours? Helen wotsername?'

'I hope so. We're good friends now.'

'She was all right that day she phoned, was she?'

'The day . . .? When was that? Recently? I haven't seen her for a couple of weeks.'

'Oh no, this was some time back. Tom spoke to her. Said you would ring back.'

Dorry frowned. 'You can't recall when this was?'

'Beginning November was it? Just a mo. I'd bought my new mack . . . so course it was a lovely weekend. I went to Bridgwater. Didn't you have a day in Bath?'

Dorry thought back. She was conscious of her heart beating fairly hard. 'Yes . . . that's right, we did.' She forced a smile. 'I don't think I ever had that message, Rainy. Typical of Tom!'

'Well . . . it didn't sound much. I shouldn'ta listened in but I was still in the treatment room and picked it up just as Tom . . . he checked she was all right.'

'And she must have been, of course. I saw her just after.' Dorry shook her head and repeated, 'Typical.'

Somehow it was the final straw. That Tom could deliberately have forgotten Helen's telephone call was so mean she could hardly believe it. She had been trying to find some firm foothold to begin trusting him again. It was as if she had slipped and

174

fallen on her face. But it explained so much; his absolute refusal to meet Helen became crystal clear.

Mrs Raines swilled the dregs of her tea and upended the cup in its saucer. 'Let's see what the leaves has to say,' she grinned at Dorry. 'Anything to cheer you up, my girl! You look like a dying duck in a thunderstorm lately!'

Dorry laughed and listened to a forecast given with affection rather than judgement. And then Mrs Raines said straightly, 'He hasn't seen her again, you know, Dorry. I had a word with him and he put her off and she hasn't been here since.'

Dorry looked at the elderly cleaner and knew she should feel anger at such interference. Then she shook her head helplessly. 'You shouldn't have said anything, Rainy. You know how he hates plain speaking! I know the kind of woman she is. Poor old Tom didn't stand a chance.'

'Then why you looking so miserable?' Mrs Raines replaced her cup with a click. 'My old gran used to say it's as easy to be happy as it is to be unhappy!' She looked closer at Dorry and added sharply, 'You're not ill, are you?'

'No. I don't think so, anyway.' Dorry stood up and collected the cups and saucers. 'I feel better since that tea-leaf job!' She grinned over her shoulder as she made for the door. 'I know now what I'm going to do at Christmas. I've really got a surprise for Tom this year!'

Aunt Mildred arrived in a flurry of forgiveness. Her cursory dismissal from Helen's bedside, over a year ago, was to be forgotten. And the fact that she had

175

anticipated immediate and enormous financial compensation for the accident was nothing she was ashamed of, then or now.

'I had no idea the compensation would come in instalments,' she explained with a brazen honesty that was almost innocent. 'Of course, there wasn't enough money for you to buy a half-share in my place. It's enormous. As for help . . . I expect –' she squinted at the wall which divided Peggy's cottage from Flatners '– I expect – in the circs – she doesn't charge very much?'

Helen was proud of herself for laughing. 'Not half enough,' she agreed. 'Anyway, Aunt. Your room is ready. It's the one at the top of the stairs.'

'Cosier than down here I expect. It's all right for you, dear, but of course it's rather . . . barren, isn't it?'

Helen was tempted to say, 'Well then, it really is all right for me, isn't it?' but she smiled instead and nodded agreement. 'I'll make some tea while you unpack,' she said. And wondered how on earth she was going to put up with Aunt Putrid for two whole days. She hoped that the Gormans, who would be staying in Peggy's cottage, would somehow neutralize Mildred's awfulness with some of their own. She thought longingly of Dorry who would be coming for tea on Christmas Day. She would make the whole thing bearable. If only she could have stayed until after Boxing Day as well . . . but Helen was well aware that she must have had to do battle with Tom for the one visit; no hope of two. Some other time she must tell her about Josh Harrison. And, maybe, Harry Vallender.

She and Mildred were drinking tea when Peggy, Rosie and the Gormans arrived. Peggy had very cannily fitted in the journey with a driving lesson, and Helen sat, smiling brightly, listening with all her ears to the sounds of people going in next door, waiting to hear Harry's voice. This was the fourth time he had taken Peggy out; the fourth time he had been within a stone's throw of seeing Helen, yet had not made that effort to do so.

Mildred repeated in a higher register, 'Helen dear! I asked you what sort of bird you've bought for tomorrow's meal?'

Helen forced her smile from ear to ear. 'Turkey, of course, Aunt. Peggy has already partly cooked it. I am doing the vegetables here. It's all organized.'

Aunt Mildred looked sentimental. 'Your dear Uncle Ern always said you were a born organizer,' she said.

Helen actually opened her mouth to say, 'Bollocks!' and then changed it to a simpering, 'Did he? How sweet.'

And then there was a tap at the door and Peggy's key opened it.

'Everything is fine. Rosie is settling them in. Are you all right, Helen?'

'Fine. This is my aunt. Mrs Wilson. And this is Peggy who looks after me so well, Aunt.'

Peggy came in and shook hands. The door blew open.

'Oh dear – do close the door!' Aunt Mildred said.

Peggy turned. 'Oh, I thought Mr Vallender was behind me. He wanted to wish you both a happy Christmas.'

Helen pushed her chair forward and the wheel caught on the table. The teapot juddered; Aunt Mildred squeaked. Helen said, 'Sorry – do tell him to come in, Peggy!'

And there he was. Just as before, standing awkwardly inside the door, tall, all angles, his dark face hiding everything. Helen waited to feel that power again; it did not come. She was conscious of her hands shaking on the drive wheels of her chair. Behind her Aunt Mildred was mopping up around the teapot, flustered and unnoticing. Peggy said, 'Are you all right, Helen?' and Helen said, 'Yes . . . Hello . . . Harry.'

He came forward instantly, leaned down to her level and took her hands in his. Hers were warm, his were freezing cold. He said quickly, 'It's all right.'

'I know.'

She wanted to tell him it wasn't really all right; that she hated not being in charge; that she had earmarked Josh Harrison for Peggy and when she mentioned the driving lessons nothing had been said about coffee at the Spinning Wheel. And why the Spinning Wheel anyway?

Yet in a way it was all right. When his ice-cold hands were being warmed by hers, when he crouched before her looking at her with his dark enigmatic eyes, then it was all right.

He said quietly, 'Pain?'

'No.'

'You feel ill?'

'Not really. No.'

Aunt Mildred had finished and was waiting to be introduced; Peggy was standing by uncertainly. He said, 'After Christmas. May I call when Peggy's finished her driving? I'm going to resurrect the flatner.'

She felt her heart leap in its cavity. Her hands stopped trembling. She smiled.

'That would be . . .' She searched for a word and fell back on Josh Harrison's. 'Nice,' she said.

He too smiled; it was almost startling. 'You'll come with me.' It was not a question; it declared a certain confidence. She thought, confused, the power is there, but it has passed from me to him.

'How can I?' Her voice sounded like a bleat, she lowered it huskily. 'It's difficult enough to get in and out of the car . . .'

Aunt Mildred said, 'I am Helen's aunt. Mrs Wilson. And you are . . .?'

He did not move; his eyes were on her face. He said gently, 'I will carry you. Of course.'

She drew in a short breath and held it. She must protest, of course. To do anything else would be . . . surrender.

He stood up. 'And I am Harry Vallender. A house agent from Bristol.' He took Mildred's hand; his smile did not quite die. 'Helen has spoken of you.'

For the life of her she could not remember whether she had told him that Mildred was known as Putrid. She looked helplessly at Peggy and Peggy said quickly, 'Mr Vallender owns the cottages here, Mrs Wilson. He sold Flatners to Helen and is letting me rent the one next door.'

'How nice.'

There was that overworked word again. Helen heard herself giggle.

179

Aunt Mildred said sternly, 'Perhaps you would like a cup of tea, Mr Vallender? I understand you are giving this young lady some driving lessons.'

Peggy, dismissed, looked at Helen. 'I'll pop back and make sure Mother and Dad . . . Will you come round to me for supper? Rosie would like that.'

'Oh Peggy, so would I.' Helen suddenly felt on top of the world. She put both hands on her flaccid legs, suddenly not hating them any more. 'Can you manage, really?' Aunt Mildred behind them was recounting the details of her train journey to Harry Vallender. He seemed mesmerized by the information.

Helen murmured, 'She really is putrid, Pegs. Absolutely putrid.'

Peggy grinned from ear to ear. 'Grandma Gorman will deal with her,' she promised. She waved her hand at the other two and then said, 'No-one's called me Pegs since I was a little girl.' She leaned down to Helen. 'Bring Mr Vallender if he will come,' she said.

There was no need for the lowered head and voice: Peggy could have issued that invitation herself. So she guessed. Helen's face was giving her away.

She turned her chair and wheeled herself slowly back to the table. Mildred had got as far as Swindon and the station's total lack of ham sandwiches.

'I said to the girl – is it beyond your capabilities to cut a slice of bread, spread it with butter and . . .'

Harry Vallender turned and looked at Helen. Helen said breathlessly, 'Did you hear what Peggy said? Will you stay for supper?'

'Helen dear, I am just telling Mr Vallender about the complete lack of courtesy—'

He said, 'I don't think I'd better. Do you?'

It was as if he'd punched her in the midriff. She blurted thoughtlessly, 'But you asked me to go out with you in the boat.'

Mildred took another piece of cake and said, 'All these courses they go on – we didn't need courses to teach us common courtesy . . .'

'Later. It's all too much for you now.'

What was he really saying? That she couldn't cope? Or that he couldn't cope?

Mildred touched her lips with a napkin. 'I told her. I said we were taught manners before we could walk or talk, my girl, and it's a great pity that nowadays those lessons are left until people are grown-up and past learning anything!'

Helen said calmly, 'Well, never mind. Perhaps another time.'

'She didn't know what to say to me! She really didn't know what to say!'

Harry Vallender smiled. 'I'm sure she didn't. I really must leave now, Mrs Wilson. May I wish you both a very happy Christmas.' He did not lean down this time. 'I know you're looking forward to seeing Mrs Latimer tomorrow, Helen. Peggy has mentioned it several times.'

Helen opened her mouth to tell him that Dorry would have Tom with her and would stay only an hour or two. Then she said, 'Yes. It will be . . . nice.'

'I'm sure it will.'

She watched him walk to the door and shrug into his mack. She could not believe he was going like this. And yet . . . what had happened? Nothing. Absolutely nothing.

'Well, what a very pleasant man, my dear. So respectful.' Aunt Mildred looked roguish. 'And *not* trying to get his legs under your table!' It was a joke against herself and she laughed uproariously. Helen stared at her.

They sat in armchairs around Peggy's open fire. No alterations had been made to this cottage and they were almost shoulder to shoulder in the small parlour next to the front door. The little dining-room was taking the brunt of the storm and it was blessedly peaceful while Rosie was given her bath upstairs and put to bed. May Gorman listened with tight lips as Aunt Mildred went through her train journey yet again. When it came to the customer relations bit she nodded vigorously, obviously very much in tune with Mildred's opinions.

Mr Gorman said quietly, 'You've done wonders for our Peggy and Rosie, Helen. I want you to know that we're both very grateful.'

Helen gave up wondering just why Harry Vallender had not stayed for supper, and smiled warmly.

'It's good of you to say so, Mr Gorman—'

'Call me Alf. Please.'

'Alf. But it's a two-way thing. I could not have come here to live without Peggy and Rosie.'

'I'm not sure about Rosie.' He looked furtively at his wife.

'She makes all the difference. I promise you. Without her Peggy would be tied here. As it is she is making a home for her daughter.'

'Helen, I must warn you . . . May would like

the child to come and live with us.'

'Peggy would hate it – oh I do hope Mrs Gorman won't mention it and spoil her Christmas!' Helen glanced at the door where, at any moment, Peggy would present Rosie in her dressing-gown to say good night. 'Alf – can you try to talk her out of it? Peggy won't agree to it, but she won't want any arguments.'

The door opened as expected. Rosie was carrying an empty stocking to hang on her bed. There were a lot of hugs. Helen glanced at Alf, hoping he would understand what an enormous difference the child made to the situation at Stormy Point. He caught her eye and nodded slightly.

Mrs Gorman held out her arms. 'Come and give your old grandma a big kiss,' she commanded and when Rosie's arms were around her neck she said audibly, 'How would you like to come and stay with Grandma and Grandad after Christmas?'

Rosie smiled innocently and slid off her grandmother's knee. 'Mummy can't leave Helen,' she said matter-of-factly.

Mrs Gorman smiled. 'But darling, you could come on your own now you're such a big girl, couldn't you?'

Helen glanced at Peggy. Peggy said indulgently, 'Perhaps you'd like to take some of your new games over to play with Grandma. Let's see what Father Christmas brings you, shall we?'

Mrs Gorman opened her mouth and Alf said quickly, 'Perhaps you could fit in a trip with your next driving lesson, Peggy?'

Peggy smiled. 'It's a thought,' she agreed. She

turned the smile onto Helen. 'He wouldn't mind. He's so nice, isn't he, Helen?'

Helen nodded and then turned to stare into the fire. Nice. That's what Harry Vallender was. He was nice to Peggy and he was nice to Helen. He was probably nice to everyone.

She said, 'Time we were getting ready for bed too, Aunt.' She looked at Alf. 'I hope you will be comfortable here – not woken too early by Rosie!'

Mrs Gorman did not laugh with her husband. Aunt Mildred said, 'We really should go to church, you know. But I suppose being stuck out here, it's out of the question.'

Helen said, 'Not at all, Aunt. I will drive you to the village if you like.'

'Oh, I'm not sure I want to go that much.' Aunt Mildred cowered in mock terror at the thought of being driven by Helen.

Helen hung on to her temper with difficulty and allowed herself to be wheeled outside. And there, parked by the front door of Flatners, was Dorry's battered old car.

Helen gave a cry and let herself into the big room.

Dorry was sitting by the low cooker; waiting for some milk to heat.

'I thought I wouldn't interrupt you next door. I've made myself at home.' She stood up, smiling crookedly. 'I've come to stay for Christmas, Helen. Is that all right?'

Helen said gladly, 'Oh Dorry, of course!' She whirled forward and took Dorry's hand in hers across the counter. 'Oh Dorry, I'm so pleased . . .' She met Dorry's round eyes and paused. Then said,

'Have you . . . you haven't left Tom?'

Aunt Mildred, closing the door and putting her umbrella in the hatstand, came forward exclaiming loudly. 'Burnt milk – oh, what have you done?'

Dorry looked down and pulled the frothing saucepan to one side. Then she started to laugh.

'I really don't know,' she said and put a hand to her mouth to stop the hysterical giggles.

Nine

Christmas Day was an enormous success. The dress Helen had made for Peggy looked wonderful and Peggy was as happy as a child. Rosie's doll's pram was wheeled endlessly between the two cottages, her new doll held up to see the waves, the bright yellow hair combed assiduously. Dorry was on top form, teasing Rosie and jollying Alf and May Gorman into accepting her suggestion that both Peggy and Rosie should return with them for the New Year.

'But what about Helen?' Peggy said doubtfully.

'I'm here until January the third,' Dorry said. 'We get an extra day because the first is on a Sunday. You don't have to worry about a thing!' She met Helen's gaze and said quickly, 'That's if it's OK with Helen.'

Helen said, 'Of course. Obviously.'

'Please come, Mummy!' Rosie had resigned herself to going back to Bristol with her grand-parents, but her mother's presence would make all the difference.

'Mr Vallender said he would pick us all up next Wednesday.'

'I'll take you into Bristol. And you'll be that much closer for your driving lessons with Mr Vallender.' Dorry smiled brilliantly at Peggy. 'How are you getting on?'

'Very well. He says I'm ready to retake the test. And of course if we were at Grandma's, it would mean he could take me out oftener, perhaps.'

'We'll ring him. See what he says.'

Dorry seemed to be fixing everything. She insisted on running Aunt Mildred to the station, although that lady would have liked to stay until the New Year. She phoned Harry Vallender to arrange driving lessons for Peggy and she took them all back to Bristol the day after Boxing Day.

And then she seemed to give up. She returned in the afternoon and collapsed in the chair opposite Helen's, looking as crumpled as a burst balloon. In spite of Helen's attempts at conversation, silence scttled in the empty house and enveloped the two women like down. That night, it was Helen who put away the presents and stacked the decorations into their boxes. Dorry sat by the dark uncurtained window, her hands around a mug of cocoa as if warming them.

Helen said, 'We'll take the tree outside tomorrow.'

She was surprised when Dorry said, 'Not until Twelfth Night. It's bad luck.'

Helen made herself a drink and took it to the table.

Finally grinning ironically, she said, 'D'you want to talk?'

Dorry did not smile. All the gaiety of the last three days had been used up. She shook her head slowly. 'There's really nothing to say.' At last a small smile curved her long mouth. 'Do you mind if we just sit? The quiet . . . it's a kind of insulation.'

Helen wanted to ask – insulation against what? She wanted to say – have you left him for good? What is happening? For God's sake, Dorry, what is happening?

She said quietly, 'Of course I don't mind.'

So they sat and looked out at the unquiet darkness which emphasized their own stillness. At nine o'clock Helen began to get ready for bed. Dorry did not seem to notice the long business of undressing. When Helen, breathing heavily, transferred herself to the bed, Dorry stood up slowly. 'I'll make tracks,' she said vaguely. And she went slowly to the stairs.

The next day the weather was still stormy. Helen woke from a fitful sleep to see Dorry slipping out of the door. Somehow she struggled into her chair and made for the bathroom. It was seven-thirty and still dark. Suddenly she was conscious that Peggy was not next door. She shut off the thought quickly and began the exhausting process of showering, drying, dressing . . . Her chair was a refuge when she eventually got into it. She leaned down and began fitting her legs into trousers. There was no sign of Dorry. She wheeled herself into the kitchen, filled the kettle and plugged it in, slotted bread into the toaster. It was almost nine; a grey windy day with squalls of rain flinging themselves at the windows every now and then. Helen thought momentarily of the muddy cliff edges and the steep slides of shale towards the end of the Point. She made tea and told herself not to be such an idiot.

Sure enough Dorry came in before half-past nine, wet to the skin but looking more normal. Helen informed her almost tersely that the tea was probably still hot enough and there was marmalade if she preferred it to honey.

'Helen, I'm sorry! You've had to cope on your own – I've taken Peggy away and not made any attempt to fill her place!'

'It's not that –' though Helen was surprised at just how much she was missing Peggy's cheerful presence '– I was worried about you.'

'I didn't think you heard me leave.'

'Of course I heard you leave!' Helen watched morosely as Dorry made toast and fresh tea. She sighed sharply. 'You know, six months ago, I would have thought this was wonderful. Your undiluted company twenty-four hours a day. Now I'm not so sure.'

'It's because I've been so odd. I'll be all right now.' Dorry nodded as if they were talking about her recovery from a cold. 'I had to be frenetic for Aunt Putrid, didn't I? But now that we're by ourselves, we can be peaceful and natural —'

'That's not natural!' Helen flapped her hands. 'We're not peaceful, you and me! We're – scratchy – and – quite unpeaceful!' She put her hands in her lap. 'Anyway, your calm is about as convincing as your social veneer! You're as peaceful as a volcano.' She waited but Dorry did not respond. So she said bluntly, 'I take it Tom had an affair with that Eileen woman. And you found out. And you can't forgive him.'

Dorry looked up as if surprised. 'Well . . . yes. I suppose that's what it is. It sounds very simple put like that. Except for the last part. I think I could forgive him if he admitted it and said it was over and he wanted us to be as we were. But although I've seen

189

. . . certain things . . . he still says there's nothing happening between them.' She poured more tea. 'It seems to me that he's living a different life . . . a different plane. What he sees as truth and reality are not the same as my truth and reality.' She sipped and glanced at Helen. 'You telephoned me. Back at the beginning of November. Something must have happened that you wanted to discuss. But he did not pass on that message.'

Helen lifted her shoulders. 'I know. In a way, I can understand that. At the time . . . I was using up a great deal of your life.'

'You knew? That he was a liar? Why didn't you tell me?'

'Dorry! Your sense of proportion has gone haywire. He kept back that message because he wanted you to himself! Is that such a crime? I coped with my problem – no problem as it turned out – and he knew I would.' She smiled. 'The trouble was, he knew I hadn't told you – he knew I wouldn't. But it meant he could not meet me. He felt too guilty.'

'Quite.' Dorry's mouth was a long thin line. 'He did not come with me to the bonfire and as soon as the Thorne woman saw me leave, she moved in.'

Helen frowned. 'You can't mean she is living in your house?'

Tiredly, Dorry explained. 'The trouble is,' she concluded, 'he is covering his tracks extremely well. Not even Rainy – Mrs Raines who cleans – she thinks it was simply a momentary thing. And believe you me, Helen, what Mrs Raines doesn't know about our affairs isn't worth knowing!' She tried to laugh, but Helen still frowned.

'It doesn't sound that bad, actually. He's explained the incident on Bonfire Night. And you say yourself she looked ill when he helped her into the taxi.'

'Helen, he does two afternoons of home visits. He's happy now . . . which he wasn't always. She is making him happy!'

'Dorry!' Helen mimicked Dorry's tone. Then sobered and went on, 'She is much older than he is—'

'So it's very flattering that she has fallen for him. And anyway, don't you see? She appeals to his sympathy and he's got lots of that. And between them they fixed it so that they spent Christmas Day together. Oh . . . I just know, Helen. Sorry. But I do.'

'Don't be sorry. It shows how close you are to Tom. Which then shows – proves – that you can't give him up just like that.'

'The final straw of course, is now.' Dorry pushed her untouched toast away as if it were her final reserve and stared at Helen across the breakfast table. 'Don't you see? I didn't come home Christmas Eve. I've been here now for four days – this is the fifth. And he hasn't telephoned or come to find me—'

'He doesn't know where you are, presumably.'

'I couldn't be that tough on him. I left a note.'

'So he knows where you are and he's not worried.'

'For God's sake, Helen! He should be worried! He should come and find me and beg me to go home!'

They stared at each other. Dorry's round eyes were bright with unshed tears. Helen's blue ones were narrowed, considering.

Helen said slowly, 'Supposing he is having . . . what shall we call it . . . a fling? It will end. You know it will end. What then?'

'Helen, I'm not proud. But it's a question of self-respect. He drops her and picks me up? And if he's done it once, he could do it again. And again. Am I supposed to countenance that?'

'No, of course not. But you've been married for how long?'

'Six years.'

'And this is the first time. And it could be because of me.'

'Oh for goodness' sake—'

'All right. But I gather your work load is ridiculous. You don't spend much time together.'

'We had a day at Bath. In November.'

'And if he had passed on my message, you wouldn't have had that.'

'Helen, if you're trying to find excuses—'

'Reasons.' Helen pushed herself away from the table and went to the kitchen where she began to clear up noisily.

'I telephoned you to tell you that Harry Vallender was the snowdrop man. He was also the bridegroom in the car that killed my parents. And Miles.'

She ignored Dorry's gasps and the flood of questions that followed.

She said levelly, 'He's attracted to me. Guilt. Pity. Who knows? The thing is, I was flattered – am flattered. Like your Tom. So I think I understand a little bit of what's happening.'

Dorry was silent and very still. Helen finished loading the dishwasher and put her hands on the low counter, clenching her fists. She said quietly, 'I know that if I encouraged . . . it . . . then Vallender would fall for me. In a big way. Except . . .' She glanced up momentarily and grinned. 'Except that he couldn't do much about it.' She stopped smiling. 'But Tom can.' She put her hands back on her driving wheels and went to the cupboard containing her painting things. 'You tell me that Eileen Thorne is widowed, alone and unhappy. Tom is sorry for her. She mistakes that for something else. And . . . and . . .' She laid out brushes and paper on the table. 'And she goes for it.'

Still Dorry made no comment. Helen began to mix acrylic paint in a saucer. She said conversationally, 'You told me once you trained as a nurse. You're hopeless in that capacity. I just mention it in passing.'

Dorry burst out, 'I'm not going to nurse Tom, if that's what you mean!'

'I didn't. But by this time in the morning, Peggy has taken Rosie to school, checked I'm up and helped me to shower and dress, massaged my legs and made coffee!'

She looked up and held Dorry's penitent gaze. Her mouth twitched. They both started to laugh.

On New Year's Eve Helen put her half-baked plan into action. In the long hours with Dorry she had made some doll's clothes. She would take them in for Rosetta. And then on the way home she would call at the house in Falcondale Road and confront Tom Latimer. What would happen then she had no idea. But she could no longer bear the stalemate of

Dorry's inaction. Something had to be done.

If she expected opposition from Dorry she was disappointed. She explained elaborately that Peggy was probably feeling rather beleaguered with the older Gormans and that Rosie would not be able to go out much in such a built-up area. Dorry nodded, smiled and said she would get tea ready and not to stay out too long after dark. Helen got into her coat and gloves, manoeuvred herself out of the door, unlocked her car and began the exhausting business of transferring herself and her chair inside. She muttered irritably, 'Either you are getting used to Peggy fussing, or Dorry is completely uncaring!' She knew neither of those things was quite true, but she also knew that she would be very glad when Peggy returned to the cottage next door. She was almost ashamed at the way her spirits lifted as she drew closer to the belt of trees that sheltered the village from the winds, negotiated the narrow road between the trees and went past Rosie's school. There was a glorious sense of freedom she hadn't felt since the accident. She pulled into a lay-by for an oncoming car and waited impatiently for it to pass so that she could drive on. But the car seemed to be drawing over to her side of the road. She frowned sharply and flashed her lights. It drew up carefully alongside hers. It was Harry Vallender's Rover.

'Hello.' They wound down their windows in perfect synchronization, as if the simple action had been rehearsed. He smiled. 'I was going to visit. What a good job I recognized the Ford.'

'Yes.' Her mouth was suddenly dry.

'Is everything all right?' His face, so familiar to her

now, leaned closer. 'Is Mrs Latimer not well?'

'No. Yes . . . I mean everything is fine. Dorry is resting. I just felt like . . . driving.'

'Anywhere in particular?'

'Well . . .' She swallowed. 'I did wonder about calling on the Gormans.'

He smiled, imagining he understood. 'Of course. What a splendid idea. You visit Peggy and Rosetta and help to heal the breach.' He nodded. 'Peggy and I have been driving. I thought I'd come and tell you how well she is doing.'

'Oh.' She could think of nothing to say and added tritely, 'That's nice.' She cleared her throat. 'How is she?'

'Finc. Her mother-in-law would like Rosie to stay on there, but Peggy isn't letting it get to her. She is quietly confident that Mrs Gorman will accept the situation as it is eventually. Helping you – making her own home – it's giving her such self-respect. She seems to be blossoming.'

Helen said again, 'Oh.' She was glad, of course. Hadn't she talked to Peggy like a Dutch uncle – or aunt – not so long ago? But that Peggy was blossoming for Harry Vallender was not quite what she'd had in mind.

He said, 'I've got an idea. Why don't you lock up your car and let me drive you in? It'll be dark soon and I imagine this car is faster than yours.'

She should have declined. She tried to remember Eileen Thorne. She must not be like Eileen Thorne.

Still she said, 'Yes. I would like that.'

He was out of his car in an instant, had opened her door, and gathered her up as if she were Rosie. She averted her head and closed her eyes against the sheer poignancy of his closeness. He smelled of soap and fresh air. He wore a car coat and her nylon jacket slid against it sibilantly. He placed her in the passenger seat with infinite care, arranged her useless legs in the well beneath the bonnet. When he went back to her car to lock it she dashed her knuckles across her eyes and reached for the seat-belt as if it were a shield against all her stupid emotions. He settled himself by her, fastened his belt and then spoke quietly.

'Shall we just enjoy the drive? Not think about anything else?'

She swallowed saltily. Then said, 'Yes. Of course.'

He pulled out of the lay-by and threaded the car through the lanes and out onto the motorway. 'Not so interesting, but much quicker if you want to see Peggy and family.'

'Yes.' She put her hands on her lap and pressed down. 'I'm missing them.'

'Well, of course.' He glanced sideways, brows raised. 'Did you think you wouldn't?'

She said honestly, 'Well, I rather thought it would be a break. In a way.' She moved her hands to her knees and added apologetically, 'You know . . . from Peggy's fussing.'

He sounded reproving. 'She fusses – as you put it – because she cares about you.'

'I know. I'm an ungrateful beast. It's doing me good to realize just how much she does do for me.'

'And Mrs Latimer is there. You're all right?'

'Of course. Absolutely fine.'

The car passed the service station at Portishead and

climbed easily up the incline of Avonmouth bridge. She looked across at the coppice of chimneys; the tide was out and the muddy banks of the Avon gleamed darkly below them. It couldn't have been a much grimmer view, yet, for her, it was beautiful.

He said suddenly, 'You often do that. Press your hands onto your thighs. Have you any pain?'

'No.' She put both hands by her sides. 'No. Sorry. It's just that . . . Peggy massages my legs and she tells me to apply pressure. Now and then.' She looked straight ahead at the tailgate of a lorry. 'There is no sensation.'

'I'm sorry, Helen.'

'I think I'm used to it now.' She flashed a smile at him. 'You don't need to be sorry. Honestly.'

He too turned and met her eyes for an instant. His were full of pain and she realized he was sorry for himself. Regret or remorse or something similar.

She looked away. 'We're simply enjoying this drive. Remember?'

'Yes.' He turned off at the bottom of the bridge and they drove onto the old Portway alongside the river. He told her about the railway line which still operated from Bristol. She told him that this was one of Wordsworth's many Bristol walks.

'He would take the ferry across to Pill and then walk up the hill to the ridgeway and back into the city. Probably a round trip of twenty miles or more.'

'He was a great walker.' Harry Vallender drew up outside the Gormans' semi-detached and turned to look at her. He said very deliberately, 'Did you enjoy walking?'

She checked an involuntary gasp. Even Dorry's

197

directness had never gone this far. She forced herself to reply. 'Yes. Very much.'

He released her seat-belt. 'Then you'll enjoy the trip in the flatner,' he said. 'It will be like walking on the water. And the wind and elements are all around you.'

'Oh . . . I thought you might have shelved the idea. You haven't mentioned it again.'

'I haven't seen much of you. I've told Peggy. She thinks it's great.'

'Oh. Does she?'

He glanced at her, surprised. 'Of course. Did you think she would disapprove?'

'I . . . don't know. I am just surprised that you talked to her. About me.' She felt her face growing hot and added lamely, 'Like that.'

He smiled and as usual his face was transformed. 'You are the main thing we have in common,' he said simply. He undid his seat-belt and opened his door. 'I'll let them know we're here. Then I'll come back for you.'

She waited. Her breathing was audible in the empty car. She watched as he knocked, saw Peggy come to the door and exclaim with delight, kept her gaze studiously on Peggy as he came back down the path to her door. And then, again, his arms were around her, and the twin sensations of being high off the ground and cradled close to his body were almost too much. Rosie ran down the path in her slippers and had to be flapped away by an anxious Peggy. Alf Gorman was at the sitting-room door and even May Gorman smiled as she indicated the armchair by the fire.

Harry Vallender put her down with infinite care.

'Your back,' she gasped. 'This is absolutely no good for your back!'

'He's strong, Helen!' Rosie said, jumping around the chair like a dervish. 'He swings me right off the ground. Don't you Mr Vallender? And Mummy too!'

'Put the kettle on, Alf,' May Gorman instructed. 'Stop flusterating Miss Wilson, our Rosie. Peggy, there's the Christmas cake in the tin.'

'No. Please. We've just popped in for a few minutes.' Helen was still trying to imagine under what circumstances Harry Vallender might have swung Peggy off the ground. He too began to protest. But May Gorman was determined to show her hospitality.

'And did your aunt get home safely?' She settled herself against a cushion and fished out her knitting. 'A very nice woman.'

Helen made a mental note to phone Aunt Mildred. She should have done it before.

'She enjoyed meeting you too,' she said diplomatically.

The short call creaked into a longer one. Tea and cake were brought. Helen found the doll's clothes and presented them to Rosie and the child sat in front of the fire struggling to dress her new doll. Peggy said conversationally that they would be returning to their cottage on Monday to get ready for school. May Gorman said there was no need to go till Tuesday. Alf Gorman cleared his throat and enquired what the traffic was like and Harry Vallender said it was surprising how much there was. Rosie gave up on the doll and started to hop and jump again in spite of all persuasions to the contrary. Helen began to feel rather ill.

'Time we were going.' Harry put her cup onto the mantelpiece and leaned over her.

She whispered, 'I'm all right, honestly.'

And he said, 'Sorry, but I have to get back.'

There were more flurries and she was in his arms again and Alf was unlocking the car door and she was safely tucked in.

'See you Monday!' Peggy called firmly, waving and holding Rosie back.

Helen waved too, then subsided as they left the house to the dusk. 'You should have said that you were in a hurry,' she said. 'That took an hour. We need not have gone in.'

'Slightly less than an hour.' He glanced at her. 'I'm not in a hurry. I thought you'd had enough. Are you all right?'

'Of course I'm all right!' Her head throbbed. She thought of her car waiting in the lay-by opposite Rosie's school and shuddered. She must pull herself together.

'Close your eyes. Relax.'

'No thanks. I'm fine.'

'You're tetchy.'

'It was the noise. People. Dorry and I . . . we're so quiet.'

They drove onto the motorway. He maintained a silence which she refused to break. The car was dark inside so that she could only see the outline of his profile, but if he had turned his face to hers she would have known. He had withdrawn into his own darkness.

They left the motorway and reached the narrow lane which led to the village. There was no way he could avoid transferring her into her own car and she wondered how this silent alienation would be maintained.

And then he spoke. His voice held none of the tension she was feeling herself. He sounded completely natural.

'Rosie has learned the hokey-cokey. She likes to be lifted right up at the end.'

The remark bore no relation to anything that had been said, yet she knew instantly the reason for it and replied without thinking, 'Peggy too?'

He laughed suddenly. He knew she was jealous! She was furious with herself. And with him.

'Peggy too. Inadvertently I might add.'

She did not want to pursue the subject. But still she said, 'It was fun. Obviously.'

'Fun?' It was as if he was unfamiliar with the word.

'You sound amused by it all.'

'And you sound very accusing.'

'Not at all. Perhaps your forte is swinging women off their feet.' She heard her own voice, childishly stiff.

He drew up alongside the Ford and held out his hand for the keys. She scrabbled for them in the glove compartment and handed them over without touching his fingers. He got out, still without speaking, unlocked the wide door at the driver's side and reached in for her wheelchair.

'I shall need that!' she bleated.

He did not hear. He unlocked the boot of the Rover and put the chair inside.

'What are you doing?' she said querulously as he rejoined her.

'You're in no state to drive along that headland,' he said shortly. 'Mrs Latimer can come back with me and bring your car back.'

'I am perfectly all right!'

'You're tired. And very irritable.'

She wanted to respond with something really scathing and could think of nothing. Like a sulky child, she sat hunched away from him as they drove down to the cottages. Then he got out, fetched her wheelchair and put it by her side.

'I take it you would prefer to do this under your own steam?' he asked.

It was a rhetorical question. She slid across without too much difficulty and by the time he had closed her door she was already letting herself into Flatners.

He refused Dorry's offer of a meal and they left almost immediately. Helen whirled around, cutting sandwiches, cursing Dorry for not having prepared a thing, cursing everything for being stubbornly inanimate. And then she realized that Harry had not wished her a happy New Year. She drooped suddenly over the bread board and stared into space. Two years ago – just two short years – Miles and she had danced in the New Year of 1993. He had whispered ridiculous promises into her ear. And then he had said, 'This year . . . 1993 . . . it's going to be a year we'll never forget.'

She blinked hard and cut the sandwiches carefully into triangles. Perhaps it was as well Harry had said nothing about 1995.

Dorry let herself in twenty minutes later, her

brows right up in her hairline with bewilderment.

'What's going on?' she asked, taking off her coat and looking over her shoulder as Helen continued to fuss around unnecessarily.

'You and Harry look about ready to explode! Have you had a row?'

Helen recounted the small events of the afternoon, curtly. 'We had tea and cake at the Gormans' so I'm doing coffee now. Is that all right?'

Dorry said, 'I don't get it. I thought you rather liked the idea of Harry Vallender falling for you—'

'What rubbish! As if he would! He's sorry for me – that's all!'

'But you're practically raw – your nerve ends are showing!'

Helen pushed her chair to the window and gazed out, suddenly still.

She said slowly, 'I've behaved badly, Dorry. I'm jealous of the attention he's paying to Peggy—'

'But it was you who arranged the driving lessons!'

'I know all that. I know how unreasonable I am. What's more, so does he. He carried me into the Gormans' sitting-room but he made sure I used the wheelchair when we got back home. But what I really hate is that I lost my upper hand.' She turned and grinned fleetingly at Dorry. 'I felt in control of the situation, Dorry. It was the first time I'd been in control of anything since the accident!' She tried to laugh. 'A man . . . a personable man . . . falling for me! It didn't matter why – his motives.' She looked back at the dark window. 'And then, somehow . . . I fell for him. And that's not good. It made me jealous of Peggy.' She shuddered and made a sound of self-disgust.

'Darling—' Dorry was suddenly her old self, kneeling before the wheelchair, her round eyes bright with sympathy. 'Listen. You can't do anything about Harry Vallender – except await events. But Peggy . . . that's different. You thought something might happen between Peggy and your new social worker . . . Joshua Harrison was it?' She smiled, beguiling Helen. 'You're a born organizer – no, I don't mean you're bossy, though you are of course. Terribly.' Her smile widened and Helen was forced to return it – reluctantly. 'But how about a spot of match-making? When Peggy gets back, phone up for a visit. See what happens.'

Helen's smile widened. 'This is the diary all over again, Dorry Latimer! Keeping me occupied with things outside myself!'

Dorry raised her brows. Her eyes were very bright. She said, 'Well?' Helen gazed down into the face of her friend and realized she had not called on Tom. It was just another frustration. She swallowed, telling herself that Dorry would be back at work on Tuesday and she would have the time she needed to do . . . all sorts of things. She said, 'All right. It might be fun. I'll see what I can do.'

Perhaps after all, the whole thing with Harry Vallender could be . . . put to one side. Tom and Dorry. Peggy and Joshua Harrison. Rosetta's new term . . . There were heaps of things she could think about. Make happen. She was not prepared to become obsolete just because she was in a wheelchair.

She patted Dorry's hand and smiled as she repeated, 'I will certainly see what I can do.'

204

*   *   *

They spent a quiet evening – 'like two old biddies' as Dorry put it. They both wanted to go to bed, yet it was the thing to do to wait up for the New Year. As Big Ben boomed sonorously over the air waves, Helen said, 'I wonder what this year will bring?' Suddenly Dorry leaned over and took her hand.

'Good friends,' she said. And Helen repeated as if she were making a promise, 'Good friends.'

Ten

It was good to have Peggy and Rosie back in the cottage next door. They brought a life and energy with them which somehow Dorry had lost. In any case, Dorry was working such long hours, Helen hardly saw her. She slept at the cottage, sometimes she ate breakfast, sometimes supper. But not often. Helen began to understand how Tom might have felt.

At the end of Rosie's first week back at school, Helen phoned Joshua Harrison.

He arrived on Monday morning at nine o'clock, apologizing for the early hour.

'I wondered if you'd be up!' He grinned at her as if she were an old friend.

'Peggy and Rosie came for breakfast quite early.' Helen smiled back but did not go for the coffee cups. 'Peggy got cracking this morning because she's going shopping.' She widened her smile. 'As a matter of fact your timing couldn't be better. You arriving now, I mean. She's going to wait outside the school for the ten o'clock bus from Bristol. So you'll be passing her on your way back to Weston. You could give her a lift.' It seemed to Helen that fate was definitely on her side.

Joshua looked happy about it, but glanced at his

watch. 'You wanted to talk to me. Will there be time?'

'Oh, yes. I only wanted to tell you that I've decided to have some physio like you suggested.'

'Oh, good!' He beamed.

'I've got the number of a good therapist. I'd like you to telephone and make an appointment for me.'

'Wouldn't you prefer to do it yourself? I won't know what time will be suitable.'

'Do it from here. Now.' She rummaged in her bag and produced Tom Latimer's phone number on a scrap of paper. No name. 'This afternoon would be fine. Or any time tomorrow.'

His smile died a little. 'If she's any good, Helen, she won't be able to fit you in so quickly.'

She did not correct his use of gender. 'That's why I want you to do it. I am one of your clients and in need of immediate attention. Put on your professional voice.'

He laughed but expostulated. 'Helen, really! What's all this about? You're perfectly capable of making your own appointment.'

She spread her hands as if confessing a secret. 'Look. I know I'll back out. Do this for me. Make it soon so that I haven't got time to think about it.'

He shrugged helplessly and she passed him the telephone and wondered what his reaction would be when he discovered that Tom was a man and called Latimer. When a woman's voice answered she was completely thrown. Dorry had never mentioned a receptionist. There was the cleaner . . . Mrs Raines. Helen prayed it was Mrs Raines.

Joshua said obediently, 'My name is Joshua Harrison. I am a social worker and I'm telephoning on behalf of one of my clients who needs treatment to keep circulation going.' He waited, listening. Was Mrs Raines turning the pages of an appointment book, or had she gone for Tom. Her voice returned. Joshua said, 'Is there any chance of a cancellation? This is a matter of some urgency.' He looked at Helen's face and said as humorously as he could, 'A case of now or never, I'm afraid.' He waited and then smiled. 'This morning? That is excellent. I can bring her in myself. The name is—'

Helen leaned forward and cut off the call.

He looked at her with raised brows. 'Backing out already? I'll take you – don't worry about it. It will be soothing and pleasant. Absolutely no pain. She sounded an extremely helpful sort too.'

She said violently, 'I don't want you to take me. I want you to take Peggy shopping. What time was the appointment?'

'Eleven o'clock.' He leaned forward. 'Helen. What are you frightened of?'

She almost laughed. 'I'm not frightened, thank you, Joshua. I'm anxious that you will miss Peggy. Perhaps you'd better go now. I'll phone this afternoon. Let you know how it went. OK?'

He protested. He told her he didn't get it. Eventually he left and she whirled around getting ready. So far so good. Everything seemed to be playing into her hands. The only fly in the ointment was the identity of the woman who had answered the phone.

The house in Falcondale Road was very much as she had imagined. Substantial, 1930s, very red brick, an imposing front door set in a porch and reached by four steps. A side entrance with a hanging sign announcing a waiting-room, thankfully on the level. And beyond that what looked like the kitchen.

She drove as close to the waiting-room as possible and began the laborious business of extracting her chair and transferring into it. Naturally, it was raining and she was distinctly damp by the time she reached shelter. She stopped in the lobby and brushed herself off and ran her fingers through her hair. There were two doors in the lobby, one marked waiting-room, the other bearing the single word 'Treatment'. She toyed with the idea of barging straight into the treatment room and catching him unawares; but then she might not find the identity of his receptionist. Besides which, she discovered wryly, she did not quite have the nerve.

She pushed her chair against the other door and went into a small room. One wall was lined with chairs, there was a table containing magazines, and a small desk next to another door. Apart from the furniture the room was completely empty. If Dorry had been there, surely a vase of flowers would be on the desk? But, recalling Dorry's haphazard way of living, perhaps not.

The door next to the desk opened suddenly and a woman, wearing a white coat like a badge of office, came into the room. Helen knew immediately it was not Mrs Raines. Her hair was beautifully sculpted, her brows plucked into a perfect arch, make-up tastefully applied. But it was more than artifice; this woman was beautiful. And Helen had no doubt at all she was Eileen Thorne.

She smiled charmingly. 'Ah. You must be Mr Harrison's client? He telephoned this morning but was cut off before he could give your name.'

She went to the desk, opened a book and poised her pen above it.

Helen had not planned this far ahead but she was so certain that Tom would not see her if he knew who she was that she said quickly, 'Gorman. Peggy Gorman.'

'Address? And your hospital? Date of birth?' Gradually her record was built up. She did not like it; it was something of a striptease. But Mrs Thorne was efficient and her smile reassuring.

'And have you brought your records from the hospital? X-rays? Mr Latimer would particularly like X-rays.'

Helen was aghast. 'He didn't say – Joshua – my social worker – didn't tell me to bring anything.' She rallied herself. 'Look. It's just that I'm supposed to keep the circulation going in my feet and legs. There's no cure or anything. I don't honestly think X-rays are necessary.'

The woman looked doubtful. 'Well, I'm not sure. But . . . I'll see what Mr Latimer says.'

Helen gripped the driving wheels of the chair and closed her eyes until the door re-opened. Mrs Thorne was smiling yet again. Helen thought of Harry's serious face and was grateful.

'Yes. Mr Latimer can give you a preliminary massage. But if there is another appointment, he would prefer to have the relevant paperwork.'

'Of course. Certainly. I do apologize.' My God, she

was even sounding like Peggy now. She coughed and deepened her voice. 'Shall I go in?'

Mrs Thorne held the door wide and Helen bowled her chair expertly through into the treatment room. And then stopped. There appeared to be three cubicles facing her. Two were probably occupied as the curtains were closed around them. The third contained a treatment bed . . . and Tom. He was so obviously waiting for her that she knew at once he was suspicious. After all, how many paraplegic women of her age did he treat? Especially ones with fair hair who lived at Weston. And she would have known him anywhere from Dorry's description. His floppy brown hair and English face reminded her of someone.

He came forward. 'Miss Gorman.' He held out his hand and she put hers into it. A good dry clasp, not too tight. 'I'm pleased to meet you. Did someone recommend me?'

He knew; of course he knew. And he wasn't going to admit it. Dorry was right, he would duck the truth for as long as he possibly could.

'My social worker. I'm supposed to have physio. Circulatory problem and so on.'

'Then let's get you on the bed, shall we?'

It was an easy voice, at once unaffected yet professional. He pumped the bed down to the level of her chair and as she sat on its edge, he swung her legs expertly into position and then cradled her head as she lay down.

'Good. Very good.' He was entirely professional now, examining her neck, shoulder and arms. He slid off her shoes and trousers. She felt her face

211

becoming hot, of course this was what she had come for. She must not forget that.

'Can you feel this, Miss Gorman? This . . . this?' She could see he was moving his hands over her legs. She could feel nothing.

'I'm going to turn you over. I need to work on your calves and heels. Then I would like to examine your spine.'

Suddenly she was terrified. 'I don't think that's a good idea. Mr Edwards, my surgeon—'

'It's all right. I know him personally. I can assure you I would never undo his work.' He positioned her expertly, made sure her head fitted into the padded hole of the bed, massaged the nape of her neck until she relaxed. 'Don't be frightened.' His voice was unexpectedly gentle. 'You are perfectly safe.' From the next cubicle came a gentle ringing sound. 'Excuse me. I must attend another patient.'

He disappeared and she heard him talking to someone. It gave her time to get herself together. She was doing this for Dorry. She must not worry about herself.

He came back and she felt a tension at her waist.

'I am pulling your legs away from your trunk. Nothing fierce. Just relieving any pressure that is building up.' The sensation at her waist ceased and she felt his hands there. She was staring down at the floor. She closed her eyes.

He said, 'You can feel that, can't you?'

'Yes.'

'My hands are actually on your hips. Now my thumbs are moving below that area. Can you tell?'

'No.'

She felt him again at her waist, moving into her spine. He appeared to be counting her vertebrae. She tried to breathe normally.

'Have you been offered surgery for this spinal kink?'

He had not seen her records so how did he know about the kink? Unless Dorry had told him.

She spoke in a strange voice because of the pressure on her face. 'We discussed it. The risk was . . . too high.'

He seemed to probe again for a long time. Then his hands slid up her spine and fanned out onto her shoulders. She felt unutterably relaxed.

He said, 'I agree. But I don't think manipulation will be sufficient to undo this damage.'

She spoke pantingly and in time with those hands which again swept up her spine and over her shoulders and now followed her arms to the wrists, slid over the thumbs and stretched the fingers. 'It's all right. I know it's incurable.'

'I didn't say that. With exercise and massage the body could well heal itself. But I think you should know that I can guarantee nothing.'

'I understand.' But in spite of her words her heart leapt. She had started this whole intrigue because if Dorry would not come to see Tom she must. It had not occurred to her that his treatment might indeed help her.

He returned to her neck. 'I'm going to work here today. The tension is very strong.'

The inference was that she would be coming

again. Did that mean she need not force the issue this time? She closed her eyes and surrendered herself to those fingers.

Afterwards he left her under a heat lamp while he saw to the other two patients. And then she heard him greet someone else and take them into a free cubicle. It was hopeless, she would never be able to talk to him this time. She would have to come again. And she did not mind.

He returned, swishing the curtain open and shut. 'That is all for this time. My receptionist will help you with your clothes and make another appointment. And then we will arrange some hydrotherapy.'

He turned her and propped her on the pillows. His eyes were close to hers. He knew who she was, she was convinced of it. Why didn't he say so?

Mrs Thorne came in and tried to dress her as if she were a rag doll. Helen smiled and took the clothes from her. She fastened her bra, pulled on her sweater and lifted each leg in turn to feed on her trousers. She could not control her heavy breathing after such hard work, but she smiled briefly at Mrs Thorne, not admitting anything.

That lady said, 'My goodness, you're expert.'

'Practice makes perfect.' Helen said in Aunt Putrid's voice. Then smiled again and added, 'Do you live in, Mrs Thorne?'

The woman was definitely startled. Not only by the direct question but the use of her name. Then she decided that Tom must have mentioned it.

'Yes, dear. Mr Latimer needs help twenty-four hours a day, as you can imagine.'

Helen wondered what would happen if she

214

screamed, clawed the woman's face and insisted on Tom returning with her to Stormy Point and Dorry.

She smiled instead and said, 'He's going to arrange for me to have hydrotherapy!' She felt ridiculously excited. Something was happening. In spite of reservations Tom had given her some hope; maybe not for a cure, but hope all the same.

'That's nice, dear. Let's see. When is the best time for your next appointment?'

They arranged for the following week at the same time. And Helen edged herself into her chair and bowled outside. She had accomplished nothing. Yet she felt strangely elated.

Tom sat opposite Eileen in the kitchen that was still Dorry's.

He said evenly, 'The girl in the wheelchair. That was Helen Wilson, Dorry's client.'

He watched Eileen blanch. It was a word he had seen written, now he saw it happen.

She said, 'Your wife sent her. To spy on us!'

Tom shook his head. 'That's not Dorry's style. She knows nothing of this. Helen Wilson came to see whether you were here.'

'Oh my God.' Eileen looked at him blankly. He no longer noticed her perfect bone structure or the artistry of her make-up. He might have thought he loved her for a short time. Then Dorry had disappeared and he had been like a rudderless boat. Now, he was simply grateful to Eileen for taking all the appointments, for cooking and running the house. Dorry shouldn't have left him. She should never have left him. She hadn't done much to help him, heaven knew, but she must have guessed he could not manage without her. So it served her right that Eileen had proved so efficient.

He said slowly, 'If I could help Helen Wilson . . . however minimally . . . Dorry might come back.'

She almost whimpered, 'Oh Tom . . .'

He said quickly, 'She won't. Of course she won't. And anyway, if she did, it would be the same old thing. She was never at home.'

'You couldn't manage without me now, could you, Tom?' Eileen asked.

He responded obediently, 'I couldn't. Definitely not.'

Peggy mentioned very casually that Joshua Harrison had been passing the school and had given her a lift to the shops. Helen made a non-committal noise and waited for some questions. None came. But on Thursday, Joshua turned up just after their shared lunch and though Peggy tried to look surprised, it was obvious the call was prearranged.

'Well. All ready? We can have two hours if we start straightaway. Pick Rosie up on the way back. OK?'

Peggy was bright red. 'I didn't think you'd come so early! I'm not ready or anything.'

'You look pretty good to me.' Joshua grinned. 'Come on Peggy – we don't want another argument.' He turned to Helen. 'I had a terrible job to get her into the car on Monday. Told her it was all your idea.'

'Oh.' Helen avoided Peggy's gaze. 'What's happening today?'

'I offered to give her some extra driving lessons.'

Helen was delighted. 'Between Joshua and Harry Vallender, you'll be ready for your test very soon.'

Peggy said awkwardly, 'Actually, I cancelled Mr Vallender. Josh said he had the day off on Saturday and nothing planned and why didn't we take Rosie out to Brean and get some practice there.'

'You cancelled Harry,' Helen said slowly. 'Well, of course, if Joshua has a day off . . .'

Joshua was all enthusiasm. Peggy's colour remained high but less with embarrassment; much more with excitement.

Helen watched them go and told herself that Peggy had missed out on her girlhood and this was her chance to catch up. And anyway, Helen hadn't wanted to come face to face with Harry after the New Year's Eve outing which had turned so sour and peculiar. So it was just as well he wasn't coming to pick up Peggy.

She wheeled herself to the window and wondered whether to have a rest or work on Rosie's dress. She chose the dress, immediately stabbed her finger with a needle and said, 'Damn! And you thought you were so clever, Helen Wilson!'

On Saturday Rosie pestered for Helen to come with them to Brean. Helen said she would wait at home in case poor Dorry came home early. Then she regretted it. After all, Rosie would be playing gooseberry so an extra one would have made no difference. The day stretched ahead interminably. She thought about her next appointment with Tom on Monday and whether she could force the issue this time and invite him to Flatners. Anyway, what good would it do when Eileen Thorne had moved in?

She stared out of the window and saw that the weather was still and grey and the sea was calm, the tide receding slowly over the mud. Perhaps she should put away her sewing and wheel herself down to the beach. But then Dorry might come in, and they had so little time together it would be a complete waste if Dorry thought she'd gone off with Pegs and Rosie. She said again, without anger, 'Oh damn. What's the good?' And then like an answer she heard a car engine.

She bowled to the door and peered through the side window. Her heart hammered fit to burst. It was Harry's Rover coming along the ridge, descending the gravel track. She pushed herself away from the window and into the bathroom. Comb. Lipstick. Some cologne.

He should have knocked by now. She went back to the window. The Rover was parked on the other side of the track and there was no sign of Harry. She slumped back in her chair. He had gone to the Coastguard cottages to check up on them. Of course, he knew about Peggy's outing with Joshua Harrison and it wouldn't occur to him that she would stay at home. 'Blast!' she said wildly to the empty room. And then she wheeled herself back to the window and picked up her sewing. She was behaving like a very foolish teenager. He had come today because he was so certain she would not be in. Hadn't she told him that there was no future for them? Didn't he know it anyway?

And then he knocked on the door and she stuck

the needle into her thumb again and dropped everything on the floor in her hurry to answer the knock.

He stood there, looking at her expectantly. He
made no attempt to come in; not surprising as he was
wearing rubber boots which came right up his
thighs, and an oilskin above that. He carried some
sort of baggage. She stared up at him and said feebly,
'Hello.'

His eyes were unguarded, surprised. 'Aren't you
ready? I told Peggy midday.'

She shook her head, totally confused. 'Peggy's not
here. I thought she'd cancelled you. She's having a
lesson with my social worker, Joshua Harrison. I'm
so sorry, Harry.'

He grinned. He looked so different in all his get-
up; he was different. Carefree.

'I know all that. I told her if it was decent weather
we'd go out today. With the tide. At midday.'

'Go out?'

'It's flatner-day, Helen.' He stepped inside at last
and closed the door. 'Can't take these off,' he
nodded down at his waders. 'But bring your stuff
over to the door. I'll help you.' He held up his
bundle and she could see it was two life-jackets.
'We'll put these on when we get to the beach. I've
left the boat there. Moored to a stake. It will be all
right. But we need the outgoing tide, so don't dilly-
dally.'

She continued to stare at him while a kind of wild
joy, starting from her waist, soared up into the rest
of her body. At last she said, 'What – what should I
wear?'

'I told Peggy. Lots of layers. Wool. I've got a spare

oilskin which will keep out the wind. Thick socks and boots. Two pairs of gloves, a woollen hat – I've got a spare sou'wester—'

She whirled over to her bed and tugged a curtain across it, opened the cupboard. And there, neatly laid in piles, were the clothes he had listed. She called back, 'I shall murder her when she gets home! She hasn't forgotten at all! All the stuff is ready for me! I'll be two minutes!'

'Are you sure you don't need help?'

'Quite sure.' Already she was wriggling out of her track suit, smiling at nobody, thinking of Peggy who had known about this for at least three days. She bundled her hair into a woollen ski cap and wound a scarf around her neck, and said aloud, 'The biter bit!'

'Sorry?' came his voice from the door.

'Nothing. Thinking about Peggy. And how she has turned the tables on me.'

She pushed aside the curtain and bowled over to him. He grinned again at the sight of her and opened the door. Side by side they went down the garden and then onto the track which led to the small, uncovered beach. And there was the flatner. It was barely more than a raft with a lip around the edge, just deep enough to house a punting pole and a pair of oars. It could have blown away if there had been much wind, except that it was embedded in the thick mud which was exposed when the tide was going out. It looked incredibly fragile.

She was dismayed.

'It – it's like a sledge!' she said.

'And that's how it's used.' He handed her an

oilskin and began to buckle on his life-jacket. 'No fishing this time. Is that all right? I thought it was quite enough for us to go boating! If I began to throw eels onto the duck board you might be put off!'

She fastened her oilskin and he immediately manhandled her into her life-jacket.

'I won't be able to stay in that!' she bleated. 'There's no support . . . it will be like sitting in a saucer!'

But he laughed. He was so different. Not only carefree, but uncaring. He dipped into her chair and gathered her up and there was none of the tenderness of before. She clutched at his shoulder as he crunched over the shingle and then gave an involuntary gasp as he dumped her into the stern of the shallow boat. She grabbed at the gunnels to hold herself steady against the rocking and tried to sound funny as she said in a strained voice, 'Where's the seat-belt on this thing?'

He did not bother with a reply. He stood behind her, bearing down on the stern so that the prow lifted very slightly out of the mud. Then he gave an almighty shove which pitched her back against his chest, and the boat slithered forward. The mud was yielding its surface water so that the shove became a glide and he left the stern and moved alongside until the impetus lessened, then he put one leg over the side and with an adroit movement was kneeling in front of her, reaching for the pole, feeding it ahead of the prow and standing without apparent effort. He held the pole loosely in one hand, with the other he reached behind him and touched Helen's cheek and then shoulder.

'Are you all right?' he asked.

'I think so. Just.' She was almost shocked by the launch. It had been fast and frightening; utterly dependent on his expertise. They could have both landed in the mud if he'd made the slightest mistake.

The flatner passed the upright of the pole and he began to push it forward, gently at first, accelerating towards the end of the push so that they did not lose speed during the business of hauling it up and planting it ahead of them again.

'Sorry I didn't warn you,' he was breathing quickly. 'I thought you might want to back out. And I was frightened I might lose my nerve!' He got his breath and turned to look at her. 'I haven't actually done this for three years!'

She felt her hands ache with the effort of gripping the shallow sides of the boat. 'It . . . it's obviously like riding a bicycle – something you never forget!'

'That's OK so long as you don't fall off!' He smiled and his dark face lit up as usual. She knew in her bones he did not smile like this for other people. It was a gift for her. She beamed back though she was still terrified.

He turned and began the next push and she held her breath because the boat was no deeper than a saucer and as it went flying across the shallow sea she had horrid visions of being tipped into that mud which, she was certain, would suck her down and suffocate her. Then, against all logic and common sense, she found the next push slightly exhilarating. And the one after that more so, making her give a little shriek and laugh up at him when he turned to check on her.

'It really is like a sledge!' she discovered. 'It doesn't float or sail, it skims!'

'It will float when we get beyond the Point into deeper water.' He pushed again and smiled as she relaxed and screamed with delight. 'We'll have five minutes out there – no longer.'

He took the boat across the bay and then turned a tight circle, leaning on the upright pole and bringing the flatner around his body in a glorious swing so that she could not scream but gasped and clutched and even shut her eyes. The wind suddenly freshened and rushed at them. She felt the uneven waves lifting them crazily, and then Harry laid the pole across the prow and scrambled down to sit facing her while he unshipped two short stubby oars.

'There are two ways of doing this.' He rowed quickly, taking the boat straight out so that she now bucked the waves. 'Mostly you stand in the stern and use one oar. I thought this way would be best for our first time out. We'll try the conventional way next time.'

'Next time?' Spray slapped her face and she gasped and shook her head. Her hair streamed across her eyes.

'We'll have to choose our times. Weather. Tide.' Suddenly they were past the Point and the waves were no longer breaking. He lifted the oars and they rolled easily over the swell.

Helen risked using one hand to dash her hair away. She looked down at Harry as the stern was lifted high. 'Oh my God!' She replaced her hand just

223

as the prow climbed the next swell and he rose above her. 'Oh my *God*!'

He said, 'This is one of the best bits, Helen. Look ahead – watch the horizon.'

She had been skiing years ago and had even tried her hand at windsurfing. This was something else. They were riding the swell like birds; like driftwood. Now and then Harry would dip an oar to keep the prow straight on; the horizon would disappear; he became her horizon. And then it would reappear and he would sink almost vertically beneath her. She shouted, 'We're part of it! We're a wave! We're the sky!' Seagulls wheeled above them and she added, 'We're birds! We're flying!'

He laughed and began to row again, stern first, towards the enormous expanse of the choppy bay. She protested. 'Oh Harry – not yet!' But he shook his head.

'The flatners are built for skimming the saturated mud. They blow off course like shells once they're in the open sea. Besides, it's your first time. Mustn't overdo it.'

The sea began to break up around them as they rowed gently into the shelter of the Point and the coracle shape rocked and protested while Harry stood up again and reached for the pole. He took them slowly along the shore of the Point and Helen was delighted to see it all from a different perspective.

'Rosie *said* they were fields!' she called to him as they slid past the grassy slopes, roughly partitioned by boulders. 'The buttercup field. The cowslip field. Mushroom meadow . . .' She freed one hand again

224

to scoop her hair back. 'Pegs and I – we couldn't see it. It was just the side of the cliff. But from here . . . you can see that they are separate fields.'

'She's very observant.' He rested on the pole and the flatner gently turned around it. 'When she's in the car she plays spotting games. You know. Horses, cows, thatched houses. She's good at it.'

Helen said, 'Miles was like that. He saw something just once . . . he sort of photographed it in his head.'

He was silent. She said quickly, 'I wish I hadn't mentioned him. I don't think about him now, you know. Especially with Peggy and Rosie. He's sort of . . . assimilated.'

He smiled wryly down at her. 'I was only thinking . . . that's how it was for him when he saw you. He photographed you. He couldn't get you out of his head. Peggy . . . Rosie . . . you were superimposed on them.'

She cried out at that. 'How . . . awful! As if I . . . obliterated them!'

'Helen. Don't be absurd. You knew nothing of them. But that's how it was for Miles. Perhaps.'

She stared up at the huge hump of the Point, undulating quietly against the grey January sky.

'Perhaps. Poor Miles.'

'Yes.'

There was a silence. He pushed them on their way again and the muddy beaches slid past them. She could see their own stony cove now, a hundred yards ahead, skirted with a border of mud.

He said quietly, 'Cheryl – the girl I was to marry – she married someone else. Last summer.'

'Oh.' She tightened her hold on the shiny wood of the flatner. 'I don't know what to say, Harry. Are you hurt?'

'No. I told you . . . we had nothing in common any more.'

'Yes, but you could still feel some pain. Regret.'

'I didn't. She married another of the . . . chaps.' He smiled slightly, almost to himself. 'That's what we were. The chaps. Mick and I . . . we grew up together. He loved flatner fishing.'

'And she married Mick?'

'No. Mick is dead. He was driving, that day. Cheryl married Arnold Davison. The construction engineer.'

She bit her lip. All this past life of Harry's. She knew nothing of it until the terrible instant of the crash. And Mick was the driver of the car. She could still see it: balloons and people flying . . . flying.

She said hoarsely, 'When you came out here with Mick, you actually fished?'

He pushed gently on the pole. 'Eels. They're in the mud. You flick them out with a curved knife.'

'Oh dear. Oh . . . dear.'

'Yes. I don't think you would care for it.'

He leaned forward, took hold of the pole as high as he could and swung them expertly onto the bare mud of the beach, then leapt out while the boat was still skidding and drew it up to the pebbles. He held it steady and looked down at her.

'You did well, Helen. Did you enjoy it?'

'You shouldn't have to ask.'

'No.' He smiled at her; not boyishly this time. 'You look wonderful. Your colour is . . . colourful!'

She laughed and held up a dank lock of hair. 'Mud?' she asked.

He reached down for her, lifted her strongly and held her against his chest.

'I had to tell you about Cheryl. After Peggy, I wanted you to know.'

She looked into his dark eyes, on a level with hers. She said slowly, 'You have to come to terms with it, Harry. That's what Pegs has done for me. Somehow you must find a way.'

His mouth lengthened. 'Don't you realize, that's what you do for me? You told me once that my obsession with bringing you back to life was selfish. You were right. If you had died, I would have been lost.'

She whispered, 'Then I am glad I did not die.'

He put her down in her wheelchair and then kissed her. For a moment she sat there, head raised, simply receiving the kiss. And then feeling stirred; she put her hands to his head and held him, opened her mouth, moved against him. For another moment he was with her completely, his one hand supporting the back of her head, the other cupping her chin. And then he flinched away; she released his head, he straightened slowly.

'Helen. I'm sorry. I forgot . . .'

'Forgot . . . what?' she held onto the hand that had cupped her face. The thickness of gloves, of scarves, of the life-jackets, made everything teeter on the edge of absurdity. She could not read his dark face. 'Forgot what?' she repeated insistently.

He began, very matter-of-factly, to release her from the life-jacket. 'Forgot you are Helen.' He smiled. 'Unattainable.'

She fought her way out of her oilskin. She could have wept. It was so true. So horribly true. She watched him go back to the shore and begin to pull the flatner above the high-tide mark. Suddenly she could not look at him any more. She turned the chair and began the laborious job of wheeling herself back up the cliff path. She had done it before but this time it proved too much and she would have rolled down again if he hadn't come behind her and grabbed the back of the chair.

'I can do it.' She had to sieve the sobs out of her voice. 'I've done it before!'

'You've been using the strength in your arms to grip the sides of the flatner. It's far more tiring than you realize.'

As they came within sight of the house, the patio window was shoved back and Dorry emerged explosively.

'Where the hell have you been?'

Her face seemed shrunken with worry and her hair was spiked by anxious fingers. She stared at the two muddy figures, the filthy waders, the life-jackets dangling from Harry's shoulder.

'You've been out,' she accused furiously. 'I thought something terrible had happened! I ran along to the Point – I saw you but I didn't realize for one moment that you would be crazy enough . . .' She directed all her anger at Harry. 'I thought you might have known better!'

Harry said, 'Dorry, I'm sorry–' And then at the ridiculous rhyme both he and Helen began to giggle foolishly.

Dorry's fury mounted. 'That's the stupid thing Tom always says! For God's sake, Helen! I came back, expecting you to be alone – I was under the distinct impression you told me Harry was taking Peggy out for a driving lesson.'

Helen said, 'I really am sorry. Honestly. Peggy went driving with Josh. And it was all a plot – they worked out the surprise for me. To go out in the flatner . . . oh Dorry, don't be angry. It was wonderful! Like tobogganing on water! You would have loved it!'

Harry said, 'Look at her colour, Dorry. All that sea air – it must have done her good.'

'Is it too much to expect some note? Just to let me know what was happening?'

'Of course not. I should have thought of it.' They drooped before her, two penitents.

She said stiffly, 'We'd better go in. It's getting damp already. I brought fish and chips. I suppose they'll warm up in the microwave.'

Helen broke into effusions of delight. They went inside and after the fish and chips, Dorry melted completely and listened while they described the trip. She even promised to go out herself. One day. And in the general enthusiasm, it was possible for Helen to forget that she was unattainable.

Harry left before Joshua brought Peggy and Rosie home. He went along to the Coastguard cottages first of all to winch the flatner back into the garage there. Then he got rid of his waders and left in his car. He did not say when he would come again.

Helen stationed herself at the side window to watch the red glow of his rear lights disappear along the ridge of the Point. She thought of the kiss.

Behind her Dorry cleared up the fish plates and stacked them in the dishwasher. Helen turned the chair and wheeled herself slowly to the kitchen counter. She leaned against it and stared at Dorry.

'I'm sorry about this afternoon. I didn't think you'd be home until after dark.'

Dorry said, 'It's OK. I shouldn't have flown off the handle like that. It's just that . . . I rang Tom. And Eileen Thorne answered the phone.'

Helen was jerked out of her self-absorption. She said, 'You rang Tom? Why?'

Dorry shrugged. 'You've been nagging. About me going there. Seeing him. Talking. I finished work early and thought I'd do just that.'

'And Eileen Thorne answered. So you're not going to do that.'

'No.'

'Blast!' Helen swung her chair to the window and gazed out at the blackness. 'Blast it! That stupid man!' She turned angrily as if it were Dorry's fault. 'He can't manage on his own. She's just there until you come back!'

Dorry did not argue. She frowned. 'Did you know she was there?'

'No. Yes. Dammit, yes. I did. She's nothing, Dorry. Maybe she's good at the things you aren't – she seemed efficient and well-organized. But bossy and incredibly dull. I bet you anything he's bored out of his skull!'

Dorry said slowly, 'My God, you've been there.'

She stared into Helen's blue eyes. 'How could you interfere in my life, Helen? What did you say . . . did you talk to her? Oh God!'

'I went as a patient. I gave Peggy's name. They don't know who I am.'

'Tell me everything!' She came to the window and sat in a chair by the table. 'I don't like being the butt of one of your schemes, Helen. Tell me exactly – exactly – what you have done!'

Helen felt somehow small. She recounted her actions and motives as best she could. Dorry said, 'So it started with Peggy. You paired her off with Josh Harrison—'

'You told me to do that!' Helen protested. 'You said—'

'I know what I said. I don't understand why that led to you seeing Tom.'

Helen made a whimpering sound. 'I thought if it worked with Peggy and Josh it might – I might be able to – you know – pour oil on—'

'Yes. All right.' Dorry got up and began to pace the room. 'I hope you realize what a ridiculous idea that was. Luckily you did not give your real name so I suppose no harm has been done . . .'

She stopped by Helen's chair and lowered her head. 'I want you to promise me here and now that you will not do anything like this again.'

Helen said in a small voice, 'I've got an appointment. Monday. Eleven o'clock.'

Dorry exploded. 'What do you hope to gain?'

Helen's voice diminished further. 'I don't know. He seemed to think he could help me.'

'With manipulation? You know that's impossible!'

'It might not be. He's going to arrange hydrotherapy.' She looked up. 'You've admitted I can't do any harm, Dorry. I like him. And he's good at his job – you must know he's good. Don't make me promise not to go.'

Dorry straightened, frowning. She said, 'I can't stop you, of course. But I don't want to know about it. About anything. It's as if . . . now I know . . . I'm spying on him.'

'I won't mention him,' Helen said swiftly. 'I won't mention you. That much I can promise.'

Dorry said, 'I think I hear Peggy and Rosie going in next door. I'm going to bed. I can't take any more today.'

'I'm sorry . . .' Helen looked at Dorry's retreating figure. 'Can I ask one more thing?'

Dorry stopped. She held the newel post and looked round warily.

'What now?'

Helen spoke falteringly. 'Dorry, you know . . . once . . . you said there were places I could go. To help with sex.' She gave a strained smile. 'A course. Sex for the disabled or something.'

Dorry said, 'Yes. I remember.'

'Will you arrange something for me? Please?'

The two women stared at each other for a long time. Then Dorry nodded shortly. 'Yes,' she said.

Eleven

Tom worked silently on the front of Helen's thighs, her knees and shins, feet and toes. He swung the hand-grip across so that she could pull herself into a sitting position while he removed the small pillow from the top of the couch, covered the hole with tissue and split the tissue down the middle. Then he turned her over and she put her face where the split was and made herself comfortable. Neither of them spoke. She had known from Eileen Thorne's face that they both knew who she was. She hoped that at the end of the session he would confront her with that fact. But if it meant the end of this treatment she felt less certain that that was quite what she wanted.

She could tell from the pressure on her face and shoulders that he was pulling her legs down; at one time she involuntarily hung on to the sides of the couch to avoid being dragged off it.

'Don't worry, Miss Gorman.' Tom's voice was reassuringly calm; he was not even short of breath. 'I won't let you fall.'

She turned her head slightly so that she could see him with one eye and tried to laugh. 'Sorry. Over-reaction.'

'It's good.' He straightened. 'Let's test normal reactions now.' He reached in his pocket and produced what looked like a spatula. It lay cold on the small of her back. 'You can feel that. Right.' It went away. 'What about that? No? And that?'

She said, 'Yes.' There was a pause. 'I can't feel anything now,' she prompted.

'No.' He replaced the spatula and she flinched slightly at the cold and grunted another, 'Yes'. There were another four times when she felt the spatula. And then she saw it being pocketed again.

'Miss Gorman, I am going to make a mark on your back which will show how far you have registered sensation today. It won't wash away. Is that all right?'

'Of course.'

She waited while he made the mark; she felt it quite painfully. Then he scooped her around onto her back and passed her the hand-grip. She pulled herself upright.

He said, 'I think there is slightly more sensation than last time. But I need to be mathematically certain.' He did not look at her face. She held the thin sheet to her chin like a blushing bride. She could almost feel her own eyes blaze with sudden hope. He must have known that, because he said immediately, 'It probably means nothing. If there is a slight difference however, I must speak to your consultant. I would like to try localized traction. Not without his permission, obviously.' He turned to go. 'I'll send in Mrs Thorne. I think another two appointments this week. Perhaps Wednesday. And Friday.'

He was gone, almost running into the next cubicle before she could say a word. Of course he had no idea of the promise she had made to Dorry. She sat there, hanging on with one hand to the grip, feeling elation in the sudden thumping of her heart. For some reason he was interested in her case; he was hopeful – whatever he said to caution her, he was hopeful. She looked down at her legs beneath the covering sheet and tried to imagine them crooking towards her, swinging themselves off the edge of the couch, supporting her as she stood up. So often she had imagined that very thing; in fact it had been easier to imagine her legs working than not working; she had found it difficult to believe in the dead meat she had to drag around with her. Now, unexpectedly and quite shockingly, she could no longer imagine herself walking again. Paraplegia was the norm; people who walked around on legs were not. She felt physically sick and forced herself to go mentally through the actions of standing up. It was so difficult. She closed her eyes . . . first her hands would go behind her to lever her body around . . . then she would bend her knees . . . or would she? Would she just swing them over the side? She could not remember . . . she simply could not remember. Her heart jumped again, this time with sheer terror. It was a nightmare and she was trapped inside it.

Eileen Thorne swished the curtain aside and came in. She carried Helen's neatly folded clothes over one arm, the appointment book beneath the other. She put them both down on the end of the couch, carefully not meeting Helen's gaze.

'Two more appointments this week,' she said brightly. 'Mr Latimer is trying really hard, isn't he?' It was said in an indulgent voice that minimized the whole gigantic effort into sweets for a child. A consolation prize. Reassurance that there was still one person in the medical field who hadn't given up.

Helen reached for her clothes and began the arduous task of dressing herself. Any effort like this forced her to face her helplessness. She closed her eyes again, fighting tears of despair. She hated Eileen Thorne. But more, she hated Tom Latimer because he had given her false hope.

She forced herself to speak. 'No.' She forced her arms into the stubborn sleeves of her favourite red sweater. When her head emerged from the turtle neck, she added, 'It's no good. I can't go on. Tell him to forget it.'

Eileen Thorne allowed herself one glance at Helen's face and almost ran for the wheelchair. Helen swung her car coat around her shoulders and heaved herself into it. Eileen bleated, 'Miss Gorman – please – let me have a word with Mr Latimer.'

Helen barged her chair into the waiting-room and out into the lobby. She turned on the pursuing Eileen.

'We both know my name is Helen Wilson,' she said coldly. 'We both know why I came.' She tugged furiously at the outer door and Eileen reached across her head and held it open. 'Thank you,' she said ungraciously. Then added, 'I shouldn't have come in the first place. Dorry has made me promise not to interfere. And there's just no point . . .'

She pushed herself furiously outside and up to the car door. Tears were rolling ignominiously down her face. She kept her head down while she unlocked the car and shifted herself inside. And then, to her amazement and chagrin, Eileen Thorne was there, folding the chair, putting it neatly into the back. Dammit, she was more efficient than Dorry.

She said nothing; stood back and waited for Helen to reverse out of the drive. She was still there when Helen drove past the gate and up Falcondale Road towards the Downs.

Helen recounted the whole episode to Dorry that evening. 'You'll be relieved to hear I'm not going again. I can't bear to think about myself as . . . a cripple. I have to try to live with it, Dorry. Not fight it. Do you understand?'

'Of course I understand.' Dorry was frowning prodigiously as if the effort gave her a headache. Or perhaps it was the omelette she was cooking. 'But it's so difficult . . . I mean, I'm glad you're not seeing Tom. Because you were just complicating things. But you believed he could help you . . . and it sounds as if he thought so too. And now, quite suddenly, you, Helen Wilson, the warrior queen, you talk of not fighting. In your case, that means surrender. Is that what you're doing? Surrendering?'

'I don't know.' The emotional upheaval of the morning had exhausted Helen. Rosie had been in her most exuberant mood that afternoon. She was tired to the bone. 'If we're talking of giving up, that's your role, surely? It was only because you wouldn't go and see Tom that I went! I still think you should go. Declare war!'

'You still think it's a game, don't you?' Dorry folded over the cheese omelette and lifted it out of the pan and onto her plate; she too sounded weary. 'You don't seem to understand that if Tom has to be coerced into having me back, then I don't want to go.' She pushed a fork into the fluffy omelette and steam clouded her head and made her eyes run. 'Helen, the only way I am going back to Tom is if he comes here on bended knees and begs me to.'

'Are you crying?' Helen asked. 'My God, I didn't want to make it worse! I thought you'd like to know what an odd situation it is there! That's all! I mean, Tom is not keen. He really is not keen. She's his receptionist and nothing else – I'd swear to it. I can see why he doesn't throw her out – she's doing a good job for one thing. But mainly it's because she's clinging on like a limpet.' She pulled several tissues from a box and handed them to Dorry. 'I don't think it's a game. Especially not now.' She waited while Dorry blew her nose. 'To allow myself to think that Tom could succeed where others have failed—'

'That's not fair, Helen!' Again Dorry stopped eating. 'Mr Edwards said you might have to wait—'

'But I have waited! It's almost two years now since the accident!'

'My God, that's nothing!' She looked at Helen and added hastily, 'All right, it's a damned long time. But you need not simply mark time, Helen. Find another osteopath – go to the hospital physio department—'

'I can't. After Tom . . . I can't. Listen to you – as if physio is some kind of occupational therapy! To keep my mind off the real issue! Which is that I'll never walk again!' Helen closed her eyes. 'You don't think I'll get better, do you? You've never thought so!'

Dorry sighed sharply and put down her fork.

'We've been here before, Helen. You know that isn't true. But if you're feeling despair now – and I can see you are – can't you see how your life has opened up? You can drive, live independently, go flatner-fishing . . .' She half-smiled but Helen did not reciprocate. Her mouth thinned as she tried to control tears.

'I don't live independently. I drive an adapted car. And I could never have gone out in that ridiculous boat without Harry.'

Dorry pushed her omelette away. 'Oh, to hell with it! Go back to Tom – force yourself! He was obviously giving you something I can't! Enjoy the treatment, let him give you some hope, do all the spying you want to! But don't tell me anything else about it. Please! You're talking about my home and my husband. And I don't like it!'

There was a long fulminating silence. Then Helen said quietly, 'Sorry. Eat your supper – please.'

Dorry looked at her levelly, drew her plate back and began to eat.

Helen waited until the omelette had gone. Then she said, 'Now you know how I felt. This time last year. When you talked to people, found out about me.'

Dorry considered this and at last smiled.

'Let's put on our dressing-gowns. And have some cocoa,' she suggested.

It seemed the epitome of companionable spinsterhood. They both laughed.

The week passed slowly. Harry phoned; he had a cold and would not call, in case he passed it on. He sounded awful and she longed to go and see him, look after him.

On Saturday Joshua called and took Peggy and Rosie off for the day. Peggy's confidence seemed on the wane again and she was due to retake the driving test in two weeks. Helen held her hands and whispered, 'You can do it! Don't look like a rabbit confronted by a snake!'

Peggy managed a wavering grin but it was Rosie who said, 'We're going to see Josh's Mam. Aren't we Josh?'

'Didn't Peggy tell you?' He was ebullient, like a schoolboy with a secret. 'We're going over the bridge to Swansea, man!' He laughed and Rosie laughed with him.

But Peggy's experience of mothers was not good and she looked sick. It hurt that she had not told Helen.

Helen forced herself to whisper, 'Tell her you come with the very best references!'

She watched them clamber into Josh's car and reverse up to the ridge. It was only three weeks since their first 'driving lesson'. She could not quite believe that one of her schemes was working out. Peggy was still so terribly vulnerable. Helen said aloud, 'If it doesn't come off, it'll be your fault, Miles! If you've spoilt Pegs for anyone else, I'll murder you!' She smiled at her words and went slowly over to her worktable and Rosie's new dress. She realized that she had never talked to Miles about Peggy in quite that way before. And with humour too. Miles had had a good sense of humour. She had forgotten that.

Dorry arrived home before midday. Her afternoon visits had been cancelled and she suggested that they drive along the coast to Dunster and Blue Anchor. It was windy but sunny and they ate a late lunch at Blue Anchor and Dorry wheeled the chair along the bleak promenade and told Helen what fun it would be in the summer.

On the way home they passed the new hospital in Weston. Dorry pointed it out and reminded Helen that it was where she would go for physio if she decided to try that. They bumped down the gravel drive to find Joshua's car parked outside Peggy's cottage. Peggy came out and asked them to come in for tea. She looked almost happy. The meeting with Joshua's 'Mam' had been a great success. Only Rosie seemed a little subdued, and that – Peggy told them quickly – was because she was overtired. Helen felt the same. The atmosphere of celebration was exactly what she had hoped for . . . she must remember to tell Miles about it later. But she could not enter into it wholeheartedly, simply because she was so tired.

She and Dorry went home as soon as Joshua left. They got ready for bed, made the cocoa and sat quietly by the window looking at the dark sea and the lights of Weston beyond it. And then Dorry put a piece of paper on the table and turned it so that Helen could read it. She did so, aloud.

'Leaze Hospital, Room 10, February the fifteenth,

241

two o'clock. Seminar on sexual enablement.' She looked up at Dorry, her eyes enormous. 'Oh my God,' she said.

'Yes.' Dorry opened her diary. 'It's a Wednesday. Just over four weeks. I'll take you.'

Helen swallowed. 'That was why you pointed out the hospital this afternoon.'

Dorry nodded. 'It's not an enormous, frightening place. You could see that for yourself.'

'I don't care if it's the size of Buckingham Palace. It's just . . .'

'What? I shouldn't have thought you would be embarrassed by matters sexual, Helen.' Dorry spoke rallyingly.

'No. But this isn't quite . . . right. This is artificial sex. It's . . . somehow . . . forcing me to accept my . . . sterility.'

'That's exactly what it's not doing. That would mean permanent celibacy. This is offering an alternative.'

'What sort of alternative?'

'I don't know. Listen, would you like me to have the day off and come with you?'

'No. No, if I go at all, it will be by myself. Absolutely by myself. But I'm not sure . . .'

'It's what you wanted. I've gone into it – Dr Simmonds is running it. She is excellent.'

Helen was silent, looking at the appointment slip, then at Dorry, finally through the window again.

She whispered at last, 'It's for Harry. Not for me. For Harry.'

'I know.'

'And maybe I'll never see him again! He says he's got a cold. It could be he doesn't want to see me!'

'Each time you see him you seem to think it will be the last!'

'I have to imagine it. In case it happens.'

Dorry's face melted. 'Oh Helen,' was all she could say.

Helen nodded. 'I know. Oh I know.'

Rosie said, 'I found these. They was wild, Helen. Almost underneath a rock.'

Helen admired the three tiny snowdrops. 'Out of the wind, I expect,' she said. 'Listen. Could you put them into your picture? I could take it down and put it on the table. Or you could stand on a chair. What do you think?'

Rosie opted for the chair. She stood before her daffodil picture, gnawing her thumb and considering an unexpected problem.

'I can't paint white, Helen.'

'No. It wouldn't show on the white paper, would it?' Helen smiled. 'Keep looking. You'll find the answer if you look hard enough.'

The small girl stood on tiptoe and tried to look down on her sea of daffodils. And then she carefully got down from the chair and looked up and said sadly, 'You only see them against something else! So I got to paint the rock. And I wanted just flowers on the picture!'

Helen nodded. 'That's fine. So you see one flower against another flower.'

Rosie's smile was a joy to see. She gathered up her

paints and put them on the window-sill, then began the laborious business of outlining a snowdrop bell on the lower rank of daffodils.

Helen watched her, smiling slightly. It was almost a month since her last appointment with Tom and nothing spectacular had happened. She had somehow come to terms with the soaring hope and the resulting despair. At first, every morning, she had put her hands on the small of her back where Tom's had been and tried to find the exact place at which sensation died. But it had been a fruitless and pointless exercise and for the past two weeks she had given up and tried not to think about herself at all. Just Harry.

'Make the paint very thick so that it covers the yellow,' she said aloud to the small artist. Rosie's tongue protruded as she began the more pleasurable job of colouring her flowers.

It was Rosie who had suggested to Harry that he might like to spend weekends in the Coastguard cottages so that he could keep Helen company when she and Peggy were out with Josh, and Dorry was working. Helen's smile deepened as she recalled the weekend just past. Harry had suggested that Rosie stayed at home on Saturday so that he could give her a trip in the flatner. Dorry had been there too; there had been a lot of screaming and they had all needed showers when they got home. It had been terrific for Dorry; she hadn't laughed like that since long before Christmas. And Rosie enjoyed every moment of the hair-raising ride. But mainly Helen's own pleasure had been in watching Harry regress from

244

solemn thirty-five-year-old to schoolboy. He had spoken very briefly about his friend, Mick, whose craziness had resulted in four deaths. But suddenly Helen could understand something of the friendship between Mick and Harry. Mick had craved excitement and adventure, Harry had gone along with him, getting him out of the inevitable scrapes . . . enjoying him. And just as he had taken the blame for so many of his friend's escapades, so now he was taking the blame for that fateful day on the motorway.

Yesterday the weather had been glorious and they had walked almost to the end of the Point before Harry drove back to Bristol. On a tiny spit of land above the Channel, he had knelt by her chair and they had taken it in turns with his binoculars to pick out the landmarks of South Wales, the humps of the Holme Islands, the neighbouring headland of Brean Down.

'Are you warm enough?' he asked as the mild breeze whipped her hair across his face.

'Yes.' She turned to him making the trite words significant. 'I am quite warm enough.' She had kissed him very deliberately, which she did often, telling herself that each time she did so, she was helping him to overcome the guilt of the accident. After their first time in the flatner, he had not responded to her kisses. It was as if, on that January afternoon, he had called her 'unattainable' to remind himself of everything that was against them. But yesterday, with the wind blowing from the west and the smell of spring in the air, he had quite suddenly straightened onto his knees and kissed her back. The flare of passion between them had startled and frightened them both with its sheer intensity. On the way home they were silent and wary. It was as if the quiet time of burgeoning friendship had gone and they were on the verge of something else. Or nothing else.

Rosie said, 'Does that look right from where you are, Helen?'

Helen squinted 'Yes. Fine.'

'But they're all in the front.'

'They might not be. There might be lots more behind the daffodils, but of course you can only see the ones that are in the front.'

'Oh yes.' Rosie marvelled. 'You are clever.'

'Not a bit. I've just got into the way of looking. And if you look long enough then you see.'

Rosie nodded, understanding. Then she said, as she had said nearly every day since her visit to Swansea last month, 'I'd rather stay here than live in Swansea.'

Helen rolled her eyes. 'How many times have I told you that Joshua's mother lives in Swansea and Joshua lives in Weston?'

'I'd rather live here than in Weston,' Rosie said.

Helen was silent for a while, then she said, 'I think Mummy would, too.'

But Rosie said with a worldly wisdom far beyond her years, 'Grown-ups change their minds.'

They had never got this far before. Helen could offer no instant comfort on that one. She waited until Rosie had finished painting, and then, paint and all, she took her onto her lap and hugged her. And it was Rosie who said, 'It'll be all right, Helen.'

Helen gasped a laugh. 'Of course it will be! And darling, don't say any of this to Mummy, will you? It's so lovely to see her getting happier and happier.'

'Like the snowdrops,' Rosie said.

'Yes.' Peggy was as unlike a snowdrop as possible with her red hair and fox-brown eyes, but her emergence into life was as tentative as any flower's, and she seemed to have found her sheltering rock in the raw young social worker.

'I won't say nuffink,' promised Rosie. 'But if we do live somewhere else, can I come and see you sometimes, Helen?'

'Oh, yes please,' Helen said.

'Even if you marry Mr Vallender?' persisted the small girl.

'I don't think that will happen,' Helen said lightly.

'But if it does?'

'Whatever. Yes.' Helen hugged her again. 'So how many hotels does that give you? Joshua's Mam. Grandma and Grandad Gorman. Me. Anyone else?'

'My best friend at school . . .' Rosie was giggling now, putting her paint-stained fingers on Helen's face to make patterns. She jiggled delightedly and Helen gasped.

'Darling, hop off now. You're heavier than I thought!'

Rosie went to the bathroom to wash and Peggy came in from next door.

'Raining again,' she commented. 'February fill-dyke and no mistake.'

She admired the snowdrops and gathered Rosie up. 'Supper and bed for you, young lady.'

But Rosie had been thinking.

'Helen . . . how did you know I was getting heavier?'

Peggy said, 'When you sit on someone's lap, they always know you are getting heavier, Rosie!'

Rosie looked at her mother. 'But Mummy, Helen can't feel her lap. Can she?'

'She can feel you on her arms, in her shoulder blades and through her head, I should think!' Peggy went to the door. 'If Dorry isn't home by the time you want to eat, give me a ring,' she said.

Helen sat very still after they'd gone. She looked around the familiar room, the clear space from door to table, from table to kitchen counter and from there to bed and bathroom. She stared at the pictures: the prints she had brought from her Bristol home; photographs of her parents; finally the painting of daffodils by the big window with its new addition of blobby snowdrops.

She whispered, 'Yes. I felt her in my arms and at my waist. Didn't I?'

Carefully, she prodded her thighs. She could feel nothing. She flung back her head and closed her eyes. In two days' time she had the appointment at the hospital.

Dr Simmonds was in her mid-thirties and almost beautiful in a pale Swedish way. But probably in

248

deference to her task today she had done everything possible to make herself plain and sterile. Her ash-blond hair was pulled so tightly into her neck that her eyes and mouth seemed to be stretching with it. Her nose was long like Garbo's and her skin shone with recent soaping.

She tried a reassuring smile and introduced her 'team'. Two men and one other woman. Nobody took in the names. There were half a dozen people there. Helen tried not to look at them.

Dr Simmonds kept the reassurance going. 'We like to meet you as a group, so that you realize you are not alone with the general problem. But obviously every individual has individual needs . . . requirements. So after this session, coffee will be served and you can socialize – or not as you feel inclined – while my colleagues and myself talk to you separately. Does anyone want to say anything at this stage?'

A dark misshapen man, who had emerged from a minibus with several others just as Helen arrived, said jokingly, 'Is there any tea? Coffee is so addictive.'

Everyone laughed with relief and Dr Simmonds said, 'Tea. Fruit juice. Anything except alcohol.' She tried a different smile: matey. 'Later in the course, it might be an idea to meet in a pub somewhere. Have a drink together.'

A black girl who appeared to suffer from cerebral palsy was understood to say she did not want anyone to know she was looking for sex; especially people in a pub. Everyone laughed again.

Dr Simmonds said earnestly, 'That's one of the things we want to get rid of. A sense of shame about this. Sex is a basic need for all of us. We must remember that.'

The dark man glanced at his companions. 'We're here because we can't supply that basic need naturally. We're rather . . . anxious . . . not to be seen as perverts.'

He was obviously the spokesman for a group of them. Helen realized that he was voicing one of her terrors. She shrank into her chair as they murmured agreement. Dr Simmonds shook her head, still using one of her selection of smiles.

'That's a problem we'll have to deal with then, isn't it?' She nodded at the spokesman. 'Would you like to talk to me about this? Or would you prefer someone else from the team?'

He nodded towards an older man who had the sleeve of his jacket pinned to the lapel so that he looked like a First World War veteran.

'Are you staff?' he asked.

'I am.'

'I'll take you.'

The older man moved matter-of-factly to a door and held it open, then he looked over his shoulder. 'The lady on the right is my wife. If anyone is interested.'

Helen would have liked to talk to her. She was plump and maternal and it was quite possible to imagine her chuckling as her one-armed husband made love to her. It was impossible to imagine Dr Simmonds allowing a man within a yard of her pristine body. But of course, it was Dr Simmonds she ended up with.

'Mrs Latimer asked me to have a word with you at this stage.' The perfect legs preceded Helen into a small office and Dr Simmonds moved two chairs to make room for the wheelchair. Helen thought grimly that she would murder Dorry for making her a special case. 'Everyone has a natural reluctance to attend this sort of course. At first. But believe me, that will go. We are talking about a bodily function. Like urinating. And I understand there was a time when you relied on a catheter. So you already understand what we are trying to do here.' She sat down and leaned towards Helen. She radiated keenness. 'Can you look at it like that? We are trying to find a sexual catheter for you.'

Helen's mouth and throat were so dry she had difficulty in croaking, 'I see.'

Dr Simmonds beamed. Perhaps Dorry had told her that Helen could be difficult at times. Helen dropped her eyes and stared down at her useless lap; how could she have thought for one moment that the flat surface might have felt Rosie's weight?

Dr Simmonds stopped being keen and addressed the top of Helen's head with unexpected sympathy.

'OK. I know it's hard. Worse for you perhaps because you can remember a time when . . .' she cleared her throat, '. . . you can remember other times.'

Helen did not speak. Any effort she made now would result in tears and that would be seen as a plea for sympathy.

Dr Simmonds said quietly, 'Look. Do you want to get used to the idea of coming here? Do you want to have the next week considering the catheter idea? I mean . . . have you had enough for this time?'

Helen nodded.

'Then that's all right. That is perfectly all right. We realize what an enormous hurdle it is just to be here today. It's going to be easier next time. You're going to start looking at the whole thing practically.' Dr Simmonds sighed audibly. 'Until we know each other very much better, we have to deal with practicalities. You're finding that impossible – I can see. You are associating the sexual act with someone special, someone you love. Try . . . next time . . . not to do that. To think of it solely from your point of view.'

Helen still could not trust herself to speak. She nodded again.

Dr Simmonds said slowly, 'All right then. I'm not sure whether to let you go at this point. Whether I shall have lost you.' She paused. Helen did not respond. 'What do you think?' she said.

Helen looked up. The ice-maiden eyes swam before her. She mumbled something.

'What?' The ice-maiden leaned across and put her palm over the back of one of Helen's hands. It was not cold at all. It was warm.

Helen gasped, 'I said . . . I *could* . . . just open my legs.' It sounded unbearably coarse. As if Harry would condone it. She added frantically, 'But he wouldn't . . . he wouldn't agree . . .'

Dr Simmonds said, 'I would hope not.' She tried another smile and this time it worked. It was

252

mischievous. 'That's the good thing about sex. It takes two.' Unexpectedly she picked up Helen's spare hand and placed it on top of hers. Then she covered it with hers. It was what Rosie called 'a hand-sandwich'.

She said, 'Try not to worry about this, Helen. There are so many ways of enjoying – showing – love without the actual sexual act.' She nodded at the four hands. 'This could be one of them.'

Helen could no longer stop the tears. Dr Simmonds did not move. After a while she removed her top hand and reached for tissues and very gently mopped Helen's face. Then she released her and handed her the box of tissues.

She said, 'I wonder if during the trauma of your accident you were able to mourn the loss of your parents. Did you cry much then?'

'Not at all. And when I did it was for Miles . . . my fiancé.' Helen trumpeted into a tissue and smiled over it. 'I'll be all right. I'd like to leave now. If I may.'

'Of course you may!' Dr Simmonds actually laughed. 'And Helen . . . if you can come back next week, you might even begin to find it can be fun. So many people who are disabled forget that sex can be fun.'

Helen nodded again and turned her chair. Outside in the reception room, the others milled around all trying to talk at once, obviously excited by what was happening. The dark man lifted a bottle of Coke to his lips and then said, 'Well . . . we can always masturbate, I suppose.'

And suddenly Helen was on the edge of the abyss again. She bowled her chair through the foyer. Just inside the automatic doors to the car park, there was a phone at her level. She recognized that she was having a panic attack but she was unable to control it. Somehow she found a ten-pence piece and thrust it into the coin box. She dialled the Bristol code and, thank God, remembered Tom's number.

He answered the phone on the third ring.

She said, 'It's Helen Wilson. Where is Eileen Thorne?'

'Mrs Thorne has left. Soon after your last appointment.' Tom's voice was cold . . . bitter. He could no longer avoid the truth. He could no longer prevaricate.

Helen said wildly, 'I'm at the hospital at Weston. I have to see you, Tom. It's hopeless . . . I can't masturbate – I can't even bloody-well *masturbate*!'

He said, still coldly, 'What the hell are you talking about? Is Dorry there?'

'I'm on my own. I've been to a course. On sex for the disabled. Tom – I can't bear it! You can help me, can't you? You thought you could – you made the mark on my back and—'

'Shut up, Helen!' His voice was suddenly strong. 'You know what I can offer. Do you want me to come and get you?'

'No. I've got the car. Can I come now? You're the only one—'

'You can come now. But for God's sake drive carefully.'

He did not need to tell her that. She sobbed as she hung up the receiver and manoeuvred through the doors. But then, she was all right. The air was unexpectedly mild. She could smell flowers under the earth waiting to be born.

She sat for a while, as usual temporarily exhausted after loading the wheelchair. And then she reversed slowly out of the disabled space and drove to the A38. Tom really was her only hope.

Twelve

Tom was waiting at the side of the house. He opened the car door almost before Helen drew to a stop. She looked at him, her face drowning in despair, and he undid her seat-belt and scooped her out of the car without a word.

She gulped, 'What about your other patients . . . no receptionist . . .'

'I cancelled them.' He was very strong but had no breath to spare for more until he put her on the treatment table. She lay back, exhausted; tears trickled either side of her face.

'I'm so terribly sorry. I never cry . . .'

'For God's sake, woman. Cry.'

She sniffed a laugh. 'You sound like Dorry.'

'I am Dorry.' He put his hands either side of her shoulders and looked into her face. 'That's what you don't realize . . . she doesn't realize. She thinks she's just me. But it's a two-way thing. I am her.'

She knew he was trying to make her think of something else; but even the thought of Dorry made her lower jaw quiver with more tears. She said, as if excusing herself, 'I tried to make her come and see you. She wouldn't. That's why I came. I wasn't a spy. Honestly.'

'I hoped you were. If she'd sent you it might have meant something.'

He was admitting the truth at last; she forgot her tears and said resolutely, 'Tom, you have got to come and see her. Tell her these things yourself. That's what she needs. In fact – that's the deal. The only deal.'

He straightened suddenly, looked at the ceiling. 'She hit me, Helen. And then she left me. Doesn't that tell you something?'

'Of course. But why didn't you come on Christmas morning?'

'There was a lunch arranged . . . oh, it sounds piffling now. But it was my way of pretending nothing had happened.'

'All right. But the next day then? Or the one after? Or any of the days that have gone by since then?'

'She moved in. Eileen. She was a wreck. I had to look after her . . .'

Helen turned her head tiredly into the pillow. 'I can imagine.'

He was angry. 'No, you can't. But I thought Dorry would. Christ, it was the Dorry in me that couldn't turn her away! The carer! The priest offering sanctuary!'

She said disgustedly, 'Don't give me that, Tom! You slept with Eileen Thorne. Go on, admit it. Just to me. Just to shrive your soul – or whatever metaphor you're living by at this moment!'

He was silenced. After some time she squeezed her eyes to wring out some vision and saw he was standing, one hand high on the cubicle rail, staring down at the floor. His overall sleeve had fallen back and the muscles in his forearm stood out from elbow to wrist. She wondered how such a physically strong man could be so emotionally weak. And then she wondered why she had turned to him. For all his fine words he had eventually failed Eileen Thorne; he had certainly failed Dorry. Now . . . now was he about to fail her?

He felt her eyes on him and turned towards her.

'I'd like to be able to say that I sent Eileen packing. But if we're playing the truth game, then . . . I didn't. Not really. You were the one who made her go. Who made her see what it was all about.'

She said flatly, 'I don't get it.'

'Oh, I told her all about you. How Dorry cared more for getting you back on the rails than she did for me.'

Helen uttered a protesting sound but he ignored it; he was determined now to bare his soul. 'She thought I'd refuse to see you again. And when I didn't . . . then she knew that I was doing it for Dorry.'

Helen said wearily, 'Put me back in the car, Tom. I want to go home.'

'For God's sake, why? I haven't started yet!'

She spoke in the same tone as before. 'I'm not being anyone's sacrificial lamb. If you want Dorry back you're going to have to deal with her directly. Not through me. I'm never going to recover from that car accident anyway, so you're on a losing wicket.'

He slid her shoes off and began to massage her feet. 'Never mind me – or Dorry. This is for you.' He bent her toes towards her shin. If she'd had feeling she knew it would have hurt. 'Tell me exactly what happened this afternoon. Try to explain to me why you were in such a state when you phoned.'

'I wasn't in that much of a state—'

'You were terrible. I thought you would deliberately crash the car. I cursed myself for not phoning the admin people at the hospital . . . telling them to hang on to you until I got there.'

She watched him manipulate each of her toes in turn. She should be used to it by now; the horror of being half dead . . . she should be used to it.

She said, 'It was brilliant really. Dr Simmonds was brilliant. Honestly. She said that perhaps I hadn't grieved for my parents . . . enough. It was so awful . . . Miles. You know. The feeling of guilt. Then Peggy sort of coming into existence. And Rosie.' She felt her mouth working again. 'Dr Simmonds just said that perhaps I . . . I . . . I . . .' She was gasping for air. He propped her up and reached for tissues. She cried aloud like a child in pain. 'I didn't mean to let go again! I'm sorry . . . sorry . . .'

He said, 'Let it go, Helen. Let it go.'

'I – I can't keep it back.' She held his shoulder for support, lifted her face to the ceiling and howled. He said, 'Good girl . . . good girl . . .' and she dug her nails into his overall and drew a strangely unemotional comfort from his closeness.

At last he laid her down.

'Come on. Ease off your trousers. We're going to make up for all those lost appointments.'

She obeyed him, hiccoughing on sobs, her face

259

feeling bloated but some kind of peace easing gently into her head.

He worked on her shins and then her thighs.

She said, 'Mummy always said I had useful legs. Strong, not beautiful, but useful. They would carry me through life.'

'They might still do that, Helen. You haven't given up, have you?'

'I did today. They – the others – they knew it was the only way for them. And I thought – what makes me any different?' She gasped a little laugh as he turned her onto her front. 'It was when they were joking about having to make do with masturbation . . . that's when it hit me. Because even that . . . well, it's no good for me, is it?'

He had his spatula on her back and seemed to ignore the question. 'Nod when you feel anything. Right . . . OK . . . fine.' He put the spatula away. 'I'm going to make another mark, work on your back, then test again.'

He worked for a long time. She began to feel exhaustion setting in for both of them. The frontal bones of her face ached where they were pressed against the tissue-lined hole on the bed. When he finally stopped he was panting; she felt something drip on her shoulder blade and knew it was his sweat. He tested again with the cold spatula and then drew a mark quite painfully.

He said, 'Does Dorry bath you?'

'No. Peggy.'

'I want Dorry to see these marks, Helen. Will you do that for me?'

'Are they good?' Hope, that insidious friend and enemy, surged around her diaphragm.

'Half a centimetre. There are three lines there now. And half a centimetre between the top and the bottom.'

She closed her eyes. 'Tom . . . what does it mean?'

He said, 'I don't know yet.' He drew a stool under the curtain and straddled it. He looked exhausted. 'I spoke to Mr Edwards. When I thought I was going to see you last month. He said it might be possible, after another three treatments, to start you on traction. Localized traction. Between the sensate line and the insensate line.'

'Traction of half a centimetre?' She was incredulous, turning her face to see him better.

'Maybe more by then.'

'Before . . . when Mr Edwards talked about it before . . . he mentioned the possibility of an operation.'

'It's risky. You realize that.'

'Life and death risky?'

'Could be,' he said unwillingly.

'Then if you are considering pulling the kink straight with traction, that will be risky too?'

'No. Not in the same way. Traction cannot, in itself, straighten your kink. But it might – just might – relieve pressure long enough for the body to do its own reshaping.'

She reached for the grip and turned herself, then sat up.

'It makes sense.'

'It will be done in conjunction with a series of

X-rays. So that we know what is happening. All the time.'

'I see.' She flicked her trousers towards her feet and began to draw them up.

'I would like to fit in some hydrotherapy as well.'

'Sounds like a busy time ahead.' But she smiled as she stuck her head through her sweater. There would certainly be no time to attend the course on sex for the disabled.

Tom smiled back. He helped her on with her car coat and then gathered her up. When he had settled her in her car he said, 'Does Dorry still work through the weekends?'

'Depends. You know Dorry.'

'Will you try to let me know when she is home?'

'And you'll come to see her?'

'She might come to see me first. When she sees the marks on your back.'

'Ah . . .' Helen shook her head. 'So you're still using me as a pawn, Tom?' She started the car and checked her mirror. Then she said, 'She won't come here, you know.'

He waited by the side door until she had gone. It was going to rain; the sky was darkening in the west and a brisk wind blew down the long road. But he thought he could smell spring.

Dorry listened to Helen's account of the afternoon and obediently went behind her chair to examine the marks on her back. She did not smile. But neither did she criticize.

'Well. How do you feel about it all?' she asked when Helen sat back, tired again at the recollection of all that had happened within the space of six hours.

'I'm trying not to get carried away. Of course.' Helen tried to sound very objective. 'The fact that Mr Edwards is in on it, is . . . hopeful. Perhaps.'

'If he is,' Dorry said, just as objectively. 'Consultant orthopaedic surgeons are not in the habit of discussing their cases with osteopaths.'

Helen flushed. 'I knew you'd be sceptical! Tom's doing all this for you, Dorry! Can't you see that? It's his way of showing you that he understands your work – your friendship with me.'

'To quote you, my dear . . . balls!' Dorry came back.

'He's coming to see you. So you can thrash it all out with him. I refuse to be your intermediary any longer.' Helen wished that she had had a stair lift put in so that she could now leave Dorry to it. It was dark and raining so there was no chance of going outside. She bowled herself into the kitchen area and began to assemble the cocoa cups rather noisily.

'How far did you have to twist his arm to get that concession out of him?' Dorry asked across the counter.

'Dorry, aren't you being rather unreasonable? You said the only way Tom could get you back was if he came here and begged on his hands and knees.'

'Ha!' Dorry commented.

'He's got rid of Eileen Thorne . . . you can tell that immediately because the place is a mess.'

'And that doesn't tell you anything?' Dorry asked. 'Doesn't it say to you that he needs me back to organize Mrs Raines . . . do some cooking?'

Helen ignored that. 'And he's facing up to the

truth! Admitting everything! Wasn't that one of your stipulations?' Helen whipped the milk saucepan off the stove just in time. 'Perhaps at the bottom of your heart, you don't want to be married at all?'

Dorry said slowly, 'Perhaps I don't.'

Helen was aghast. 'Dorry . . . you're only half the person you were! You used to laugh and tease me and – and – you were so different!'

'Maybe I didn't live in the real world then.'

Helen brought the cocoa to the table and said pleadingly, 'Well . . . be pleased for me. Can't you do that? I won't have to go to that awful course again. I might get enough sensation to be able to—'

Dorry interrupted incredulously. 'Not go to the course? Has he talked you out of that too?'

Helen was angry. 'Weren't you listening? It was awful – agonizing – I couldn't bear the thought of going through that again!'

Dorry leaned forward, took the cocoa cups from her and put them on the table. 'Darling Helen. It wouldn't be like that again. It's a process of going forward . . . a progression. Just as Dr Simmonds says, there are things you have to go through. Grief for your parents. You've been able to cope with the Miles part of it by growing to love Peggy and Rosie. But your parents have been almost put aside. And the pain – the stab wound if you like – of hearing that man talk of masturbation . . . that won't happen again. Can't you see that?'

Helen stared at her friend. She spoke slowly. 'Attending something like that . . . it presupposes a lifetime of paraplegia. And you want me to go.'

'Don't accuse me of preaching acceptance yet

again, Helen. Please. I simply want you to keep every option open. You've been closeted away from people for far too long. And these people . . . are you frightened of them? Did you talk to any of them?'

'I told you – it was horrible.'

Dorry picked up her cup. 'I'm going to take this upstairs. I've got some notes to write up.' She gathered up her bag and stood at the foot of the stairs. 'Helen, ask yourself just what was horrible. Think about it. Actually, from what you've told me, nothing horrible happened today until you got to Falcondale Road. And then you were hustled into an exhausting programme that would cut out the counselling you are likely to get at the hospital.' She climbed the stairs wearily. 'Give me a shout if you need help getting to bed. And don't be too long, Helen. You look totally exhausted.'

Helen felt exhausted. And petulant too because Dorry had been able to walk out on her instead of the other way around. In fact, everything suddenly seemed to be Dorry's fault.

The next day the weather mirrored her mood with squally storms and fleeting sunshine. A small gull was hurled against the patio windows while Peggy was rubbing her legs and after the initial shock and horror, Peggy brought it in and they made a nest for it in a cardboard box. Helen defrosted some fish and put it in with the gull and they placed the box outside the front door which was protected from the winds.

At midday Rosie's teacher telephoned to say that

Rosie had a sore throat and was weepy. Peggy fetched her immediately. She begged to lie down on Helen's bed where she had a view of the sea outside the big window. She was much too anxious about the gull and Peggy spent most of the afternoon going back and forth to look in the box and report the bird's progress, or rather lack of it. Harry, arriving in the middle of a particularly fierce storm, enquired about the box of fish on the doorstep. The bird had flown.

'He's blowed away!' Rosie said tragically. 'He'll be dashed on the rocks and killed dead!' She told Harry about the gull and Harry reassured her as best he could. The fact that he had brought fish and chips for their meal did not help. Peggy decided that hot milk and sponge fingers might be a better option for Rosie. She let Harry carry Rosie next door, apologized to Helen and followed them.

Harry returned and surveyed Helen, his mouth turned down.

'Do I gather all is not well?' he asked. 'Rosie obviously sickening for something, you looking tired to death and Peggy a bag of nerves.'

'I'm all right. And Peggy . . . I didn't notice anything. Probably she's worried about Rosie. But I think it'll be all right after a good night's sleep.'

'Peggy's nerves have nothing to do with Rosie,' Harry said. 'And Rosie's sore throat is doubtless psychosomatic. Don't forget it's the driving test tomorrow!'

'I didn't know.' Helen gazed up at him blankly. 'Nobody tells me anything any more! How did you know?'

Harry looked uncomfortable. 'Well actually,

Peggy did say. Last week. We were in this room. You've forgotten.'

Helen leaned her head back and closed her eyes. 'Yes. I've forgotten. Too concerned about my own affairs, I expect. That's what Dorry would say.' She opened her eyes. 'Where is Dorry? We can't manage all those fish and chips ourselves.'

'She'll be back soon. I'll put them in the oven, shall I?' Harry went into the kitchen and busied himself. Helen watched him with dull eyes. He said without looking at her, 'What is it? Has something happened?'

She found she could not tell him about Tom nor about the course at Leaze Hospital. She shook her head dumbly. He said gently, 'Have you and Dorry had a row?'

'I suppose we have.' Helen sighed mightily. 'I suppose it's as simple as that.'

He said thoughtfully, 'Perhaps it's time for Dorry to find herself a flat. Close to the office.'

Helen was aghast. 'Harry! It wasn't as bad as that! We're bound to have disagreements now and then.'

'She's got too much on her mind. You. Tom. Her work – the journey into town takes almost an hour with the traffic. And her own uncertainty about whether to cut herself free entirely and start a new life.'

Helen looked at him, her eyes intensely blue. 'I thought she found some kind of sanctuary here. I didn't realize it was all adding to her burdens!'

'Of course she finds sanctuary.' He smiled but she did not respond. 'But often sanctuaries become . . . something else.'

'Prisons? Yes, I can see in Dorry's case that could be so. She is tied to me. Just like Peggy and Rosie.' She widened her eyes more. 'Just like you!'

He said steadily, 'Nobody is tied to you, Helen. Any more than you are tied to them. I meant that Dorry might feel so comfortable here, she won't make the effort to be independent. And that's what her move away from home was really about. Don't you think?'

Helen tried to stay very calm. She had the oddest feeling that the little haven she had created at Stormy Point was disintegrating around her. And her relationship with Harry, always so nebulous, so fleeting, so entirely ambiguous, might well be at stake.

She said, 'Perhaps you are right. If she found independence was not what she really wanted, she would go back to poor Tom, wouldn't she?'

'I really don't know, Helen.' But he sounded doubtful. 'That would be up to Dorry.'

'Of course.' She felt snubbed and determined not to show it. 'Well . . . perhaps you are the person to help her. Have you got anything on your books that might be suitable?'

'Probably. When she's ready she might mention it to me. Then Margaret could post things to her. You know.'

She wondered if that was another snub. Or if she was being paranoid. Or what.

Harry gave her one of the tentative smiles that made her heart melt. He said, 'Shall we take our supper next door so that Peggy can have hers?'

It was almost the last straw. She could have thought of it and hadn't. Or better still, he could have said how good it was to be just the two of them.

She said, 'What a good idea. And you can test her on her Highway Code.'

They packed up the fish and chips and Harry draped her coat around her shoulders and put his own back on. And she thought: I'm trapped in the situation that I have made for myself. My only hope is Tom.

At that moment Tom was dishing up his own meal. For some reason he had felt like sausages. Probably because Eileen had insisted on cooking delicious little dishes far removed from the homeliness of Dorry's menus. The sausages were spattering uncontrollably in the pan because he had forgotten to prick them, and he saw with dismay that the pristine stove left by Eileen was now covered in globules of fat. He wondered whether he could phone Mrs Raines and suggest that as Mrs Thorne was no longer in residence, she might care to come back to her old job. He cut bread and butter and fetched the sauce bottle. He knew she would not return now unless Dorry was there.

He set to on the sausages. He was hungry. He'd cancelled most of today's patients in order to keep an appointment with Richard Edwards, Helen's consultant. He wished now that he hadn't spun her the yarn about all that official approval. Edwards had finally examined the X-rays and suggested that Tom's course of treatment was 'a shot in the dark'.

However, he had not vetoed it and had nodded agreement when Tom suggested that regular X-rays should be taken.

'Miss Wilson is a free agent, obviously. If she has decided this is what she wants . . . In any case, she is due for another examination quite soon.' Edwards had practically squinted suspicion in Tom's direction. 'I suggest I see her before you begin this intensive massage. And then again, after the first session of traction.'

Tom had tried to make his usual charming smile even more winning.

'Absolutely,' he enthused. 'I think any therapy Miss Wilson undergoes should be monitored by you.' He felt the smile becoming a smirk and straightened his face quickly. 'My name was put forward by her social worker. I wondered if you had recommended me.'

'No. I assumed Miss Wilson would come into the hospital for physio. However' – Edwards appeared to be having his words dragged from him – 'I understand you are fully qualified and have an excellent reputation.' He hesitated. 'It is simply . . . you realize that false hope is sometimes worse than none at all?'

Tom said robustly, 'While there's life . . .'

'Quite. It's just that when Miss Wilson left here, she was dealing – psychologically – very well with her disablement. She had come to terms with it. It would be a pity if that . . . acceptance . . . confidence . . . were undermined in any way.'

'Absolutely,' Tom said again. 'Let us build on that confidence rather than undermine it.'

There was a silence. Edwards now looked down at

his notes and pursed his mouth consideringly. Then he nodded.

'All right. I'll get an X-ray arranged. My secretary will telephone her.'

Tom smiled more naturally and left. But the whole thing had taken its toll and he was tired to the bone. Tired of this silly rift between him and Dorry . . . tired of Eileen, Mrs Raines. Most of his women patients. Except Helen. He was determined he was going to help Helen for whatever motive.

He speared the last sausage and ate it from the fork like a lollipop. And, through his chewing, he heard the key in the front door.

It had to be bloody Eileen. She must have taken a key with her. It was so typical and he was so angry he actually stood up and went to meet her. She wasn't going to get past the hall this time. It *was* all her fault; the whole damned thing.

And there was Dorry, standing by the hall cupboard looking around her as if she'd never seen the place before. He was overjoyed. He lifted fork and sausage into the air as he opened his arms to her.

'Dorry! Oh Dorry – how lovely!'

She might well have walked into that outstretched welcome if he had left it at that. But it was difficult for Tom. And he had to add, 'I knew you'd come!'

The words had no subterranean meaning, but she stopped in her tracks and looked at him, her round eyes narrowed into almonds. She was wearing one of Helen's old coats and it was much too long for her. A beret covered her short hair. He had not realized how much he had missed her rather odd shabbiness.

Eileen's svelte appearance was somehow wearing.

He said, 'Dorry – come on – let's kiss and make up!'

It sounded good to him, but still she made no move and he spotted the sausage and held it towards her. 'Have a bite?' he suggested humorously.

It seemed to snap her out of her trance. She brushed the sausage aside and walked past him into the kitchen. He suddenly saw it all through her eyes. The hall was still neat and untouched since Eileen's departure but the kitchen had the accumulated mess of two weeks' neglect. It was bordering on squalid.

She drew out a chair with a kind of grim stoicism and sat down.

'No evening patients?' she asked in the most neutral voice he had ever heard.

'Er . . . not today. I cancelled them. I had an appointment with Richard Edwards and I didn't know how long it might—'

She interrupted. 'Ah. So you did lie to Helen. I take it this visit was . . . what shall we call it? Retrospective?'

'Not at all! It was a follow-up as a matter of fact.' He improvised with as much dignity as he could muster. 'Anyway, never mind that. I'm just so pleased you've decided to—'

'I haven't come back if that's what you're going to say. I'd rather not hear too much from you, actually. I'm going to talk to you. And I want you to listen very hard. Can you manage that?'

He began to feel hard done by and annoyed. He waved the sausage in the air. 'Look here, Dorry. If you've come to have a row why did you come at all?'

'To ram home what I wish you to hear. The telephone wouldn't have done it. A letter might, of course. Yes, I'll reiterate what I'm going to say in a letter.' She moved three dirty mugs and spread her arms on the table. Her eyes were slits; he had not realized Dorry could look evil. He leaned away from her and to show her he didn't care a damn what she had to say he took a bite of the sausage. She waited until the chewing got under way. He felt ridiculous, like a child insolently chewing gum.

'All right now?' she asked as he swallowed. 'Right. It won't take long. But I want it to be very clear. You are not to see Helen Wilson again.'

He was so astonished his mouth literally fell open. He stammered, 'But I thought you'd be so pleased!'

'She said you were doing it for me. I couldn't believe my ears. If it's true then I can only assure you I don't want you to do anything for my sake. Especially treat Helen.'

'I thought you were fond of the girl! Don't you want her to get better? To walk again? Especially . . . so it would seem . . . to have sex again!'

He knew as he spoke he should not have said that. Dorry's face flamed furiously and between her slightly parted lips he saw her teeth practically click together. He tried to apologize. 'It was just something she said, that's all. And you'd sent her to some God-awful clinic—'

'You *creep*! You total *creep*! I think I'd temporarily forgotten why I left on Christmas Eve. And now you've reminded me!'

273

'Dorry – I'm sorry.' He tried to laugh at the familiar rhyming gag and it emerged as a giggle. 'Dorry, she rang me from the hospital—'

'I know all that! And I will tell you something. Helen is in love. She does not even realize at the moment how deeply she is in love. It is precious and it is special. And the man she is in love with is as crippled as she is – mentally rather than physically. They can help one another. It is a fluid and difficult situation. It does not need interference from you or anyone!'

'So you sent her to a sex clinic!' He was angry now. Angry that Helen was in love because she had seemed so specially his . . . angry with Dorry who was so completely unjust. 'That wasn't interference I suppose?'

'She asked me to arrange it. She hated the idea. She was doing it for him.' Dorry made a sound of disgust. 'You wouldn't understand that.'

'Don't you think I've tried to do things for you? Not just helping Helen! Getting rid of that woman—'

'Don't keep lying, Tom. Eileen Thorne left because Helen was here. Is that another reason for tying Helen to your apron strings? To make sure Eileen Thorne does not come back?' Her face was like flint. She had changed. His sweet, caring Dorry had changed. She went on stonily, 'You thought I was Eileen Thorne, coming back, didn't you? Well, she won't be coming back, Tom. You can relax. She's found someone else.'

'Who?' He did not mean to sound aghast and added bluffly, 'And how do you know anyway?'

'Because I've made enquiries. I've kept tabs on you and your – your – mistress, since I left. This is my home, Tom. I want to know what goes on in it!'

'You've spied on me!'

'Yes. I suppose I have. But at least I didn't use Helen to do my dirty work for me. Like you have!'

He felt suddenly helpless. Used and manipulated by three women at once.

'I've done no such thing. She . . . I care about what happens to Helen, whatever you might think. And how do you know . . . about Eileen Thorne?'

'There are plenty of private investigators around, Tom. Some of my paranoid clients use them, you know. The one I engaged is a woman. She simply made an appointment with you for a body massage and kept her eyes and ears open. She now visits Eileen's doctor privately. Eileen is very happy with him. He is divorced and I think they might make a match of it.'

He groaned aloud, 'Oh my God.'

She said, 'What really gets to me, Tom, is the way you've talked Helen out of continuing with that course. It's a way of understanding other people. Can't you see that? There are all kinds of disabilities there, hers not so bad as some. She needs to know that. To realize that in partnerships there are often inequalities. One partner making up for defects in the other.' She shifted her gaze to the sausage still held aloft. 'I think you know exactly what I mean, don't you? From personal experience.'

'Dorry—'

She said quickly, 'Don't read anything into that. I'm going now.'

He said, 'Dorry, I can't let Helen down. Not now. She's relying on this course of treatment and whatever you say, Edwards did go along with it. I swear that to you. And Dorry – I haven't spoken to her about the bloody sex therapy – she hated it – she thinks if *I* can restore some sensation below her waist, she won't bloody need it!'

She did not speak for a long time. Then she said, 'All right. But don't say too much to her. Please. Just treat her, consult Mr Edwards, and leave it at that.'

He said, 'I'll talk her into going back to the sex clinic, shall I?'

She shook her head at him sorrowfully. 'I repeat. Don't *talk* to her, Tom. Let her make her own decisions. *Please.*' She went to the door and looked back at him. He hated to think how he must look, pleading, angry, uncomprehending. She said quietly, 'Good luck, Tom.' And then, 'Eat your sausage and cheer up. We're not quite at the end of the world yet.'

He half stood, hoping she meant something special by that. But she must have run down the hall because the front door slammed almost immediately. He went slowly into the little sitting-room where they had so often made love in front of the fire. She had parked in the road. It was raining and one of her wipers was not working.

He let himself cry. And then he ate his sausage.

Thirteen

Peggy passed her driving test the next day and quite suddenly life changed for the four of them at Stormy Point. Helen started going with Peggy and Rosie to school at least once a week, then continuing on into Weston to help Peggy with the shopping. And Dorry found a flat overlooking the Clifton Suspension Bridge in Bristol and moved out of Flatners Cottage.

Helen and Peggy had spent a lot of time together of necessity; but it had always been in the cottage or along the headland or in the cove. Now they were together sharing a joint task, discussing food and household cleaners, looking at new carpets. As Peggy said with her usual naïvety, 'We're just like two women together!' Helen knew exactly what she meant. Peggy had come into her own; she knew she was good at her job – she had seen for herself at Christmas that Helen had been delighted to have her back. And she had been capable enough when it came to catching buses and buying the weekly groceries. But this was different. She was driving the two of them; she discovered a knack for manoeuvring into difficult parking spaces, for finding a route out of town that wasn't jammed with other cars. And though Helen loved the freedom of being able to drive by herself, it was very pleasant not to have to worry about loading in her own wheelchair or being responsible for her own vehicle. And she had a flair for shopping which she had forgotten all about in the last two years. In one of the small Weston streets she discovered a fish shop which sold at least twenty different kinds of fish. 'Look at their eyes,' she advised Peggy. 'If they try to avoid your gaze, they're not fresh!' Peggy's giggle was exactly like Rosie's. Helen smiled and pointed to a large trout. 'My mother was brilliant with fish. She would have known that trout was giving us the glad eye!' Peggy doubled over. 'You're awful, Helen,' she said delightedly

Harry's words on the day of the storm had prepared Helen for Dorry's possible departure so that when Josh took Rosie and Peggy 'over the bridge' to Swansea for the next weekend, she was not surprised that Dorry too was to be away on Sunday.

'I'll ring Harry, shall I?' Dorry looked anxious. 'He'll probably be coming to the Coastguard cottage anyway. The tide's right for a trip in the flatner – he won't want to miss that.'

Helen said, 'Look . . . when you leave I'm certainly not going to ask Peggy to give up going out with Josh, am I? The phone is there if I need anything. For goodness' sake don't bother Harry.'

'What do you mean – when I leave?'

Helen lifted her shoulders slightly. 'Well, you won't want to stay here for ever, will you? I hoped Tom would come and see you . . . as you know. He hasn't, so I suppose that's that. You'll be looking elsewhere.'

Dorry stared at her. The round brown eyes were

concerned. 'As a matter of fact, that's what I'm doing today. I've got the keys of a flat in Clifton.'

'Were you scared to tell me?' Helen grinned somehow. She had accepted now that Tom would never come and beg Dorry to come back to him. Sometimes, even when his powerful, probing fingers were dragging sensation down her spine until it disappeared at waist level, she hated him for his stupid schoolboy pride. But she had never mentioned Dorry again; and neither had he. In fact they barely spoke during their time together.

'Not scared. No.' Dorry sighed. 'Unwilling . . . yes, very unwilling.' She sat down suddenly opposite Helen; she was looking wearier each day. 'I knew I'd got to go when I discovered I didn't want to!' She grinned. 'That's the sort of thing Peggy says. Sometimes Peggy is so wise, simply because she is so basic.'

'Yes.' Helen swallowed. 'This flat . . . did Harry find it for you?'

'No.' Dorry sounded genuinely surprised. 'I didn't think of mentioning it to him, actually. It was in the paper. Furnished flat, bedroom, sitting-room, kitchen and bathroom. View.'

'Furnished?'

'Well I can't take any of the stuff from Falcondale Road, can I? I wouldn't want it. This will do for . . . I don't know . . . possibly a year. Then I'll have got myself properly together and I'll probably buy something.'

Helen said slowly, 'Have you definitely given up on Tom?'

'I don't know. I don't really *know* anything any

more, Helen. I fell for Tom because he made every-thing seem easy and fun. He had a family and I hadn't. But he doesn't appreciate the family. And life isn't always easy and fun. I've got to stand on my own feet.'

'Yes. Yes, I do understand.' Helen smiled. 'Though I think I've forgotten about actually using my feet!'

'Helen, I'm sorry—'

'Don't be. But let me come with you to see the flat. Like we looked at this place.'

'It's upstairs.'

'All right, I'll stay in the car and you can tell me all about it – call out of the window or something.'

But in the event, the downstairs tenants were two medical students; mid-twenties and built like oxen. They carried Helen and her chair up the stairs with evident enjoyment and assured her they would keep an eye on Dorry if she decided to take the flat.

'Clifton Village just around the corner,' one of them said. 'Good pubs.'

'Oh well, that's all right then,' Dorry said with relief, and they all laughed.

When they were alone, Helen wheeled herself around, much more enthusiastic than Dorry herself.

'It's really rather nice,' she announced. 'The bed has a frilled valance! I mean . . . a frilled valance!'

'Shut up, philistine,' Dorry advised. 'And come and look at this view.'

The small casement window looked across the gorge to Leigh Woods. The bridge leapt across the ravine like a spider's steel web and, far below, the ebb tide was leaving banks of black mud shining in the

March sunshine. Underneath the window, Sunday-afternoon traffic crept up the hill and joined the queue for the Zoo.

'I think so,' Helen said quietly. 'Don't you?'

'I'll stay at Flatners if you want me to,' Dorry offered suddenly.

'I know. And I know that I'm not going to be able to rely on those two lads downstairs to hoist me up here every five minutes. But I still think this is right for you. You're scared . . . don't deny it, I can tell. But you'll be all right, Dorry. You're tired . . . this place will let you rest.'

Dorry shook her head. 'That's silly. I can't sleep anyway.' She made a dismissive gesture at Helen's expression and said, 'Listen. I want to say thanks. If I hadn't had you . . . what should I have done?'

'Gone to a hotel. Found a flat.'

'I needed . . . you.' Dorry went to the window and stared down. 'Let me say it, Helen. *Thanks.* OK?'

'OK. And thanks to you too.'

It was as if they were saying goodbye then and there, and in a way they were because then they told each other there was no need of goodbyes; they were within half an hour's drive of each other. And they both were bidding farewell to their old relationship; nothing would be the same now. It was impossible to know what would happen next, but it would be different.

Dr Simmonds said, 'Don't apologize, Helen. You're not expected to come every week. We're here on Wednesday afternoons and you can come and see us when you need to.'

'Well, it's not exactly that I need to . . .' Helen had not been to Leaze Hospital since that first appointment on 15 February. She could hardly confess to Dr Simmonds that she was only coming now for Dorry's sake. Paradoxically, because Dorry had left and couldn't badger her any more, she felt bound to come.

Dr Simmonds walked ahead of her down the corridor to her office. She scooped her hair into a severe pony-tail as she walked so that when she eventually sat down opposite Helen, her eyes were tilted and almond-shaped again. Helen sighed.

She drew some notes towards her, nodded and said, 'Just to bring you up-to-date . . . generally we have concentrated the past two sessions on getting to know each other and – in most cases – discussing our problems – whatever they are – openly. Freely. And certainly without embarrassment.' Dr Simmonds smiled and her mouth paralleled her eyes. 'We've played silly games. We wrote down the names we use for our genitalia and the various bodily functions. Childish names. Clinical names . . . whatever. We put the paper in a hat and drew out a few to read aloud. Actually, it was very funny.'

Helen thought: I cannot bear this, I shouldn't have come.

Dr Simmonds straightened her smile. 'I don't think that was your thing really – perhaps it's as well you missed it. But you will understand it did help several of the group to express themselves bluntly and to the point.'

Helen tried to look at her watch without being obvious.

Dr Simmonds tried a different smile. 'It's all right, I'm not in any hurry,' she said almost humorously. 'But I can see you might be.' She became professional. 'Listen Helen. I'm going to give you an exercise I'd like you to do in the next week, and then go into the other room and sit there for a while. I'm not asking you to make an effort to socialize. But if anyone speaks to you – tries to start a conversation – promise me you won't snub them. They might not seem as vulnerable as you feel, but I can assure you, they are.'

She – or the words – made Helen feel small and mean. She swallowed and nodded curtly.

'Good. Now the exercise. I would like you to note down all the intimate actions that – in your experience, or in your imagination – precede and follow the sexual act. Don't simply write the word "caressing" or "fondling". Think about it carefully. Describe the caress. Where is it? What would evoke the most feeling from you? The palm of a hand against your cheek perhaps . . . it can be as simple as that. If it is kissing, describe the kiss.'

Helen felt sick. 'I'm afraid I shall get a C minus.'

Dr Simmonds shook her head. 'No-one will see it except you. Unless you wanted to discuss it, of course.'

'I would still get a C minus.'

'Why do you say that?'

'I think the sexiest thing in my experience is a look.' The words were wrung from her abruptly. Just to end this ridiculous conversation. But Doc Simmonds opened her Swedish-blue eyes wide with pleasure.

'That is exactly what I mean! We're on the same wavelength, Helen!' She saw the change of expression and laughed. 'That doesn't please you, obviously. But like it or not, we are.' She leaned forward. 'Helen. The word sex is used a lot – it's what most people expect. Practical help with the actual act. I can see that turns you off. Will you think . . . romance . . . When you are making your list, think . . .' Her voice paused significantly. 'Romance.'

Helen stared across the desk; her fingers ached from gripping the wheels of the chair and she was stiff all over with more than embarrassment; with distaste. Now, as if the word freed her in some way, she felt her upper body beginning to relax. From the very beginning she had felt the tension between herself and Harry; had recognized it for what it was; had flirted with it, let it change her mood from low to high; from high to low. And as time went on, her inadequacy had seemed blatant. The relationship could go no further because of it. Now, with almost shocking unexpectedness, Dr Simmonds' single word – 'romance' – triggered a shift in perspective. Suddenly she saw the whole of the past eighteen months from Harry's point of view. The first surreptitious visit when he had told her she looked plain and beautiful. She had pretended pique at that description and he had said helplessly, 'I mean . . . you were plainly beautiful.' And then the flowers because he wanted to force her to live. And the cottage . . . and the trips in the flatner across the mud of Bridgewater Bay.

She repeated in a whisper, 'Romance . . . romantic . . .' It described Harry perfectly. It was like discovering the combination of a lock. Everything about him, his dark mysterious nature, was opened.

Dr Simmonds said, 'Yes. Will you do it?'

Helen found herself nodding.

'And will you wait . . . just five minutes in the other room. Just in case someone would like to talk to you?'

'You make me feel . . . ungracious,' Helen said unwillingly.

And suddenly Dr Simmonds laughed and it was natural and free. 'Oh, you're certainly that!' she said. 'But then, so is everybody at some time in their life!'

Helen turned her chair to leave and then turned back to say, 'Thanks. Sorry. And thanks.'

Dr Simmonds said warningly, 'We're not there yet.'

And Helen said, 'Well . . . I know that all this talk of the sexual act does not apply to me. But perhaps I didn't think there could be anything else.'

The almond eyes lifted into the blond hairline.

'Did you think I was offering romance as an alternative?' She shook her head decisively. 'Not a bit of it, Helen. I told you, we're not there yet. It's a long road.'

Helen looked at the perfect face, searching for the spurious optimism that meant – in the end – nothing. But Dr Simmonds was giving nothing away. She smiled and Helen waited for her eyes to lift up and sideways; when they did not she realized that the silky pony-tail had escaped from its rubber band.

Helen smiled. 'I think you might be human after all,' she said and bowled herself through the swing door and down the corridor. And there, as if waiting for her, was the girl with cerebral palsy.

'Hello.'

She sat in her wheelchair, slightly askew, a pretty girl in a red woollen shift, her hair cut as short as a schoolboy's. Helen stared into round eyes as brown as Dorry's.

'Did Doc Simmonds ask you to talk to me?' she asked directly.

'No.' The girl rounded her eyes still more. 'I thought . . . you haven't come the last two times. I thought you might have been ill.'

Her legs were twitching, moving from side to side. Helen said, 'Sorry. I'm a bit touchy . . . didn't mean to be.'

The girl gave a wonderful lopsided smile. 'I wanted to talk to you. My name is Alice.' Her speech was slurred but comprehensible. Unexpectedly her left arm shot sideways and she pulled it back in, laughing. 'That's Fred,' she said of her arm. 'The other one is Joe. They only fly about when I'm nervous.'

'I make you nervous?' Helen had to smile. Alice looked about nineteen; she had buck teeth and Helen had had a small girl in one of her classes with buck teeth.

The girl was suddenly serious. 'Well . . . you're glamorous. You look like a film star.'

The arm – Fred – shot out again and punched the wall. The girl flinched.

'Oh . . . what bollocks!' Helen grabbed the other wheelchair and pulled it away from the wall. 'Let's look at your hand.' The small knuckles were skinned. 'If Fred insists on waving around the place, you'd better keep clear of walls.'

But Alice was entranced. 'Language!' she commented admiringly. 'You don't look as if you could come out with something like that!' She experimented herself, 'Bollocks . . . it's like an explosion, isn't it?'

Helen fished in her bag and found her moisturizer. She smeared some on the knuckles.

'You'd better not tell anyone I said that!'

'A secret!' Alice was even more delighted. 'What's your name then?'

'Helen. Helen Wilson.'

'Are you here cos you got a boyfriend?'

'I'm not sure. I think so.'

'I've come cos I want one,' Alice said frankly. 'I want to get married and have a family and be like everyone else.'

'Yes . . .' Helen watched as Fred and Joe shot away from each other and Alice's mouth stretched uncontrollably. 'Yes . . . that's what I want too.'

'You'll be OK.' Alice spoke with conviction. 'You could have anyone. You're beautiful.' She folded her top lip over the recalcitrant teeth and considered. 'Least . . . when they got to know you, you could. You're not stuck-up or frightening at all really, are you?'

'No.' Helen said. 'And as for being beautiful, I'm not that either. But you – you've got something very special. You're full of life – look at Fred and Joe, they want to be doing something all the time! And you twinkle. As if you're always laughing inside.' She grinned. 'I bet you could have anyone . . .

287

anyone at all. So mind you pick the right one!'

Alice started to giggle and couldn't stop. She was still laughing when the large comfortable lady came to take her in for a 'chat'. Helen wheeled herself outside and frowned with concentration as she transferred herself into her car. Had she been 'professionally optimistic' to Alice? She shook her head slightly as she pushed the folded wheelchair behind her. Alice *did* have something special; in a strange way her unco-ordination was part of it. And obviously the pale Scandinavian Simmonds thought she was quite capable of becoming one part of a couple. Helen clipped on her seat-belt and muttered to the steering wheel, 'Why shouldn't she have a normal life like everyone else? Children . . . a home . . .'

She switched on and glanced in the mirror. Her own eyes looked out at her. Deep-sea blue and full of secrets. She thought, surprised, that perhaps she *was* beautiful. But she was definitely plain as well. She indicated right and said loudly, 'My God, that Simmonds woman knows what she's about after all!'

Tom was even more silent than usual and his expression only just short of taciturn. Helen guessed he had heard that Dorry now had her own flat. He knew – as she did herself – that though Dorry was physically closer to him, in actual fact she was now further away than ever. When he removed her pillow, put a tissue for her face and turned her over, she risked speaking to him.

'She has to be independent, Tom. It's a furnished flat so it's not permanent.'

'What?'

She turned her head and registered his complete surprise. There was no point in trying to cover up now.

'I thought you must know. Dorry has moved into a flat in Clifton.'

'She has?' His face lit up and she felt a pang of real sympathy for him. 'My God. That's only up the road. I might see her.' She said nothing. Unless Dorry wanted to see Tom, there was little chance of them meeting. 'Can you give me her address?' he asked tentatively.

'I don't think so, do you? She is my friend and I know she wouldn't want that.'

'But I'm her husband . . .' The petulant note was still in his voice. He probably heard it himself because he stopped speaking and began to work on the back of her legs. After a while he said, 'You must miss her terribly.'

'We didn't see much of her, you know.'

It was true but it did not answer his question. She added honestly, 'Yes. I do miss her.'

He continued massaging as usual, then turned her again and fitted the traction corset. He switched on and she felt the upper half of her body tighten; nothing apparently happened in the lower half. He saw from her face that nothing had changed since the last treatment and he turned to go. 'Five minutes, Helen. The bell will go as usual.'

'Right.'

He did not draw the cubicle curtains and she watched him go to the other end of the room and open a folder. He seemed unhurried to the point of being lethargic. She remembered the first time she had come here at the beginning of the year when Eileen Thorne had answered the telephone, swished the curtains back and forth, searched through a full appointment book. For the past month there had been no other patients during her appointments. The telephone had not rung and dust lay over the magazine table in the waiting-room.

He was taking some pages out of the folder in front of him: X-rays. He pegged them up and switched on a light. Three of them in a row. She knew they were hers. He gave them his whole attention until the bell on the traction machine pinged, then he carefully unpegged them and put them away in the folder before coming back to her.

'Where are you feeling the pull?' he asked as he always did.

She pointed to her waist and let her fingers trail up to her clavicle. 'Same in my back,' she added.

'I see.' He kept disappointment out of his voice but she saw it in the set of his wide shoulders, even the angle of his head.

She said, 'Those were my X-rays, weren't they?'

'Yes. Of course.' He looked at her. 'You are my sole remaining patient. Didn't you know?'

'Of course I didn't know!' She was aghast. 'Why? I don't get it!'

He shrugged. 'I'm not sure myself. I couldn't cope with the phone . . . everything seemed hard work . . . I cancelled people. They must have gone somewhere else.'

She pulled herself up with the hand-grip. 'Tom . . . you cancelled people so that you could come with me to the hospital . . . see Mr Edwards . . .'

'Some of them. Not all of them. I couldn't be bothered – I needed to get a cleaner and a receptionist . . . it didn't seem worth it.'

'You fool!' She was so angry she stammered. 'If you think you can get Dorry back by letting yourself go—'

'I haven't let myself go!' He flushed under her furious gaze. 'For goodness' sake, Helen! I've looked after you . . . got meals . . . washed and dressed.'

She could not speak; there was a frightful pain in her chest. She fell back on the bed.

'Stay still – I haven't undone the traction corset yet—' He whipped the velcro fastenings away. 'Breathe normally. You're all right.'

'I am not all right! I've got a terrible chest pain!' But she was better; she lay back not knowing whether anger had caused such sharp agony or whether it was the constriction of the traction corset.

He took her pulse. 'I can't find anything wrong. Do you want me to call a doctor?' He was anxious now, hovering over her.

She hauled herself up again. 'No . . . it's OK. It happened before when Rosetta sat on my lap. I suppose the traction has the same effect. As I pointed out to you just now, the sensation goes from here to here.' She trailed her fingers from waist to breastbone again.

'You mean when anything affects your legs, you experience sensation – even pain – in your chest?'

She stared at him. She knew, suddenly, that this was important. 'I'm not sure,' she said slowly.

He said, 'We all know about referred pain . . .'

She said very quietly, 'Ages ago, Mr Edwards said something about my – my functions – like sweating and urinating – they were on automatic pilot. Sort of.'

'And this might be the same . . . a kind of echo effect,' he suggested.

She said nothing, just stared. He picked up her hand and held it between his. 'I have to tell you, Helen, the X-rays are showing no improvement at all. I'm sorry.'

She swallowed. After a long while she said, 'Hooray.'

'Why?' he looked bewildered.

'Tom Latimer admitted an unpleasant truth!'

He tried to smile. 'Oh . . . Helen.' His mouth worked uncontrollably.

'Don't cry. Please don't cry, Tom. I'm not going to.' She patted his hand and then released herself from him. 'I'm going to concentrate on the echo effect. From now on, I shall be making a note every time it happens. OK?'

'Helen, there's no point in keeping this up . . .'

'Don't you dare run out on me, Tom! You've let down two women in your life! I'm buggered if I'm going to be the third! We keep going. Is that understood?'

He tried to laugh. Then he walked away from her back to the table. He ran some water into the basin and splashed his face. She watched him while he towelled dry. She thought fiercely: he's kind . . . he's weak too, but he's kind . . . and stupid . . . oh God, poor Dorry, poor Dorry.

He fed her legs into her trousers while she

struggled into her sweater. Then as usual he carried her out to the car. She said, 'I'll see you on Friday. Think about the echo effect, Tom. Think about it all the time. You can use it – can't you? It's possible to build on it.'

He sucked his mouth inside out in an effort not to weep again. Then he nodded.

She did not turn right into Falcondale Road, she turned left and made for Westbury village. Ever since her last exchange with Dr Simmonds she had wondered how she could share her feelings with Harry. She wanted him to understand that their relationship must grow . . . or die. Somehow it was static, trapped just as she was trapped in the wheelchair. But now – at last – she had a sense of events moving. Tom and the echo effect. Doc Simmonds and . . . romance. She drove to Blooms Best and sounded her horn. An assistant came out to her and she took two twenty-pound notes from her purse.

'Will you deliver flowers to Mr Harry Vallender? Just down the road at the estate agent's office—'

'Yes, I know the place, madam.' The girl was all smiles. 'What would you like? This is a great deal of money.'

'I'd like something quite small. Each day. Are there any snowdrops left?'

'Oh yes.'

'Then snowdrops for the rest of this week. And then next week, daffodils. And if there's any money left, tulips after that.'

'Is it a late Valentine?' the girl said, smiling.

Helen thought about it. 'Yes. Yes, it is.'

293

She drove slowly home over the Suspension Bridge and through Ashton Park to the old country road through Long Ashton. The March sunshine was all around her. She felt a gentleness inside and outside her body; it contained sadness and a kind of contentment. When she bumped down the gravel drive and Rosie came flying out to meet her, she knew a moment of piercing happiness.

That night when Peggy and Rosie had left her, she watched the tag-end of a dark red sunset that heralded frost the next morning. She waited until it had gone and the stars took over, then she switched on her lamp and drew pen and paper towards her.

She printed at the top of the page, the words 'Eye contact'. And then she whispered, 'Thank you, Miles.'

Fourteen

The telephone rang the next morning after Peggy and Rosetta had left for school. Harry's voice came across the wire at once, familiar and exciting.

'I opened up at eight-thirty and the snowdrops arrived at nine. They're . . . wonderful. Thank you.'

She said demurely, 'I'm glad you like them.'

'I like them.'

'Describe them to me.'

He was surprised. 'They – they're snowdrops. White. Green sheaths. She – the florist – has arranged them in real moss which completely hides the plastic container . . . a sort of saucer.'

'Tell me the colours again.'

'White. And green. Isn't that what you asked for?'

'Oh yes. But there's far more than white and green and I want you to look at them when you've got spare minutes throughout the day. And then tell me about them.'

'Am I going to have to paint them? Like Rosie paints flowers?'

'You could do, of course. That is when you really see things.' She was smiling at the sunshine which was glinting in from the left side of the window, turning the marmalade on her plate into liquid gold.

There was a silence on the other end of the phone.

295

Then he said quietly, 'Only one thing matters about these snowdrops. And that is . . . you sent them to me. That makes them unique.'

She was convinced she felt her heart physically expand. 'So . . .' she cleared her throat '. . . you don't actually like the flowers?'

'Helen . . .' his voice was a murmur '. . . learn to be . . . quiet.'

She wanted to ask him whether he was telling her to shut up. But it was as if he was drawing her down into that silent well of his being. She already knew that when there was nothing to be said or done about a situation, he remained silent. There had been times in the last four months when she had forced words from him, but they had come uneasily and from the depths of the turmoil which he kept tightly lidded.

She waited, staring at the molten marmalade until she had to close her eyes against its brightness. Then she whispered, 'How can I communicate with you if I am silent and you are silent?'

He said, 'I am looking at the snowdrops.'

And then he replaced the receiver.

She said aloud, 'Damn!' because she had wanted to ask him if he would be calling in that evening. She knew he would; hardly a day went by without a visit from him. But she needed to ask him; she needed him to tell her. She looked at the marmalade . . . she needed him.

Margaret brought in his coffee and some mail.

'You look as if you're learning to smile again,' she said, smiling herself. 'They say time heals everything but I had started to wonder if you might be the exception to that rule.'

He shook his head at her more in sorrow than in reproof. She had been his father's secretary so had to be allowed that kind of remark.

'It's Miss Wilson, isn't it?' Margaret pursued unwisely. 'I didn't think she'd want anything to do with you but she's like a moth around a flame. I suppose those snowdrops are from her?'

He felt himself withdrawing; he knew he should be angry and tell her to mind her own business, but anger involved passion and he no longer allowed himself any passions.

He took one of the letters from her hand. He recognized the signature. 'What's this? Request for a survey?'

Thankfully she was diverted. 'From that friend of yours. Arnold Davison. He wants to buy something in the area. That would be nice, wouldn't it?'

He could think of nothing worse than Arnold – and that now meant Cheryl too – living within calling distance.

'Leave it with me,' he said dismissively. And at last Margaret got the message, put the rest of the mail in a neat pile on his desk, next to the coffee cup, and departed.

But her words lingered on. She had described Helen as a 'moth around a flame'. He took Arnold's letter and went to the window, his face darkening introspectively as usual. Moths eventually burned to death from their attraction. Was Helen attracted to him because he represented death to her? He recalled the perfect oval of her face, the dark blue eyes and the full mouth which was so often set with sheer determination. Because of him she had almost died. But also because of him she had hung on to life and wanted it back again. And that was when he should have left her to find what she really wanted, instead of haunting her like some ghost of her past. But he could not leave her now because, for him, she represented something far above the agony of the accident; it was almost as if she represented life . . . a certain kind of life . . . after death.

He read Arnold's letter. It was informal, friendly. He wanted a survey done. The house was an Elizabethan manor on the south-facing slopes of the Mendip hills. It was a big job; an excellent commission. He threw the letter into the bin. And then he picked up the arrangement of snowdrops and looked closely into them. Helen was right, of course. Besides the palest of greens in the shadows of the white bells, there were purplish veins; gold too. He closed his eyes and let the earth-fresh scent roll into his head. He did not need to look that closely to know that the snowdrop was purity. Like Helen herself.

At last he replaced the small container on his desk, picked up his coffee cup and drained it.

The first time Helen went into the heated pool, she was consumed with a basic terror of drowning that made her flounder helplessly to the side and hang on to the safety bar for dear life. The therapist – called Hilda and as stalwart as her name – slid in beside her.

'It's all right. Did you expect to swim immediately?'

298

Helen nodded, unable to speak.

'Some people do. Others, like you, find their paralysed limbs act as a dead weight. They won't pull you down, but you've got to get used to them. Let's put some floats underneath you.' She reached up to the side and pulled down a bright orange float, gathered up Helen's legs and laid them onto it. 'Don't release the bar just yet. Get used to that position.'

Helen panted, 'I've no intention of releasing the bar at all! I want to get out. Now.'

'Oh, come on. Give it five minutes at least.' The therapist beckoned a helper over. 'Liz, can you support Helen's head? Now . . . you can let go, Helen.'

'No!'

'Just one hand. I'll hold it. That's it . . . I'm going to move it up and down in the water.' She paused and looked at Helen's wide eyes staring obsessively at the roof of the poolhouse. She said gently, 'You are in a world of sensation now, my dear. Feel the water as your hand moves against it. Feel the buoyancy in the small of your back and your shoulders. Liz is barely supporting your head, but she is there. And I am here. You are absolutely safe. Lie back and enjoy it.'

The words were strangely familiar; they were the kind of words Helen herself used when she wanted someone to look at colours and shapes. But still she said, 'I can't – I can't! My legs will come off the float! They will pull me down.'

'They won't do that. But you will feel their weight. So in a way you are feeling your legs. You are conscious of your legs for the first time since the accident. Isn't that rather interesting?'

Helen risked turning her head and focused her stare on the older woman. Hilda was wearing a regulation black swimsuit; she was large-busted and comfortable; completely different from the blond skinniness of Dr Simmonds. But they had a lot in common.

Helen panted, 'No-one told me you were a psychologist!'

And by the time Hilda finished laughing, Helen had released the bar with her other hand and was moving that in the water involuntarily. She looked down the length of her supine body. Her legs were beneath the surface, trailing like puppet's legs from her waist. The water gave them a life of their own, they bobbed up on the float and submerged again.

She gasped, 'Hilda – Hilda, can Liz hold my other hand?'

Liz did so and they moved into the middle of the pool. The legs came too, wavering after her on their orange float, part of her, yet not part of her. She had not been able to do anything for them for so long; Peggy, and now Tom, regularly rubbed them, but she could do nothing. Now she could. She moved her upper body from side to side and after a split second they followed suit, twisting back and forth in the water as if saluting her ironically. She laughed and lay back again, looking at the ceiling, already working out that if she could make them twist behind her like that, she might eventually use them to swim.

Suspended between the two women she felt safe

300

at last and closed her eyes, trying to recapture her old love of the water. This was why she had enjoyed the flatner. The heavy medium of water provided a buoyancy the air could not. She tipped her head back and let a film of it wash over her face.

They reached the other bar and held on to it.

Hilda said, 'See if you can push yourself out from the bar – don't let go. I want you to push out, then pull back in, so that your legs float out behind you.'

'Without the float?' Helen was nervous again.

'Yes. You're holding on. Nothing to worry about. I want you to see for yourself how they will behave. You've got to get to know them.'

'But won't they sink? They're not buoyant without the float.'

'They are if you use the water and your own body. You will learn all these things. I promise you. Give it a try.'

So Helen spent the rest of her half-hour's hydrotherapy pushing herself to arm's length on the safety bar, turning her head to watch her legs, and realizing that, slowly but inexorably, they floated out behind her.

'Next time,' Hilda was quietly confident, 'next time, you'll be swimming with a float. And the time after that, without one. And each time you come your arms will be stronger so that you will swim faster. With regular training sessions you might be picked for the Paralympics next year.'

Helen looked at her face, suspecting irony; there was none. In the changing room she sat on one towel, used another on her top half, while Liz patted her legs dry with a third.

'You know, when you get the use of these back –'
Liz used the towel on her calves like a band-saw.
'You'll be almost instantly mobile. The muscles
aren't wasted at all. You must have daily massage.'

Helen thought of Peggy with deep gratitude. 'I
do,' she said. It was much later that she recalled Liz's
first words. Liz and Tom were the only people who
simply assumed that she would get back the use of
her legs. And Tom had changed his tune since the
last lot of X-rays.

Peggy and Rosie were at Flatners and the table was
laid for a high tea. It looked wonderful.

'How did it go?' they asked practically in unison.

Helen nodded. 'Brilliantly. I'm going in for the
Paralympics next year!'

Rosie hopped around the table laughing her
congratulations. Peggy said, 'That's great.' Helen
told her that it was all due to her massage tech-
niques. 'That's great,' she said again.

Helen looked at her. 'Is something up? Harry
can't come down tonight?'

Peggy smiled. 'He'll be here any minute now.' She
poured water into the teapot and her face disappeared into the steam.

'What then?' Helen persisted.

'Nothing.'

Rosie said, 'Josh wants to come and live with us
next door and Mummy says no.' She spoke the words
in all innocence but cast a dark look at her mother.
'His feelings are very hurt,' she added.

'Oh.' Helen looked at Peggy, wide-eyed. Peggy
shrugged. Her freckles had been absorbed in a full-
blown blush of embarrassment.

Helen accepted a boiled egg from Rosie and said, 'I think Mummy would rather not talk about it, Ro. Right, Pegs?'

Peggy smiled gratefully. 'Right,' she agreed.

But when Harry arrived and Peggy and Rosie prepared to leave, she unexpectedly leaned over and brushed Helen's cheek with hers.

'It's exactly the way I came by Rosie,' she murmured. 'I don't intend to let that bit of history repeat itself.'

And Helen, looking up, surprised and delighted by the salutation, said, 'Perhaps it's just that Josh lacks . . . finesse.'

Peggy actually smiled. 'You can say that again!' she agreed.

Helen thought: another merit mark for Doc Simmonds . . . romance would have done it. I must talk to Josh.

Harry said, 'What was all that about?'

'Peggy and Josh. Peggy's hopeless at talking about herself, so we shall never really know.' She touched her cheek. 'That is the first time she has kissed me.' She looked at Harry, smiling. 'Kissing is quite wonderful, isn't it?'

He stared at her, his dark eyes bright with intensity. 'So are snowdrops. And now daffodils,' he said.

Unexpectedly, she blushed. Like Peggy. She wanted to laugh at herself and tell Harry about the romance thing. Instead, she put her hands to her face and said, 'Harry – why are you looking at me like that?'

'I want to see you. You told me to look and keep

looking if I wanted to see the snowdrops properly. And I want to see you.'

She tightened her lips against a rush of emotion. 'Oh . . . Harry,' was all she could find to say. But the words, and her covered face, seemed to bring him out of his reverie. Suddenly, as if he was trying to reassure her, he said, 'It's all right, Helen. You know how I feel about you. I would never do anything to hurt you. I promise that.'

She wondered what he meant. The trouble with being romantic was that you never quite knew where you were and what was happening. She said with a catch in her voice, 'You know I'm having counselling. It could help . . . us.'

'No, I didn't know.' He frowned. 'I don't think you need counselling. You cope so well. I take it for granted now that you use your wheelchair like a spinning top . . . sew, cook . . . paint . . . drive your car. But I thought you were . . . content. Surely all this counselling guff is not for you?'

Her face was still warm; the multi-compliments confused her further. She forced her hands into her lap and looked at them. She had long wanted to tell Harry about Tom's treatment and the echo effect, about Doc Simmonds, about Alice. The only thing was, he would surely understand immediately why. And then somehow, the romance would be gone. But had the romance served its purpose?

She lifted her head and tried to look at him levelly.

'You must know that I am more than content. I am . . . still capable of excitement. Ecstasy.' She said the last word deliberately and he knew it. It was his turn to look away. He said nothing. She waited; his silence became a wall.

She blurted at the wall, 'You must know that my excitement – my ecstasy – is because of you.'

He looked up at last. 'Helen—' His voice held an unfamiliar note; was it desperation? 'My dear, don't torture yourself like this. I understand what you mean . . . none of that matters. Not to me.' He gestured with his hands; it was so uncharacteristic of his normal stillness. He was physically searching for words. 'You just said yourself . . . a kiss is a wonderful thing. It can be . . . enough.'

She closed her eyes against the intensity of his. She knew, in that instant, the terrible depth of his . . . alienation. She had been able to reach part of him. Suddenly she was frightened she might lose that small part. She said in a low voice, 'I'm not on a pedestal, Harry. I'm no saint. I have feelings . . . sexual feelings. Strong sexual feelings. A kiss is not enough.'

'It is for me.' She felt him come close; his lips brushed her hair, her forehead, her eyes; then moved to her mouth. She turned her head away sharply.

He drew away, hovered above her. 'What's wrong?'

'I don't like being segregated.'

'Helen!'

'Just because I can't feel my legs . . . can't feel my vagina . . . does not mean I cannot *feel*!'

Though by now there was space between them, she sensed his further withdrawal. It was so close to distaste that it made her words tawdry, vulgar.

She said wearily, 'Sit down, Harry. At least that puts us on the same level.'

He sat down. He looked at her as if he had not seen her before. He said, 'Helen, I'm sorry. I don't know how this started. I don't really understand. You talk of happiness. Ecstasy, even. But it's obvious that you are not happy with things as they are. And I am sorry.'

She felt incredibly tired; her arms were heavy on the chair, her head had to be consciously held upright on her neck.

'I simply wanted you to know that . . . things will be different.'

'And I wanted you to know that it doesn't matter to me.'

'That is . . . defeatist.'

He reached for her hand. 'Or realistic.'

'No.' With the last of her strength she pushed his hand away. 'No. Acceptance, in this particular case, is further disablement, Harry. *You* are disabling me.' She sighed hopelessly. 'You should be going to the sex counselling, not me.'

'Sex counselling? Is this Dorry's doing?' His distaste was now obvious. She forgot that distaste – revulsion – had been her first reaction too.

She responded angrily. 'Yes! I've met people there who can laugh about all this! Because it is funny, you know, when you have to use man-made aids to get an erection! To get an orgasm! And they are the lucky ones – they are teaching me to laugh now! Because man-made aids are no good to me! And you – you

306

will disable me all over again because you won't make love to me—'

'Helen!' His protest was also a cry of agony. 'How could I use your body like that! What do you think I am?'

'It won't be like that.' She leaned forward now, supporting herself on her elbows, her tiredness in check for a last plea. 'Tom says there could be an echo effect! When Rosie sat on my lap I felt it in my chest – in my shoulders! And when the traction corset—'

She had broken through into his inner self at last. He said incredulously, 'Tom? Are you talking about Tom Latimer? My God, what is Dorry playing at, letting you loose on some quack who's messed up his own marriage! What's he done to you? Tell me!' He had her by the shoulders, he was shaking her.

She gasped, 'Nothing to do with Dorry. I chose to go to Tom! By myself!' Her hair tossed around her shoulders and over her face. 'I make my own choices!' He let her go and they were both still; panting. She pushed her hair behind her ears. She stared at him defiantly; her eyes were dark with pupil. 'I chose you. Do you remember that? When I came down to the office? You must have known then that I was choosing you.'

. 'Christ . . . oh Christ . . . what have I done?'

'I don't know.' She lifted her chin and spoke in a hard voice. 'Do you want to go to bed?'

'No! Christ! Helen, don't talk like that!'

She shrugged as if she did not care. 'That's your choice then.' She relaxed and, with shocking unexpectedness, smiled at him. 'Harry. Go home. Have another look at the flowers. Let's start again. You sent me flowers when you wanted me to live. Now I want us both to live.'

'I can't leave you like this!' His dark eyes were open to her now; they were full of pain and bewilderment. 'We need to talk, Helen – please—'

'I cannot talk any more. Not now.'

'But . . . I can't just leave you! I – I was violent, Helen . . . oh God, I am so sorry. Did I hurt you?'

'Of course you didn't hurt me. But I can't go on talking. I must rest. Please go now.'

'Helen, I'm desperately sorry. I don't know what to say – what to think—'

'Good night Harry.'

He got up and moved to the door like a man in a dream. He shouldered into his coat, opened the door and turned to look at her. And she knew that his dark eyes were full of tears.

She did not expect to see him the next day, but when two more days elapsed and he had not phoned either, she felt a terrible sense of loss. Tom took her for further X-rays. When she went swimming she hardly noticed the joy of the different element; she forced her upper body through the water as if she were already training for the Olympics. Liz was warm with congratulations; Hilda less so. 'Take it more slowly next time,' she advised. 'You didn't even watch your legs.'

'I knew they were behind me,' Helen said with humourless irony.

It was Wednesday again and she said to Alice, 'Any luck with a boyfriend?'

Alice blushed. 'Stewart asked me for a cup of coffee.' Stewart was the small dark man who seemed so in command of every situation. 'What about your bloke?' Alice asked.

'I don't know. I sent him flowers. Haven't seen much of him since. Don't send flowers to Stewart!' They both laughed, but then Helen found herself saying, 'We had a row. About this—' she moved her head around the room, encompassing all that it meant. 'He couldn't take it.'

Alice lifted her thin shoulders; her arms went with them. 'They can't.'

'They?'

'The non-disabled people.' Alice's arms – the recalcitrant Fred and Joe – shot out sideways. 'They should come with us. Here. But they don't think they need that.' She looked serious and it was unusual for Alice to look serious. 'You might have to let him go. It's a bit like me being black. 'Tisn't everyone who can integrate. Some blacks have to be with blacks. Some whites have to be with whites. P'raps your bloke won't be able to cross over.'

Helen felt her diaphragm flutter as if with a premonition.

She said, 'Sounds as if you're talking about a great divide. We're all human.'

Alice grinned again. 'Yeah. But some are more human than others.' She said, 'I got a motor on my chair now. Race you to the foyer!'

Harry could not raise Dorry on the phone. The Social Services office said she was out on calls; when he rang the flat a young man answered, obligingly offered to go upstairs and knock the door down, but then said as her car wasn't outside she must be making calls. He could not bear to wait until she returned either to the office or to the flat. He put down the phone, picked up his coat and went downstairs.

Margaret said, 'Are you going to see Mr Davison?'

'No. Why?' He stared at her uncomprehendingly.

'The letter I put on your desk this morning. It was from him. He telephoned just after you'd left last night. He thought we hadn't received his first letter.' Her eyes were heavy with reproach; she looked like a bloodhound.

'I ditched it.'

'He won't take no for an answer.'

'I think he'll recognize a cold shoulder after a while,' Harry thrust his arms into his coat and opened the door. Margaret came at him full sail.

'Look at you! It's raining outside! At least turn up your collar.' She put actions to words. He flinched away. She fell back, rebuffed.

'I thought you were getting better,' she said, half angrily, half excusing herself.

'I am.' He forced a smile. 'I am behaving like a normal male. For the first time in two years.'

And he went outside to the car.

He drove slowly – he would always drive slowly now – and drew up outside the Falcondale Road house at eleven o'clock. He checked the time because he wanted to be certain Tom would be in the middle of his morning appointments and not sloping off for an early lunch. He pulled into the kerb outside the drive. It was an imposing red brick house, with a porticoed front door and wide side entrance leading to a garage. And there, horribly familiar to him, was the small Ford Escort especially adapted for Helen.

He almost heard his heart beating. He knew he was angry and fought to control himself. How often had he told Mick about control; he had made up an epigram, pretending that it came from the East: 'He who is not master of himself is master of no man.' Mick had been spoiling for a fight with a gang of street yobs at the time; he had laughed crazily and gone in with fists flailing and Harry had been forced to join him. They had both landed up in hospital. But Harry now knew how Mick had felt.

He waited at the edge of the kerb, engine running for almost five minutes while traffic manoeuvred around him. Then he drew out again and parked in the first side street, locked the car and walked back to the house.

Next to Helen's car was a door marked 'Waiting-room'. He tried the handle; it was locked. He hammered on it with his fist; nothing happened.

He stood back, looking up at the side of the house and breathing heavily. Then he went to the front and used the bell and knocker simultaneously. There must be a receptionist, especially with Dorry not there. But the door remained unanswered. He stood there, alternately ringing and knocking, only just managing to stop the urge to kick the door.

At last he went around the house, past Helen's car to the garage. A wrought-iron gate – padlocked – guarded the rear from intruders. It was head height but he climbed over it without too much difficulty. He found himself in a large garden conventionally laid out with lawn and herbaceous borders. A clothes line was festooned with dripping shirts and pants. It was raining quite fast now. He wiped his face and tried the back door. It was locked. To the side of it was a window; he peered through. He was looking into a kitchen; immediately beneath the window was a sink unit and a long working surface. Every inch of the surface was covered with used crockery. In a saucepan of water, cutlery was stacked. The sink contained two more saucepans. Beyond that was a deal table. It held a bread board and a loaf, butter in a plastic carton, a marmalade jar with the lid by its side and a packet of cereal. He thought of his own sterile kitchen without pride. Somehow Tom's squalid mess looked as if someone was living in it. Or even dying in it. Certainly not simply existing.

He moved to his right. A large French window, its paintwork flaking, framed a dining-room. The sideboard, mantelpiece and table were dusty and obviously unused. Vaguely Harry remembered Dorry saying something about a cosy front sitting-room; this one needed new windows; it was draughty. He looked down: the bottom of the frame was rotten; the bolt not even shot. He put his foot against it and applied pressure. There was a splintering sound. He pulled the handle and the door swung creakily towards him.

Just for a moment, he paused, wondering what he was doing. Breaking and entering was the emotive term that might be applied to the old Mick but never to him. And then he thought of Tom Latimer, doubtless smoothly handsome in an erotic, unbearable way. Tom Latimer, who had doubtless discussed the possibility of orgasm with Helen. And had he done anything else . . . had he demonstrated what he meant?

Harry had felt sick ever since he left Flatners. Now, as he stood in the Latimers' unkempt house, he knew the first thing he must find was a bathroom. He could almost smell the decadence with the dust; it was horribly easy to imagine Helen, naked and vulnerable here. He stepped into the room and moved swiftly to the door. This opened onto a big old-fashioned hall. The floor was tessellated, the stairs heavily banistered. Beneath the stairs was another door which he thought was the downstairs cloakroom; he opened it and found himself in what was obviously a treatment room. In contrast to the kitchen and sitting-room, it was neat and clean. He retreated, shut the door and took the stairs two at a time.

He was still in the bathroom when he heard a car outside. He had been swilling his face and as the engine note drew nearer he wondered if the outgoing water would give him away. By the time he had raced into the bedroom to peer through the net curtains like any nosy neighbour, the car was still closed and no alarm was being raised. He peered down: presumably it was Tom Latimer's car, a much newer model than Dorry's and better kept too. Neither of these facts endeared Tom to Harry. He very gently unlatched the sash window and lifted the bottom pane two or three inches. Then he remained statue-still, his eyes burning with concentration. Nothing happened for a long time. Then, when he was thinking that somebody must have already emerged from the car and gone elsewhere, the driver's door opened and a man got out. He was completely unlike Harry's mental image of Tom Latimer, there was nothing of the seducer about him. His hair was mouse-brown and flopped over his forehead like a schoolboy's; from above, even foreshortened, his face looked typically English. Yet his powerful shoulders were as Harry might have imagined and his professionally cheerful voice identified him immediately. He leaned down and looked at someone inside and said in a hearty, jolly voice, 'Cheer up, Helen! I know Dorry is dead against it, but we'll go on working – I promise you I won't run out on you!' And then he gave a laugh that was completely phoney.

Harry gripped the window ledge and closed his eyes; behind his lids a red light burned. He had not seen that light for a long time but knew it was anger. Then came the sound of a car door being slammed and he opened his eyes quickly. Tom Latimer had closed his door and was rounding the bonnet to Helen's side of the car.

Harry changed position slightly so that he was peering directly beneath him. He had an excellent view when Tom opened her door and reached inside – the shoulders and arms only too obvious – and emerged with Helen. Helen clung to him – of course she had to – but it was also obvious that she was weeping. Harry did not know how to bear it. Her head was tipped back so that the fine rain fell directly onto it. If she had not been blinded with tears she would surely have seen the net curtain moving in the breeze and would have felt his gaze on her. He had to do something; he moved the net and pressed his forehead against the cold glass. But already Tom was opening the door of her car and settling her inside. Harry felt a pang of pure anguish. She was going to drive home, weeping and unhappy. That unfeeling swine was going to allow that. He dropped the net and turned to run down the stairs to intercept her. But by the time he reached the hall he could hear her reversing into the road. He ran into the cluttered kitchen and looked through that window; Tom was in the road, holding his hand up to the traffic so that she could reverse out safely. Harry held the edge of the greasy sink and groaned aloud. She had been rejected by him and she had turned to Tom. What for? Why had Tom promised not to run out on her? Harry groaned again.

He heard the key in the waiting-room door and pulled himself together somehow. He must try to stay calm; he had to find out what was happening before he actually hit Tom Latimer. To run into the treatment room and grab him now would be . . . what was the phrase? Counterproductive. He sat down at the kitchen table and waited.

When Tom came through the door under the stairs he did not immediately make for the kitchen as Harry had expected. He went to the telephone in the hall and Harry heard him punch out a number quickly, obviously from memory. And then he spoke, eagerly.

'Dorry? Listen. I've done what you said. We're just

back. The X-rays did not appear to show any difference and I told her I couldn't do anything else for her.'

Dorry. So he knew where to reach her, and it sounded as if she was master-minding this thing . . . whatever it was.

'Yes, well, it wasn't quite like that . . . no – no, listen Dorry, – please! She was in a state anyway – don't know why – and she went completely to pieces, so I had to . . . well, I had to, didn't I?' There was a pause, then he said, 'Of course I didn't promise her the earth – I told you – but I did say we would go on. For a while.' Harry could hear Dorry's protest from inside the kitchen and Tom interrupted her loudly and insistently. 'I had to say something, Dorry! For God's sake! She was crying and begging me not to desert her! What d'you mean, you don't believe me? I know a part of Helen you don't! Certainly I do! Helen is a highly sexual woman who needs me and I do not intend to—'

He got no further. Harry's advantage was that of surprise. He gripped Tom's muscular shoulder and turned him easily on the tiled floor. His left hand – always his strongest side – came up from thigh-height with terrific force. It connected horribly audibly with Tom's chin. There were two grunts, one of surprise and one of pain and Tom's knees buckled and he collapsed by the newel post, still holding the phone.

Harry almost collapsed by him; his limbs seemed to be shaking independently of each other. He stared down at Tom, wondering if he had killed him, and saw immediately that he had not. Dorry's voice, disembodied and frantic, spoke from under Tom's tousled brown hair. 'Tom! Tom? What is happening?'

Slowly Harry leaned over, felt Tom's pulse, then his jaw, then retrieved the telephone and said, 'It's OK, Dorry. It's me, Harry. I've just knocked Tom out.'

There was a long pause. Harry hung on, waiting for the onslaught that must happen. And then a strange noise came from the receiver.

It was some time before Harry realized Dorry was laughing like a hyena.

Fifteen

Dorry arrived in ten minutes by which time Tom had
come round and was propped up against the banisters, feeling his jaw and making noises of
bewilderment in the face of Harry's grim silence.
She did not go to him immediately but looked at
Harry.

'Are you all right?' she asked.

Tom burst forth indignantly at that. 'Is *he* all right?
What about me? I'm the one with the broken jaw and
several teeth missing! And who the hell is he anyway?
Do you actually know him?'

'This is Harry Vallender, Tom.' Dorry spoke
formally as if introducing the two of them at a business meeting. 'Harry, you probably gathered, this is
my husband. I suppose I should say, my estranged
husband.'

'Dorry!' Tom protested. 'I'm injured! Aren't you
going to help me?' He looked darkly at Harry. 'I've
heard of you. I don't know if you've gone
temporarily mad or what. I shall sue you, of course.'

'I don't think so.' Dorry crouched by Tom at last.
'There are no teeth missing and I don't think you
could keep up this continual chatter if your jaw was
broken.'

'Chatter . . . my God,' Tom groaned despairingly.

318

Dorry said briskly, 'Harry, can you help me get him into the front room. It'll be warmer there – the sun, you know. Can you manage that?'

Harry nodded once. He had managed to control the trembling in his body but he could not trust his voice.

They frog-marched Tom to an armchair by the empty grate. Dorry was not gentle and he flopped back, relieved to be released.

'Is it explanation time yet?' he asked with ironic politeness. 'Am I to be told why a complete stranger has broken into my house and attacked me in the most cowardly way—'

Dorry interrupted him. 'Shut up, Tom. Harry is Helen's close friend. I am also Helen's close friend, and I have told you repeatedly that to offer Helen hope, only to have to withdraw it, is the most cruel and unnecessary piece of ego-based drama I have encountered for a long time. Even from you. Obviously Harry has only just discovered what you have been doing and he has responded . . . shall we say, emotionally?'

'He responded physically – let's be under no illusions about that!' Tom felt his jaw tenderly again. 'I could do with a coffee,' he mentioned plaintively and without much hope. 'I had to get Helen to the hospital by ten and there was no time for breakfast. And of course the coffee machine wasn't working.'

Dorry turned to Harry. 'Actually, I expect we could all do with a coffee.' She closed one eye at him and smiled, 'D'you think you could find your way around that dump he calls a kitchen, Harry? There probably isn't any milk, but we can manage with it black, I expect.'

'Yes. OK.' Harry knew she was giving him a chance to escape; he touched her arm gratefully. This whole thing was becoming more like a bad dream by the second.

Tom said, 'Oh he speaks, does he? I was beginning to wonder. Helen has some odd friends but this one takes the bloody biscuit!' Harry had already opened the door. He turned and looked over his shoulder at Tom; he could hardly believe that Dorry could have allied herself to someone so ineffectual. Tom wilted under the dark gaze. He said hurriedly, 'Sorry. Actions speak louder than words. I accept that.' He nursed his jaw again.

Harry closed the door behind him. Dorry went immediately to Tom and knelt by him.

'You are all right, aren't you?' She put her fingers beneath his earlobes and ran them down to his chin. He groaned. 'Come on, Tom. Pull yourself together – this is a crisis and you need to think what you're doing!'

He opened his eyes wide. 'I know it's a bloody crisis, woman! I'm the crisis! Why haven't you called a doctor for God's sake? Exactly what is going on here? Whose bloody, blasted side are you on?'

'There's only one side, my darling, and that is Helen's side. And you don't need a doctor – if you're still in pain tonight you can go to the evening surgery or get yourself X-rayed at Casualty . . . you know the ropes as well as I do.'

'Dorry . . .' he sounded like a child. 'Please . . .'

'Please what?'

'Please be nice to me! You've just discovered me lying on the floor after a brutal attack! Surely you should be holding me to you . . . weeping at my pain . . . *some*thing!'

She laughed softly. 'Oh Tom. Is that how you see it? The reconciliation scenario? All is forgiven when I discover that I truly love you after all!' She held his hands. 'We both know that I love you, Tom.' She shook her head at his whoop of joy. 'Surely we also both know that I don't like you. And I don't like you so much I cannot bring myself to live with you?'

For the first time since he opened his eyes on the hall floor, he looked ill. He stared at her, his forehead twitched as if wincing with pain, his colour changed subtly. He said in a low voice, 'She's gone, Dorry – she's been gone for yonks! Aren't you ever going to forgive me?'

'It took you so long to admit she was here! That's what I didn't like.' Dorry sat back on her heels and put her hands on his knees. 'I didn't like the way you saw yourself as her saviour, the young Lothario who made her forget her loneliness. What was it, Tom? Did you see yourself as a sex therapist?' She paused and opened her mouth slightly, then went on. 'Of course. That's why Harry hit you. He's got the impression that you are acting as Helen's sex therapist! Oh my God! Poor Harry!'

Tom tried to assemble some dignity. 'Look here, Dorry, I don't know what you're talking about, but it wasn't like that with Eileen Thorne. And it certainly has not been like that with Helen!'

Dorry nibbled her bottom lip consideringly. She was surprised to find that she no longer cared

321

tuppence about the Eileen Thorne business.

'You see, what worries me is your attention span,' she said slowly. 'You get tired of things so quickly, Tom. Your role as Eileen's saviour . . . how long before you were bored with that? And now Helen . . . it's all more complicated than you thought, isn't it? Liaising with Mr Edwards and the hospital, cooking up these theories to encourage Helen. And now of course Harry.'

Again he felt his jaw; he looked anxious.

'I still believe I can help Helen, Dorry. Honestly. That's why I told her we could go on. It's nothing to do with – with some kind of self-glorification or whatever you think . . . I like Helen – I admire her. And the only hope she has now is this echo effect. It's no theory that I have cooked up. It happens, Dorry. We might be able to increase that with time – don't you see how important it is for her? Can't you understand that?'

She was silent, holding his knees, looking at him searchingly. Her hair stood on end and her cardigan sleeves were too long. He thought she was the most beautiful girl he had seen. Tears filled his eyes.

She said, 'Tom . . . please. It almost worked before until I discovered that your eyes were running because I'd hit you. Now Harry has hit you and they're running again. It won't work, Tom!'

He said brokenly, 'Dorry . . . I don't think I can live without you. I'm sorry. I know that sounds like another drama, but . . . that's it.'

She continued to look at him for a long half-minute. Then she sighed deeply and stood up. 'So you want me to come back, clean up that kitchen, get Mrs Raines here again, and pretend nothing ever happened?'

She saw his Adam's apple move convulsively as he swallowed. He said at last, 'I suppose . . . yes. I suppose that's what I want. But I realize that cannot be.' He stood up slowly, pushing himself out of the armchair without any exclamations of pain. He faced her. 'Will you keep in touch, Dorry? If it became . . . a possibility . . . that you might be able to come home . . . you would not know . . . unless you kept in touch.'

She smiled slightly. 'Oh Tom. You want me to pop in, see what a good boy you are being, congratulate you on what you are accomplishing with Helen . . . and *then* fall into your arms?'

His eyes were swimming again. 'Oh Dorry. Yes. That would be marvellous!'

She had to laugh at his sheer naïvety. And while she was laughing he put his arms around her and kissed her. She fought against him for a second, then remained very still and unresponsive.

When he released her, she said steadily, 'Well, I don't think Harry has done any permanent damage to your jaw, do you?'

He could not look away from her. 'No,' he said.

She heard Harry at the door and went to open it for him. Her legs worked, she spoke and acted as usual. But the remembrance of his familiar body against hers was surprisingly poignant. She knew it had taken an act of will not to melt into that embrace.

Harry said, 'I found some biscuits. And some powdered milk.' He glanced at Tom. 'I hope you have never given Helen anything from that kitchen.'

Dorry said, 'He's never offered anyone anything from the kitchen yet, Harry.' She dealt with the coffee tray and went on, 'Come and sit down. I think you need to know quite a lot of what has been happening. And I think you must try to understand the situation between Tom and Helen.' She glinted at him as she passed his cup. 'Whatever we say and do – the three of us – matters not at all. Helen has decided she wants Tom to go on treating her. And we know how strong Helen is.'

Harry, who had had a lot of time to think while he found cups and tried to do a temporary repair on the French doors, nodded and sat down. He had to believe that even if this quack was offering some kind of sex therapy, Helen would never accept it.

Tom hesitated and then sat down too. Both men looked expectantly at Dorry.

As soon as Harry left Falcondale Road he headed for Stormy Point. The whole time he had been forced to stay at that house he had had visions of Helen driving home, weeping, distressed. Now that he knew the full story and understood that distress, he could not wait to see her. He went across the Downs, took the steep snaking road to the Portway and made for the motorway.

The last time he had used the motorway had been at Christmas when he had taken Helen into Bristol to see Peggy and Rosie. He had thought that journey had put an end to the nightmare of motorway driving. He discovered now that it had not. Helen's presence by his side then, and the lack of traffic, had made the experience completely different. Now, with this sense of urgency driving him on and a feeling that Helen was slipping away from him, that terrible day nearly two years ago was reincarnated. When he took a left-hand curve leaving Gordano, it was as if the northbound traffic occupied the same carriageway as the southbound. It was an optical illusion soon dispelled because the two carriageways split their levels, but for a blinding instant he nearly drove the Rover onto the central reservation in a desperate effort to avoid a family saloon that could so well have contained a middle-aged couple with their daughter and their daughter's fiancé . . .

He pulled himself together with a physical effort and slowed down to a steady 60 m.p.h. as the road swooped down to Clevedon and began the six-mile stretch across the old Levels. It had been an absurd morning; he tried to visualize the whole series of events as if they were in a Chaplin film but that merely increased the unreality of it all. However ludicrous it seemed, he had hit a man and knocked him out. The deep inner involvement he felt for Helen had burst out like a volcanic eruption. He should be able to smile at it; to feel kindly towards Tom who, it appeared, was doing his best to help Helen. But he could not smile and he could not feel anything towards Tom except a certain incredulity.

He left the motorway gratefully and took to the quieter road that led to the wooded lane past Rosie's school. It was two o'clock. Helen and Peggy would have finished lunch and she would be resting. He did not know what he was going to do except put his arms around her and hold her close against all the pain and frustration she was feeling. What would happen if she demanded more, he could not begin to imagine. Somehow he had bottled up the awfulness of the other night but the memory of his violence still haunted him and he was only too aware that all the suppressed emotions of the past two years were no longer under his complete control.

Before he took to the gravel drive he realized with a pang of terror, that Helen's car was not there and Peggy's was. Helen must have left Falcondale Road by eleven-thirty and it was now two-thirty. She should have been home at least an hour ago. It was raining still, an incessant misty fall that hid the big bay and made the sea look like a vale of tears. It all added up to poor driving conditions; he dare not let himself think beyond that. He drew up behind Peggy's Fiat and scrambled out to ring the doorbell and then peer through the side window while he rang again. He thought grimly that it must be his day for trying to get into empty houses.

Then Peggy's door opened and she stood beneath her small porch, a newspaper held ineffectually over her head.

'She's gone to the hospital, Harry. Come on in here.'

She turned and went inside and after a moment's hesitation he followed her.

'I have to fetch Rosie soon . . .' Peggy preceded him into the tiny front room and shook the newspaper. 'Sit down. There's time for a cup of tea. Will you wait for her?'

He could not sit down. His tall thin frame seemed to make the ceiling lower. 'Hospital? What's wrong?'

His eyes were no longer still and opaque; they seemed to dart around the room in search of clues, answers.

Peggy looked at him, noted all these things, and blushed deeply.

'You know. The course. The – the counselling course.'

His voice was steely. 'You mean the sex therapy?'

'It's not quite . . . it's more a general discussion on how each individual . . .' Peggy had never really come to terms with the concept of the course. She began to repeat Dorry's words like a parrot and then stopped.

Harry said, 'Yes. I see. Is it at Leaze Hospital?'

'Yes. She'll be home about four. If you want to wait.'

'No. I don't want to wait.'

He did not even say goodbye. On the way back down the ridge to the woods, he passed Josh Harrison's car. He thought that there was just enough time before meeting Rosie for Josh and Peggy to . . . how might they put it . . . get it together? That's all it was, getting it together. To feel sick about it was ridiculous. He and Cheryl had got it together often enough; he knew that Miles and Helen had slept together often. And Dorry with that ridiculous husband of hers . . . He closed his eyes momentarily and heard a car horn blare at him on the narrow road.

He saw the Ford in the car park for the disabled, and he parked the Rover to the left and behind it. He could see the hospital entrance and he could see Helen's car. All he had to do was to sit and wait.

When the trembling started again he wondered whether he was ill. He had to remind himself that he had eaten nothing all day and drunk only the bitter instant coffee at the Latimer house. It would account for the nausea too. He hung on to the steering wheel and conquered both trembling and nausea with sheer effort of will.

The big automatic doors to the foyer slid open at exactly four o'clock and instead of the previous one or two people who had been coming and going sporadically since his arrival, a group of ten or twelve emerged, very together, some of them obviously disabled. Two men were on crutches, another man and three girls in wheelchairs. He saw Helen immediately. She was with another girl in a wheelchair: black; cerebral palsy from the look of her flailing arms. They paused under the overhang and looked out at the rain; the girl was laughing and Helen leaned forward, captured both her arms and held them. A small dark man came up to them and pushed Helen's chair. Harry leaned forward with a muttered curse, but then the two girls were using the impetus of the push to spin around joined by their hands. They spun faster and faster. All the others drew aside and were laughing and clapping. The small dark man made urgent signs of encouragement. Then the doors breathed open again and a tall, skinny fair woman came out. Although she too laughed, the spinning chairs slowed down as if deferring to her and then stopped. Helen did not release her companion immediately; she looked up at the fair woman with her head angled challengingly. The woman moved hers slowly from side to side as if in resignation.

Then she walked out into the rain, bent against it and hurried into the main car park. Helen put the other girl's hands carefully back onto the arms of the chair and let her own chair roll down the ramp; then she sat still, head tipped back, apparently drinking in the rain. Behind her, under cover, the others were all laughing and talking at once. A minibus appeared and Helen got out of its way and began to move towards her car. Harry watched as she unlocked it, transferred from her chair to the driver's seat, folded the chair and humped it behind her. By this time the minibus had lifted the others aboard; there was a toot; Helen waved. She was alone. Still he watched, unseen. She did not produce her keys or attempt to belt herself in; she sat there, looking through the windscreen, her hair wet rats' tails around her face. When he moved and began to get out of the Rover she noticed him for the first time; he watched her face transform and come alive.

'Harry! Oh Harry . . . how lovely!'

He knelt on the wet tarmac and put his arms around her waist. She was wearing a track suit; it was damp and smelled of oil paints. He pressed his face into it, felt the soft resilience of her breasts under his cheek, tightened his hold and lifted his face until he could kiss her throat.

'Harry . . . it's all right.' Her voice was muffled by his hair. She moved her mouth to his forehead and felt its waxy coldness. 'Darling, what has happened?'

He moved his hands from her waist upwards, cupped her breasts through the thickness of her track suit, pushed them together and pressed his face into them again. She gasped with the sudden pain. He lifted his head slightly, though he did not release her. His mouth covered hers. The kiss pushed her hard against the head rest. She tried to resist him. He pushed harder, moving around so that her mouth was twisting beneath his. There was no longer stillness in him; he was fighting time and was consumed with a passion and desire that was close to anger.

She turned her own face so that she could pant, 'Harry . . . you're hurting me!' and at last he seemed to register what he was doing. He leaned away slightly and stared at her as if – just for an instant – she was a stranger.

'It's all right . . . all right.' It was as if she understood his urgency; his desperate race against time. She whispered, 'Get in the car, Harry.'

He stood up; his knees were muddy and wet. He went to the passenger door and doubled himself up to get in beside her. She switched on and revved the car into life. She whispered, 'It's all right . . . plenty of time.' But she did not believe herself because she took the Ford out of the car park at a screeching angle and headed for the dark grey sky that overhung the sea as if they had only minutes to live.

He said, 'I shouldn't let you do this. So much has happened today. I knocked Tom out. Oh Helen . . .'

'It's all *right*!' She did not seem surprised and she was certainly not curious. She drove much too fast along the Promenade until they came to the Uphill beach. The beach car park was closed for the night and the barrier was down. She drove up to it very gently until the bonnet was touching the wooden bar, then she clutched and revved alternately three times. The bar splintered and fell into the sand and she drove over it and into the murk of rain and sea-fret almost to the old ferry point. Grey darkness enclosed them.

He sat there, hunched and helpless while beside him she flurried into activity. He knew this was insanity and tried desperately to put an end to it.

'Helen!' It was like a cry for help.

She said reassuringly, 'Do exactly what I tell you.' She was breathing heavily with the effort of taking her trousers off her useless legs. 'Put my right foot there –' she guided his hand to the shelf above the glove compartment '– and my left leg there –' she put his hand on the back of his seat.

'Helen I cannot do this . . . my God, what are we thinking of?'

She grabbed his head and kissed him first of all fiercely, then slowly and slower. And then she stopped.

'Don't take it so seriously, my darling. It's all right. It's meant to be fun . . . not a desperate business . . .' But it was desperate and they both knew it. He was shaking again and realized that she was too.

And then a light came on and a hand rapped imperatively on Helen's window. Time had run out and they had not quite got it together.

The interview room at the police station was box-like and overheated. The policewoman seemed unim-pressed by Helen's insistence that she had seduced Harry and in the end Helen was forced to telephone Peggy's cottage and ask Josh to come and bail them both out. Her tart and very loud comments in the front office regarding the actual definition of the word rape were also unappreciated, not only by the sergeant on duty but by Harry who looked grimmer and more withdrawn than ever. Josh appeared to be treating the matter lightly; of course, all he knew was that Helen had totally destroyed the barrier to the car park and had then been found in a compromising position by the irate attendant. Helen, knowing she had lost Harry, threw discretion to the winds and became so outrageous that the policewoman asked her to 'mind her tongue'.

Helen looked at her, her eyes heavy with weariness. 'Why?' she asked. 'I've got nothing to lose. Not now.'

The woman suddenly snapped back. 'Except your self-respect!'

Helen was silent at last. Josh took the handles of her chair and she did not protest. They went outside; it was raining harder now and by the time she had got back into the car and Josh had strapped her in like a baby, she was sodden. Harry waited by Josh's car, head bent, letting the rain run down the back of his neck. Josh drove him back to the hospital to pick up his car and Helen took the road through the woods and was home in ten minutes flat. Peggy was waiting for her, agog. The living room of Flatners was warm and welcoming. She left Peggy to lock the car and bowled to the kitchen counter where she put her head down and wept.

Peggy slammed the front door shut and ran to her.

'My God . . . what's happened? When you phoned

. . . you were laughing . . . we thought it was just some scrape.'

Helen turned, put her arms around Peggy's waist and pushed her head hard into the plump midriff as if she could shut the world out. Peggy stroked her hair, made sounds, waited for the storm to abate.

At last Helen said, 'It should have been a scrape! But . . . it cannot be! Harry will never be able to see me as a proper woman! Only as a cripple!' She lifted her head; her eyes were drowning. 'He'd stay by me for ever, Peggy! But I'm not going to have it! I won't be a second-class citizen – I won't be!' She hid her face again, wailing. And then, quite suddenly released Peggy, scrubbed at her eyes and sat back.

'It's OK. I'm not going to have a breakdown – nothing like that. It's so silly! So funny really. He went to see Tom – knocked him out apparently – Dorry arrived, they told him everything. About the sex therapy . . . everything.'

'I gathered that. He came here looking for you.'

'He must have felt sorry for me or something. I don't know.' She slumped in the chair drearily. 'All I know is, he went crazy for me and I thought it would be all right. And it would have been all right except we were caught.' She managed a fleeting smile at Peggy's gasp of horror. 'I didn't care. But of course he did. They were going to arrest him for rape, Pegs!' She made a dismissive gesture. 'Pegs, it's not fair on him – any of this. It's ridiculous. He must find some nice normal girl and get married and have kids. Just like he was going to before this.' She gestured at her legs.

'He loves you, Helen!' Peggy protested.

'He does in a way. But he needs . . . normality. He needs it more than I do, Pegs. He's more crippled than I am . . . and I never thought I'd say that.'

Peggy shook her head. 'He won't agree with you. He'll be here tomorrow. There's something special between the two of you.'

Helen began to wriggle out of her trousers yet again; they were wet and clingy and Peggy knelt down to strip them off her flaccid legs.

'I don't think he will come tomorrow.' Helen struggled out of her damp sweater. 'But he will telephone. I shall disconnect the phone. And on Saturday I'll go and stay with Aunt Mildred. Put some distance between us so that he knows it's over. Write to him of course. I can pretend I am disgusted with him. He won't be able to fight against that because he's disgusted with himself.'

Peggy rolled up the damp clothes and went to run a bath. When she came back her eyes were red, her sensitive skin blotchy. She said, 'In other words, you think you're dragging him down so you're going to set him free!' She spoke with unusual irony.

Helen grinned ruefully. 'Another little melodrama, Pegs! I seem to specialize in them, don't I?'

'Helen, you can't. You simply cannot throw him away like this.'

Helen said, 'There's Josh. Get me in the bath and go and sort him out, my dear. And for goodness' sake, let him stay the night – let him stay indefinitely. Make the most of him, Pegs. Please. For my sake.'

Peggy tested the bathwater and settled Helen in the hoist. She spoke in a stifled voice. 'He'll get tired of me. Like Miles did.'

Helen lay back in the warm water. Her body felt sore with tiredness.

'More likely you'll get tired of him, honey.' She closed her eyes. 'Oh Pegs . . . I'm so sorry. So terribly sorry.'

Peggy put a hand across her mouth.

'You mustn't say that. You mustn't feel it. I don't know whether I will live with Josh or not. But I do know one thing. I love him – properly. I was swept away by Miles. But Josh . . . I liked Josh before I fell in love with him.'

Helen smiled. Peggy said, 'I won't be long. I'll tell him what's happening. Don't go to sleep before I get back.'

Just for a split second, Helen considered the possibility. Going to sleep in the warm water and slipping beneath its surface. The second passed. She reached for the soap.

Aunt Mildred was put out, then intrigued, then very pressing.

'All this talk of money,' she scolded. 'My goodness, if I can't have you to stay without being paid for it—'

'I must insist, Aunt.' Helen even managed a grin into the hall mirror as she spoke the words. Aunt Putrid would never change. 'I have to have such a lot of help – and a bed downstairs of course – I could not dream of putting you to such inconvenience and expense.'

'Well, my dear, if, as you say, you insist . . . I have a man to do the garden. He can bring a bed down. And there is an excellent nursing agency in the town who will supply a nurse. I will arrange it. And you can give me the money to settle the bill.'

'That sounds excellent.' Helen put the phone down and wondered how she could possibly find Aunt Putrid even remotely amusing when her heart was breaking. The thought of the pristine house in the small village in the Cotswolds, where everyone knew everyone else's business, was appalling. Why on earth hadn't she gone to one of the hotels specially adapted for wheelchairs? But she needed someone of her own; even Aunt Putrid was better than no-one.

There was a tap at the door and her heart bounced uncomfortably. She looked through the spyhole; a woman, and behind her a van marked 'Blooms Best'.

She opened the door and took in the enormous bouquet. It was so unlike Harry she had to read the label to make sure they were from him. They were.

She buried her nose in the hothouse carnations and closed her eyes.

'Oh Harry . . . poor Harry.' It was the first time he had sent her flowers as an apology. She bowled into the kitchen and began stripping off the cellophane wrapping and cutting the stalks. She had hoped that somehow he would do or say something which would make everything all right. But the flowers confirmed that nothing would ever be all right between them.

She took out a little clump of freesias and put them in a separate glass.

'Nothing is ever wasted, Harry,' she said steadily. 'You must know now what you really want.' She took the flowers to the table and put them in the centre.

Then she stared at the view. And at last she saw. She had always known that if you looked long enough, eventually you saw and understood. And she understood now that this was not really to do with Harry 'crossing over', as Alice had put it. It was to do with Harry's life; to do with Harry being free of the accident, of his enslavement to her real love. Her love was holding him . . . imprisoning him. She lowered her head with the pain of what she was doing. But at least now, she knew it was right. At least now, she knew what real love was.

Sixteen

The journey to Oxfordshire was endless. Peggy trav-
elled with Helen; Rosie and Josh came behind.
They stopped frequently but Helen was exhausted
by the time they drove down the long street at
Bussington and drew up outside Aunt Putrid's door.
It was good to have Josh there to carry her inside
and put her on the bed in the front room.

Aunt Mildred flapped around smugly.

'I thought you'd like the view of people rather
than countryside, my dear,' she said, a duster still in
her hand. 'See, the bed is right in the window. You
can watch the world go by!'

Helen quite liked the thought of seeing people
but if she was depriving Aunt Mildred of her front
room, did that mean she would have to share it in
the day? She lay back on the banked pillows and
smiled her thanks.

'I'm not bed-ridden you know,' she said. 'But I
must admit this is very pleasant.'

'We'll have tea in here, I think.' Aunt Mildred
sat the others down at regular intervals around the
room. 'Rosie, you can come and help me push in
the trolley. Isn't it lucky Auntie Helen decided to
come on a Saturday? It's such a pleasant drive.
Now when I visited you, I had to take a taxi to

Oxford and a train down to Swindon and then change there for Bristol . . . my goodness I had a dreadful time at Swindon. They had no sandwiches!' She shepherded the small girl through into the hall.

Peggy said, 'Are you really going to be all right, Helen?'

Josh said, 'You could have a fake relapse and we could say we had to get you back to your consultant.'

'I shall be fine.' Helen was already feeling sick at the thought of Peggy and Rosie leaving her here. 'But just remember, the whole thing will fall flat on its face if you tell anyone. Anyone. Dorry, Tom – even Mr Edwards.'

'And especially Harry,' Josh chanted. 'Honestly, Helen, you're forcing me to be extremely unprofessional.'

'I know and I'm sorry, Josh. But he won't get my letter until Monday. Till then he might try to find me.'

Peggy said with unusual emphasis, 'He'll try to find you anyway, Helen. He's not like Tom Latimer.'

Helen smiled slightly and shook her head. 'No. He's not a bit like Tom Latimer. But he won't try to find me, Pegs. Not when he reads my letter.'

Peggy's brown eyes were concerned. 'What have you said?'

Helen touched her arm. 'Only what I had to in order to free him.' She widened her smile. 'Here's my aunt and Rosie. As soon as you've had something, please go, Pegs. It's like waiting on the platform for a train to go out.'

Peggy's eyes filled with sudden tears and she

blinked hard. When it was time to leave she whispered fiercely into Helen's ear, 'A phone call. That's all it takes and we can be with you in two hours.'

Helen watched them piling into Josh's car, Rosie waving frantically from the back window, Aunt Mildred flapping her duster. She felt as if her world was slipping away.

On Friday morning the flowers arrived again for Harry; dark red camellias framed by their dark green leaves. He sent another bouquet himself, bigger than Thursday's. He was filled with self-loathing and fear. When he telephoned yet again and still heard the high-pitched whine, he rang the exchange. They investigated and told him she must have unplugged her telephone. He rang Peggy's number and she confirmed that the phone was unplugged. She said nothing more; no excuses or explanations. He asked if he could come and see Helen and she said quietly, 'Not yet.'

On Saturday morning there were no more flowers. The message was nevertheless loud and clear. He cleared his paperwork as quickly as he could then got into the Rover and drove to Stormy Point. When he found both cottages empty, he did not know what to think; he certainly did not know what to do. He peered into all the windows through cupped hands, then wandered around like a lost soul. Peggy's car was there; Helen's was not. It was most unusual for the two girls to take Rosie out in Helen's car; the wheelchair took up most of the back seat. But it was just possible, in which case they would be back soon. He drove across to the

Coastguard cottages, parked the car where it was not immediately visible, and unlocked the cottage he kept for himself. He put on overalls and tried to go on with some painting started two weeks ago. It was difficult to do anything and keep an eye on the ridge for possible arrivals. He gave up quite soon and sat on a beach chair in the tiny front parlour, his eyes fixed unwaveringly on the top of the headland. He tried to rehearse what he would say but his thoughts were so jumbled he could not sort out a single coherent sentence. He had never been so totally confused and bewildered; even in the darkest time after the accident, he had had a clear vision of his situation, however grim it was.

The morning wore on and became afternoon. He had hardly eaten since the frightful Wednesday morning when anger had driven him over the edge and he had attacked Tom Latimer. He knew only one thing: he had to see Helen. It would have been better if he could have talked to her first and discovered how she felt; but now that that was no longer a possibility, he just had to see her.

At six o'clock as it was getting dark, headlights emerged from the belt of trees and a car began the long jog along the ridge. Harry moved his cramped limbs and discovered he was cold and his eyes hurt. He closed them hard and moved his shoulders. When he opened them again, the car was turning into the gravel drive serving Flatners. It was not the Ford.

Harry frowned and got out of the beach chair with some difficulty. He made for the back door and stood outside, less than a hundred yards from the

341

other block of cottages. The headlights on the car were doused and the doors opened. Rosie's voice was plain to hear. 'Can we have fish fingers, Mummy? And please can Josh stay the night again?' Peggy and Josh emerged from the front of the car; Peggy helped Rosie with her seat-belt and lifted her out. 'We'll see,' she said non-committally. They closed up the car and Josh used a remote control to lock it. Helen was not there.

The small overheard exchange was enlightening. They had taken Helen somewhere; they had not eaten a meal; Josh had been staying with Peggy. Harry recalled belatedly that Helen had phoned Josh at Peggy's; therefore Helen knew Josh was staying . . . he tried to sift this information for clues about Helen's whereabouts and could find none.

Lights went up in the middle cottage. Then smoke appeared from the chimney. He imagined Josh kneeling in the parlour laying paper and sticks, Rosie in the bath upstairs, Peggy taking fish fingers from the freezer. It was so domesticated; so happy; so utterly unattainable. Before Wednesday it would have been a possibility for Helen and himself; domesticity was probably one of the sides of marriage that would flourish in the absence of . . . other sides. He squeezed his eyes again on the thought of himself on his knees in the mud grovelling with Helen's breasts. He felt cold sweat on his face and grabbed the roof of the Rover to steady himself.

And then, with an unexpectedness that almost stopped his heart, Peggy's voice spoke from the other side of the car.

'Harry. I know you're there.' He must have exclaimed because her voice quickened. 'It's all right. It's only me. The others don't know. I saw the shadow of the car.'

He breathed heavily and rested his head on his arm.

'I thought I'd hidden it.'

'You have. But I've been looking out for it. I thought you'd come on Thursday. Or yesterday.'

'I tried to telephone to see if I could. You know that.'

'Yes. But it wasn't enough. Don't you remember last Christmas? Dorry. How she waited and waited for Tom to come for her. And he did not.'

'I'm here now, Peggy.'

'She's gone away. For a complete break.'

'Where? I'll go there. Now.'

'No. I promised I wouldn't tell anyone. And I'm not going to, Harry.'

'Then why are you here? I gathered that she'd gone away – I can see that. Why have you come to tell me what I already know?' He heard his own voice, raw and angry.

'Because on Monday you will get a letter. I don't know what she has said to you but she is quite certain it will end the relationship for good. So it must be quite . . . devastating. The letter. Devastating.'

'And you want to warn me? Thank you very much.'

Her voice was still steady and very gentle. 'I simply want to tell you, that whatever she has said, she believes she is doing something good.' Peggy's hand reached across the car and covered his. 'I think . . . I think she loves you better than she loves herself.

343

And that is important. Because for the last two years – almost two years – she has been forced to think of herself first. Her needs, her sanity, her own life . . . can you understand that?'

'Of course. Of course – that's what we wanted – surely? The alternative was death.'

'Yes.' Peggy moved his hand slightly. 'Harry, will you talk to Dorry about this? Don't read the letter and despair. Please. Dorry will explain – I'm no good at talking.'

Harry looked into the darkness. He could see Peggy's milky skin, almost luminous in the frame of her springing hair. He said slowly, 'You underestimate yourself, Peggy. You know Helen. You share so much with her . . . experiences . . .'

Peggy said simply, 'Yes.'

He squeezed her hand gently then released it. 'Thank you.'

'Will you come in? Have supper with us? Thaw out? Your hand is freezing – how long have you kept this vigil?'

'I don't know.'

'We left early. About nine. We had to stop often on the road.'

He wondered if she was giving him clues. If so they were not clicking in.

'I think I arrived about ten. I did some work first. I should have left it.'

'Have you eaten?'

'No.'

'Please come in, Harry. You can sleep in Helen's place.'

He knew suddenly that this was what he wanted more than anything. He nodded once.

Helen noted in her diary that on Sunday 26 March it was Mother's Day and Aunt Mildred wheeled her to church. The afternoon was taken up with Aunt Mildred relaying news about the congregation.

'That small woman – red hat – you must remember her – it was such an unsuitable colour for Lent I thought – she is married to the man who does my garden. D'you remember I told you he would fix up the bed for you downstairs?'

'I didn't see him – I would have thanked him.'

'Oh my dear, he never goes to church. Not Fred Barncs. Doreen always says she prays for both of them but of course she only comes so that she can claim acquaintance with the Honourable Mrs Dowty. *She* was in the front pew. Lots of veiling.'

'Yes, I did notice her.' Helen smiled genuinely. 'It hasn't changed since Jane Austen's time, has it?'

'I don't think I knew her, dear. Was she in your uncle's time?'

For a split second Helen imagined sharing that with Harry. Then she changed the name to Dorry. Dorry would enjoy that.

The nurse came from the agency. Her name was Miss Banks and she was built like a horse. She bathed Helen as if she were still a baby and gave her an alcohol rub on her lower back and buttocks. Helen knew she was sore but could not work out how she knew. Miss Banks refused to enter into a discussion about it.

'You're tired. The clocks went forward last night and you've got an hour to catch up on. Early bed, dearie. That's my prescription!'

On Monday the washing dried 'in five minutes' as Aunt Mildred said, because it was sunny and windy. Helen went into the garden and let the breeze blow through her hair. It was coming from the south-west. The sea outside Flatners would be choppy; the tide would be going out and the exposed mud would be alive with eel and lugworm. And Harry would receive her letter. She shivered slightly and Aunt Mildred said, 'I saw that. Indoors this instant. The rector's coming for coffee, I don't want you sneezing over him.'

On Tuesday they woke up to snow. Incredibly, a thin covering of snow was everywhere. Rain washed it away and after lunch they went for a walk down the village street and stopped to speak to people, buy bread and rubbing oil because Helen was quite certain the alcohol was burning up her skin in spite of Miss Banks' reassurances.

Helen was surprised by the constant stream of callers at the house. Aunt Mildred specialized in a brand of inquisitive interference that also offered practical help and advice. When Doreen Barnes called, aghast at unexpected visitors arriving the next day, Aunt Mildred produced a cake from her freezer and promised a casserole would follow. 'Home-made stuff, dear,' she explained to Helen later. 'People expect it when they come to the country.' But in return, Doreen was expected to furnish almost intimate details of her visitors. And

Fred had to prune the apple tree as an extra. 'Well, there's nothing much for him to do this weather,' Aunt Mildred said as if she were giving him a present. 'He'll be pleased to have a proper job for once.'

Helen nodded. It was all so logical when Aunt Mildred put it like that. Perhaps she was less putrid than Helen had thought. Certainly the rhythmical village life suited her very well; her bossiness was accepted as good organizing. Helen found if she went along with that organizing, life was not unpleasant. It was empty but not unpleasant. She began to put on thick socks and boots ready for the afternoon walk. It was today that the WI held their tea in the village hall. She looked through her things for a scarf that would brighten her black sweater.

Harry did not read Helen's letter twice. Although he understood her motive and Peggy had told him it was because she loved him better than she loved herself, the letter still did its work. It was so honest, so clinical, so polite. And it was grateful too. He recalled certain phrases with a strange horror. 'I know that without you I might have given up. Between you, you and Dorry forced me to live. I have not always been grateful for that. Now I am. I thank you from the bottom of my heart.' It was too polite for Helen; there was a horrible finality to every sentence.

Then, it seemed, his 'protectiveness' had emphasized her disadvantage. She recounted small incidents he had forgotten. It seemed he rarely came down to her wheelchair level. He did not let

347

her carry things . . . even the trip in the flatner emphasized her disability. 'Dorry makes a point of not helping me. She walks away when I get out of the car. At Christmas she made sure I looked after her.' And then she reached that awful time of last week. She acknowledged she had wanted sex. 'The final equalizer' she called it. But when it had so nearly happened . . . when she had had to place her legs . . . then she had realized it was the final unequalizer. She told him she had been disgusted. Unable to share that frantic desire . . . horrified by the sordidness of the car and the denouement of being discovered. He felt sick as he read on; she spared him nothing. And at the end of it all she told him briefly that her only hope of equality was to live with a community of disabled people. 'I want to gift Flatners to Peggy. I know you will not mind and it seems the obvious move. She will eventually marry Josh I think, and they can settle there very happily.'

The only clue in the letter was the reference to a community of disabled people. The other faint hope was that she would contact her solicitor about gifting Flatners to Peggy. Surely she had a local solicitor? Dorry would know that. And if she had gone to some sheltered housing or something, Dorry would probably know that too. After a terrible day when he worked like an automaton on an extensive survey of a house in the city, he telephoned Dorry's flat in Clifton. There was, of course, no reply. He remembered that Dorry did a lot of her work in the evenings. He continued to phone at intervals until nine o'clock, and then grabbed his coat and got into his car to drive to the Falcondale Road house.

The front of the house was in darkness but a light reflected on the garage door from the rear. He drove on a few yards, turned left and parked his car in the familiar cul-de-sac.

He walked down the drive, tried the wrought-iron gate, found it open and went through into the back garden. Tom was working on the damaged French windows. As the gate squeaked he leapt in the air and turned at the same time, trying to hold a hacksaw in a menacing way. He landed awkwardly, dropped the hacksaw in order to clutch for support at the open window, the blade nicked his wrist and the new door handle came off in his hand.

He recognized Harry at the same time as he crashed against the door and broke a pane of glass. Harry pulled him upright and reached down for the door handle, gabbling apologies and reassurances at the same time.

'Christ Almighty!' Tom bawled the oath furiously, and held out his bleeding hand. 'Look what you've done this time – last week it's a broken jaw, this week it's a lacerated hand! Do you realize my hands are tools of my trade? D'you realize that? And as for this bloody window—' He turned and would have kicked out another pane if Harry hadn't restrained him. Even then he backed away nimbly under the impression that Harry was attacking him.

'Listen – hang on –' Harry held up both hands in an attitude of surrender. 'I'm sorry. Let me see to the hand. I've come to talk to you – wrong foot again –'

Tom was only partially reassured. He mumbled something and made for the door, pushing it irritably with his foot. 'Is this your work? I suppose that's how you bloody well broke in last week, was it? Christ, Helen's got her hands full with you!'

'Helen's gone.' Harry followed slowly, examining the broken door as he came. 'Look. I'll see to this. And we can put some cardboard or wood across this break for tonight.'

Tom went straight to the tap in the kitchen and held his hand beneath the running water. Harry was amazed to see the kitchen had been cleaned.

Tom said briefly, 'There's plasters in that top cupboard – first aid tin – can you see it?'

'Yes.' Harry put the tin on the scrubbed table. 'It's all very . . . neat.'

'I'm getting the place together. Trying to see patients. Mending that bloody door. She's popping in at regular intervals. Checking on me. If I pass the test she might even come back.'

'Dorry?'

'Who else?'

Harry fastened a plaster across the cut; it was not deep. 'Well . . .'

'I know, I know.' Tom sat down suddenly. 'Women mess up your life. I'm finished with them.'

'Dorry's a woman.' Harry put the tin back.

'Dorry's a wife. The sooner you marry Helen Wilson, the better. She'll drive you mad while she's still a woman.'

Harry smiled bleakly. Tom was making a gargantuan effort, that was certain, but basically he could not change.

He said, 'I've been trying to get hold of Dorry. Helen's disappeared. Dorry might know where.'

'Helen's disappeared?' Tom looked up, his own

troubles forgotten temporarily. 'That's why she cancelled. I thought it was you coming the heavy.' The petulant lines of his face softened. 'I'm sorry.'

Harry was surprised. 'Are you? I thought you might think I deserved everything I got.'

Tom grinned fleetingly. 'You do in a way. Dorry's told me about you. You've become obsessed with Helen and she with you. She's got the sense to put some space between you.'

Harry said sombrely, 'She wants the space to be permanent.'

Tom turned his mouth down. 'You've done something she can't take.'

'Yes.' Harry wondered how he could be talking like this to Tom Latimer.

'Another woman?'

'No.' Harry could have smiled at that.

'You're not going to tell me.'

'No,' Harry agreed.

Tom sighed. 'You're a man of few words but plenty of action.' He stood up. 'Listen, if you fix that door – now – I will not only make sure Helen gets a letter from you, I will scramble some eggs and make coffee. I'm very domesticated.'

Harry said, 'You know where she is?' He fought an urge to take Tom by the shoulders and shake the information from him.

'No. But you're right, Dorry will know. And I'm practically certain I can talk her into forwarding a letter.'

Harry knew he should be more grateful than he was. He had wanted to get in the car and drive to Helen that night, wherever she was.

351

He said, 'All right. Thanks. Tools?'

'Probably scattered all over the garden after the shock you gave me.' Tom went into the other room and began to gather tools and put them into a box. 'OK? I'll be about half an hour.'

Harry looked at the wrecked door. 'I'll be longer than that. And you'll have to paint the repair tomorrow and see about a glazier.'

Tom felt suddenly cheerful. He said, 'It's all underwhelming. But never mind.' He went back to the kitchen and assembled food on the table. Then he went into the front room and lit the fire. Just in case Dorry popped in later after work. He had a lot to tell her, she might even stay the night.

Helen opened Dorry's thickly-filled envelope and blanched as Harry's letter fell onto the duvet. Dorry's scribbled note said, 'Sorry about this. Harry mended the door for Tom on the understanding that Tom would arrange for a letter to be forwarded. I've said it must be a one-off. How do you fancy Torquay? There's a hotel there which sounds rather fun. Doc Simmonds recommends it. Haven't got round to the sol's yet – very busy.'

Helen said, 'Damn you, Dorry, you're stalling on that! And your so-called explanation about Harry's letter is rubbish!' She held Harry's letter on the palm of one hand as if weighing it. She should tear it up but of course that was impossible.

Aunt Mildred trundled in with a trolley containing breakfast. Helen tucked Harry's letter away while they discussed the day's 'programme'. Helen had been in Bussington almost a week and had thought she was quite enjoying it. Now, suddenly, she was bored. The thought of Miss Banks arriving soon, bathing and rubbing her back was an ordeal. And then, the early lunch and the Easter play performed by the local schoolchildren outside if dry . . . it was all so ideal for someone in a wheelchair. Cosy and enclosed and secure. Wasn't that what she wanted? She let herself imagine the flatner skimming over the mud of the bay and meeting the first of the waves and her heart contracted with equal amounts of pain and excitement and grief.

As soon as Aunt Mildred disappeared, she read Harry's letter. It was as economic as he was himself. It said, 'You know I love you. You know more about that Wednesday afternoon than I know myself. You know I will live by any rules you care to make. Yours, Harry. P.S. I am glad you cancelled the flowers. P.P.S. I will always kneel or sit – I will do anything to look into your eyes again.'

She folded the letter carefully and put it in its envelope and then in Dorry's envelope. Like any lovesick girl, she held it momentarily against her heart. She knew it was the best love letter she had ever received.

Harry took her reply to Falcondale Road the next week. He thought wryly that he was spending more time with Tom Latimer than with anyone at present. He drove the car up the drive and parked alongside Tom's car. It was disappointing that Dorry's car was not there; it was Dorry he wanted to see.

He went through the patients' entrance and realized that Tom was treating someone, so he went around the back and examined his work on the French doors. A glazier had replaced the broken pane but Tom had not got around to painting yet. Harry took off his jacket and went into the small utility room where Tom kept his tools. He was already familiar with the ramshackle store cupboard full of paint. He found a brush and some white spirit, some sandpaper and undercoat, and went back to the window. When Tom came in an hour later he had rubbed down and undercoated one of the doors.

Tom was delighted.

'I say, you don't have to do penance indefinitely!' he said, grinning from ear to ear. 'It was worth an aching jaw to get those old windows repaired!'

Harry managed a responsive half-smile. 'I wanted to see Dorry. Can't get a reply on her phone again.'

'Well, you know what she's like.' Tom stripped off his white coat. 'Can you just begin to see my point of view about our marriage? The woman puts her clients before anyone. And I mean anyone.'

Harry sighed. He did not want to agree with Tom, but twice now he had wanted to see Dorry quite desperately and had not been able to find her. He said, 'That's why she's so good at her job.'

Tom grunted. 'Matter of fact, she will be along later. I told her I'd got an evening appointment. She said she'd bring in some fish and chips.' His grin became sheepish. 'She's checking up on me. She was pleased about the kitchen and the housework generally. Now she wants me to build up the practice again.'

'You let it all go then?' Harry picked up a rag soaked in turps and began to clean his hands.

'Everything seemed so pointless. There was just Helen.' Tom looked sombre for a moment. 'If only I could have helped Helen . . . it would have all been worthwhile somehow. The whole mess.'

Harry said unexpectedly, 'I know what you mean.'

Tom looked up. 'Is that how you see her? Dorry said I was making use of Helen. To justify myself in some way. Is that what you've been doing?'

Harry pulled the window almost closed and began to gather up his things.

'I'm not sure any more. It could have been like that in the beginning. All I know now is that I love her.' He said it so simply it was not embarrassing to either of them. For once Tom made no comment. He picked up the newspaper Harry had put down and turned for the kitchen.

Harry said, 'You'd better not close the doors until you go to bed. Should be dry by then.'

'Right.' Tom bundled the newspaper into the pedal bin. 'I was going to light the fire in the front room anyway. Join me when you've cleaned up. We can wait for Dorry together.'

So it was that Dorry, arriving just as it was getting dark, found them sitting either side of the fire in the small front sitting-room, sipping drinks and discussing, of all things, the weather.

She stared at them in amazement. 'Such a picture of domesticity!' she said.

Tom was immediately on the defensive. 'We might as well be comfortable. Harry's done a paint job on the window and I had a patient . . . we don't have to be working all the time like you!'

Dorry held the door jamb and began to laugh. She had been unhappy for so long; and now in the midst of it all, Tom and Harry, as unhappy as she was, protagonists as dissimilar as it was possible to be, were sitting together remarking on the sudden bright spell of April weather! She felt her laughter tremble towards hysteria and cut it off abruptly.

'Sorry. You're quite right . . . it's been a lovely day.' It sounded so inadequate she almost started to laugh again. Instead she thrust forward the large bundle of fish and chips. 'I didn't get any for you, Harry. I didn't know you'd be here.'

Tom sprang up and took the bundle. 'I'll make it go round. You must eat, old man. You're looking . . . not good.' He leaned forward and kissed Dorry's outdoor-cold cheek. She did not avoid him. 'Harry wants a word with you. I'll keep these warm and make some tea.'

She drew back, her eyes bright. 'Tact. A clean kitchen, the patients coming back. And now tact.' He sensed sarcasm and moved past her but she detained him for a moment with a hand on his arm. 'Thanks Tom. I knew you could do it.'

He looked at her sharply. 'That sounds as if you might be considering coming back for a longer visit?'

She smiled impishly. 'Mrs Raines will only have her old job back if I'm here. And I know how much you miss Mrs Raines.'

His face lit up and she put a greasy finger over his

mouth. 'Don't say anything yet, Tom. We need to talk about it. OK?'

He pressed the finger to his lips then nodded. 'OK. Supper coming up.' He went out.

Harry too looked pleased. 'I'm glad, Dorry . . . you've sorted it out? I mean in your head . . . it's OK now?'

She came to the fire, wiping her hands on a tissue. 'No, it's not OK, Harry. Nothing is solved. Not really. Tom's doing his best here of course – trying to earn Brownie points as it were. But he'll get fed up again with my unpredictable hours.'

Harry frowned. Dorry said, 'I came to the conclusion some time ago that nothing is ever actually *solved*. You have to live with problems. Get used to them. Cocoon them – like oysters – make pearls of them perhaps.' She sat down in Tom's chair. 'All I know for certain is that Tom is unhappy without me and I am unhappy without him.'

Harry leaned across the hearth and took her hands but all he said was, 'Ah . . . Dorry.'

She shook his hands gently and drew away. 'Tom and I. You and Helen. Thank God for Peggy and Josh!'

'Yes.' Harry drew out Helen's letter from his pocket. 'This came. The gist of it is . . . I am to find someone else. Without impairments. And live happily ever after.' He passed across the single sheet of paper. 'I knew she had some quixotic idea like this. I've got to see her, Dorry. You must tell me where she is.'

Dorry scanned the paper and looked up. 'I

shouldn't read this – it's for your eyes only. But can't you see what she's saying? Can't you begin to visualize how much she loves you? It's nothing to do with being quixotic. It's to do with your eventual happiness.'

He said tiredly, 'I can't debate this, Dorry. She's wrong. She's trying to twist the future unnaturally.' He closed his eyes and Dorry felt as if a light had been cut off. 'Tell me where she is. That's all I ask.'

'I can't do that. And in any case, you know Helen well enough . . . nothing you could say would bring her back now.'

He opened his eyes, startled. 'My God! What are you saying? That I am to give up – I'll never do that!'

'No. I'm not saying that. Helen has to come home of her own accord.'

'How?' He sat up. 'Have you got any ideas, Dorry?'

'Yes.' The door opened and Tom came in pushing a trolley ahead of him. Dorry smiled at him then looked back at Harry. 'Do exactly as she says, Harry. I'll make sure she knows.'

He frowned. Tom said, 'There were too many chips anyway – plenty to go round.'

Dorry said, 'Marvellous. Harry could you put some coal on the fire?'

He did so, but as Tom handed round plates and cutlery, he said, 'I don't get it. Sorry.'

She smiled again and combed her fingers through her short hair until it stood on end. 'There was a time before – when she thought you might be attracted to Peggy . . . she hated it. And she did something about it.'

Harry ate his supper in silence. He knew there was

no-one else he wanted to be with. Dorry simply did not understand. Somehow, he had to discover where Helen had gone.

He had to manoeuvre carefully past Dorry's car which was parked in the drive. He wondered whether it would be there all night; he hoped so. The clock on the dashboard of the Rover shone greenly on 22.30; it was a fine night, the stars gave a milky glow to the concrete road. He garaged the car and went up to his flat above the shop. And there, in the light from the uncurtained windows, he saw someone asleep on the sofa. For a wonderful moment he thought it was Helen, then knew it was not.

He peered into a round milkmaid's face topped with a riot of curls.

It was Cheryl; Cheryl who was now Arnold's wife.

Seventeen

For what seemed a long time, Harry stared down at the sleeping girl. As his eyes grew accustomed to the dusky light, he saw that she had been crying; her mascara had run and had been scrubbed into patches beneath her eyes. Her short curls were tousled – her hair was lighter than he remembered – and, even as he looked, she drew in a deep breath that shuddered on the remains of a sob.

He murmured very quietly, 'Damn,' but she heard and opened her eyes wide, meeting his intense gaze at first without recognition and then with glad relief.

'Oh . . . Harry!' She struggled to raise herself on one elbow. 'Oh – my arm's gone to sleep—' She tried to give her famous gurgling laugh and choked. 'Oh Harry – it's all pins and needles!'

He had forgotten her assumed childishness. Perhaps he had found it quite charming at one time and she had developed it for him; and now, probably, for Arnold.

He said curtly, 'Never mind that. Why are you here? Where's Arnold?'

'I've left him.' She made the outrageous statement quite calmly and then started to cry. 'I've left him, Harry! Oh my God, I've left Arnie!'

He knew he should ask her why, and then he

should listen to her endless analysis of her six months of marriage. Instead he said in the same curt voice, 'Well, you can't stay here, Cheryl.'

She wailed at that. 'Where else can I go?'

'Your mother's, I should have thought.'

'Oh my God, Harry! My mother's? You don't know what you're saying! She was the one who angled for me to marry Arnie! She kept inviting him round to console me after you'd jilted me at the altar—'

'It wasn't like that, Cheryl.'

'Oh, yes it was!' Her voice hardened into bitterness. 'And somehow you made me feel it was my fault!' She managed to control her sobbing and began to rub her arm. 'It wasn't my fault Mick had too much to drink – as usual – and thought it might be amusing to drive over the central barrier! It wasn't my fault you all went out on a binge the previous evening and made it last all night and half the next morning! And it certainly wasn't my fault that four people were killed and a girl was crippled for life!' He closed his eyes momentarily and Cheryl said swiftly, 'And it wasn't your fault either! We could have got married – oh, not while you were in hospital, of course, but later. Nothing had changed!'

He said in a low voice, 'Everything had changed. I thought you understood that. When we talked—'

'You talked!'

'All right, I talked. I thought you listened.'

'I did. But you didn't make sense. You never made sense!' Her voice dropped suddenly, 'Mummy said it was a waste of a wedding dress and – and everything. She said just because Arnie had so much money it would not stop him feeling dreadful about

Mick. And I could make him better. Cheer him up.'

Harry summoned his reserves and said rallyingly, 'And you did. And you have.' He walked to the door and switched on the light. The room looked sterile and sparse. Cheryl put her arms around her shoulders and shivered; tears welled again and began to move slowly down her face. He pretended not to see.

'I did. And I suppose I could still do so. But . . .' she looked up. Her blue eyes appeared to be drowning. 'Arnie's not a gentleman, Harry. He seems to think . . . he thinks he's – he's *bought* me! I can't bear it any more, Harry!' She stood up suddenly and cast herself on Harry's chest. He recoiled, but her arms were around his waist; she was pressing herself frantically against him. And she was so shockingly familiar; even the smell of her hair and the way she suddenly reached up and held his head and rubbed her nose against his, laughing through her tears, was exactly the same as he remembered from two years ago. He had found her so delightful in the old days. So happy and insouciant. She had had a gift for making him believe that everything she did was especially for him. She established small routines like the nose-rubbing and then maintained they were his. He knew that now he should hold her head in turn and kiss her and call her his little Eskimo woman. And then she would put her arms around his neck and wrap her legs around his and he would support her buttocks in the palms of his hand and they would stagger about ridiculously, laughing crazily and kissing crazily until they collapsed on the sofa.

But his hands stayed by his side. He knew with icy certainty that if she curled her slim legs around his body, he would actively hate her. Simply because she could do that and Helen could not. He thought of Helen and her abrasiveness; he remembered her awful behaviour in the police station; he saw again the horseplay with the black girl, the spinning wheelchairs, the laughter. He remembered his own stupid behaviour and lack of understanding and her reaction to it . . . 'D'you want to go to bed?' He knew now the kind of courage behind her brazenness. The same courage that she had displayed, much more obviously, when she had placed herself in his hands – literally – and sat so gingerly in the stern of the flatner. She had to summon that courage every day, every hour of her life. And she did so. Her sheer indefatigability made him stagger as Cheryl locked her hands behind his neck.

He reached up and disengaged her grip.

She said in a high little-girl voice, 'Harry! You've forgotten! You made me begin the nose-rubbing. Then you went on with it and I—'

'For God's sake, Cheryl!' He walked away from her. 'Can't you see? That's in the past! It's finished!' He heard her catch her breath but he went on. 'I suppose we were in love. We must have been. But . . . it was another life, Cheryl.' He turned and faced her and put a clenched fist on his chest. 'This man – he's not the same! You're not the same.' He made a sound of exasperation as she began to weep in earnest. 'Be honest – just for once, be honest! You

363

could not love me as I am now! You could not bear to be with me for longer than a few hours! You would be bored to death. I sit and stare, Cheryl. For long periods of time. Could you stand that?'

'I'd change you! Cheer you up—'

'Just as you've so obviously cheered Arnie up.' He hated his own sarcasm, but could not continue this futile conversation any longer. 'Did you have a coat? I'll take you home.'

'I'm not going back to that house!' She threw herself on the sofa again and looked up at him. He wondered how serious her desperation was. 'Let me stay here tonight, Harry. Please. Just tonight.'

He hesitated. He was very tired and longed to be alone.

He said, 'I'll leave you to it, then. You know where everything is.'

'Harry – don't be silly! I'll stay in here – you can have your own bedroom!'

He could imagine the seduction scenes that would take place during the night.

'Margaret will be here at eight-thirty. I'll arrive soon after. Good night, Cheryl.'

He ran back down the stairs. He took the motorway to Weston and was no longer conscious of its dangers. He thought – as he constantly thought now – of Helen and the small group of friends she had surrounded herself with. He had been one of them. And now he was not. And ironically she had told him to find himself another girl. And, as if by magic, there was Cheryl.

He smiled grimly through the windscreen as he

bumped down the gravel path to the Coastguard cottages. If Dorry could have seen Cheryl just now, she would imagine he had taken her stupid advice.

He glanced across to the other cottages. Peggy's bedroom light shone across the front of Flatners and revealed no sign of Helen's Ford. But Josh's car was there.

Tom brought Dorry's breakfast upstairs on a tray lined with a pristine cloth. She could see her face in the side of the silver teapot and the toast, stacked neatly in a new rack, was crustless.

Tom said, 'Doesn't this feel right? Tell me the truth, Dorry. Doesn't this feel exactly right?'

Dorry smiled her thanks as she took the tray. 'Of course it does. Breakfast in bed always feels right! Idiot!' She relented and pecked his snub nose. 'I know what you mean. Last night – all last night – was wonderful. But you do know that I'm not giving up my flat just yet, don't you?'

He looked crestfallen. 'Why? Dorry, it's ridiculous – what's the matter – stubborn pride or what?'

'Don't be daft, Tom!' She cupped his cheek with one hand and picked up the teapot with the other. 'We've got to take it slowly. That's all. You say you've turned over a new leaf. And I can see you have. I'm proud of you, Tom!'

'Well?'

'Well, darling, I haven't. Turned over a new leaf, I mean. I'm still working all hours, still driving my poor old car—'

'I'll see to it, Dorry, I promise—'

'Tom – I'll be delighted, but something else will drop off quite soon. Things happen to me.' She drank her tea and eyed him solemnly through the steam. 'D'you know, Tom, I have lost four umbrellas since we separated.'

He looked bewildered. 'I don't see the connection.'

'There is none. Except that I lost you as well.'

'But we're back. Together. I don't get it.'

'I don't want you to get fed up with me too soon, darling. That's all. If I live in the flat during the week, you won't expect me to come home for meals. You won't even know if I lose an umbrella.' She held her teacup to his lips. 'And Tom, the weekends will be so wonderful.'

He sipped obediently, choked and said, 'But you often work at weekends, too!'

'Not any more. I've made new rules—'

'You won't keep them!'

She put the cup down. 'Don't you want me home at weekends?' she asked.

'Yes – yes – yes!' He waved his hands. 'I want you home all the time. The split-home idea is mad! And irrelevant!'

'No.' She bit into some toast. 'This is heavenly toast, Tom. Lovely, lovely, lovely toast. I've never tasted such lovely—'

'Listen fishface. I have to go. And I want you to be here in between your appointments like you used to be.'

'Tom. I'm not going to be. *I* want you to go on organizing everything like you're doing now. You're – you're becoming quite – splendid, Tom.'

366

'Stop messing about.'

'I mean it. And I'll go on trying to get organized too. And then—'

'Just come home tonight!' he pleaded.

'Darling, I want to see Harry. He needs to talk, otherwise he's going to go off into the countryside looking at all the hostels and hotels for the disabled—'

'You promised. You said Mrs Raines would only come back if you did! And I'm desperate for Mrs Raines!'

They stared at each other and started to laugh at the same time.

'All right. Tonight. And I'll bring Mrs Raines with me.'

When he had gone she got up and had a bath and put on yesterday's clothes. Then she took them off and fetched a linen suit she'd bought last summer. The sun was shining. It was just about suitable. She combed her short hair flat to her head and applied a coat of lipstick. It was nine o'clock. If she could not give Harry time this evening she would give him time now. She grinned. He would not recognize her. She took her tray downstairs and cleared it away, then glanced with pleasure around the kitchen. Tom was like a small boy behaving well in order to earn a reward. That was the trouble, or one of them. Small boys were notoriously demanding; once he got his reward how long would it be before he wanted more?

She sighed deeply and went through the repaired French doors to pick up her car. How marvellous it must be to be as certain as Peggy and Josh. She paused in the act of climbing into the driving seat, realizing how stupid that particular thought had been. Peggy with all her hang-ups – doubtless Josh had his share too – and Rosie . . . Rosie was the one who would ultimately decide her mother's course of action, and Rosie was the most volatile of them all. Dorry sighed again and clipped on her seat-belt. If she had learned anything from her work, it was that every choice one made was hedged around with chance. Every choice was a gamble. She edged the car cautiously into the road and joined the stream of traffic going downhill. Was she willing to gamble on another effort at making her marriage work? And would Helen – dear Helen – ever be able to gamble on any kind of marriage? She turned into the village and concentrated on finding a parking space. It was just past nine o'clock and the offices of Vallender and Son were open; the window cleaner was at work on the plate glass and Margaret was going through a stack of letters.

'Hi!' Dorry grinned at the window cleaner and swung through the door. 'Lovely morning! I've come for a quick word with Harry. Is he upstairs?'

Margaret's face tried to give nothing away at this point.

'You look very nice, Mrs Latimer. Summer has come!'

'Not quite.' Dorry's grin widened. 'I'm freezing, actually. But it seemed a good idea when I got up.' She modified the grin. 'Is everything all right, Margaret? Harry not well? He's been under such a strain lately.'

'I'm sure I don't know how Mr Vallender is this

morning,' Margaret said in a suffering voice.

'Oh.' Dorry was nonplussed not so much by the answer as by Margaret's tone. She hesitated at the foot of the stairs. 'I'll go up then, shall I?'

Margaret dropped all pretence and gave Dorry a frank grimace. 'It's very awkward, Mrs Latimer. I went up to remind him that Mr Davison is expecting him out at the Mendip house this morning – he's reminded him twice and Mr Vallender throws his letters away but I can't believe – or I couldn't believe – that he would turn down a job for his friend. So up I go, not ten minutes ago, and who answers the door of the flat but . . . Mrs Davison! And in a pair of men's pyjamas, would you believe!'

Dorry stared. She had no idea who Mrs Davison could be. But Harry's pyjamas said quite a lot.

Margaret sat down suddenly as if it was all too much for her.

'Mrs Davison is Mr Davison's wife,' she said flatly.

Dorry nodded. 'As I thought,' she murmured.

Margaret became impatient at Dorry's lack of reaction. 'Mr Davison is Arnold Davison the building contractor. Rolling in money. Mr Vallender's friend . . . with him in the car when the accident happened . . .'

Dorry's brown eyes rounded. 'Oh,' she breathed.

'And that's not all,' Margaret continued triumphantly. 'Mrs Davison was Cheryl Mason who was going to marry Mr Vallender before – before – it happened.'

'Oh my God . . .' Helen had mentioned Cheryl. Cheryl was to Harry what Miles had been to Helen. Except that Cheryl was obviously very much alive.

And in what looked like Harry's pyjamas!

Dorry said, 'I think I will go up, Margaret. This is important.'

'Quite,' Margaret said, heavily sarcastic.

'No, but important in other ways . . .' Dorry swung around the newel post and stared down at Harry's right-hand girl who had been old Mr Vallender's right-hand girl and probably knew as much about Harry as anyone. She said, 'Oh Margaret, I told him to find someone else. To make Helen jealous, you know – bring her back to Bristol quickly. But I didn't think he'd actually do anything like this! And of all people . . . she is probably the one girl in the world that Helen will take seriously . . .' She went on up the stairs, leaving Margaret to digest this latest nugget of information.

Cheryl answered the door, still in the notorious pyjamas. She had thought that Margaret was Harry; now she thought that Dorry must be. Her face fell prettily. Dorry saw that she was, indeed, very pretty. Uncomplicated . . . easy to be with. Probably the kind of person Harry needed. Oh God.

She did not feign surprise; it was obvious that Margaret would have told her what to expect.

'Sorry to interrupt.' She kept her voice brisk. 'May I have a word with Mr Vallender?'

Cheryl shook her head and her curls bounced. 'Sorry. He's not here. He let me stay the night. But I've no idea where he went.' She glanced at an expensive wrist watch. 'He should be coming in at any minute.'

'May I wait?'

'Well . . .' Unaccountably the girl was reluctant to

admit anyone. Was Harry in there all the time? '. . .you could always wait downstairs. With Margaret.'

Dorry used her most winning smile. 'I just thought . . . a little talk. I'm a social worker you see and—'

Cheryl's face cleared instantly. 'Oh . . . do come in! I thought . . . ' She stood aside, giggling like a schoolgirl. 'I thought you must be his latest lady-friend!'

Dorry walked through the small hall and wondered what the linen trouser suit would bring forth next. She went into the sitting-room and made for the gas fire. 'Aren't you his lady-friend?' she asked directly, smiling, one girl to another.

'I want to be.' Cheryl knew that one of her charms was her frankness. 'I'm working at it. But Margaret came upstairs just now and was spluttering something about Helen! So I assumed you were Helen.'

'No. I'm Dorry. Dorry Latimer.' Dorry moved slightly away from the fire in case she scorched the trousers. 'As a matter of fact I was Helen's social worker when she was in the hospital in Bristol.' She looked Cheryl in the eyes. 'Helen was the sole survivor. In the other car.'

Cheryl gave a gasp, then stared back at Dorry for a long time. At last she said, 'I see.' She continued to stare. 'She was crippled. For life. Wasn't she? And Harry . . . feels responsible. And has gone all quixotic about her. Yes . . . that's Harry.'

Dorry lifted her shoulders lightly in an acquiescent shrug. She had to admire the way the girl summed up the situation so quickly. Simplistically, that was exactly how it was. She was tempted to tell her how deeply Harry loved Helen, how deeply

Helen loved Harry. But she did not.

'And you're now married to Arnold Davison,' she said instead. 'And you're going to the Mendip house with Harry to do a survey this morning? Am I right?' She knew she was not. She was offering Cheryl a way out of an awkward situation.

'Well . . .' Cheryl fiddled with the cuff of the pyjamas. 'Actually . . . I've left Arnold. My husband. At least . . . I thought I had. I thought Harry would be – might be – pleased to see me. After so long. I thought I could . . . sort of . . . break through his with-drawnness. Arnold asked him to our wedding last autumn. He didn't come.' She looked helplessly at Dorry and shrugged. 'That could have meant he was still in love with me. Couldn't it?'

'Yes.' Dorry said. 'Yes, it could have meant that.'

Cheryl smiled. 'I didn't expect you to be so under-standing. I mean, if you are this girl's social worker—'

'I was. I was Helen's social worker. Now I am her friend.'

Cheryl opened her eyes. 'Oh,' she said.

Dorry smiled. 'When she bought Harry's cottage at Weston she was out of my area. But it has made very little difference.'

Cheryl's eyes could not open wider but her eyebrows reached her mop of curls. 'Oh,' she repeated. Then she said, 'Harry owns four or five cottages. Which one did she buy?'

'Flatners,' Dorry replied.

'Flatners.' Cheryl's voice dropped. She turned to the window and stared down into the busy High Street. Harry's pyjama trousers sagged around her ankles. Dorry tried to imagine Helen standing upright beside her. Helen would be taller; Harry's pyjamas would not be enormous on her; her pale daffodil hair would splay over the collar and after a traumatic experience such as Cheryl had just had, she would look pale and drawn. Cheryl looked like a child on an adventure that might have gone wrong.

She said suddenly, 'I think this is Harry. Arriving. What shall I do?'

Dorry came behind her. Harry's Rover was nosing through the early-morning traffic. She said briskly, 'Why don't you go and shower? And then dress. I will tell Harry you are going with him to look at the Mendip house.'

Cheryl looked round. Her face was tragic in the way a child's face was tragic when deprived of a lollipop. She said, 'Are you sure?'

'Yes.' Dorry smiled comfortingly. 'You know, I don't think you'd like to be married to Harry. He . . . he can be difficult.'

'But he's good at looking after people. He always looked after Mick, you know. Until . . . well, until he died.'

'And you? Did he look after you?'

'Oh yes . . . He made me feel . . . safe.'

Dorry sighed. She looked down to where the Rover was now parked and Harry was emerging.

She said, 'I rather think Harry needs looking after too.'

Cheryl said eagerly, 'Well, Helen can't do that, can she? After all, she's in a wheelchair for the rest of her life!'

For a moment Dorry could have walked away from this stupid girl. But then she said very gently, 'Helen is the only one – the only one in the world – who can look after Harry. Believe me. Please.' She held Cheryl's gaze for a long moment, then went on, 'I don't know your husband. But surely he came to your rescue after the accident? Surely this house – wherever it is – is for you?'

Cheryl said in a low voice, 'But I've left him! He knows I've left him!'

Dorry shrugged. 'He might be very pleased to see you back then. After all, you will have been the one to persuade Harry to do the work for him.'

Cheryl said strongly, 'It might give him a bit of a shock too. I'm not just a – an ornament! He might realize that now!'

'Quite,' Dorry agreed.

There was another little silence. Suddenly Harry's steps could be heard coming upstairs.

Cheryl said swiftly, 'I'll go and shower. Can you tell him – make it all right?'

'I expect so.' Dorry smiled. It was so much easier when it was someone else, after all.

Miss Banks was like a bulldozer; she kept going through all objections.

'I can assure you, Miss Wilson, your skin is not even red! I have always given alcohol rubs to inhibit bedsores of any kind. And it is working on you just as it works on everyone else!'

She rolled Helen onto her back with an expertise that apparently took no effort at all. She then straightened her legs.

Helen lay back like a beached whale, feeling helpless and almost hopeless.

'It's just that Peggy – my friend you know, she always uses lanolin or baby lotion and it is much more soothing than—'

'And not so efficacious, I'll be bound!' Miss Banks was already pulling Helen's pants up over her knees. She got into trouble with the word 'efficacious' and sprayed Helen liberally. 'Anyway, if you will excuse my bluntness, I don't see how you can tell whether it is soothing or not around your buttocks!'

'Well, I can,' Helen maintained stubbornly. She put a hand on Miss Banks' shoulder and hauled herself into a sitting position. 'I think it's what my physio calls an echo effect.' It seemed years since those days when Tom had given her hope and life had been exciting in spite of everything. Even when that hope had faded.

Miss Banks passed her a lacy bra with a hint of disapproval and started on jeans and socks.

'Physios,' she said with veiled scorn.

'He was good.' Helen heard her own voice; almost a bleat. But Tom had been good. And she knew why Dorry loved him. She said, 'I must write to his wife . . . phone her. To thank them both.'

Miss Banks held a sweater at the ready and Helen dived into it.

'I'll say this for you, Miss Wilson . . . left arm . . . I said left!' Helen's head and arm emerged together. Miss Banks continued grudgingly, 'You're not a moaner. And you try to help yourself. But you must accept that we professionals know best.'

Helen felt as if her spine were tingling from the

inside. She wanted quite desperately to cry but after Miss Banks' words that was impossible.

She said, 'I know. I'm sorry. Thank you.'

She lay back exhausted after Miss Banks had gone. How on earth had she managed at Flatners? Shopping with Peggy, hydrotherapy, driving into Westbury to see Tom and then to Weston for Doc Simmonds' sessions . . . and yet there had been long periods of blessed silence; of watching the sea come and go, of looking at everything with the intensity of a painter . . . She said aloud, 'I drew energy from that . . .' And immediately Aunt Mildred's head came round the door and she said, 'You drew energy from what, dear? A nice cup of tea . . . biscuit?'

It was too difficult to explain. She said, 'That would be very nice, Aunt.' How useful Josh's word had become. Everything was nice at Bussington. It truly was. Nice. But how much longer Helen could bear it, she did not know.

'Palm Sunday next weekend,' Aunt Mildred said wheeling in the trolley. 'So I've made some Easter biscuits. This afternoon we'll take some to poor Doreen. Her sister always comes for Easter and she can't make biscuits to save her soul!'

'That will be nice,' Helen murmured.

'Yes.' Aunt Mildred smiled. 'And there's still quite a lot of pruning her Fred can get on with. In return.'

Helen smiled responsively and wondered what Aunt Mildred would expect from her 'in return'. She was paying handsomely for what Mildred called her 'keep', but Helen knew it would not end there.

She murmured, 'Easter . . . I hadn't realized it was so soon.'

Aunt Mildred said smugly, 'Everyone says how Christmas and Easter creep up on them! I always prepare well in advance. I don't like being caught on the hop.'

'No.' Helen felt another tremor inside her spine like a premonition. She said suddenly, 'I think I should go home for Easter. There are friends I promised to see . . .'

Aunt Mildred's eyes opened in horror.

'My dear, you're not fit to make the journey! And anyway, I thought you were giving your little cottage to that friend of yours? Surely it will be awkward just to turn up there now?'

She was right, of course. Dorry could well have started the legal business of gifting Flatners to Peggy and once Peggy knew about it, then it would be impossible to take advantage of her and use it again. The tingle became a dull ache. She had burned her boats. She knew she could not see Harry again, but she wanted desperately to go home and see Dorry and Tom and Peggy and Josh, and Hilda at the swimming pool and Alice at the counselling clinic. And she could not.

So it was wonderful when Dorry arrived two days later, her arms full of daffodils, looking better than Helen had seen her for ages.

'What has happened?' she greeted her as they embraced through the daffodils.

'I'm sort of back with Tom.' Dorry put a hand to her lips as Helen exclaimed. 'Hang on. I'm keeping the flat. It's got to be slow. Careful. Tom's damned optimism gets in the way.'

Helen laughed then sobered. 'That's what I miss. Tom's damned optimism.'

Dorry delayed her news. 'Come back then,' she said.

'You know I can't do that.'

'I didn't say – come back to Harry. I said – simply – come back. Come back home.'

'There's no home there any more.'

Dorry exploded a sigh. 'I haven't got in touch with your solicitors yet. Peggy knows nothing about your plan. She won't accept the cottage anyway – you know that.'

'She will. When I've seen her, she will.' Helen's face was set in stubborn lines. 'I can't think of Flatners as mine any longer. And that's that.'

Dorry made up her mind quickly. 'Well, you'd better come and live at Falcondale Road for a while then. In fact that might be better. Nearer the centre of operations, as it were.'

Helen misinterpreted her. 'Operations? You mean Mr Edwards wants to operate?' Her face lit up. 'Tom was right then! Something is happening . . . the kink . . . it can be straightened!'

'No!' Dorry put her hands to her face. 'Oh God – I'm sorry, Helen. Nothing like that. Tom hasn't seen Edwards since you left. Oh, my dear, I'm so sorry . . . so sorry. What a fool I am!'

The light in Helen's face had died as soon as Dorry spoke. She shook her head as if to clear it. 'Don't be silly. I'm the fool – it's just . . . you know, you coming to see me unexpectedly. I thought perhaps . . . oh Dorry, do stop looking like a tragedy queen and tell me everything! You – Tom. Rosie . . . have you seen them at Stormy Point? Is Josh still living there? And did you tell Doc Simmonds that I'd moved? I want to get hold of Alice's address – I think it's a hostel – I must write to her—' Helen ran out of steam and looked at Dorry's face which was more than just remorseful. She said slowly, 'Something has happened. To Harry? Oh my God, don't tell me something has happened to Harry.'

'No.' Dorry was quick with that reassurance, knowing exactly what Helen meant. Then she said, 'Well . . . yes, in a way. But he's fit and well, so don't worry about that.' She paused. 'Actually, he looks awful. I don't think he's eating very often and he's always thin so you can imagine—'

'I thought you'd keep an eye on him.' Helen's voice was instantly accusing. 'I know you're up to your eyes, but I thought you'd find time to take him out for a meal.' She too checked, then smiled ruefully. 'What's the matter with us? I'm sorry . . . I forgot about you and Tom.'

Dorry took her hands. 'Let's start again,' she suggested. She spoke calmly because she guessed her news would cause some kind of eruption from Helen. 'I thought you should know . . . you're the only one who can help him. Harry's one-time fiancée has turned up. Apparently she was married to one of Harry's friends. Last autumn. It hasn't worked out and she says she is still in love with Harry and she moved herself into his flat above the shop, two days ago.'

Helen looked stunned. She held on to Dorry's hands hard; her eyes were almost navy-blue. 'Cheryl,' she breathed. 'Cheryl . . . Mason, was it?'

'I think that's what Margaret said. Cheryl Davison now.'

'Margaret?'

'Margaret told me about it. Harry's Girl Friday.'

There was a long pause. Dorry waited for the eruption.

Helen said quietly, 'And Harry?'

'He's trying to help her. Of course.'

'Of course. Dear Harry . . .' Helen smiled slightly. 'I told him he tried to help me too much. I told him I needed my independence.'

Dorry returned the hand pressure. 'I don't think Cheryl wants independence,' she said. And then she had a sudden pang of conscience at using Cheryl to manipulate Helen and she added, 'Actually, she's quite a nice girl. You might even like her. Later.'

Helen blinked. 'Later?'

'You know . . . when you and Harry get it together . . . she might become . . .' Dorry swallowed at Helen's expression of complete bewilderment. 'She might become a friend.'

Helen said slowly, 'You think this will force me into coming back to Bristol?' She made a hideous face. 'Fight for my man? Is that it?'

'Darling – Helen—' It was Dorry gripping Helen's hands now. 'It sounds dreadful when you put it like that. But you can't – you simply cannot – stand by while Cheryl Davison dithers about between—'

Helen said quietly, 'Be quiet a moment, Dorry. Think about this. Think about it properly. Never mind how I am feeling about Harry – about Cheryl – about anything. Think of Harry.' She waited. Dorry was silent, round eyes looking almost frightened.

Helen went on, slowly, carefully, putting her thoughts into words as if they were bricks to be piled into something complete.

'Harry has to come to terms with the accident, Dorry. It was easier for me because it was linked to those—' She nodded almost dismissively at her legs. Dorry made a little sound of distress and Helen tugged at her fingers humorously. 'It's OK. I am beginning to own them again – especially when I swim.' She took a deep breath. 'As I came to terms with them – before I came to terms with them – I was accepting what had happened. I remember Doc Simmonds telling me I hadn't grieved enough for my parents. After that, I did cry for them. But they were part of me . . . like my legs. As my legs stayed with me yet were unfelt, so did my parents.' She looked down at her trousers again with some speculation. 'Perhaps if – when – I can stand again, it will be because of them. *For* them, too. But you see what I mean? You know the rest . . . Peggy and Flatners and – and of course Harry.' She was silent again then took another breath. 'D'you know, Dorry, I am thankful for Miles. Miles taught me things. About being in love . . . about looking . . .'

Dorry sobbed, 'Helen—'

'It's all *right*! Honestly. All I'm saying is that all this – this – rehabilitation, is it? It's been happening for Harry too. He helped me. I like to think that I might have helped him. Maybe in some ways he couldn't walk either, and I've—' She laughed. 'I've put him back on his feet!' She shushed as Dorry would have spoken. 'Harry has got to accept that accident, Dorry. It's harder for him because of his sense of

381

responsibility.' She paused. 'Yet, I had that too, didn't I? My silly wedding dress . . . Peggy . . . Rosie.' She blinked. 'Somehow I used it. Made us into a family. For our sake. For Miles' sake. For the sake of May and Alf Gorman.' She smiled almost blindly. 'We are a *family*. That's true. You're part of it, Dorry. That's why I'm missing all of you so much.' She turned the smile on Dorry. 'My God, I didn't realize I'd got so many blessings to count!'

Dorry said, 'Helen, he's not interested. She turned up but I told her about you and I think she realizes. They went together to look at a house . . . that's all . . . there's nothing more to it . . .'

Helen said quietly, 'Give them space and time, Dorry. Don't you see? Harry has to go back. Has to accept a lot of things that happened. Not find instant salvation in me. I can't give him what he needs. I can't say to him, all is forgiven. Because I'm there, without the use of my legs. I'm going to remind him all the time that he hasn't forgiven himself.' Dorry made another sound and Helen went on, her voice quickening with conviction. 'He has to go back and find the Harry that was in that car in the first place. The Harry that was going to marry Cheryl.'

Dorry bleated, 'But she's married to someone else, Helen!'

Helen released one of her hands and made a dismissive gesture. 'And she still loves Harry.' She held up the hand. 'And before you say another word, it *is* possible that Harry still loves her.'

Dorry wailed and began to blabber that she had jokingly advised Harry to find someone to make

Helen jealous and the next thing she knew – as if she had wished her there – Cheryl had been ensconced in Harry's flat.

Helen released the other hand but managed a little smile.

'So . . . you see me as the jealous type, do you? What was I supposed to do? Crash into some manufactured love-nest in my wheelchair?'

Dorry sobbed, 'Helen, please! Can you honestly imagine Harry with anyone else? Be honest now!'

Helen put her hands flat on her lap and bore down. Harry had asked her why she did that . . . Harry had known so much about her . . . everything there was to know. And she had always known that she knew very little about him.

She said, 'No. But you see, I do not know the Harry Vallender who was going to marry Cheryl Mason.' She smiled again. 'There is only one woman who might suit Harry . . . help Harry . . . be right for Harry. And Cheryl is that woman. And you have got to give it a chance, Dorry. Whatever you might feel or think, you have got to give Harry the chance to cast off the horrible burden that he has carried for almost two years, and find some kind of guilt-free happiness. You must promise me that.' She stared at Dorry. 'Promise me now.'

Dorry said, 'I can't – it can't end like this, Helen! You and Harry – you're – you're right—'

'You haven't listened to a word I've said.'

'Yes, I have. But you're wrong. Harry loves you . . . you! You must know that's true—'

The door opened and in came the inevitable tea

trolley. Aunt Mildred said, 'I can see I'm interrupting a deep discussion! But everything stops for tea!' She trilled the last few words and manoeuvred the trolley between the two girls. Dorry stared helplessly across it. Aunt Mildred said, 'Will you be mother, my dear? And Helen . . . you look tired. Why don't you lie on the bed for a while. We've got the palm crosses to make this evening.' She beamed at Dorry. 'I always make the palm crosses for Palm Sunday. And it's excellent therapy for Helen. Don't you agree?'

Dorry said faintly, 'Yes. Yes, I suppose it is.'

Helen moved her chair slightly so that she could see out of the window. She said, 'There's such a lot going on here, Dorry. The place is full of interest. Like Cranford . . . or Middlemarch.'

Dorry looked at the densely blue eyes of her friend. They signalled no special message. They were suddenly rather like Harry's dark eyes: opaque and withdrawn.

Dorry wanted – quite suddenly – she wanted Tom.

Eighteen

After Dorry had left, Helen knew a time of such desolation she could hardly eat her meals or respond to Aunt Mildred's constant commentary on her neighbours. She tried to hold on to the the idea of being a character in a book about village life; she tried to find it amusing when Doreen Barnes smilingly accepted the Easter biscuits but announced that she had made a perfect batch at last and would pass these on to her less fortunate neighbour. She managed to agree with Mildred that Doreen's sudden independence made it very awkward to suggest to Fred that he could do the extra pruning, but when Mildred said, 'Of course, dear, if you suggested it – as a favour – I know he would do it. He thinks the world of you. Because of the accident, you know,' she said nothing. She felt nothing. The old fire was no longer there. She gazed bleakly through the window at Doreen hurrying off with her booty of biscuits, and wondered if the family of friends at Stormy Point had existed only because of the accident. Were all her recent friendships because of the accident?

Aunt Mildred prompted her and she said obediently, 'If you think it would help, Aunt.'

'Oh it would, dear. Everyone in the village thinks you are just marvellous.'

Helen transferred her gaze to Mildred's energetic face and thought tiredly that probably everyone thought Mildred was marvellous for having her. And why not? And if that made the two of them just marvellous, then why not stay here? She could 'invest in the house' as Mildred had suggested before, and gain a spurious independence that way. Or even buy some land and have a functional bungalow built nearby. Bussington had a lot to offer. Until the news of Cheryl Davison's arrival, she had found it mildly interesting, even amusing at times.

The Mendip house was a small Elizabethan gem beneath Victorian additions. In spite of himself, Harry became interested in it and crawled around the roof space and cellars looking for rot or woodborers, delighted when he found neither. As he emerged into the dark hall Arnold and Cheryl looked almost translucent against the oak panelling. They had had very little to say to each other since their meeting two hours ago; but at least they were still there waiting for him.

Harry put the damp-meter in its case, slung it over his shoulder and dusted his hands.

'It's going to take longer than I thought.' He tried a grin in Arnold's direction. 'You didn't mention it was a baronial hall!'

Arnold said very clearly, 'I gave the exact specs actually. I understand you threw them away. I've got my own architect, you know. He could have surveyed it for me, but I thought it would do your business a bit of good.'

Harry was suddenly furious. He had been lumbered with this problem through no fault of his own, just when he wanted to concentrate his whole energy on finding Helen. And now Arnold was talking like some would-be benefactor.

He shouldered his equipment again and said sharply, 'Then you'd better get him in double-quick, Arnie. My business certainly does not need any injections from you!'

The two men confronted each other; quite suddenly both were breathing heavily. Harry was the taller, but Arnold was heavier and very obviously stronger.

Cheryl giggled. 'You look like a couple of bulls pawing the ground,' she said, managing to sound both cross and pleased. 'If you're really quarrelling over little me, then please don't.' She registered Harry's expression and said quickly, 'I'm sorry . . . I shouldn't have brought you my problems, Harry. It's your own fault though. You were always so good at helping me out.'

Harry's grim expression did not change. 'Right,' he said.

Arnold's snort was indeed bull-like.

'Do I gather you two spent the night together?'

'You do not.' Harry turned to go. 'Cheryl used my flat. That's all. I went . . . home.' It was the second time he had slept at Flatners since Helen left. He had slept easily and dreamlessly on her bed and then had wept when he awoke to the knowledge that she was not there.

387

Arnold waited till Harry reached the heavy oak door then said quickly, 'Hang on, old man. I don't want any other surveyor. I want you. I trust you.' Harry had tugged the door open and the spring sunshine streamed in. Arnold raised his voice. 'I trust you Harry! D'you hear me?'

'Yes. But I haven't got time . . .' Harry turned and made a gesture of surrender. 'Let's take it as said, OK? You two – sort out your problems. Without me. I have to – I have to find someone.'

Cheryl called, 'Harry don't go! Please! I think we might be able to help you – Arnie and me. Dorry told me . . . about Helen. Arnie's got contacts. We might be able to find her for you.'

Harry paused at last. Arnold said, 'What's going on?'

Cheryl said, 'Harry needs some help this time, Arnie. Can't we forget us for a bit. Have lunch somewhere. Talk about it.'

There was a moment of hiatus. Harry held the door and a cloud went over the sun so that the hall was suddenly cold. Cheryl had taken her husband's arm and he looked down at her hand and then towards Harry. He teetered on his feet.

'Well . . .' he said at last, heavily. 'If that's OK with Harry, it's OK with me.'

The nearest village was Axbridge and they sat in an ancient pub and ate Cheddar cheese and pickled onions and green salad with hunks of new bread, washed down with cider.

Cheryl said, 'We used to do this.' Her voice was small and shook slightly. 'Mick . . . it was the only time he seemed content.'

Arnold glanced at her and put an arm casually along the back of her chair.

Harry said suddenly, 'Mick didn't have much time for contentment. Excitement. That was the name of the game for Mick.'

Arnold said heavily, 'Well, I should think that last drive was the ultimate then. For him.'

There was a silence. Harry stared down into his glass. He thought, surprised, Arnie isn't over it. Any more than I am.

Cheryl said in a smaller voice still, 'What a price to pay for excitement.'

Arnold nodded. 'All those deaths. And the girl . . .'

Harry realized that Cheryl was weeping. He said, 'But don't you see . . . Mick has also taken the responsibility? For the first time in his life he took the consequences of his actions?' He reached across the table and covered Cheryl's hand with his. 'Don't you remember how often Mick dragged me into his scrapes? You probably thought I was like him . . . I wasn't. Not a bit. Ever since we were at school together I'd tried to bale him out. But I was never like him.' He grinned suddenly, 'I'm a dull dog, Cheryl. I need someone else to bring excitement into things. You couldn't put up with me . . . honestly.'

She nodded. 'I know that. Arnie and me . . . we get on all right really. Don't we, Arnie?'

'She keeps me on the straight and narrow.' He tried to match Harry's grin. 'I have to change my shoes when I go into the house, Harry! Can you imagine that?'

Harry could imagine the constant bickering that

passed for excitement. He thought of the long hours of quiet with Helen, lightened by the wonder of their trips in the flatner. Helen seemed to make everything exciting. He thought of the sexual tension between them that she had fought so hard to fulfil, and the ham-handed way he had responded.

Arnold had his arm right around his wife now; she wept freely onto his shoulder.

He said, 'Look, we all know it was Mick's doing. Can't we leave it at that? Do we have to be haunted by it for the rest of our lives?'

Harry shook his head to clear it. 'We were there. So it will haunt us. But . . . we're talking about it. That's good, isn't it? Perhaps we should see more of each other. Perhaps then, we can let Mick . . . do his stuff. Absorb the whole thing in some way.'

There was another long silence. Cheryl said, 'You've shut yourself away for so long, Harry. And now suddenly . . .' She gave her silly laugh and – typically – skipped ahead of the conversation and added, 'Will Helen like me, d'you think?'

Her trite words opened up a new world for Harry. A wonderful yet ordinary world. A home with Helen; visiting friends; cooking meals.

He smiled. 'Not at first,' he admitted honestly. 'But later . . .' His smile widened as he imagined Helen's efforts to be 'nice' to Cheryl. She would do it for his sake; because she would think it good for him to befriend Cheryl after the awful repudiation two years ago.

Cheryl laughed ruefully and ran her fingers through her curls. 'Don't blame her. After all, it's normal to be jealous.' She looked frankly at Arnold.

'I'm glad you didn't have anyone before me.' She saw his expression and added, 'Anyone official. You know. A proper relationship.'

Harry wondered how Arnold could bear this sort of speech. But he was smiling indulgently; and then he actually leaned forward and rubbed his nose against hers.

Then he leaned back to look at her.

'Now. What about trying to find this Helen for Harry? You're the one with the ideas, Cherry-ripe. What do you suggest?'

'I suggested you, darling!' Cheryl protested, all eyes and rounded lips again. Harry thought wryly that the moment of understanding between the three of them had gone, probably for ever. Not that it mattered. It had happened. And Helen would understand. That was the great thing about Helen, she would always understand.

Arnold said, 'Look, Harry, old man, leave it with me for a couple of days. Will you do that? She's gone somewhere within a radius of a hundred miles – right? You said they'd driven her wherever it was, and then come back, all in one day.'

'It's probably a hostel – accommodation either owned by or recommended by the Social Services. Dorry must have known about it.' He explained who Dorry was.

Arnold said, 'And Dorry's not letting on?'

Cheryl said, 'Dorry won't split on Helen if she's promised not to. I met her for about half an hour this morning and I can tell you that much.'

Harry nodded. 'No-one's letting on. I think possibly if I put pressure to bear on Peggy . . .'

'Who is Peggy?' Cheryl asked, immediately diverted.

Harry began to explain. As he ploughed on through exclamations from Cheryl and rumbles from Arnold, it occurred to him that he was doing an awful lot of talking. He concluded by saying, 'You see, Helen and Peggy are . . . good together. First of all, they had just Miles – and that could have joined them or divided them. But now, it's more. They're so dissimilar. But there's something . . .' And then he wondered if that was why Arnold and Cheryl were no longer to be avoided: because they had Mick in common.

Arnold said heartily, 'We'll find her. If it's the last thing . . .'

'And I'd like to go on with the survey of the house,' Harry said. 'Some of the rainwater goods look original. Fascinating place.'

Cheryl said, 'We thought it might give us . . . stability.'

Arnold was more direct. 'We thought we'd raise our family there.'

Harry nodded. 'Good idea,' he said. It still annoyed him when Cheryl blushed and giggled. But not quite so much.

He was still working his way through the Victorian outcroppings of the house three days later when Dorry arrived back from Bussington.

She had succumbed to Tom's pleas to stay at home and rest for twenty-four hours so that he could look after her. She had told him about Helen and there had been a blessed relief in having him there to dry her eyes and tell her that everything would be all right in the end.

'Your infernal optimism used to get me down,' she admitted, controlling her sobs with difficulty.

'Eternal, sweetheart. Not infernal,' he murmured, knowing that this whole affair with Helen and Harry was at last in his favour.

'No. I meant infernal,' Dorry hiccoughed. 'Oh Tom, I'm sorry. You just wanted to help Helen after all. And now – and now—'

'Darling one, I still think I can help Helen. While you were away I saw old Edwards again to discuss those last X-rays. And – believe it or not – he has to admit that the kink is less of a kink and more of a curve.'

'What!' She pushed away from him. 'Tom – d'you realize what this means? If Helen can walk again, she'll come back! She'll – my God – she'll jolly well claim Harry – she'll probably kidnap him at gunpoint or something! Oh Tom—'

'Steady on, old girl! Who's being infernally optimistic now? We're talking of years rather than months. And possibly an operation at the end of it. You mustn't say anything to Helen yet. You could raise her hopes for nothing . . .' His voice trailed off. They stared at each other.

She said, 'That's my line.'

And, for once, he said nothing.

Dorry went late to Vallender's office the next morning. She had taken officially two days off work and this was the fourth day. She wondered if she might get the sack.

Margaret said, 'Oh Mrs Latimer. How nice to see

you. You've just missed Mr Vallender, but he'll be back midafternoon.'

Dorry was amazed. Last time she had seen Margaret there had been epic horror in the air.

'What's happened to Cheryl?' she asked directly. 'And Harry – did he take her home? Or what?'

'Better still. They went straight up to the house in the Mendips and met with Mr Davison. It's done Mr Vallender a power of good. He seems so different. Relaxed – even happy.'

'You mean . . . he and Cheryl . . . they're surely not back together?'

'Oh no. He seems to have patched their marriage up somehow. But it's certainly done him good to see her again. And Mr Davison as well. This is the fourth day he's been to the house. They usually go into Axbridge for lunch. After all, they were good friends once.'

'Yes . . . yes.' Dorry was somehow affronted at the sheer normality of what was happening. She felt she had stepped out of tragedy into farce. 'Can you give me a few directions? I must see him as soon as possible.'

And so she arrived at the enormous old house built into the hillside below Crooks Peak and found the solid front door open to the morning sunshine. Harry's car was parked outside, but there was no sign of life and Dorry spent a long time walking along galleries and dark passageways calling his name, before he emerged from the wine cellar, hung with cobwebs but grinning from ear to ear. This was a Harry she had not seen before.

She blurted, 'You shouldn't leave the door wide

open like that! I could have been anyone!'

He began to dust himself off. 'Arnold usually arrives about now. We eat in Axbridge. You must come with us, Dorry. You did not see Cheryl at her best the other morning.'

She was horrified. 'Are you and Cheryl – I mean – what about her husband?'

'Arnold? He understood, I think. She's always been immature and when things didn't go well, she turned to me because there was no-one else. He knows her well enough to accept that.'

Dorry puffed her relief. 'I thought, for a moment, you and Cheryl might be back together.'

His grin died. 'Don't be ridiculous, Dorry.'

'But you're doing this work for them! And you look happy!' Her voice was a bleat.

He said simply, 'They're going to find Helen for me. You can't stop them – or me – Dorry. So don't try. I'm going to find Helen and take her right away.'

Dorry began to cry. 'She won't come. She was almost pleased when I told her about Cheryl! I thought she'd be jealous and want to come back and – and . . .' she hiccoughed. 'She really does want you to be happy. And live a normal life with a normal woman—'

He laughed shortly. 'There's only one woman who fits that description. Helen is normal by all my criteria.' He gathered Dorry to his dusty shoulder. 'Come on now. It's going to be all right. I know you can't break a promise and tell me where she is. But Arnie's got contacts in the building world and she's bound to need work done – wheelchair access, that kind of thing—'

Dorry blubbed incoherently, 'She's at Bussington. Near Oxford. With Aunt Putrid. And she doesn't like it and she has to pretend she does and it's such a mess, Harry.'

He held her off by her shoulders. 'Aunt Mildred? Where did you say – near Oxford?'

Dorry gave the address, parrot-fashion.

He stared into her button-round eyes for a long time while she stammered that she knew she was breaking a promise but she didn't care because if Helen had gone temporarily mad then she had to be cured any way at all.

She sniffed loudly and said, 'They keep a spare key on a ledge in the roof of the porch.' She added defiantly, 'You need to know that because Helen won't allow Aunt Putrid to let you in!'

He murmured, 'Ledge in the roof of the porch . . . halfway down Bussington High Street on the left . . .' Then his voice strengthened and Dorry could almost see energy coursing through him. He said, 'When Arnie gets here, tell him I've gone. I've almost finished here. The house is worth having. I'll do a report later.' He kissed Dorry smackingly. 'Thank you, dear Dorry. I love you.'

He left her standing there in the dust-moted hall. She heard the engine of the Rover start up, tyres spitting gravel, and then the car rounded a bend and was gone. She went slowly to the stairs and sat down. She said aloud, 'What have I done?'

Harry went back to the flat immediately; he talked to himself on the way. 'Hotels on route . . . flowers for now . . . clothes for me . . .' He was nearing the A38

396

and a herd of cows suddenly appeared ahead of him. He slowed and stopped, frowning prodigiously. A lad in corduroys and cap and bright green wellingtons came to the car window and he lowered it automatically.

'Sorry sir. Vet's just arrived for inspection – can't do nothing about it.'

Harry realized the frown had been misinterpreted.

'I was working on a problem,' he confessed. 'And I think I've solved it.'

'Good for you, sir!'

He moved away as the last of the cows flicked a dismissive tail. Harry put the car into gear and edged over the resultant mess. 'Wedding dress!' he said quietly but emphatically. And the frown had gone.

Nurse Banks had been using lanolin for almost a week and Helen's back was still sore. She did not complain; she felt sore all over these days; her neck was stiff and twice she asked Banks if there was a corn on her toe.

'Clean as a whistle,' the nurse replied. 'You're lucky. I've seen some paralysed limbs in an awful state. Look at these pink feet! Lovely!' She gave them a congratulatory pat and Helen flinched. She knew her feet hurt even if she could not feel them.

She cried off the usual afternoon outing and as soon as Aunt Mildred walked past the window, waving coyly, she reached for the phone and punched out Peggy's number. There was one ring and then Peggy's voice came over the line.

'Is it you?'

'Yes. And this time I can talk properly. Aunt Mildred has gone out on her own for once.'

'Dorry's back. She planned to see Harry today. She sounded awful when she phoned.'

'Yes. Listen, Pegs, don't let's go through all that again. You and I know why Harry has to go back to Cheryl. We can't expect Dorry to understand.'

'I don't see why not. She's obviously going to patch things up with Tom.'

'I'm not discussing it, Pegs. I wanted to ring you to tell you something. I asked Dorry to arrange for a legal transfer of Flatners. To you. Has she mentioned it?'

There was a small silence then Peggy blew up. 'How dare you try to put me into such a position, Helen! I thought you knew better than that! Our friendship is based on the fact that we are equal! In that way—'

Helen interrupted quickly. 'It's OK, you need not go on about it. I am ringing to tell you it's all off! Does that please you?'

She could hear Peggy breathing. 'I just wish you hadn't told me.'

'I was worried Dorry might have mentioned it. But I think I need Flatners, Pegs. I can't come home yet, of course. This whole thing with Harry . . . poor Harry's going to have lots of complexes about me now! But later I must be able to come back. You understand that, don't you?'

Peggy said impulsively, 'Come back now, Helen. Please. Harry need not know – nobody need know. He won't come out to the Coastguard cottages and even if he does, we can put your car behind our block and stick a tarpaulin over it or something.'

Helen was terribly tempted. She said abruptly, 'I'm not happy. I admit it, Pegs. I feel I want to sit in that window at Flatners and paint myself into something else. But I also want to go swimming and see the counselling people. And I can't do that if I'm hiding out.' She sighed. 'It's OK, I can stick this for most of the summer.' She forced a laugh into her voice. 'If I sound like Aunt Putrid when I come home, you will let me know, won't you?'

Peggy said, 'I can't bear it. You being there when you could be here.'

'You're not likely to swan off with Josh, are you? You will still be there come the autumn?'

'Things are different this time, Helen. Rosie and I have a home here. If Josh wants to share it, we are very happy about that. But those are the terms.'

'Nothing to do with me.'

'Nothing. And everything. And I am not going to discuss that!' Peggy laughed. 'Listen. We'll come and see you for Easter. Some more money came through this month and I promised Rosie we'd stay at the Bussington Arms and have a picnic.'

'Oh Pegs . . .' Helen could have wept.

'Josh is going to Swansea. So I'll be driving.' Peggy repeated the last words. 'I'll be driving. Did you hear that, Helen Wilson?'

Helen knew she was indeed weeping now. She said quietly, 'I heard.'

She spent some time that afternoon looking through the diary she had kept in hospital and remembering those first visits from Peggy. Peggy's very existence – Rosie's too – had changed her feelings for Miles. Had made the way clear for Harry. Yet Harry had surely been the one man she should never have loved.

She almost smiled at that. Because after all, it was true. And then she wept again.

Aunt Mildred was worried. She came home full of news about the Honourable Mrs Dowty and it was obvious, even to her insensitive ear, that Helen was not interested.

'I think you must be sickening for something, my dear,' she announced when Helen shook her head at the fresh rhubarb crumble as it appeared on the supper table. 'We'll see how you are tomorrow. Miss Banks will advise us. We might have to have the doctor.'

'I'm a bit down, that's all, Aunt.'

'It's since that Dorry called in on Monday, isn't it? Did she bring bad news?'

Helen lifted her shoulders. 'Made me feel a bit . . . homesick, perhaps.'

'This is your home now, Helen. We're all that remains of the family, dear. I've been thinking a great deal lately about you making your home with me. We could have an extension built . . . a granny flat . . . you know the sort of thing . . .'

Helen let her go on. A granny flat. She could never be a granny.

'I think I'll have an early night,' she said.

'Oh dear. You are sickening for something. That serial you like is on tonight. Last episode.'

'You can tell me about it tomorrow,' Helen said.

She did indeed feel bone-tired. Somehow she undressed and got into her nightie. The bed felt cold and she shivered slightly as she pushed her head into the pillow. She knew for certain that behind the curtain of non-feeling, her feet were cold. She worried about that for a while; why was she so concerned with her feet? Was there something awful happening down there beyond her ken, as it were? She hauled one of her legs up until her knee was almost touching her chin, then rubbed experimentally at her foot. Her hands, warmed by now, reported that the foot was indeed cold. The foot itself told her nothing.

She felt the hot tears again behind her eyes and hated herself for being a wimp. 'You wimp!' she whispered under the bedclothes. 'You stupid, lovesick wimp!' And she closed her eyes and thought of Alice and the small dark man with the wicked sense of humour whose name had turned out to be Wilfrid. 'Let it be all right for them,' she hissed into the darkness. 'Is anyone up there listening? Mummy? Dad? Miles? Let it be all right for them!'

She had no idea what time it was when headlights lit up the chintzy curtains at the window. Nothing ever stirred in Bussington after ten o'clock so she was instantly awake. She was not conscious of an engine note but when the lights died, it was obvious the car was outside the house and her first thought was that Dorry was back and something dreadful had happened. Ten seconds later she heard the key in the front door and her worst fears were confirmed because Dorry was the only one beside herself and Aunt Putrid who knew where it was kept. She reached for the pull-switch of her light and propped herself on an elbow. Her heart was hammering frantically. Peggy had driven over the cliff; Rosie had pneumonia; Harry was . . . she stopped her thoughts and closed her eyes. If anything had happened to Harry she knew she could not bear it.

And then hands fumbled at her door in the darkness of the hall, and it opened.

Harry's unmistakable length came in, blinking against her light. He shut the door behind him.

She whispered a scream. 'Harry! My God, what's happened . . . oh Harry!'

He said almost curtly, 'I've come to take you away. Where are your clothes? I'll help you dress. Then you must write a note for Aunt Putrid. We're going to Gretna Green. We're going to get married.'

Nineteen

Helen stared at him numbly. Relief at seeing him mingled with fury at her own needless terror. And then there was a sudden sense of being complete again; her incompleteness without Harry had been so different from the physical incompleteness of not feeling her legs. It had ached; constantly ached. A void that threatened to grow until it annihilated her. And the sight of him instantly filled the void so that she could do nothing to express relief, anger or pleasure except to put her hands to her face and cry.

He responded instantly, dropping the curtness that had sustained him on the way across country and kneeling by her in distress.

'Helen . . . Helen, it's all right . . .'

She sobbed, as Dorry had sobbed, with anger.

'I never cried till I met you! I hate myself for being so weak and stupid!'

'You don't usually cry when I'm around,' Harry said matter-of-factly, reassured by her typical reaction. 'So it's just as well I'm here and going to be here for the rest of our lives.'

She gasped, accepting the inevitability of his words, still fighting for what she saw as 'normality'.

'You know it's not right. You and Cheryl . . . you were going to be married two years ago! Now you're together again – it makes sense, Harry! It's part of your – your – rehabilitation! I know you feel a lot for me – I'm not denying that – but with me you're only half a person! Now . . . you're coming to terms with what happened – you can be a whole person again. Oh Harry —'

'It's all right. Honestly. You've just got it round the wrong way, my love . . . my dearest love. I was half a person then. Looking after Mick . . . Cheryl . . . Now I'm half a partnership.' He leaned away from her, looked at her streaming face, smiled in a way he could not have smiled before. 'Come on, Helen. Stop using your brain and use your heart. I'm taking you away from here whether you like it or not. But I can't marry you against your will, and that's what I want. More than anything else in the world.'

She gave a little cry of shock and stared at him helplessly. She saw him as if he were under water; his dark thin face wavered uncertainly through her tears. It emphasized the unreality of this midnight meeting.

He said, 'I'm on my knees. Looking you straight in the eye. I'm going to carry you out to the car because we might wake Aunt Putrid otherwise. And besides –' he wiped her face with the palm of his hand – 'I want to carry you. I like carrying you. When you can walk again, Helen, I shall still carry you sometimes. Is that all right? That's not disabling you, is it?'

She tried desperately to find her old abrasive self. 'You're doing a lot of talking. You hardly ever talk. It's Cheryl . . . you're different.'

He seemed to consider this. 'I think you're right.

I've had to talk. To Tom and Dorry and Peggy . . . anyone who might know where you are. And then of course, to Cheryl and Arnie because they weren't seeing straight.' He smiled. 'It's your fault, of course. I couldn't have found so many words if I hadn't been desperate.' He leaned forward and kissed her. They shared her tears.

He drew back. 'So . . . did you hear what I said? I'm here, on my knees, not only to look you in the eye, my darling, but to ask you to marry me. Please, my dearest dear. My Helen . . . my wonderful, stubborn, beautiful Helen who tried to show me she was attainable, but then, when I muffed it, who tried to prove she was absolutely unattainable – will you marry me? I've got it all arranged for a wedding next week at Gretna Green. I've booked hotels en route . . . it'll be a wonderful drive. Won't you trust me?'

He fished for a handkerchief and dried her face properly. She croaked through the linen, 'Gretna Green?'

'I wanted it to be romantic, Helen. So that we can tell our children about it later. Eloping to Gretna Green . . . something rather special for them, don't you think?'

She pushed the handkerchief away and choked, 'Children?'

'Ours, Helen. Our children. I've talked to Doc Simmonds. No problem about children.'

She began to cry again. But she asked no more questions.

He did not attempt to dry her face again. He said in a low voice, 'Helen, on the face of it, I am one of the people you should not trust. But I know you trust me. You do, don't you? In spite of me being in the car that did this . . .' he tightened his hold on her. 'The car that killed your family . . . in spite of that . . . you trust me, don't you?'

She nodded blindly.

He whispered, 'Then trust me now, Helen.'

He waited. The blue eyes so near his own, focused on him through the tears. She whispered, 'You know I do. You always said that the accident joined us in some way. You were right. It's crazy. But it's true. That's why you came to see me . . . why you sent me those flowers. That's why I let you take me out in the flatner. I was terrified. But I trusted you. And I knew that if we drowned, we drowned together. Already – then – that was what mattered.'

He held her head between his hands. 'And yet you tried to send me away.'

The tears came again. 'I wanted you to have a life, Harry. I didn't think you could. With me.'

He held her gaze, marvelling at the intense blueness of her eyes. He let his thumbs trace her brows and then beneath her eyes.

She whispered, 'What are you doing?'

'Looking. With hands as well as eyes.'

'Then let me too . . .' She put her hands on his face. For a long moment they were locked together. Gradually her eyes dried. She smiled at him and drew his face towards hers.

Later she murmured into his hair, 'You said you would still carry me when I walk again. You did not say – if I walked again. You said when I walked again.'

'Oh yes.' He put his lips against the long muscle

that ran from her ear into her shoulder. 'I know you will walk again, Helen. When I saw you first through the window of your ward, I knew you would live. And when I met you that first time, I knew you would walk one day.' She could feel him smiling against her ear. 'Tom and I . . . we're almost friends now, you know, and I think Tom will be the one. He'll get you walking. He's so optimistic, nothing will stop him.'

She turned her face to his. 'Thank you, my darling. But . . . d'you know what is the most wonderful thing about this?'

Their lips brushed and brushed again. 'What?' he whispered.

'When it comes to you and me . . . and that's everything . . . it doesn't matter. I'm not disabled when I'm with you, Harry. You make me whole.'

He did not try to control his own tears and she took his head on her breast and comforted him and then lowered her own head to listen to his words.

'Likewise,' he said gruffly.

'Oh . . . Harry . . .' She lifted his head and kissed him and he kissed her, and then quite naturally he made love to her and knew that something wonderful had happened for them both.

Much later, as they lay in each other's arms, she started to laugh.

'In Aunt Putrid's house . . . of all places!'

Harry whispered solemnly, 'The moment I saw her, I knew . . .'

She told him he was incorrigible, and then said quickly, 'You know . . . I felt it. The whole passionate experience. I felt it, Harry. I'm not making that up. I swear.'

He replied calmly, 'I know you're not. I told you. I talked to Doc Simmonds.'

She tried to get onto her elbow and failed. He held her close.

'I can't believe you talked to Simmonds. You were so shocked by the whole idea of sex therapy!' She lay in the angle of his shoulder and thought about it. 'Harry! It's been only five – no, four – days since Cheryl came on the scene! And in that time you've made all these plans, seen Doc Simmonds—'

'I've done a lot.' He nodded against her hair. Then said smugly, 'I've bought your wedding dress too.'

Her incredulity was exhausted. She said flatly, 'I don't believe you. You don't know my size or anything.'

'Oh yes, I do. I haven't been looking at you – really looking at you – all these months without knowing your size.' He turned his head and kissed her ear lobe. 'I wondered if it was the right thing to do – I mean, brides like to choose their own dresses. But it might have proved another loophole. I thought if I'd done everything – every last little thing – you wouldn't be able to wriggle out of it.'

She giggled and sounded even more girlish than Cheryl.

'I'm giving up wriggling. For Lent. And I shall love the dress. But . . . oh Harry, Doc Simmonds. What did she say?'

'What you have always said. That I must not disable you. That when we were together, if we wanted to make love, then it would be fine for you.'

'Yes. It was. But it was more than fine.' This time she managed to prop herself up and look at him in the glare of the electric light. 'I think it's the echo effect. I think I should talk to Mr Edwards again. He might decide on the operation.'

'Steady . . .' He stared into the face so close to his own. He knew he must not show any fear of what might lie ahead for her. But still he said, 'Can we go to Gretna Green first and then have the summer at Flatners? Please?'

'You know we can.' She smiled at him. She said, 'Part of me feels I should have protested more, Harry. But I am so happy . . . so happy. I can take on the world, my love. You will be there with me . . . won't you?'

He swallowed. 'Always.'

'It's not going to be easy, Harry.' Her voice was exultant as if the difficulties of what lay ahead stimulated her. 'But we can do it! We can do it, Harry!'

He said again, quietly, like a promise, 'Always.'

He helped her to dress, even folded her bedclothes neatly. She insisted on telling Aunt Mildred what was happening.

'A note would be cruel,' she said. 'This way she can be in on it. She'll have an absolute ball telling everyone in the village about how she arranged the elopement.'

It was difficult for Harry because at first Aunt Mildred was appalled and resentful. 'When I met you at Christmas I thought you were such a nice man,' she accused him. 'I remember thinking you at least weren't trying to get your legs under

Helen's table! And now it turns out . . .'

Helen held on to the bony hands and felt them shake.

'Aunt . . . please. When I came here – I was running away from Harry. You must have realized I was running from something. I wanted him to marry someone non-disabled – who could walk and – yes, run – with him . . . this last week I've been very unhappy. Because I thought that was what he had done!' She laughed a little, looking at Aunt Mildred, encouraging her to respond. That lady looked grimmer still.

'I thought you were happy here. I thought we were going to share a home.'

'Aunt . . . this was my sanctuary – you were my sanctuary. Don't you realize that?'

'Well . . .' Mildred said, grudgingly.

Helen said, 'This house is where Harry proposed to me – just now. And where I said yes.'

'Proposed?' Aunt Mildred was slightly mollified.

'I've arranged for us to go to Gretna Green, Mrs Wilson.' Harry thought he had better help out. He put his hands over Helen's. 'We're staying two nights en route. And afterwards we shall live at Flatners. We'd like you to be our first guest.'

'Well . . .' Mildred said again. She was already picturing the furore this news would cause tomorrow at the Women's Institute Market. And after all when she had first met Mr Vallender, she had been struck by his grave 'gentlemanliness'. He would certainly look after Helen.

So, finally, she gave in and made them all tea and helped Helen to pack her things.

'I can't help thinking your dear mother would not approve of me encouraging you in this,' she grumbled as she fastened the last case and handed it to Harry. 'You're acting like some schoolgirl . . . you must be thirty by now. And, after all, I am *in loco parentis* as it were.'

'She knows how wilful I am,' Helen said, and she spoke without sadness. She could almost hear her mother laughing delightedly at this match, at Harry's romantic and ridiculous gesture. Both her parents would like Harry. The thought gave her deep pleasure.

And then it was time to go. Harry had put the wheelchair in his Rover and come back to lift her off the bed. Aunt Mildred twittered behind them about not wanting to go back to bed now. Dawn was washing the sky.

Harry paused in the doorway.

'I'm just about to carry you over the threshold,' he murmured. 'Please note.'

'But you're going out. Not in.' Mildred pointed out.

Helen smiled. 'We're going out into the world, Aunt.' Harry took a step. 'Now!'

'Hush, child!' Mildred looked nervously up and down the country street. 'You'll wake the whole village!'

For some reason her remark, innocent enough surely, made them laugh. They laughed so much she was surprised they didn't fall over. Somehow Harry tottered down the path and deposited Helen in the passenger seat. He did not make the mistake of trying to belt her in; that was something she could do for herself. But he did run back up the path, still laughing, to peck Aunt Mildred on the cheek.

'Please go back to bed,' he said. 'It will worry Helen to think of you being alone here and at such a loose end until the village does wake up.'

She was struck by his kindness but surprised because his own remark made him laugh more.

She said, 'You didn't strike me – before – as so – so jolly!'

'Ah.' He pecked her again and then shook her hand. 'But, then, I wasn't.'

They were gone. And she drew her dressing-gown close and padded down the street to wake Doreen Barnes. Her mother had always told her that a lady never went outside in slippers, dressing-gown or curlers, and here she was in public in all three. She did not care. After all, it was almost morning and Doreen would be delighted to be the first one to hear this particular story. A proper love story. Mildred smiled sentimentally: a real romance.

THE END

THE APPLE BARREL
by Susan Sallis

Hope and Jack Langley seem like a couple who have it all. Soon after they marry and move into an idyllic Gloucestershire village, Hope discovers she is pregnant. And, almost immediately, the glamorous Petersons, Henrik and Mandy, appear on the scene as new neighbours. Local rumour about the couple is rife: they are rich, they are Norwegian, they aren't married, they give crazy parties.

Yet to Hope and Jack they seem reassuringly normal and kind, and soon the four of them become close. Before long the Petersons have inveigled their way into every aspect of the young couple's lives. With the birth of their second daughter, the Langleys' happiness seems complete, but appearances can be deceptive.

0 552 14747 8

THE KEYS TO THE GARDEN
by Susan Sallis

Widowed Martha Moreton was a devoted mother to her only child, Lucy, and when Lucy married Len on a golden July day, Martha tried hard to make the best of things. Len was a good man who would make Lucy happy. They wouldn't be living far away. And the arrival of grandchildren was something she anticipated eagerly.

Unexpectedly, Len's job took the newly married couple overseas, where their first child was born. But sorrow, not joy, came with Dominic's birth. On their return, Lucy's best friend, Jennifer, as flighty as Lucy was conventional, was anxious to provide her own kind of consolation . . .

Martha, who was experiencing unlooked-for and at first unwelcome changes in her own life, clung fast to the maternal bond that meant so much to herself and Lucy. Everything she had come to depend on was over-turned, however, before Martha was able to find her own kind of happiness in a very different existence.

One of Susan Sallis's most poignant and involving novels, *The Keys to the Garden* explores the mother-daughter relationship with a rare insight.

0 552 14671 4

COME RAIN OR SHINE
by Susan Sallis

There were four of them: young women, dressed decorously in black, employed at an exclusive jewellery store in the 1960s. Close friendships were forged as Natasha, Prudence, Rachel and Maisie worked together under the benevolent rule of the two Markham brothers.

Years later Natasha, newly divorced and back from America with a fifteen-year-old daughter, decides there must be a reunion. Pru, always the mysterious one, unexpectedly offers Prospect House, a property she has inherited in the Malvern Hills where they may all forgather. Rachel, married to her former boss, a Liberal MP, gladly leaves a tangled domestic situation to join the friends she hasn't seen for so long. And Maisie . . . Maisie, perhaps the most vulnerable of the four, mother of five children, wife of the unpredictable Edward, fails to arrive at Prospect House. The drama of her disappearance has a far-reaching effect on the lives and destinies of them all.

0 552 14636 6

A SELECTED LIST OF FINE NOVELS
AVAILABLE FROM CORGI BOOKS

☐ 14438 X	THE THURSDAY FRIEND	Catherine Cookson £5.99
☐ 14696 X	HARRIET & OCTAVIA	Jilly Cooper £6.99
☐ 14449 5	SWEET ROSIE	Iris Gower £5.99
☐ 14410 X	MISS HONORIA WEST	Ruth Hamilton £5.99
☐ 14820 2	THE TAVERNERS' PLACE	Caroline Harvey £5.99
☐ 14603 X	THE SHADOW CHILD	Judith Lennox £5.99
☐ 14781 8	JOINING	Johanna Lindsey £5.99
☐ 14693 5	THE LITTLE SHIP	Margaret Mayhew £5.99
☐ 14354 5	UNTIL YOU	Judith McNaught £5.99
☐ 14752 4	WITHOUT CHARITY	Michelle Paver £5.99
☐ 14715 X	MIDSUMMER MEETING	Elvi Rhodes £5.99
☐ 12375 7	A SCATTERING OF DAISIES	Susan Sallis £5.99
☐ 12579 2	THE DAFFODILS OF NEWENT	Susan Sallis £5.99
☐ 12880 5	BLUEBELL WINDOWS	Susan Sallis £5.99
☐ 13136 9	ROSEMARY FOR REMEMBRANCE	Susan Sallis £5.99
☐ 13756 1	AN ORDINARY WOMAN	Susan Sallis £5.99
☐ 13934 3	DAUGHTERS OF THE MOON	Susan Sallis £5.99
☐ 13346 9	SUMMER VISITORS	Susan Sallis £5.99
☐ 13545 3	BY SUN AND CANDLELIGHT	Susan Sallis £5.99
☐ 14162 3	SWEETER THAN WINE	Susan Sallis £4.99
☐ 14318 9	WATER UNDER THE BRIDGE	Susan Sallis £5.99
☐ 14466 5	TOUCHED BY ANGELS	Susan Sallis £5.99
☐ 14549 1	CHOICES	Susan Sallis £5.99
☐ 14636 6	COME RAIN OR SHINE	Susan Sallis £5.99
☐ 14671 4	THE KEYS TO THE GARDEN	Susan Sallis £5.99
☐ 14747 8	THE APPLE BARREL	Susan Sallis £5.99
☐ 14867 9	SEA OF DREAMS	Susan Sallis £5.99
☐ 14785 0	THE WAY AHEAD	Mary Jane Staples £5.99
☐ 14638 2	THE HOUSE ON HOPE STREET	Danielle Steel £9.99
☐ 14740 0	EMILY	Valerie Wood £5.99